# PIERS ANTHONY

# PET
# PEEVE

A TOM DOHERTY ASSOCIATES BOOK
NEW YORK

This is a work of fiction. All the characters and events portrayed in this book are either products of the author's imagination or are used fictitiously.

PET PEEVE

Copyright © 2005 by Piers Anthony Jacob
Excerpt from *Stork Naked* © 2006 by Piers Anthony Jacob

A Tor Book
Published by Tom Doherty Associates, LLC
175 Fifth Avenue
New York, NY 10010

www.tor.com

Tor® is a registered trademark of Tom Doherty Associates, LLC.

ISBN-13: 978-0-765-34311-6
ISBN-10: 0-765-34311-8

First edition: October 2005
First mass market edition: October 2006

Printed in the United States of America

0  9  8  7  6  5  4  3  2  1

# Contents

# PET
# PEEVE

# 1

# FINGER

I
t all started when the stranger gave Goody Goblin the
Finger. Goody was annoyed, in fact he was furious,
but was far too polite to show it or return it.

That was of course his curse: he was so civil that other
goblins couldn't stand him. A goblin male was supposed
to be obnoxious, foul mouthed, and disreputable, the crap
of the earth. The niceness in the goblin species was confined to females. But those pretty, sweet, and obliging
goblinesses generally preferred brutally manly males. It
was a fair division of types. Goody came across like a girl.

Oh, he had tried to overcome it. He had even gone to
the Good Magician nigh a score of years ago for a way to
abate the curse. Magician Grey Murphy had shown
Goody that he knew the bad vocabulary when Goody sat
on a curse burr. But thereafter he had avoided curse burrs,
and so did not curse, and his problem remained. He
lacked even the inclination to be crude or mean spirited.
Worse, he no longer had even the desire to change; he
was satisfied to be the way he was.

He looked at the Finger. It was in a small box with a cushioned bottom. It appeared to be a human center digit, firm and healthy, severed neatly at the base. Along the side of the box was printed MAKE ANYONE MAD—GUARANTEED. GIVE THEM THE FINGER.

It certainly seemed to work. Goody had been mindlessly enraged to receive it, for no discernible reason. There must be a curse associated with it, a spell that oriented on the person who accepted the box. He didn't even know the stranger, in fact had hardly seen him; the rage came regardless.

What was he to do? He couldn't keep the Finger, because its very nearness irritated him unmercifully. He didn't need to look at it; he knew it was there, and that made him boil.

Well, who said he had to keep it? He set the box on a fence post and took a step away.

In a moment something poked him in an infuriatingly private place. He leaped, whirling, coming perilously close to uttering one of those curse-burr words.

It was the Finger, floating out of its box. It had followed him and goosed him. Its direct touch was thrice as worse as its boxed presence. He was so angry that he felt steam rising from his head. This was no good; he couldn't handle such raw emotion; the heat would soon cook his face.

He went back and fetched the box. The Finger obligingly floated into it and lay quiescent. Now it was only normally obnoxious.

So he couldn't leave it behind. He would have to give it away to someone. But how could he do that? That would be unkind, and he was not that sort of person. He did not care to voluntarily annoy any person.

There was a swirl of smoke. "You look like a goblin with a catechism."

"A goblin with a what?" Only belatedly did he think to wonder why and how a swirl of smoke could talk.

"Annoyance, quandary, bother, imbroglio, bafflement,

nuisance, confusion, vexation, trouble, snag, pickle, muddle, enigma, pother, dilemma, flaw—" The smoke coalesced into an electrifyingly exotic female human shape. "Well, don't just let me go on forever! How many alternatives do you want?"

"I don't understand."

She frowned, her scant attire drooping to proffer naughty glimpses fore and aft. "You're supposed to suggest the word I'm looking for. Now shall we try again? Aggravation, perturbation, mystery, kink—"

"Problem?"

"Whatever," she agreed crossly. "Who are you?"

"Goody Goblin. So called because—"

"My turn. And I'm the Demoness Metria. I have a slight problem with vocabulary, but I'm more than sexy enough to make up for it."

He was catching on. "I have a problem with vocabulary too. I don't like to use bad words."

She eyed him, her eyes expanding to twice their normal size. "But you're a male goblin! Isn't that a Gordian knot?"

"A what?"

"Poser, heresy, perplexity, asymmetry, irony—"

"Paradox?"

"Whatev—no, wait, that's not quite it. Puzzle, absurdity, contradiction, stupidity—"

"Oxymoron?"

"That's it!" She put on the frown. "I mean, whatever. How can you be a male goblin without cussing?"

"It's not easy, but I have learned to live with it."

"But that wasn't what summoned me. What's that you're holding?"

"A boxed Finger."

"Fascinating! Let me look at it." She reached for the box.

Goody suffered a moment of sinful temptation. Fortunately his better nature prevailed. "You would not care for this."

"I'll be the epicure of that. Give it to me."

This time he refrained from challenging the wrong word. "I would like to, but it wouldn't be kind."

"You little twerp, stop teasing me!" She snatched the box from his hand.

There was a pause, if not pregnant, at least gravid. Then the demoness exploded into a noxious fog. "You gave me the Finger, you bleepity bleep!" The nearby foliage wilted with the heat of the language.

"Well, I tried to warn you."

"Take it back!" The Finger flew through the air and smacked into his hand.

Goody was outraged. "You outrageous—" But words failed him, as they were all well beyond his comfort zone.

Metria re-formed, wearing a different but no less revealing outfit. "Outrageous what?"

"Manure, ordure, dung, feces, stool—"

"Turd?"

"Whatever," he agreed crossly. She had come up with a word he would not have used, but which did fit the situation.

"Now at last I understand the nature of this thing," she said. "It infuriates whoever receives it."

"Exactly. That's its magic. I need to be somehow rid of it, without being unkind to some other person."

She contemplated him, her eyes remaining normal this time. "You are a wonder, Goody Goblin."

"I'm an outcast among my kind. But that's beside the point. What am I to do?"

"Obviously you need to go see the Good Magician Humfrey. Toodle-oo." The demoness faded gracefully out.

He sighed. The problem seemed intractable. Therefore he would have to take it to the Good Magician. Of course that would cost him a year's Service or equivalent, but he did have time on his hands (not to mention the Finger), and a sadness on his soul that could use the distraction.

He set out immediately. There was no point in delaying; he wanted to be rid of the Finger as soon as possible. He knew the way to the nearest enchanted path, and that would lead him safely to Humfrey's castle.

He was in such a hurry that he started a group of bunnies. They hopped out of his way, Jacks and Jills. He could tell because the Jack rabbits wore little trousers, and the Jill rabbits little skirts. It seemed they had been on their way up a hill before he so rudely interrupted them. They were highly annoyed.

Which was surely the fault of the Finger. Its proximity made him behave crudely. He held up the box, to show them the cause, but that made them glare worse.

Goody sighed. He walked away, not trying to explain further. Now he had even more reason to get to the Good Magician's Castle rapidly.

Soon he reached the enchanted path that went the way he was going. That was one of the qualities of such paths, of course: they were not only safe, they were convenient. As he stepped onto it, he encountered two human people just stepping off it. One was a young teen girl with dark brown hair and large deep brown eyes; the other was an older teen boy with tousled light brown hair and shallow brown eyes. They were obviously siblings. Both were twice as tall as Goody, being normally human proportioned.

"Here's another fine mess you've gotten us into," the girl was complaining. "This isn't the path we're looking for."

"But you picked it," the boy protested. "You know my talent."

"Your talent is failure," she retorted. "You always get the wrong answer, make the wrong decision, or pick the wrong path. So I chose the opposite direction—and it's *still* wrong! How can that be?"

"Well, your talent of dumb luck didn't fix it."

At that point they spied Goody, who was politely waiting for them to pass. "Oh, a goblin!" the girl exclaimed, appalled.

"There must be hundreds more right behind him, all bent on foul mischief."

"Which means there is only this one, and he's all right," the girl said. "I think. So let's ask him how to find our way."

"He won't know."

"Which means he *will* know. Maybe my talent led us to him." She faced Goody. "Hello, goblin. I am Song Human, and this is my brother Ownlee Human. We're lost. Will you help?"

"I am Goody Goblin. I really don't think I can help you, because—"

Song smiled at him. She was twice as pretty when she smiled, and he felt his knees turning spongy. Girls had that effect on him; he wasn't hardened against their blandishments. "But I'll try."

"How did we get lost, when I chose the opposite direction my brother chose?"

Goody was old enough to have had some experience with opposites. "There may be a reason, but it is complicated to explain."

"Don't you dare talk down to me!" Song snapped, the snaps echoing faintly off the nearby tree trunks. "I'm a grown woman."

Goody was taken aback. "But—"

"I know I look fourteen, but I'm really eighteen."

He hesitated, but she threatened to smile again, so he lurched into his explanation. "The opposite of a wrong is not necessarily a right. It may merely be another wrong. There may be only one right path, but many wrong ones."

Now she did smile. "Oh, I see! We took one of those other wrongs."

"So it seems. Where are you going?"

"To the Good Magician's Castle."

"Why so am I! Do you have a problem for him?"

She laughed, and that had much the effect her smile did. "Oh, no. We just happen to live nearby."

"We took a walk," Ownlee said. "But then when we started back—"

"I understand," Goody said. "If you don't mind traveling with a goblin, I'm sure I can lead the way there. I don't have any magic talent, so my directions are not confused."

"Oh, thank you, Goody!" Song exclaimed. She leaned down and kissed him on the forehead. He felt like floating, but managed to keep his feet on the ground.

They walked along the enchanted path. There was just room for the three of them abreast. "If you don't mind my asking, why are you going there?" Song asked.

It was impossible to mind anything about her. "A stranger gave me an ugly thing, and I need to find out how to get rid of it."

"What thing?" Ownlee asked.

"I would rather not say."

"Oh, please," Song pleaded.

Goody melted further. "But I must warn you, you won't like it." He held up the box.

Both humans peered into it. Song screamed in shock and Ownlee burst out laughing. "Someone gave you the Finger!" he chortled.

"Ownlee!" Song said severely. "That's disgusting."

"Yeah," her brother agreed, smiling. His smile was not nearly as evocative as hers.

Soon they reached the vicinity of the Good Magician's Castle. "We have to get off here," Song said. "But the next intersection is the Castle, marked by the Memorial."

"The Memorial?" Goody asked.

"Gravestone," Ownlee clarified. "Where other folk croaked."

"Ownlee!"

He was making a social mess, but Goody understood. "I'll watch for it."

"It encourages a person to mourn the tragedies of others," she explained. "It's very sad."

"I'm sure it is."

"You have been such nice company," Song said.

"For a goblin," Ownlee agreed.

Song bent down and gave Goody a hug. "Thank you for showing us the way." Her hair tickled his shoulders, smelling of colorful flowers amid new-mown hay.

By the time he recovered his perspective, the two were gone and he was walking on down the path. Song reminded him of a gobliness, pretty and nice, though larger. But that thought brought back his sadness, and he had to walk quickly to leave the mood behind.

Yet the mood stayed with him, and intensified. He couldn't escape it.

He spied the memorial stone. Suddenly he realized what was happening: the stone was causing him to mourn others. The closer he got to it, the worse it was. The grief up close was overwhelming. But then he got past it, and the awful feeling faded.

There ahead was the Good Magician's Castle, surrounded by its moat. He approached it, hoping the Challenges would not be too bad. He came to the drawbridge, which was down.

There was a sign: BEWARE THE LINE OF SIGHT. Goody shrugged; what was there to fear from a line of sight?

But as he sought to cross the bridge, he became aware of something sharp. There was a row of eyes along its rail, staring cuttingly at him. He couldn't get close without getting sliced.

This was evidently the first Challenge. The Line of Sight. How was he to get by them so he could cross the bridge without getting cut?

He looked around, but saw nothing to be used to shield himself from those swordlike beams. Could he wait until dark, and sneak by them? No, because they seemed to glow; they would stab through the darkness and get him. He had to tackle them now.

He pondered, and considered, and cogitated, and

thought. He came up with nothing. Go-Go would have thought of something, but she was gone.

Go-Go. Suddenly he was sad again. It tended to happen when he thought too much. This was not the time to be distracted by recurring grief.

Or was it? He hated this, but realized that it just might be the answer.

He faced the Line of Sight. "I have something to tell you," he observed, and saw several eyes wince at the implied pun. That was a good sign. It meant the eyes could hear and understand him, even if they lacked ears, and that they had emotions. That was what he needed.

"I am going to tell you about my beloved wife, Go-Go Gobliness. But first I have to tell you a little about me. You see, I am Xanth's only polite male goblin. It's like a curse; I simply am not inclined to use harsh language. That got me banned from my tribe, and other goblins don't like me."

He paused. "But what about the goblin ladies, you may ask. They are all very pretty and nice. Surely they would like a nice male. The answer is no; they expect goblin males to be brutish, and think there is something wrong with one who isn't. They're right; I'm simply not the ideal male of my kind. So I could not get a gobliness to marry.

"Until I encountered a mean old goblin who had a problem. He hated everything, but loved his daughter. But she was cursed to die before she was forty. No man wanted to marry her, because of that curse, though she was comely. They teased her unmercifully about it, calling her Gone-Gone. As a result she was not very choosy. We met—and it was love almost at first sight.

"We married and were happy. The storks brought us two children, and they were fine and healthy goblets. The boy was as brutish as they come, and the girl was lovely and sweet. The boy got in with a bad crowd, cursed his family, and took off. We were so proud of him! The girl lied about her age, took up with a prominent junior chief, got him in trouble, and married him. No girl could have done it better. So we were alone again, just in time, for Go-Go was starting to feel the curse. I wished I could find some magic to save her, and indeed I heard there was a Black Wave Human Magician who could reverse curses, but we did not know where to find him. So Go-Go kissed me one last time and faded out.

"I was so horribly grief stricken that I could not stand to remain at home, where everything reminded me of her. So I left and wandered alone through Xanth, trying to escape my abiding sadness. But whenever I relax, I remember, and grief wells up again. I don't think there can ever be another woman like her. She was wonderful for twenty years, and I hope when I finally fade out myself to meet her somewhere on one of Princess Ida's moons and be happy again. I have to believe that, because otherwise my life is pointless. Surely you understand."

He looked at the eyes. They did understand. They were tearing freely, their vision blurring and clouding.

Goody walked by them, across the bridge. They tried to glare cuttingly at him, but the glares washed out and drooped harmlessly to the planks. He had passed the first challenge.

But he wished he could have done it some other way. He hated sharing the memory of Go-Go. It was as if that diluted it, leaving less for him to cherish. He wanted never to forget her, only to be with her again.

The far end of the bridge led into the grand entrance gate, with no apparent barrier. The inner hall led in turn to a large parklike chamber with walks, trees, ponds, glades, and creatures. Goody looked around admiringly; if this was a challenge, it was a beautiful one.

He walked to the edge of the nearest pond. There was a lovely creature swimming in it, part human, part something else. "Hello," he said politely.

The creature swirled about to face him, lifting her bare head and bosom. Her face was pretty, with big blue eyes and green and orange tresses that would have reached well toward the feet of a human girl. She also had arms and well-formed breasts. "Hello, goblin. Are you here to straighten us out?"

"Why, I don't know. Perhaps I am, if this is a Challenge. I am Goody Goblin."

She clapped her hands. "Wonderful! My name is Mirage. I'm an exhibit. But I have forgotten my type."

"It's an esthetic type, I'm sure."

She blushed down toward her shoulders. "There was a confusion, and our identification plaques were lost. Now none of us know what we are. If you will kindly identify us, we will be ever so grateful."

This was definitely a Challenge. "I will certainly make the attempt. You seem to be a crossbreed."

"Yes, we all are. That's why it's so confusing. You must speak our types, and they will appear on the blank plaques." She gestured, and he saw that there was a mounted wooden sign beside her pool. "But you must be sure to get them right, because we will be cruelly oppressed if misidentified. For example, if you called me a harpy, I would be required to act like one, and that would truly dismay me."

So he could not afford to make a mistake. She looked like a mermaid, but not quite. It might be easy to make a mistake.

"May I get a better look at you, please? It's not that I wish to be obnoxious, but in the interest of accuracy I must consider carefully."

"I understand." She flexed her long tail and forged out onto the small beach surrounding the pool.

"You can go on land!" he exclaimed, surprised.

"So I can. But I do prefer the water."

He studied her. Her human forepart was only about a seventh of her length. Her long tail was rounded, snakelike rather than fishlike. She was able to slither on land. "Some mer-folk can make legs. Can you?"

"Let me see." Mirage concentrated prettily.

Suddenly she assumed the form of a nude woman ly-

ing on the sand. "Oh!" she cried, distressed. "I'm showing my panties!"

Goody tried to think of a polite way to tell her that this
was not the case. It was impossible to show what one
wasn't wearing. She might be an exhibit, but she was
making more of an exhibition than she cared to. But she
had already changed again, this time to a full serpent. She
slithered into the water, becoming a fish.

At least that settled him on her nature. She had three or
four forms, while a mer-person had only one or two. "You
are a naga," he said to the swirling water. "A mer-naga.
Your parents were probably a naga and a mer-person."

The plaque illuminated: MER-NAGA. He had gotten it.

Mirage's head and bosom reappeared in the water. "Oh
thank you, Goody! Now I feel competent again. I'm so
thrilled I think I'll kiss you." She swam purposefully toward him.

"That really isn't neces—"

But she was already slithering out of the water and lifting her forepart to plant a soft-fronted kiss on him. Little
hearts flung out and orbited his head as he lost his balance and sat on the sand. All he could think of in the
blissful confusion of the moment was that he had been
lucky she had kissed him in her naga form rather than her
full bare human form. He would have entirely freaked out
despite the absence of panties.

He bid farewell to Mirage and walked on to the next
exhibit. This was a section of forest where a long-legged
wolf with dainty feet ranged. The wolf spied him and approached. It had long-flowing ears and a small pearl horn
on its forehead. "Hello," Goody said. "I am—"

The wolf changed form, becoming a human woman
with long blond hair and wings, and pale blue eyes with
matching blue hoofs. "I overheard. I am Maggie. I hope
you can classify me. I don't know whether to howl or
neigh."

Goody had been exposed to quite a number of human

females recently, but had not become inured to the bare exhibit. "Please let me study your other form."

"Of course." She changed back, her second word sounding more like a growl.

There had evidently been something of an event at a love spring. He saw strong evidence of wolf, unicorn, bird, and human. But he wasn't sure how four creatures could have done it; two was more likely. Maybe an alicorn, which was a winged unicorn, and a werewolf. That would account for the wings and hoofs, though they did not appear in the same form, and the wolf and human aspects. "You must be a wericorn," he said.

The woman reappeared. "Is there such a thing?" she asked doubtfully.

"There is now," he said, pointing to the plaque, which now said WERICORN.

"Oh, yes," she agreed. "I'm so pleased, I think I'll—"

"There is really no ne—"

Too late. She lifted him up to human height and kissed him. This time the orbiting hearts were larger, with blond tresses and hooves. He really wished he could do something about his susceptibility to female charms, but it seemed to be inherent. Ever since Go-Go.

The hearts cleared as she set him down, facing the next exhibit. This was a big bird with the head of a dog. "Woof!" it said.

Goody was getting better at this. "You're a bird dog."

The plaque lighted with the designation.

The bird dog looked pleased. It approached him.

"There is no need to—"

Again he was cut off by the kiss. The creature hovered before him and licked his face with a single juicy slurp.

The next exhibit was another bird/animal combination, with the head and wings of an owl and the hindpart of a cow. "Hoo?" it inquired.

"I am Goody Goblin. It seems I am here to define your type."

"Whooii mooake HOO," it said.

Goody realized that it was talking to him, so it behooved him to fathom its message. When he allowed for the whoo and moo of its owl and cow aspects, it seemed to be saying "I make—" But he stalled on the last word.

"You make something," he said.

The creature flew to a milk pail and positioned its udder. Fluid squirted out. Then it kicked the bucket toward him.

Goody caught it before it spilled and held it up. "But this isn't milk," he said. "This is pure water."

"HOO," the creature agreed.

Then at last a bulb flashed over his head. "An H and two O's. $H_2O$. That's water! You make water."

"HOO," it agreed.

"But I need to classify you. You're obviously an owl/cow crossbreed. What would that be called? An owlco? I don't think so." Then another bulb flared. "A cowl!"

"Hoot moon!" it exclaimed, pleased as the plaque accepted the term. He had gotten another.

There was one more creature to classify. This exhibit was a large greenish melon growing in a desultory patch. As Goody approached, it metamorphosed into a sad-eyed dog.

Goody was riding a wave of success. "You're a melon-collie," he said, and it was so. He had conquered the last challenge of nomenclature.

There was an open door before him. He turned and waved. "Farewell, lovely creatures," he called. There was a chorus of responses, some of which sounded like kisses.

He turned back to the door and entered another huge chamber. This one was boxlike, square with solid wooden panels around the sides and across the ceiling. This one, like the other, had five sections, only these were all lined up across the center with separate paths leading to each.

Evidently he had to choose a path, and surely four of them would be wrong.

He stood and looked at the section farthest to the left. This had a disreputable man standing beside the path. In fact he looked like nothing so much as a giant insect. "Hello," Goody said politely. "I am Goody Goblin, and I would like to pass through your territory. Is this a problem for you?"

"Yes, I have a problem with that," the man buzzed. "I am Esso Bee, and I will stop you from passing this way."

That did not seem promising. "But I have done you no injury. Why should you seek to balk me?"

"Because I like to make problems bigger than they are."

Goody decided to risk it. He walked toward Esso.

The man pointed to a little molehill by the path. Suddenly it swelled into a mountain, blocking the way.

"That's a remarkable talent," Goody said.

"It's no bigger than my dislike for you, goblin."

Magnifying a harmless person into a significant enemy. That was consistent with the man's talent.

Goody tried to walk around the mountain, but Esso pointed to another molehill, and it swelled into another mountain. It was apparent that he would not get through this way.

Goody shrugged. "You are doing an excellent job of balking me," he said.

"Flattery will get you nowhere, runt."

So it seemed. Goody backed off and addressed the second section of the box. This path was clear, with no more than a single tree growing beside it. That did not look difficult.

He started walking toward the tree. "You'll be soorreee!" Esso called in singsong from the other section. He was clearly mean spirited.

Goody walked faster, then faster yet. Suddenly he realized that this was not entirely of his own volition. Something was urging him forward. He did not trust that.

He halted with an effort, his feet actually sliding to a stop. His body seemed to want to fall toward the tree. How could that be?

He dragged himself back along the path. It got easier as he went, until he hardly felt any pull. Now he saw a small sign: GRAVI-TREE.

The more he considered that, the less he liked it. The tree seemed to borrow from the Demon Earth's magic of attraction, hauling him in with greater power as he approached it. What would happen if he got too close?

"You'll get squished to pulp, you little snot," Esso called nastily.

Just so. This path, too, was impassable.

The next section seemed to be a vegetable garden with many fine, tall stalks. That should be harmless. He hoped.

He walked down the path. Immediately several stalks uprooted themselves and moved toward him. They looked menacing. Some glistened with fluid that could be poisonous; others were coated with ugly powder. These were not innocent, peaceful plants.

He tried to hurry, to get by them before they could close in on him. But they hurried too, forming a large but shrinking circle around him. Now he smelled something like acid. There was also some of the black powder wafting toward him. He caught just a whiff of it and sneezed violently. If a whiff did that, what would a full breath of it do?

Now he realized what the plants were doing. They were stalking him. That might have seemed funny, but for their evident seriousness.

Discretion was the better part of valor. Goody ran back along the path. A line of stalks moved to cut him off, but he leaped, hurdling them. A faint mist hovered above them that stung his eyes and made his breath tighten, but then he was past, and able to clear his lungs and eyes. But it was clear, if fuzzy from his tearing eyes: he could not pass this way either.

He oriented on the fourth path. This one passed a dark cave. What was in there?

He would surely find out. He walked along the path.

As he approached the cave, a bear emerged. It set itself in the path, blocking it.

"Hello," Goody said politely. "I am—"

"I am a bi-polar bear," the bear growled, cutting him off. "Sometimes I am high, but now I am low. I feel like destroying something. If you get near me, I will take it out on you."

Goody considered that, and decided not to argue the case. "I hope your mood improves soon," he said, and retreated. The bear went back into its cave.

The last section contained another tree, but this one was unusual. Its fruit seemed to consist of items of, well, defecation. Indeed, the sign identified it as a toilet-tree.

There were a number of creatures using the items. An elven girl was powdering her face, and a troll was sitting on a pot, straining. Even insects were relieving themselves on miniature facilities.

Well, the ugly sight and smell would not really hurt him. Goody walked toward it. As he approached he began to feel awkward in the middle of his body. In fact he needed increasingly to, well, use a toilet.

Then he realized something else. The folk availing themselves of the facilities were not moving on. The elf girl continued retouching her face, never satisfied. The troll might have done its business, but was still trying for more. The insects were not departing. It seemed that this was not a passing thing, but a required continuous effort that it was never possible to complete.

Goody halted, then backed away from the tree. This was not an avenue he cared to take either.

He paused to consider, which was a sensible habit of his. This was a Challenge, so there had to be a way through. He should not have to get past mountains made of molehills, be compressed by a gravi-tree, get stalked

by vegetables, suffer the ire of a bi-polar bear, or be
trapped on a toilet. Yet these seemed to be the only
choices offered.

But there was something he had learned in the course
of his middle-aged life, and that was that what was apparent was not always the full story. Other goblins had rejected Go-Go because she was cursed to fade before her
time, yet Goody had found her to be the perfect wife in
every other respect. She had of course wanted to marry a
normal disreputable goblin male, but had discovered that
a polite male could nevertheless have qualities to be respected. Long before the end she had told him that she
was glad to have married him, and considered herself better off than her friends. So they had both profited by being willing to avoid the stereotypes and choose
unconventionally.

It was called thinking outside the box. Goody had
avoided many difficult situations by practicing it.

And this Challenge was in a box. A bulb flashed over
his head. Did this box have an outside?

He went back to the entrance. Sure enough, the box sat
in a slightly larger chamber. There was a small clearance
around it, between its slats and the stone of the chamber
walls. Just enough for a goblin to squeeze through.

He squeezed, making his way around the outside of the
box to the other side. There was an open door into the rest
of the castle. He stepped through it.

# 2

# PARODY

A young human woman appeared. "Welcome, Goody Goblin," she said. "I am Wira, the Good Magician's daughter-in-law."

"Thank you for meeting me," he said politely. "I have come to see the Good Magician about a problem."

She smiled. "That happens here on occasion. Humfrey is busy at the moment, but you can visit with Rose while waiting." She led the way through labyrinthine passages.

"I am not certain I know Rose."

"She is the Designated Wife of the month. Humfrey rescued all five and a half of his former wives, but only one can serve at a time, so it alternates. Rose is very nice."

"Should I explain my mission to her, or to you?"

"There is no need. Magician Humfrey will know."

They came to an interior court. There was a pretty rose garden there, tended by a pretty woman in an elegant gown. She looked up as they approached. "Hello, Wira. Who is our guest today?"

"This is Goody Goblin." Wira turned to him, and in the light he saw that there was an odd blankness about her eyes. "Goody, this is Rose of Roogna."

Goody made a courtly bow. "I am pleased to meet you, Rose."

Rose was surprised. "I mean no offense, but this is not the greeting I expected from a goblin male."

"I am cursed to be polite. It is most inconvenient."

"Ah, now I remember. Grey Murphy mentioned that he once helped a polite goblin male learn how to swear."

"I am that one," Goody agreed. "However, it remains not to my taste."

Rose looked more carefully at him. "You look like a typical male goblin, with a big hard head, big club feet, and a body only half human height. Yet there is sadness about you. May I give you a rose?"

"I appreciate the offer, but there is no need."

She gestured to the garden. "Take the one that most appeals to you."

It would not be polite to demur further. Goody looked at the assorted roses, discovering many colors. There was something special about all of them, and he realized that they were in some way magical. All of them were pretty, but one appealed particularly. "This one," he said, indicating a delicate pale gray rose.

"Take it."

He reached out and grasped its stem. He twisted, and the rose came free. He smelled it, and was reminded strongly of Go-Go. That of course brought a surge of grief, but it was bearable. "Thank you."

"That is the Rose of Grief," Rose said. "Only a person in sincere grief can take it fresh without getting stabbed by its thorn. I thought that might be the one."

"It is," he agreed. "My wife." He did not need to explain further.

She approached him, bent down, took the rose, and tucked its stem into a buttonhole on his jacket. The roses were her magic; she was immune to their thorns. "It will help you bear your grief. When another woman is able to take it, you will know she is worthy, and that you will be able to love her as you loved your wife. That your grief has dissipated enough to allow this."

"I think that is not possible."

"It is possible, Goody. The rose knows."

Wira had disappeared at some point in their dialogue. Now she reappeared. "Magician Humfrey is ready," she said.

"Thank you, dear," Rose said. "Go with her, Goody."

Goody followed the young woman up a winding flight of stone steps to a dingy dark office. "The querent is here, Good Magician," Wira said. "Goody Goblin."

Something moved in the shadow. It was the Good Magician, poring over a huge dusky tome. "Ask, goblin."

"I need to rid myself of an ugly artifact," Goody said, removing the Finger box from a pocket. "It is a Finger."

"You hardly needed to come here for that," Humfrey said grumpily. "Just give it to anyone you don't like."

"That is not in my nature. I do not wish to offend anyone, or to cause distress."

Humfrey looked at him more than half a moment. "You are a goblin male?"

"A polite one," Goody said, embarrassed.

"Give it to Wira."

"Oh, I couldn't do that!"

"Evidently you are unaware that she is blind. She can't see it, therefore will not be offended."

"But she led me here without a misstep!"

"I am familiar with this castle," Wira said. "Give me the Finger."

Reluctantly Goody handed the box to her. Her expression did not change. She was not offended. She bore the box away.

"Your problem has been solved," Humfrey said. "Now depart."

"But I have not yet served my Service."

"There is no need for a Service for this. I will use the

Finger in a challenge for some obnoxious querent I wish to discourage."

"But that would not be right. You have relieved me of an unpleasant object, and I should pay the usual price."

Humfrey contemplated him again. "You are a remarkable goblin. I see Rose gave you a rose. That is a mark of considerable favor and significance."

"Rose is very kind."

"Have you ever reacted violently to provocation?"

"I wouldn't think of it."

"There is a task that needs performing. But it is a considerable challenge, and very few folk would be capable of it. Perhaps you are one such."

"I will do my best."

"The task is difficult and provocative, but its accomplishment may lead to considerable reward. You will need help. Grey Murphy will help outfit you."

"If I may inquire, what is this task?"

"To find a suitable home for the parody."

"I fear I don't quite understand."

"You will." The ancient eyes moved, spying the returning girl. "Wira, take him to Grey. He will deliver the parody."

Wira shuddered. "Yes, Magician."

She led him to another part of the castle. They entered a room where Magician Grey Murphy was working. On the table before him was a raised wooden bar, and on the bar perched a green bird. "Magician, here is Goody Goblin. He will place the peeve."

Grey jumped up. "Goody Goblin! I remember you from way back. You were one of my first cases."

"You showed me how to curse," Goody agreed wryly. "All it took was a curse burr."

"Didn't that solve your problem? What brings you back here?"

"Someone gave me the Finger, and I needed to be rid of it. Now it seems I am to find a suitable home for the

parody. I hope you have further details, because I admit
to being perplexed."

"Small wonder! I'll fill you in. This green bird here is
the parody. It's a pet peeve, and we need to find a suitable
home for it."

Goody studied the bird. It was moderately small, perfectly plain, with a downwardly curved beak, beady eyes,
and nondescript feathers. It seemed entirely unremarkable, except for the intense way it stared at him. "It looks
like a nice enough creature, rather like a small mundane
parrot or large parakeet. I should think almost any family
looking for a pet would like to have such a bird."

"That is not the case. Here, I'll stop using my magic to
suppress its nature." Grey put his arm out, and the parody
hopped onto it, fluffing its wing-feathers.

"You're such a poor excuse for a goblin it's a wonder
the harpies didn't adopt you," Grey said.

Surprised, Goody looked at him. He knew it wasn't
like him to insult people.

"In fact, you should go stick your head into a nickel-
pede nest to improve your complexion," Grey's voice
continued. But this was especially odd, because his lips
were not moving. In fact his mouth was tightly closed.

"I don't think I understand," Goody said.

"Of course you don't understand, you moronic idiot,"
Grey's voice said. "When they passed out stupidity, you
were the first in line."

Then Goody caught on. "The bird! The parody is talking in your voice."

"Exactly," Grey said. "Wira, may I give you the bird?"

Wira stepped forward and put out her arm. The parody
jumped onto it. "And you call yourself a Magician,"
Wira's voice said. "I've seen better magic in Mundania!"
Her mouth was closed too.

Wira proffered the bird to Goody. He put out his arm,
and the peeve hopped on. It hardly weighed anything.
"Only a real idiot like Hugo would have married you,

sleepyhead," Goody's voice said. "If you could see, you sightless wretch, you'd know what a pitiful bag you are."

Horrified, Goody opened his mouth to protest.

Wira cut him off with a smile. "I know that's not you talking, Goody. It's the pet peeve. It doesn't like anything."

"Least of all you, you inane excuse for a chambermaid," Goody's voice said. "You give blind stones a bad name. They should have put you back to sleep a decade ago."

She smiled again and put forth her arm. The bird jumped onto it. She brought up her free hand and stroked its back. She was evidently a gentle soul.

"And you're worse, you denatured goblin," her voice said to Goody. "Why don't you just put on a pretty dress and be done with it?"

Ouch. He hated being likened to a girl.

Wira kissed the top of the parody's head and gave it back to Grey Murphy. Now the bird was silent. Goody remembered that Grey's magic was to nullify magic. That was why he could stifle the obnoxious avian.

"This should give you half a notion what to expect when you travel with the pet peeve," Grey said. "It will insult everyone and everything that comes in range, with marvelous specificity, using your voice. Be suspicious if you ever hear a positive word from it. Are you sure you want to take on this mission?"

That daunted Goody, but he persevered. "I shall do my best. But I am concerned about the reactions of those we may encounter."

"Exactly," Grey said. "You surely observed how giving folk the Finger made them react. You won't even need to give them the bird to elicit their ire. You will need defensive magic. Wira, do you know where that bag of used four spells is?"

Wira hurried away in search of it. "Four spells?" Goody asked.

"I'll explain in a moment. I trust you realize that what qualifies you to escort the parody is that you must be one of the few folk who won't fly into a rage and wring its neck. Only a supreme pacifist can keep company with this bird for very long without suffering apoplexy or worse."

"I am coming to appreciate that."

"It may help to understand our diagnosis of its nature. The peeve has a high AQ."

"I beg your pardon?"

"Annoyance Quotient. Almost anything it encounters annoys it, and it reacts by expressing itself in hostile and sometimes vulgar language."

Goody had to smile. "I believe I noticed something of the kind."

"A sense of humor certainly helps when dealing with it. The parody is attracted to the highest AQ it encounters. The recipients of its attention hate it, much as they do the Finger, which is perhaps another reason why the Good Magician gave you this challenge. You are not a creature of hate; you are essentially a pacifist. You will need to find some responsible person who will not be outraged by receiving the bird from you."

Goody was beginning to doubt. "Is there such a person?"

"There must be, because Humfrey does not assign impossible Services. The challenge is to find him, her, or it. But it shouldn't be another pacifist, because the peeve would languish if not provided a ready source of aggravation. In other words, don't consider any low-AQ folk."

"A high-AQ person who likes the peeve," Goody said. The challenge was looming larger by the moment.

"Still, it was left here by the Gorgon, who rescued it from Hell, where it had rather worn out its welcome, and Humfrey agreed to find a good home for it. He has trouble saying no to his wives. We've gotten used to it here, but frankly will be satisfied to see it on its way."

"I can imagine."

Grey angled his head, gazing at Goody. "My talent of suppressing magic makes me sensitive to it. I need to know what I am suppressing, so as not to do corollary damage. There may be magic about you."

Goody was perplexed. "I am merely an ordinary goblin."

"I suspect you have a magic talent."

"But goblins don't have talents. Well, some have half talents that have to be matched with harpy half talents."

"Yes. But half a talent may become a full talent in time. I believe you have that potential."

"No offense, but I find that hard to believe."

"Keep it in mind. Maybe you and your wife came to share a talent, in the course of your long and close association, and you are in the process of inheriting the whole of it. Even Mundanes can develop talents in time. In fact there is now a Mundane Magician."

"Amazing!"

"Magic *is* amazing," Grey said seriously. "I came from Mundania, which provides me a certain exterior perspective. There are just so many remarkable aspects to magic. I would not believe in it at all if I didn't have constant experience with it."

"I certainly believe in magic. But it's hard to believe that I could have any of my own. Do you have any hint what kind of magic I might have or develop?"

"A hint, yes. No more. It is generally protective in nature. Not strong, but perhaps useful when needed."

Goody considered that. He had never dreamed he could have a magic talent of his own, but he was not in a position to doubt the Magician. What possible type could he have? "Protective" didn't narrow it down very far.

Wira returned with a motley bag. She handed it to Grey.

"Ah, yes, the four spells," Grey said. "These are potent, but have been used, so may be diminished in force or apt to end abruptly. So it is best not to invoke one until there is immediate need."

"Why are there four spells, instead of three or five?"

Grey laughed. "There are dozens of them. Such as

fourwarned, alerting you to danger by heightened senses of sight, smell, sound, and touch. Or fourshadowed, which provides you with four shadows reflecting your immediate past and future. Really intricate spells, but not fully reliable because of their age and wear and tear. In addition, they are all mixed up in the bag, so you can't be sure which one you're getting; you will just have to poke a finger into the bag and invoke the first one you touch."

"This seems less than convenient."

"It gets worse. Their terminations have been lost, so once invoked, they can't be turned off. So you may have four shadows far longer than you want them. But they are effective spells."

"I am not clear why—"

"Because we have a budget, and these are the most effective spells we can spare for this mission. So I'm afraid you will simply have to make do. With luck you won't need to invoke too many."

"With luck," Goody agreed weakly.

"But mainly, you will be protected by a bodyguard. We happen to have one who owes the Good Magician a service, and this is the assignment. I'm sure she will be able to get you out of most of the mischief the peeve will generate. So the spells are merely a reserve for when she can't."

"She?"

"Hannah Barbarian. A very effective warrior, and loyal to her mission in the barbarian manner. With her by your side, you won't even see most of the threats of the wilderness. They will stay clear, knowing better than to mess with her."

"But I have no desire to travel with a human woman!" Or any woman, he thought, whether goblin, naga, elf, or mer. He was too susceptible to their physical charms, and too unavailable emotionally. That was a bad combination.

Grey looked at him. "Well, you can turn down the mission. That is probably the better course."

That put him on his mettle. "No, I'll accept her protection. But I doubt she'll appreciate guarding a polite goblin."

"This is similar in a manner to the problem with the bird. We don't dare allow her to guard a normal goblin male. She would soon feed him to a dragon."

Goody appreciated the point. He also realized that the threats of the Xanth wilderness were myriad and deceptive, well worth not encountering. "I will try to get along with her."

"Then it is time to introduce you. I will take along the parody."

"But it will insult her!"

"Yes. I will have to clarify that aspect at the outset." Grey held forth his arm, and the silent bird hopped on.

"How is it that such a curmudgeon obliges your wish so readily?"

"It knows we are trying to find it a better situation. The parody is not stupid; satisfy it that a given course is best for it, and it will cooperate readily enough, out of sheer self-interest."

They made their way to what appeared to be a small arena. A warrior was practicing martial arts there with a wooden mockup. "Kiai!!" it cried fiercely. Smash with a mailed fist. Then violent chopping with a sword, and the dummy flew into pieces.

The figure paused as they approached. From up close Goody saw that it was indeed female, with a metallic halter and skirt, helmet, gauntlets, and spiked boots. The halter was full and the legs well shaped; otherwise it would have been hard to tell the gender.

Wira appeared. "Emergency in the rose garden," she told Grey urgently. "A querent got lost and stumbled into it, and the roses are slicing him."

"On my way!" Grey said. "Take the parody."

Goody took the bird, and Grey and Wira hurried off.

"What have we here?" Goody's voice said loudly. "A man in a skirt!"

Oh, no! The peeve was no longer nulled, and was having at the warrior maiden.

She faced him dangerously. "You can't recognize a healthy feminist activist when you see her? Are your eyeballs clogged?" Now it was apparent that there was long hair piled under the helmet.

"It talks!" his voice exclaimed. "It's alive! Who would ever have believed it? O the horror of it!"

"So," the maiden said, huffing into a larger size. "A mouthy goblin male."

"Oh, go chop some more kindling," Goody's voice said. "You swing like a collapsing wall anyway."

Hannah's face curled into a grim smile. "Do you know what we do to mouthy goblins where I came from?"

"Hug them and kiss them, honey pie?" Goody's voice asked sarcastically. "You sure couldn't damage them any other way. In case you hadn't noticed, you're not where you came from. No nice knitting needles here."

She advanced menacingly on him, raising her short sword. "Oh, really? I wonder how far your measly little head will fly from your body?"

"Not far enough to get clear of the smell of you, you stinking sheep in wolf's clothing."

Goody finally got his mouth open. "Wait! That's not me talking!"

Hannah paused. "You're starting to grovel?"

"You're the one who should grovel, you piece of rotten cheesecake. What a gruesome stench!"

"No, no!" Goody yelled. "I'm not saying it. It's the bird."

"Blaming it on the bird? What a sniveler!" She lifted her sword high. Its blade gleamed hungrily.

"You're the sniveler," Goody's voice said. "You're so full of snot it's sniveling on your shoes."

"Those are warrior boots, goblin. To protect my legs from flying blood." She took careful aim.

"The bird! The bird!" Goody cried desperately as he backed away. "It's imitating my voice!"

"Are you schizo?" Hannah demanded, her sword quivering in its eagerness to strike. "Make up your mind. Are you a goblin or a bird?"

"I'll give you the bird," his voice said. "Right up your piddling pink—"

Goody did the sensible thing: he fled.

"Oh no you don't!" Hannah said. "I'll cut you into such small bits they'll never know you existed." She pursued, taking much bigger steps than he could manage.

There was a set of wooden bleachers set up for spectators of arena events. Goody dived under it, still bearing the bird.

"You can't escape," Hannah said grimly. She swung at the bleachers. Chips of wood flew as she chopped them apart.

"Nyaa nyaa!" Goody's voice called in singsong. "You can't get mee, you effeminate biddy!"

"Ha! We'll see about that." She continued chopping. The bleachers were rapidly falling apart under the onslaught. In hardly more than three moments they were a pile of debris.

What could he do? There was nowhere else to hide.

Think outside the box.

Goody flung the parody at her. Startled, Hannah paused. The bird landed on her raised sword-arm and perched there, insolently eying her.

"Are you still here?" Hannah's voice demanded. "Why don't you crawl into the sewer where you'll feel at home, you ridiculous excuse for a goblin."

Hannah's eyes widened. "I didn't say that."

"The Good Magician is really scraping the bottom of the barrel to come up with you, you ludicrous imitation of a functioning creature. What made you think you could find your way out of a pigpen, let alone accomplish a quest, you awesomely stupid runt?"

Hannah eyed the peeve thoughtfully. "My voice— spoken by a bird." She looked at Goody. "This was the case with you?"

"Yes," Goody agreed, relieved. "That's a pet peeve. It insults everything, using your voice."

"Shut your face, you loathsome gob," her voice said.

"And what's your business with me, goblin?" the real Hannah inquired.

"I'm supposed to deliver this bird to a good home. You're supposed to guard me."

She nodded. "I think I can see why. Take back your bird." She shook her arm so that the parody had to jump off. It landed neatly on Goody's raised arm.

"About time, you crazy man-hating schemer," his voice said. "It's a good thing your panties don't show, because they wouldn't freak out anything."

"I gather you're not a typical male goblin," she said.

"I am the one polite male goblin," he agreed. "I always seek non-confrontation. I apologize for inflicting the bird on you, but—"

"I understand. It made you sound exactly *like* a typical male goblin."

"That's what you think, you typical petticoat slacker."

"Exactly," Goody said. "I can appreciate why you would not want to take on this onerous duty."

"No, it will be a challenge, now that I know the rules."

"You mean you'll do it?" Goody asked, amazed.

"The more fool you," his voice said. "Better to stick to your kitchen."

"I like challenges," Hannah said. "I like combat. This promises the best of both. You will certainly need competent protection."

"I certainly will," Goody agreed.

"Not that you can provide it, you sissy colleen," his voice said.

"Just for the record, I'm a feminist, not a man-hater. I believe in female rights being just as important as male rights. Do you have a problem with that?"

"I have a problem with your whole existence," Goody's voice said. "You're as poor an excuse for a female as this goblin is for a male."

"Now that's interesting," Hannah said. "You can insult your companion too? Doesn't that rather give away the ploy? How can others blame him for insulting himself?"

"Oops," the parody said, its feathers turning pink.

In the momentary silence, Goody answered for himself. "No, I believe in feminine rights. My wife—" He choked off.

"She's assertive?"

"No, not exactly. It was that anything she wanted, I wanted, so there was never a conflict. I wish she could have lived longer. I loved her."

"You're a widower?"

"Yes."

"So you're looking for another woman."

"Never! There could only ever be one Go-Go."

"But you're wearing a rose."

"It's a grief rose."

Hannah considered. "May I touch it?"

"I wouldn't recommend it. Theoretically only the woman I could love can take it. I think that means no woman."

"I understand. I don't want to take it, just touch it, to verify something."

"As you wish," he said with resignation.

She reached out with a finger and lightly brushed the stem of the rose. She winced. A drop of blood fell from her finger.

"Serves you right, tender piece."

"I'm sorry," Goody said.

"Don't be. I just verified that it is indeed magic, and that there will be no foolishness about our association."

Then Goody realized the nature of her concern. She did not want to maintain close contact with a male who might get ideas about her. It wasn't that he would ever, or could ever, force any male attentions on her, but even the idea of such interest could be embarrassing. She was a warrior, but also a very fine figure of a human woman.

"I'm glad we have come to this understanding," Goody said. "Your concern was sensible."

"You're a bleeding idiot," his voice said.

Goody and Hannah laughed together. The peeve was back in style.

"Let's get to know each other," Hannah said. "My talent is to be deadly accurate with weapons. If I strike with my sword, it will connect exactly where I intend. If I use a knife, it will score. If I use a shield, it will block the weapon of my opponent. This sort of thing is useful for a warrior maiden."

"I should think so," Goody agreed. He had just seen her effectiveness with the sword.

"So do you have a talent?"

Goody hesitated, remembering his prior discussion with Magician Grey Murphy. "I—don't know."

"Come on now. I told you mine."

"Goblins are supposed to have half talents that can't be used by themselves. But I may be different."

"Different?"

Grey and Wira returned before he could explain further, concerned about the mayhem that might have happened.

"We're ready to travel," Hannah Barbarian announced.

"Your two jaws are dragging on the ground, you incompetents," Goody's voice said. It was very nearly true.

## 3

# SPRING

They set off next morning, armed with supplies, weapons, and the parody. "Do we have a destination?" Hannah inquired.

"What kind of language is that?" the peeve demanded in Goody's voice. "You're supposed to be a barbarian. You should be uttering dull monosyllables and scratching your armpits."

"True barbarians are clean," Hannah replied equably. "It's the ignorant civilized miscreants who stink, in bodies and language."

"And not all of them," Goody added.

The parody gave up trying to insult them, because it was clear that they were no longer fooled. Ruffled, it looked around for some better target.

"But about our destination," Goody said. "I don't have anything specific in mind. But in a general way, I suspect that the enchanted paths will have mainly busy travelers, not looking for pets. So maybe the less-traveled regions are better. The relative wilderness, as it were."

"Where they aren't as smart," Hannah agreed. "Some might even think the baneful bird is cute."

The peeve ruffled further, but did not comment. It evidently wasn't used to receiving insults itself.

"Where is the most backward wilderness?"

"That would be the Region of Madness," she said. "That's south of here."

"South it is."

They left the path and cut south across field and forest. Goody hoped to find an isolated house, maybe a hermit residence, whose occupant would welcome even the dubious company of a pet peeve. He had more than a suspicion that it would not be nearly that easy.

They found a small path through a thicket. "I don't trust this," Hannah said. "It looks like a—"

"Well, look at that!" the parody said with Goody's voice. "If it had decent foliage, it might vaguely resemble a tree."

Goody looked where the path was leading. It was indeed a tree, surrounded by a small greensward. Its foliage consisted of drooping fronds or tentacles. He looked at Hannah. "Tangle tree," he mouthed silently.

She nodded. This was one of the most dangerous denizens of the vegetable kingdom. Tangle trees lured their prey within range by means of convenient paths, fragrant flower smells, pleasant scenery, and possible shelter from a storm, then grabbed them and consumed them. They needed to get well away from this.

Silently, they turned, hoping to escape before the tree realized that they had caught on. One could never be quite sure how far a tangler tentacle could reach.

"I've seen better strings on a kraken weed," the parody said loudly. "What a miserable excuse for a mop!"

The tangle tree quivered. Individual tentacles twitched. The alluring perfume intensified.

Goody and Hannah slowly stretched their lifted feet around toward the back. They needed to get out of range.

"And the stench!" the peeve continued. "Did a stink horn die here?"

That did it. Four tentacles flung out, whipping neatly around the arms of Goody and Hannah. They had not after all been quite out of range.

"My turn," Hannah said grimly. She whipped out her short sword before the vine around her sword arm could prevent it, and sliced through the opposite vine. Then she switched sword hands and severed the first.

Meanwhile Goody was being roughly hauled into the heaving green mass of the tree. "Help!" he cried as more tentacles caught hold of his limbs. Now he saw the trunk of the tree, with its huge wooden mouth and great thorny teeth. Tanglers were carnivorous plants, the pulped bodies of their victims getting digested by the roots.

"On my way," Hannah said. She forged toward him, whirling her blade.

"Pitiful effort, nymphet!" the parody called.

More tentacles flung at the warrior, but she sliced them off as quickly as they neared her. She reached Goody and hacked around him as though demolishing another stand of bleachers. Chunks of tentacle flew out and landed squishily on the ground around him. Then she grabbed him by the scruff of his shirt and hauled him out of the danger zone. Her hand brushed the gray rose, but it didn't stab her though the tips of her fingers were exposed.

"You beat the tangle tree!" he said breathlessly.

"Fighting tanglers is part of barbarian training," she said. "But we don't do it for pleasure."

"And you do a messy job," the parody said.

"Listen, birdbrain: it was going to eat you too."

The peeve considered that, and lapsed into grudging silence.

"Thank you for saving my life," Goody said.

"It's my job, remember? Bodyguard. No thanks to the bird."

Soon they resumed travel, avoiding the tangle tree. Beyond it was another tree, which wasn't surprising, considering that this was a forest. This one had regular leaves, and was covered with little fruits.

"That looks good," Goody said, getting hungry. "That looks like gum. It must be a gum tree."

"Or a variety," Hannah said. "I'll check." She picked a piece of gum, put it in her mouth, and chewed. "Better," she said. "This is a gumption tree. Serve yourself."

"Gumption? I don't understand."

"Eat some. You'll see."

Goody picked a piece of gum and chewed it. It tasted good. Not only that, he experienced a surging courage and feeling of competence. "Gumption," he agreed, pleased.

They picked a number of gums and saved them for future use, then went on, encouraged. They found a small forest path and followed it.

They encountered a man going the other way. He had orangy hair, and was accompanied by an unkempt mixed-breed dog. "Hello, stranger," Goody said boldly. "I am Goody Goblin."

"I am Rusty Human, and this is Mudgeon. He's a cur," the man said. "Don't touch me."

"And why not?" Hannah demanded, bridling.

"What makes you untouchable, dumbbell?" the parody demanded.

"That's the bird speaking," Goody said quickly.

Rusty looked confused, but bore with it. "My talent is to make anything I touch rust," he said. "A little rust won't kill you, but you wouldn't like it."

Hannah nodded. "Then we won't touch you."

"Lucky for you, metalrot," the parody said. "That goes double for your fleabag mutt."

Rusty frowned, and the cur Mudgeon growled. "Listen, goblin—"

"It's the bird," Hannah repeated firmly.

"Don't you believe it, corrosion creature," the peeve said.

Hannah put her hand on her sword.

Rusty considered her, seeing her armor and weapon, and decided to let it be. He and the dog moved on.

"We've got to stifle that bird," Hannah said.

"You and who else, doxie?"

"Do you want your scrawny neck wrung, fowl face?"

"You wouldn't dare, beef butt."

Hannah took a step toward the bird. The parody lurched off Goody's arm and flew up to land on a branch. "And where were you while this sickening slut threatened me, milquetoast?" it demanded. This time its voice sounded like the abrasion of branches rubbing together.

"Remember, it's just a dumb animal," Goody reminded her.

She nodded. "I almost forgot. I'll tune it out again."

The peeve flew back to Goody's arm. "That's what you think, harness halter."

She made a twisting motion with her hands. "I said *almost*, barf bird."

The bird decided to let the issue be. For the moment.

They moved on. Soon they encountered another person. This was a thin, stiff woman, who moved in a rather jerky manner. Yet she was quite pretty. Her face was set in a classic mode, and she had lovely hair.

"This bird speaks with my voice," Goody said quickly. "Ignore it."

"Hel-lo," the woman said jerkily. "I am Mary An-nette. I am a life-size pup-pet."

"String her up!" the parody said.

Mary's head rotated to orient on the bird. "I need no strings."

"So you say, blockhead."

"Ignore the bird," Hannah said. "Unless you'd like to adopt it. Then it would insult everyone but you."

"I can bring o-ther pup-pets to life," Mary said, "But I have no use for a nas-ty bird."

"Well, I have a use for *you*," the parody said. "Your face looks like the bottom of a birdcage."

"I think what you need is a life-size boy puppet to bring to life," Hannah said.

Mary smiled, somewhat woodenly. "Yes, that is what I need. Thank you." She walked jerkily on.

"Good riddance, you jerky piece of ash!"

It was getting late, and Goody was tired for more than physical reason. "Why don't we find a place to camp for the night?"

"I'm ready," Hannah agreed.

They came to a glade with a pool in the shape of a mundane car. "A nice car pool," Hannah said. "That should do." She set about chopping branches with her sword, and soon fashioned a comfortable lean-to shelter beside the pool.

Meanwhile Goody checked around the area, and found a nice fresh pie tree. They would not have to eat their backpack supplies this night.

Hannah gathered dry moss and kindling, then struck sparks from a stone with her sword to set it on fire, and built it up nicely. They had hot pies for supper. Even the parody seemed satisfied as it perched on a root and pecked at a pepper pie, because it made no derogatory remarks.

"You're pretty handy with that sword," Goody said. "I mean, using it to make a fire, though you handled that tangle tree effectively too."

Hannah hesitated, looking pained. She had removed her helmet so that her hair fell down around her face, framing it rather attractively.

"Did I say something offensive?" Goody asked. "I didn't mean to."

"Your whole existence is offensive," the peeve said with its ground-root voice.

"It's not that," Hannah answered, ignoring the bird. "It's just that I never traveled with anyone before, especially not a goblin, especially not a male. I don't know how to handle a compliment."

"Don't worry about it, fatal femme. You'll never get another."

Goody smiled. "I learned how from my wife. No matter what it is, you smile and say thank you. Then you find something nice to say in return."

"What a load of fresh cow flops!"

"Oh—like a return strike when your opponent tries to cut off your head."

"Too bad he didn't succeed, you dizzy dame."

"Similar," Goody agreed. "I suppose the rules for positive exchanges do resemble those for negative ones. But it is important not to get them confused."

"That lets both of you out. You're always confused."

She smiled. "I'll try to keep them straight. Is it too late to respond to your compliment?"

"It is never too late for that."

"It's way too late!" the bird said petulantly.

She put on a smile. "Thank you."

"You're welcome."

"No you aren't, you foolish floozy."

They finished their meal as dusk came. "I got hog sweaty fighting that tangler," Hannah said. "I'd better dunk my hide." She stood and undid her metallic halter.

"Wow!" the peeve said. "A strip tease!"

"Wait!" Goody said. "You can't strip in front of a man."

She paused. "Why not? You're not much of a man."

"You said it, sister!"

Goody might have preferred more circumspect phrasing, but didn't care to make an issue of it. "It—it is not considered socially polite to disrobe in company. You're a fine looking woman, and—"

"You're an overstuffed squaw!"

She smiled carefully. "Thank you."

"I mean, normally women value their privacy."

"What do you have to be private about, hussy?"

"Oh, do they? They didn't cover that in barbarian school."

"So men won't get ideas."

"As if you could ever get an idea, goblin noggin."

"But you're in grief and have no ideas," she said. "I checked. That gray rose." She resumed undressing.

"Still, as a general social rule—"

"Take it off! Take it off, strumpet!"

"I'm not good at social rules. I just like to get the job

done, whatever it is." Now her top was bare. It was spectacular. She started on the bottom.

"I've seen better cones by roadside construction."

"I should at least turn my back," Goody said uncomfortably.

"So I can scrub it? All right. Get it bare."

"Yes, bare your bumbling bones, goblin gook."

He realized that she was right. There was no reason for squeamishness. She was unconscious of any awkwardness, and he should be too. They were after all of two different species. "I suppose we're like family," he said. "I need to wash too."

"For once you're making sense. You both stink like constipated pigs."

Hannah's hand shot out and caught the bird by the feet. "You're coming too, crow bait."

"I'll fly away, you feminist garbage," it threatened with her voice.

She took a long tress of her hair and knotted it about one of the peeve's legs. "I think knot," she said, smiling. She set the bird on her head.

"I'll poop on your hair!"

"If you do, I'll dive wa-ay down deep to wash it off."

The parody looked thoughtful and kept its beak (or whatever) shut. The knot on its leg was quite tight.

They both stripped and waded into the water, which was pleasantly cool. Hannah had to go out twice as far as he, being twice as tall. "Yee-haa!" she cried, leaping up and coming down with a great splash. She was indeed barbarian.

"Watch it, harridan!" the peeve exclaimed. "You're wetting me."

"Oh, like this?" She scooped a handful of water and fired it at her own head. It smacked into the bird, thoroughly soaking it.

The peeve got the message. It ceased protesting. Goody rather admired the way she was handling it. Barbarians evidently had a knack with animals.

Then she waded halfway back, dripping from several rounded points, heading right for him. Goody hoped he had no reason to be alarmed. She dropped beside him and sat on the sand beneath so as to be his height. "I'll do your back now."

Oh. "Thank you." He turned away.

"You're blushing, goblin twerp," the bird said from her head.

Goody hoped that was not the case. His skin was of course goblin dark, but it was possible for a goblin to blush, and his surface was making the effort.

Her hands were strong yet gentle as she stroked, then kneaded his back and shoulders. "Oh, that feels good!" he said.

"Well, it doesn't *look* good! If you were any scrawnier it would take two men and a bird just to see you."

"Barbarian massage. It relaxes the muscles after a hard day's battle. You can do me next."

"Front or back?" the bird demanded.

He did her next, emulating her motions as his hands went over her tightly muscled back and shoulders. He felt the knots relaxing, and knew he was getting the job done. She was big and strong, but there were ways in which she reminded him of Go-Go. Probably it was just that she was female.

"You have the touch," she said. "Maybe it's your talent."

"Goblins don't have talents." But then he remembered what Magician Murphy had said. "But maybe I will develop one some day."

"There's love in your hands. I never felt that before."

"Why would you *want* to, cutie pie?" the bird demanded with overwhelming sarcasm.

Oh. "I was thinking of my wife. That always melts me."

"That's what I'm feeling, then."

"You got it backwards, babe. *He's* feeling up *you.*"

They finished and waded out of the water. They had no towels, but that was no problem for Hannah. She simply shook herself in place, doglike, making the water fling out in every direction.

"Squawk!" the parody protested dizzily.

But it wasn't the water that bothered Goody. His eyes locked up and his breath froze. The world went darker than the dusk.

A hand whammed him on the back, nearly jarring his teeth loose. "Come out of it, goblin! What's the matter with you?"

"The jerk freaked out!" the bird said.

Goody gasped in a breath as his eyes creaked back into focus. "This time the peeve is right. I—I think I freaked out."

"Freaked out?"

"When you shook your body. There was so much, so close, so mobile—above and below—"

"Too much hot wet meat whomping around," the bird clarified helpfully.

She was amazed. "My body did that? But I'm no nymph!"

"You could pass for one, unclothed. A muscular one. I was caught off guard. I'm sorry."

"The little louse's a man after all. Who would have thought it?"

"I freaked you out," she repeated. "I never thought I could do that to any male. I'm a warrior woman."

"A battling bawd."

"Now you know," he said, smiling wanly.

"I wonder if it would work in combat? If I was really hard pressed and needed a secret weapon."

"I believe it would work," he said. "Especially against human males."

"What a discovery!" she exclaimed, pleased.

"Thirty-six years old, and she's just discovered sex!"

The bird could be uncomfortably accurate. "I am glad to have helped," Goody said, wondering how it knew her age.

Hannah reached up and untied the loop of hair holding the bird to her head. "Go find your own perch, fowlmouth." She went to fetch her clothing where it had dried on bushes. Goody clapped a hand over his eyes before she got into her steel-mesh panties, saving himself another freakout.

They finished dressing, and things were safe again. Goody gathered pillows from a pillow bush.

"What are you doing?"

"Fetching something soft to sleep on."

The parody flew up to roost on the front pole of the lean-to. "Make her take off her halter again, idiot!"

Goody's skin made another effort to blush.

"Why bother? The ground is good enough." She flung herself down under the lean-to in her clothing and was instantly asleep.

Well, she *was* a barbarian. Goody placed his pillows beside her and lay on them. He was soon soundly asleep too.

"Well, now!"

Goody woke. That was the peeve's voice. "Is there a problem?"

"No. Go back to sleep, runty."

Hannah stirred. "The dirty bird wants us asleep? I don't trust this."

Both of them quietly got up. There was a light out on the pool. What was going on out there?

"Well, stuff me in a bottle and call me a pickle," Hannah breathed. "It really *is* a car pool."

Indeed it was. Cars were lined up on the far side, with headlights slanting toward the pool. Kiddie cars and motorcycles were sporting in the water, supervised by the full-sized cars. Sport cars were racing along the sand, and bold pickup trucks were sparking with well-upholstered limousines.

Several cars got together and made music for others to dance to. Pictures also appeared in the flickering headlights of a car labeled with the words Anni Mae, showing cars doing funny things. "Car tunes," Hannah whispered.

Something nudged Goody's foot. He looked down. There in the faint light left over from the distant cars was a miniature car, a toy, nudging his ankle. In fact there were a number of them, covering the ground before them. "What's this?"

"A car-pet, imbecile!"

It seemed the bird was right: the ground was covered with friendly little cars seeking adoption. Finding no takers here, they soon rolled on around the lake.

"It seems harmless," Goody said. "And not our business." He returned to his bed.

"Look at the tailpipe on that doxie," the parody said. "That's revving some motors."

"Forget it," Hannah said. "She's already hitched to a semi."

Fortunately Goody was too far into sleep to wonder about it.

By morning the cars were clear. They ate more pies, cleaned up the campsite, and were ready to move on.

The parody hopped onto Goody's shoulder. "You're looking good today, mop-head," it said to Hannah.

"Thank you." Then she changed her mind. "Wait half an instant. You never compliment anybody. What's wrong with my head?"

"I'll never tell, tanglehair."

She faced Goody. "What?"

"Well, your hair is rather tangled under your helmet. I suppose that's all right for a barbarian warrior lass."

"But not if I should happen to want to freak out an enemy warrior man with my body," she said, catching on. "How do I fix it so I can charm a man if I ever want to?"

"Say, you're getting those sneaky distaff ways, chick!"

"My wife used to braid hers to keep it out of the way, and coil the braid on her head." He was able to speak of his wife without sinking into an abyss of grief now; it seemed the gray rose was helping.

"That's way too much trouble. I'll just comb it out." She lifted off her helmet, plucked a comb from a bush and started ripping it through her tangles.

"Rip it all out, playmate!" the bird advised.

"If I may assist—" Goody said.

She considered half a moment. "Fix it like your wife's hair." She sat on the ground and gave him the comb.

"Braided and coiled? That would take some time."

"That's right. I forgot. Then just leave it loose."

He used the comb carefully, and soon enough had disentangled the tangles and combed her tresses out into a fair flair that flowed silkily down her back.

"You actually have very nice hair," Goody said.

"You ruined it!" the parody complained. "What a mess!"

"That confirms it," she said, satisfied as she set the helmet carefully over it, letting the tresses show below. "Thank you."

"Welcome."

They got on their way. Soon they encountered an ogre who was entertaining himself by twisting saplings into square knots. By mutual consent, they elected to pass him by, as ogres were not safe to mess with.

"What a weakling," Goody's voice said loudly.

The ogre paused. Ogres were the strongest creatures of the forest, and knew it, and liked to prove it. Then he picked up a fist-sized stone. "Who speak me weak?" he demanded.

Goody tried to fade back as the ogre's short attention span made him forget what had annoyed him.

"And smart, too."

The ogre huffed up. Cracks appeared in the stone he held. Ogres were justifiably proud of their stupidity.

Goody set himself to run. "And handsome as they come," the bird concluded. And of course ogres loved being ugly.

Juice dripped from the fragmented squeezed stone as the ogre took a step toward Goody. "Me do a job on big-mouth gob."

"I'll handle this," Hannah said.

"Please, no bloodshed," Goody said. "It's not the ogre's fault. Maybe we can apologize."

"With the pet peeve on your shoulder?" She put her hand on her sword. "Pacifism can't counteract *that*."

She had a monstrous point. "Or at least delay until we can escape," Goody said desperately.

A bulb flashed over her head. "Female wiles," she said. "Maybe they'll work. I'll distract him while you and the bird get clear."

"Spoilsport!"

"Agreed," Goody said.

Hannah faced the slowly advancing ogre, opening her halter. "Hello, you ugly brute," she said. "We were just trying to get your attention, because you looked too stupid to understand anything."

The ogre gazed dully at her, mollified. "Me see a she."

Hannah moved her head, flinging her hair about in nymphly style. Ogres liked ugly in their own kind, but were not entirely immune to nymphly charms. "Yes, we are just passing through." She inhaled.

The ogre's eyes began to glaze. The maiden's charms were working. Goody took a cautious step backward.

"She says she's seen trolls uglier, stronger, and duller than you are!" the peeve called.

That snapped the ogre out of it. He grabbed a small tree, ripped it out of the ground, and prepared to club the barbarian woman with it.

"Panties!" Goody called. "Flash them!"

She whirled, drawing up her metal skirt. Goody turned away in time, but the ogre didn't. In a moment he was frozen in place, caught in mid swing.

Back on the trail, safely past the ogre, halter back in place, Hannah murmured with satisfaction. "It worked," she said. "It really worked. I paused him with my hair, stopped him with my chest, and froze him with my panties. I'm a successful nymph!"

"Aw, you were just lucky," the parody said.

"And you didn't have to hurt him," Goody said, relieved.

They climbed a moderate hill and came to a sign partly shrouded by foliage. Goody peered at it, making it out. LOVE SPRING.

"We don't need that," Goody said. "We had better circle well around it."

"Amen."

"What's a love spring?" the parody demanded.

"What, are you asking questions now, you ill-tempered avian?" Goody asked. "Are you thinking about reforming your nasty nature?"

"That'll be the day!" Hannah said, laughing.

But Goody felt constrained to answer the question, as it was the polite thing to do. "A love spring causes any people or creatures who drink or touch its water to—"

Then the ground gave way beneath them, and they slid helplessly into the spring.

"Ha ha!" the peeve called as it hovered in the air. "I distracted you so you didn't see the overhang. You morons!"

And the two of them splashed into the water. It was deep enough for Goody to float and Hannah to stand with her head clear, so that her armor didn't sink her. They weren't hurt, but were thoroughly soaked.

"Oh, no!" Goody cried, swimming toward her. "This isn't what I want."

"If I had to choose someone to get dunked in a love spring with, it sure wouldn't be you," Hannah said, disgusted, as she oriented to meet him.

"What a laugh!" the parody chortled. "Now you're really in for it!"

"D—da—dam!" He couldn't get the bad word out; what emerged was something to do with a dike for water.

"Bleep!" Hannah swore, doing it for him.

Then, respectively floating and standing, they embraced each other and kissed passionately.

"Oooo, what clumsy smooching! Why don't you put some real oomph into it, you amateurs!"

"We can't do this here," Goody gasped as they broke for a breath.

"Or in clothing," she agreed. That had not been exactly what he meant.

"Ha ha ha!" the peeve laughed. For once it wasn't peevish, oddly.

They clasped and kissed again. The barbarian woman was really quite compelling when she tried, to his dismay. Now he wished he hadn't helped her learn how to be feminine.

"I hate this," Goody said at the next break. "I'm in grief for Go-Go." Another hot kiss as he stroked her back.

"Quit fooling around and get down to business," the parody called.

"If it weren't for the barbarian code of honor that requires me to complete my assignment, I'd pulverize you rather than do this." She put her hands on his rear and hauled him in to her halter for a heart-throbbing squeeze.

"What are you two doing in my pond?" a voice demanded.

They paused to look. It was a lovely lady standing by the edge of the pool. She wore a beautiful short dress with wet hems. She looked like a water fairy.

"We fell in," Goody said awkwardly. "We didn't mean to."

"And we wish we hadn't," Hannah said.

"The last thing we wanted to do was fall in a love spring," Goody said.

The woman laughed. "Love spring? Whatever gave you that idea?"

"That sign," Hannah said.

"What sign?"

"The one on the bank above that says LOVE SPRING," Goody said.

She laughed. "You mean the LOVE SPRINGS ETERNAL sign at the lookout ledge? I've been meaning to clip back the encroaching foliage."

Goody and Hannah exchanged a gaze of something

other than passion as they disengaged. "Part of it was covered," Hannah muttered.

"I'd be relieved if I weren't so embarrassed," he said. "We didn't have to—to—"

"Whatever," she agreed crossly.

They swam and waded to shore and emerged in their dripping clothes. The woman went the other way, wading into the water. Her dress became a fish tail. She was a mermaid!

"Perhaps we should introduce ourselves," she said. "I am Lorelei, the Siren's lesser-known cousin who was lost in the Void but managed somehow to find her way out."

"I am Goody Goblin, the only polite male of my kind, on a mission for the Good Magician."

"I am Hannah Barbarian, assigned to guard this goblin."

"It is an education to meet both of you," Lorelei said. "It does get rather quiet in this isolated spot."

"Would you like to have a talking bird?"

"Bird?"

"I need to find a good home for this pet peeve." Goody indicated the parody, who was now hovering silently above the pool.

"Why, that might be nice," Lorelei agreed. "Is it housebroken?"

"Housebroken!" the peeve exclaimed, outraged. "I'll poop in your pool!"

"Don't you dare!"

But she was too late. A nugget plopped into the water.

"Unfortunately it's obnoxious," Goody said.

"It certainly is!" Lorelei agreed. "Shoo! Get away from here, bird!"

"And what if I don't, you wet piece of tail?"

The mermaid put her hands together. A jet of water shot up, scoring on the bird.

"Awk!" The parody tumbled through the air, righting itself barely in time to land on Goody's shoulder. "You fishy wench!" it sputtered with Goody's voice.

"We'll take that as a no on the bird," Hannah said.

"Do you have any idea who might be interested?" Goody asked.

"Maybe someone in the Region of Madness," Lorelei said as she gingerly scooped up the bird dropping and hurled it into the brush. "They'd have to be mad." She washed her hands off vigorously.

That about covered it.

# 4

# No Man's Land

They found a private glade where they could strip and dry, no longer sensitive to the problem of exposure or the bird's risqué remarks. Hannah found some fireweed that was useful for heating and drying their clothing, but they didn't dare hang it so close as to burn. It was easier to wait.

"I wish to apologize for my behavior in the mermaid's pool," Goody said.

Hannah shook her head. "You really are polite! I was as much at fault as you."

"It is amazing how influential suggestion can be. We saw the sign, and assumed we were compelled."

"We should have known better."

"If we are ever in a similar situation—"

"We'll stop and check to see if it is real, before we act."

"Before we act," he agreed.

She hesitated. "Now don't misunderstand, but—"

Goody felt himself trying to blush again. "We are definitely not cut out to ever be a couple."

"Right. You're a goblin and I'm a barbarian. But—"

"But it was fun kissing."

"It was fun kissing," she agreed. "Let's never do it again."

"Agreed! What this suggests is that we are perhaps more ready than we thought to find appropriate partners, if they exist."

"That's it exactly. A nice goblin girl for you, a brutish barbarian lout for me. Too bad Jordan's taken."

"Jordan?"

"A barbarian male. There's a whole book about him somewhere; he's become part of the legend."

"Maybe he has a brother."

"And maybe there's a goblin girl who likes politeness."

"There's always faint hope," he agreed.

"Fat chance, you dunces."

"And maybe a bird for you," Hannah said to the parody. "What gender are you?"

"None of your business, strumpet."

Their clothing was dry. They donned it and were ready to travel again. "Are you familiar with the Region of Madness?" Hannah inquired.

"I have heard of it, of course, but never ventured within it."

"The same for me. I understand that truly weird things exist in that area. Are you sure you want to venture there?"

"Is there any better chance to place the bird?"

"Asked and answered," she agreed ruefully. "Only a madman would be crazy enough to want to adopt this miscreant creature."

"You said it, hussy!"

They marched south, toward the dread Region of Madness.

There was a trembling in the earth. Hannah put her hand on her sword and stood ready, while Goody stayed back and watched. There was no telling what they might encounter as they approached Madness.

The ground gave one last quiver. Then a hole opened almost under her feet and a blue snout poked out. *A greeting, fair maiden.* Goody heard it in his head, and was sure Hannah did too.

"What outside of tarnation are you?" Hannah demanded.

The snout was followed by a green and brown worm-like body with squat red legs. *Vortex Dragon, you delicious creature.*

She was astonished. "You're a dragon? You don't look like any dragon I've ever seen."

*Your legs are lovely, but let me get separate so I can concentrate.*

Hannah hastily jumped back, realizing that the dragon was peering up under her skirt. "Is that you talking in my head?"

Vortex coiled, snakelike, holding his head high. He was about one and a half human people long, from snout to tail-tip. *Let me attune.* "There: is that better?"

Goody came forward. "Now you're talking!"

"I am projecting my thoughts into your mind, phrasing them to emulate a verbal voice."

"Mind reading!" Hannah exclaimed.

"I am telepathic, true. It is one of my aspects. My full description is medium-small suction tunneling friendly telepathic male dragon. And you are?"

"Goody: polite male goblin."

"Hannah: barbarian female human."

"Go soak your snout, worm-face."

The dragon oriented on the bird. "I believe you would make a good meal, parody."

"Don't try to threaten me, you pitiful imitation monster. You don't even have any teeth."

"Nor do I require them." The dragon lifted his snout. It widened, becoming a flaring tube. Dusty air sucked in, spiraling, forming a miniature tornado. The whirling air extended toward the bird. It tugged at Goody's clothing and hair. It was about to suck in the peeve!

Hannah drew her sword.

"Wait!" Goody cried. "This bird is not for eating."

The tornado faded. "Are you sure? It seems too obnoxious to allow to live."

"My job is to find it a good home. I can't afford to let it get eaten."

"In that case I will let it go, against my better judgment."

"I never heard of a telepathic sucking dragon," Hannah said. "Are you from the Region of Madness?"

"No, I am part of the recent dragon immigration facilitated by the Muse of History. It seems that an affliction decimated the original dragon population, so we were asked to colonize from Dragon World. Being of alien derivation, we have qualities that are not identical to those of the locals. We are still spreading out, settling into our ecological niches, as it were. I apologize for inconveniencing you."

There was something about this creature that appealed to Goody. "We are glad to make your acquaintance."

"I shall be on my way. If you should change your mind about the availability of the peevish bird for consumption, please give me a mental call." He pointed his snout at the ground, then seemed to dive into it as if it were water. In not much more than a moment and a half he was gone, leaving solid ground behind.

"Good riddance!" the peeve called, after the dragon was safely gone.

"I didn't realize there was a dragon immigration," Goody said.

"Neither did I. But come to think of it, a couple years back I encountered fewer dragons than usual. So maybe a plague did thin them out."

"He wasn't fooling about having different qualities. Sucking in prey, tunneling through the ground—"

"And telepathic. That's not unknown in dragons, but I got the impression it is routine for his world."

They walked on. Soon they came to an archway. Above it was a decoratively curving sign: LET NO MAN ENTER THESE OUR PREMISES.

"I would not want to intrude where I am not wanted," Goody said. "We must find another route."

"Aw, go ahead, spoilsport," the peeve said, ever alert for mischief.

"It's solid prickly tangle east and west," Hannah said. "I've been keeping an alert barbarian eye out. We'd have to make a long detour, and the day is getting on."

"But the sign says—"

"Technically, you're not a man. You are a male goblin. Maybe it's just human louts it doesn't want."

"I don't approve of invoking technicalities."

"Chicken! Buk buk buk BAWK!"

"Shut your beak," Hannah snapped. "We're trying to make a decision here."

"I'll help you, sour skirt." The peeve launched into the air and flew through the archway.

"Bleep!" Hannah swore, pursuing it.

Without thinking, Goody followed. As he passed under the arch, something peculiar happened to his clothing.

Hannah stood in the path, the peeve on her shoulder. "Oops," she said.

"What a sight!" the bird said, its beady eyes staring.

"I don't understand," Goody said, trying to adjust his shirt, which had become uncomfortably tight across the chest.

"Let's just get you on out of here," Hannah said, hustling him back through the archway.

"It didn't work!" the peeve cried, delighted.

"What didn't work?"

"It didn't change you back," Hannah said, looking half stunned.

"Back to what? I'm still Goody Goblin, aren't I?"

"Back to a man."

Goody looked down at himself. His shirt bulged out

with two rounded projections on his chest. His legs had
thickened, especially in the upper thighs. His hair felt
longer. "To a what?"

"Take off your shirt."

He was glad to, to alleviate the constriction. Then he
saw the problem: his chest was now formed into two full
female breasts.

"Get a load of those boobs!" the peeve cackled.

"Check your hardware."

He felt inside his trousers. There was nothing there.

He felt faint. "What—?"

"You are now a woman."

"I can't be!"

"It seems that's what the arch sign meant. Not that no
man should enter, but that no man could. Because it
changes genders."

"And doesn't change back!" the bird exalted.

"This can't be," he protested.

"It didn't affect me," she said. "Just you. It seems to be
a one-way transformation. You will have to get used to
being a girl."

"Ha ha ha ha ha!"

Goody grabbed for the peeve, but it flew up out of
reach.

"Come on, I'll help you adjust. There is suitable clothing beyond the arch, maybe by no coincidence." Hannah
led him back through. This time his body did not change.

She outfitted him—he might have a female body now,
but he still thought of himself as male—with a small bra,
panties, blouse, skirt, slippers, and a ribbon to tie back
his longer hair. "You helped me be female," she murmured. "I'm returning the favor."

He winced. "Thank you." He put his backpack back on.

"Let's be sensible: if there's a no-man's-land, there
must be a no-woman's-land too. We just have to find it."

Goody brightened. "That would help."

They followed the path toward wherever it was going.

It seemed routine. They saw fat butterflies and thin margarine flies, winged oblongs of yellow substance. On the ground were dull ignor-ants and excited ant-icipations. There was a bat flying from cookie to cookie in a cookie field, knocking them off their stems: a cookie batter. A bush by a pond was covered with ticks. Goody recognized a loon-a-tick, whose bite would cause a person to feel compelled to dive for fish. They passed a field of candy corn, with a lady farmer made of candy. Nothing out of the ordinary.

"Maybe let's not mention my, ah, origin," Goody suggested. "I'm really not used to it."

"Agreed."

They found a campsite. A woman was there before them. "Hello," she said. "You must be new here. I'm Hazel; my talent is to change the color of my eyes." She demonstrated as she spoke, her eyes going from hazel to blue, and back again. "Welcome to No Man's Land. You will never be bothered by a man here; it's a sanctuary."

"What crap," the peeve said with Goody's voice.

Hazel's mouth tightened. "How's that?"

"It's the bird," Hannah said quickly. "It borrows our voices to insult people."

"Don't believe it, harridan!"

"We're looking for a good home for it," Goody said quickly. "It's a bit awkward to have around."

Hazel squinted at the peeve. "I can appreciate that. I don't think anyone here would want such a creature."

"What the bleep do you know, pooch?"

Hazel's face hardened. "Maybe you folk had better move on with your bird."

"We'll do that," Hannah agreed.

"The goblin's a boy," the peeve said.

So much for privacy; it was impossible with the bird.

"Not anymore," Hazel said. "Didn't you see the warning sign?"

"The bird flew in, and he had to follow," Hannah explained.

Hazel nodded. "Why don't you simply feed it to a nest of nickelpedes?"

"So much for you, you vomit-faced Jezebel! No more Nice Bird! Now I'll really cuss you out!"

"We admit to being tempted," Hannah said quickly. "But our mission is to place it in a good home."

"No good home would accept such a wretch."

"This dump accepted *you*, you fixed canine."

"Is there anywhere I can get turned back into a man?" Goody asked. "We'll be happy to go there immediately."

Hazel considered half a moment. It was obvious that she wanted the bird to be far away, soon. "You might try No Woman's Land. I haven't been there, of course, but I understand it has a masculizing effect."

"Not that a butch like you needs it."

"Thank you," Goody said eagerly. "Where is it?"

"Somewhere beyond here. That's all I know."

"We'll find it," Hannah said grimly.

They departed the campsite quickly. "I wonder if we could tie string around the bird's beak to keep it shut," Hannah said.

"You wouldn't dare, you hotted up battledore."

Hannah reached toward the parody, but it flew up out of the way. It was merely a gesture; she hadn't moved as fast as she could have, and in a moment the bird settled back down to perch on Goody's shoulder. Their quarrels were becoming ritualized.

A swirl of smoke formed before them. "What's aloft?"

"What's this?" Hannah asked, surprised.

The cloud solidified. "Elevate, above, buoy, build, ascend—"

"Up?" Goody asked.

"Whatever," the shape agreed crossly.

"What the bleep are you?" Hannah demanded.

"The Demoness Metria," Goody said.

A luscious female form clarified. "And who are you, goblin girl?"

"Goody Goblin in drag," the parody said.

The demoness transformed into a glowing lightbulb, and back to herself. "Of course! This is No Man's Land. Not worth the stumble."

"Worth the what?" Hannah asked.

"Loss of balance, misstep, movement, passage, voyage—"

"Trip?"

"Whatever. There are no men to torment here, so what's the point?"

"What a nincompoop!" Goody's voice said.

The demoness oriented on him. "How's that again, goblin?"

The parody answered before Goody could speak. "Nitwit, dope, clod, ass, pinhead—"

"I know the bleeping word!" the demoness snapped, fire flickering on her breath. "Do you want to live another millisecond, goblin?"

Hannah interposed herself. "It's the bird, using his voice. Her voice. Whatever."

The fire eased into hot coals. "Oh. So what does he/she want?"

"I want to get back my gender," Goody said. "Do you know where No Woman's Land is?"

"It won't drudge."

Goody hated this, but was stuck for it, because he wanted her help. "Won't what?"

"Strain, pull, exert, labor, do a job—"

"Work?"

"Whatever! You can't get from here to there."

"But I have to change back!"

"Too bad. Oo-toodle." Metria faded out.

"Oo-toodle?" Hannah asked.

"She gets her words confused," Goody said.

"Didn't you notice, poop-for-brains?"

Hannah flicked a finger at the bird, reminding Goody oddly of the Finger that had started him on this adventure, and the parody twitched a wing as if ready to fly.

"So it seems we have a problem," the barbarian said.

"We?"

"Less of one for me. Do you think you can complete your mission as a gobliness?"

"No!"

"But you know your personality already matches. You can make a very good lady goblin."

"Something's missing."

"Fortunately it doesn't show."

"Haw haw haw!" the peeve laughed.

Goody didn't find it all that funny, but realized that the bird hadn't meant him to be amused. "We've got to get to No Woman's Land."

"But the demoness said—"

"Metria may not have had quite the right word."

She looked at him with masked pity. "Very well. We'll search for the route."

They walked on. Soon they came to a dog whose body was in the shape of a numbered dial with a long pointer and a short pointer radiating from its center. It was sitting and scratching ceaselessly.

Goody had sympathy for animals in trouble. "What's the matter?" he asked it.

The dog glanced at him as if he were an idiot and went on scratching.

"I believe that's a watch dog," Hannah said.

"And it's got ticks," the peeve said.

Goody realized that there was no cure for what ailed the dog, because when the ticks stopped, so would the dog. So he walked on, hoping this was not a clumsy parallel to his own situation.

Next they came to an olive green girl sitting beside the path. She was holding a baby. This seemed odd, because the storks normally did not deliver to children.

"Let's leave the peeve out of this," Hannah said. "Better that you talk to her alone."

"Bleep!" But the bird fluttered to her shoulder, knowing that nothing would happen until it did.

Goody walked on. The girl continued to croon to her baby.

"Hello, little girl," Goody said, wondering whether it would be polite to inquire about the baby. Probably not, but he could ask about No Woman's Land.

"Hello, goblin girl," the child replied.

"I am Goody. I was wondering—"

"I am I love you."

That set him back. "I don't think I—"

"Olive Hue," she repeated carefully. "Because I'm green."

Oh. "I apologize for mishearing."

"That's all right. Everybody does. I'm green because I envy all you normal folk with real friends. What's your talent?"

"I'm not sure I have one. Most goblins don't."

"Mine's to make imaginary friends. This is Lorlai."

"Lorelei?" he asked, surprised, because that was the name of the Siren's sister.

"Lorlai Fiona," she said carefully. "She's 4.7 months old. She needs me."

"I apologize for—"

"Everybody does. I can make others."

"Others?"

"Imaginary friends." The baby faded out.

Goody was finding this exchange to be more challenging than anticipated. "Uh, all right."

Two bigger girls appeared. They were evidently twins, one of light complexion, the other dark.

"Hello, Goody," the dark one said. "I am Olive's imaginary friend Suretha. My talent is to turn day to night." The light of day faded, and the scene became dark.

"And I am her sister Sharina," the other girl said. "My

talent is to turn night to day." The darkness abated, and it was day again.

Goody digested this. Imaginary friends with real talents? That gave him a wild notion. "I am impressed. Maybe you can help me."

"Sure. But my friends don't last." The twins faded out.

"I am looking for something and don't know where or how to find it. Would any of your friends—"

"Sure."

An older woman appeared. "Hello, Goody. I am Mysteria. My talent is to create what is needed, but I don't know what it is or how to use it."

Goody wasn't sure about that, but maybe it was better than nothing. "Would you be willing to create what I need?"

"Certainly." An object appeared in her hand. She proffered it to him.

Goody looked at it. It was a small statuette or a large key in the shape of a person. "Thank you."

But Mysteria was already fading out. The object, however, remained.

"Uh, may I keep this?" he asked Olive, who now had the baby back.

"Sure. It's yours." She resumed crooning.

"Thank you." He walked back to Hannah and the peeve.

"About time!" the bird carped. "Day and night passed waiting on you, you slacker."

So the effects had been real for the others too. Those were truly remarkable imaginary friends!

"Any luck?" Hannah asked.

"Some, but I'm not sure what kind." He showed the statuette. "This is what I need."

"What does it do?"

"I don't know."

"How do you use it?"

"I don't know that either."

"What an ignoramus!"

"And is its purpose and application clear to you,

peeve?" he demanded as he pocketed the object. That shut the bird up, for a while.

"Well, maybe the answers will come," Hannah said dubiously.

They walked on. They came to a field of hot crossed buns that looked delicious. It was midday, so Goody picked one and bit into it.

The thing puffed into foul-tasting smoke in his mouth that burned his tongue. "Yuck!" he exclaimed, blowing out a blot of smoke in the shape of a cross.

"That's a hot crossed pun!" Hannah said. "Are you going to be emitting smelly puns for a day?"

"I think I spat it out in time."

"I hope so. The bird's bad enough already, without that."

"What do you call a big drum carried by two nuns?"

She looked at him suspiciously. "Is that a—"

"A conundrum!" he said. "Co-nun-drum."

"Ugh! You swallowed some of that crossed pun!"

"I suppose I did," he agreed ruefully. "I think I got it all out now."

"What a stinker," the parody said with satisfaction. "Got any more?"

Hannah peered ahead. "There may be real food across that river."

Goody looked. "But how do we get across? I see colored fins."

She nodded. "Not worth trying to swim. But there must be a way."

They walked along the bank, and the colored fins paralleled them. Those were likely loan sharks, eager to take an arm and a leg if given opportunity.

A woman was sitting on the bank, flipping small coins to the loan sharks. "Don't feed the fish!" Hannah said. "That will make them lose their fear of man."

"There are no men here," the girl pointed out. "Do you need to get across?"

"Yes. Do you know a way?"

"Of course. I am Brigitte. I make bridges appear. That's my talent."

Brigitte—bridge-it. Goody wondered if the girl had partaken of the hot-crossed puns. "We could use a bridge."

Brigitte gestured. A bridge appeared, spanning the river. "Welcome. That's why I'm here."

"You call that a bridge? I've seen a better span on lace!"

"Really?" The bridge disappeared.

"It's the bird!" Goody explained. "It imitates my voice to insult people. It's a fine bridge."

Brigitte looked unconvinced.

"Try it yourself," Goody said desperately. "Take the bird on your arm and listen."

"Oh, all right," she said. "But I don't believe it."

The parody hopped onto her lifted wrist. "Did you ever see a snottier looking goblin girl?" her voice inquired. "You'd swear she's a man in a dress."

Brigitte nodded. "Now I believe."

"Would you like to adopt the bird?" Goody asked. "We're looking for a good home for it."

She laughed. "No way! They'd boot me out of No Man's Land! Take it on across the river." The bridge reappeared.

Goody took back the peeve. "Thank you."

They walked onto the bridge. It was solidly constructed and seemed more than adequate, but close to the surface of the river. The loan sharks swam in close.

"Ignore them and maybe they'll go away," Hannah advised.

"Hey, you lubbers! You call those teeth? I've seen better on a keyhole saw!"

The sharks' colors intensified. They gnashed their teeth, which were considerably larger than described.

"And those fins—I'll bet they make stinking soup!"

Goody hurried, but now the sharks were really enraged. One big blue one leaped high enough to land on the bridge. It swiveled around, trying to slide across the planks to reach them.

"And what happened to your tail? Did it get caught in a grinder?"

Goody backed away as the shark snapped at his legs.

Another shark made the leap, landing behind him. This one was red, and larger than the first. Now he was trapped between them.

Hannah stepped in, her sword drawn. "Now we can do this one of two ways," she said to the sharks. "You can slide back into the water on your own, and keep your hides intact. Or you can be filleted for our dinner."

"Don't you believe it!" Goody's voice cried. "She's got good-tasting arms and legs."

The red shark gnashed its teeth, sending out a shower of sparks. It wasn't being bluffed.

"Perhaps a small demonstration," the barbarian said. She stepped forward, her sword-point blurring. The letters H B appeared on the shark's hide.

"She carved her initials!" the parody chortled. "Maybe she'll do her whole name next: Honey Bunch."

The shark chewed on that a moment, then slid off the bridge, followed by the blue one. Hannah had made her point.

They continued on across the bridge, unmolested. "Could you really have filleted them?" Goody asked.

"Of course. But I didn't really want to. Loan sharks taste terrible."

They reached the far bank and turned to wave thanks to Brigitte. Then they surveyed the plants growing here. There was an assortment of pie plants, milkweed, and cookies. Exactly what they needed.

They settled down for a considerable snack. "Honey Bunch?" Goody asked.

"When I was a girl, a mean boy made that up to tease me. Now they call him tongue-twister."

"But that's not a tongue twister."

"Because he never was able to get the knot I tied out of his tongue."

"He he hee!" the peeve laughed.

Hannah glanced at it. "I haven't lost the knack."

The bird's beak snapped thoroughly shut.

Stuffed, Goody found he had a problem. "I need to—"

"Poop!" the bird said helpfully.

"No! But—"

"Squat by a bush," Hannah said.

"But—"

"You can't do it the way you used to. You're a girl now."

"And you've got pan-ties!"

Goody found the whole business uncomfortably awkward, especially with the goading of the bird, but managed to get through. "I thought I got what I needed," he said, glancing at the statuette. "But it didn't help at all."

"Such artifacts are usually valid. Just keep it in mind as we search." But the barbarian's assurance lacked conviction.

They came to a central plaza. There was some kind of monument, a big block of polished stone. On it were the words THINGS EQUAL TO THE SAME THING ARE EQUAL TO EACH OTHER.

"What does it mean?" Goody asked.

"Beats me. But it surely means something."

"Duh!" the parody said.

She turned to the bird. "Do you know something, or are you just mouthing?"

"Small object, big object, put them together, cretin."

Goody brought out the statuette and considered it more carefully. "I just noticed something: this is male on one side, female on the other."

"I just noticed something too: there's a doll-shaped cavity in the top of this block."

"Double Duh!" the bird repeated.

"So we put them together?" He brought the small object to the big object. The cavity was just the right size for it. "Which way up?"

"I am getting a wicked notion," Hannah said. "It has to go one side up or the other. Could that be important?"

"Let's find out." Goody laid the doll in the hole, female side up.

Nothing happened.

"Now try the other way," Hannah said.

He lifted out the figure and replaced it male side up.

Something odd happened. His shirt loosened and his trousers constricted him uncomfortably in the crotch.

"Oh, no!" Hannah exclaimed.

"I'm back!" Goody cried. "I've got my male parts!"

"You don't say," Hannah said heavily.

He looked at her. Her halter hung loose and her skirt dangled on her narrow hips. Her arms and legs had developed knotty muscles. "You're a man!"

"Ha ha ha ha ha!" The parody laughed so hard it fell off Goody's shoulder and lay twitching on the ground. "How you like them apples, hero?"

"That's why the bleeping bird was so helpful," Hannah said. "It knew this would happen."

The peeve flew back to Goody's shoulder. "Well, it was a lucky guess, dolt."

"We can change you back, Hannah," Goody said. "But—"

"But then you'd be a girl again."

That gave him pause. "I gather you don't want to be male any more than I want to be female?"

"Right on, buster."

A bulb flashed over his head. "I can leave. You can stay here and change it back once I'm out."

She/he nodded. "That should work. Let's do it this way: I'll escort you out, then return here to change, then rejoin you as female."

It was decided. Except for one thing: "What about the gender key?"

"Let's experiment." She lifted it out. Nothing changed. "It seems it remains where set; this is only a key, not the whole magic. Let's take it with us, so no one else can use it before we're clear."

"Awww," the parody said.

"Now I think I understand what the demoness meant," Goody said. "We couldn't go to No Woman's Land, because it didn't exist. But we made it come to us."

"So she did wangle a confusion."

"Demons do tend to be devious."

They foraged for new clothing, storing the old in Hannah's barbarian backpack.

They walked back the way they had come. They came to the river and waved. A bridge appeared, and they crossed. On the far side was a man who looked like Brigitte's brother. His clothes fit perfectly. "Did you find what you were looking for, brothers?" he inquired jovially.

Goody sent Hannah a Significant Glance, then answered. "Yes, thank you."

They went on, and came to a little green boy playing with another boy. "Hello, Olive."

"Hi, fellows." He continued playing, paying them no more attention.

"Now he makes imaginary boys, not girls," Hannah murmured.

They came to Hazel, who was now male. "How does it feel to be altered?" Goody asked.

"What?"

"To change from female to male?"

"What are you talking about? I've always been male. Everyone's male, here in No Woman's Land."

Hannah returned the Significant Glance to Goody. The inhabitants didn't know!

"What a crackbrain!"

"And you boys still have your bleeping bird. I thought you were going to get rid of it."

"No such luck, yet," Hannah said.

They went on. "Did you notice how their clothes fit?" Goody asked. "They must have changed with the people. Why didn't ours?"

"Because we're outsiders. That's why we're aware of the change. Probably if we stayed here a while, we'd lose track too."

"I find that scary."

"So do I."

They continued on out the gate, which now said NO WOMAN'S LAND. Even the stone had changed! "I'll wait here," Goody said. "With the parody."

"That will help. I'll hurry." She/he disappeared back through the gate.

Goody settled down for a snooze. This had been quite enough of a day!

Then he thought of something. The parody had never changed. Did that mean it was neuter, or that it was impossible to tell its gender? Well, did it matter? Its nature was obnoxious regardless.

He woke as Hannah returned, female again. "Let's get the bleep away from here," she said. "This place gives me the creeps."

"Impossible! You're already a creep."

"What did you do with the key?"

"I've got it in my pack. Should we leave it here?"

"Let's keep it, just in case we should ever have to return here. We don't want to be subject to another involuntary change."

"Agreed."

They walked away from No Man's Land.

# 5

# BOUNCE

Once they got well away from No Man's Land,
they relaxed. They found a field of daisies and sat
there, resting. "I thought I was afraid of nothing,"
Hannah said. "But I'm afraid of turning male. What a
horror!"

"You look good as a barbarian lout, damsel."

She flung a pebble at the bird, which missed. It would
have hit, had she wanted it to.

Goody nodded. "Likewise, only vice versa." He
picked a daisy flower and sniffed it. From up close he realized that it was actually in the shape of a letter E. That
was curious.

Then Hannah was hustling him out of there. "Those
are daze-E's!" she said.

Goody looked around dazedly. "Like what?"

"Sniff them and you're dazed. We can't camp in that
field. We'd never get organized."

He was recovering his equilibrium. "Oh. Yes."

There was a big sign at the edge of the field. Goody tried to read it, but it didn't seem to have words, just what appeared to be the beaks of assorted birds, some of which were falling off.

"Ho ho ho!" the peeve laughed.

"I must still be too dazed to focus," Goody said.

"No, you see it clearly enough. It's a billboard."

Goody groaned. "I just want a safe, peaceful place to stay the night."

Hannah pulled a bill off the board and unrolled it like paper. "What does this say?" she asked, showing it to him.

"You can't read it yourself?"

"Barbarians are illiterate."

"They are?"

"It's in the Barbarian Handbook. Not that I've read it, of course."

Goody was not at all sure of that, but let it go. "Leigh and Anne," he read. "Room and board for a good tale."

"That sounds good. Where's their house?"

"Behind the billboard," he read.

She took the paper, rolled it back into form, and plugged it back onto the board. Then they walked around the billboard. There was a neat cottage they somehow had not seen before.

They went to its door. Goody knocked. It opened to show a girl of about seventeen with a solid nice figure, cream-colored hair that fell short to her ears, and large innocent blue eyes.

"What a dizzy chick! Did her hair get caught in a bucket of sour milk?"

Oops. The parody was at it again. Goody opened his mouth.

"Oh, a goblin, a barbarian wench, and a talking bird!" the girl said. "Wonderful. Do come in. I'm Leigh. I'm sure you have a fascinating tale."

They didn't argue. They entered. Inside was another girl of similar age, with long auburn hair with copper streaks. Her body was extremely shapely, as were her features, but she seemed to be too shy to speak.

"Curves to die for," Hannah muttered. "Good thing I'm not envious."

"This is my younger twin sister Anne," Leigh said. "She does as she is told."

"I am Goody Goblin. This is Hannah Barbarian, and the bird is—"

The peeve opened its beak to say something nasty, but Anne smiled at it, lighting the room, and the bird was silent.

"A pet peeve," Goody continued, amazed. "Looking for a good home." Could this be it?

"Anne, go set the table for our guests." The girl obeyed. "We don't want a talking bird. But we'll listen to your fascinating tale tonight."

Obviously the elder, plainer twin was the boss of this establishment. Goody did not feel it was his place to argue. But had he been human, the younger twin could have made him do anything, just by smiling. She had stifled the obnoxious bird; even the peeve was unable to be peevish in the face of such loveliness.

They had just settled down to eat a delicious meal when there was a tramping sound outside. Goody was ready to jump off the high stool they had set up for him, because there was a familiar thud to it. All goblins knew and feared the sound of ogre tromps. "Anne, see what that is," Leigh snapped.

Anne, who was on her feet because she was serving, walked to the wall—and through it, disappearing.

"A bleeping ghost!" the bird said.

"No, that's her talent," Leigh said. "She can diffuse until she is ghostlike. It's handy when we want to check something without making a commotion."

Anne returned through the wall. "An ogre is coming," she said. "He says he's Rek King, going to meet his queen at the Rek King Ball."

"Well, he can't stay here," Leigh said. "We've already got company."

Hannah stood. "Ogres don't like to hear the word No," she said. "I can go out and——"

"I'll handle it," Leigh said. She walked to the door, and through it, but not in the manner of her sister. She left a person-sized hole in it, with splintered wood at the edges.

"That's her talent," Anne explained shyly. "To make herself so solid she's like a brick wall."

"So I see," Hannah said. It was becoming clear why these sisters were not concerned about abusive visitors. One was too solid to gainsay, the other too ghostlike, when they chose.

There was a crash outside, like that of a mighty acorn tree falling on a boulder, or two dragons smashing in midair. Then Leigh walked back in through the door. "We collided," she said. "He changed his mind."

Goody couldn't think of what to say, so he generated a compliment. "There are qualities in the two of you to be admired."

"Thanks," Leigh said gruffly, and Anne smiled. Goody felt bathed in sparkling warmth.

After the meal, they settled down to tell their tale. Goody explained about the Finger, and his agreement to find a home for the parody. Then it was Hannah's turn.

"I'm thirty something," she said, "and life got dull. So I decided to have a really good barbarian adventure, before thinking about settling down. The wildest adventures are by those performing Services for the Good Magician, in exchange for Answers to their Questions. So I made up the stupidest question I could think of and went there."

"What question was that?" Leigh asked.

"What is the nature of ultimate reality?" she said.

"Why would a barbarian care about something like that?"

"I told you it was stupid."

"Did he give you an Answer?"

"Humfrey told me that I would know it once I completed the Service, and the Service was guarding Goody Goblin while he shopped the obnoxious bird around. So far it's been pretty good."

They continued with the story of their adventures so far, including the embarrassing love spring confusion and No Man's Land. Every time the parody got ready to comment, Anne glanced at it with the hint of a smile that stifled it. The twins agreed it was a fine tale, worthy of the night's lodging.

Then it was time to sleep. "You'll use Anne's room," Leigh said. Then, before Goody could get out a protest, "She'll join me, of course." Oh.

In the morning the smashed door had been replaced, by what agency they didn't know. They had a pleasant breakfast and resumed their journey.

They spied a small boy doing something odd. His head did not seem to be quite even, but that wasn't it. He was standing by a small pond, gesturing.

"Get a load of the brat."

"Maybe he's lost," Goody said.

"I'll ask." Hannah approached the boy. "Hello. I am Hannah Barbarian. What are you doing?"

He looked up at her. "I'm Colt Human. I'm throwing snow fakes."

"What a faker!"

"But there's no snow here."

"Snow *fakes*," he said. "They make people act unlike themselves. See the fish."

Goody and Hannah stared. The fish were leaving the pond and walking upright on its bank.

"How can that be?" Goody asked.

"It's my talent. See." Colt blew a small white flake toward Hannah.

A peculiar expression crossed her face and departed for parts unknown. "Oh, you dear child!" she exclaimed. She picked Colt up and half smothered him with kisses.

Goody stared. This was totally unlike the barbarian warrior. She was acting like a fond mother.

"Ooo la LA!" the parody exclaimed. "Honey Buns got sweet on the brat."

"Ugh!" Colt said. "I thought it would make you go away."

"Not till I run out of kisses." Fortunately that occurred soon, and she set the boy down.

"That's a nice talent," Goody said. "Now we must go." He managed to catch Hannah's hand and urge her away.

"Thanks," she gasped. "That was awful. Promise never to tell."

"I promise. As far as I'm concerned, you've always been a heartless warrior."

"Thank you. Now let go of my hand, or I may lose control and smooch you. The mood hasn't completely passed."

Goody hastily let go. "I'm just glad he didn't blow that snow fake at me."

They continued along the path. "Something occurred to me," Hannah said.

"We're not making much progress on placing the peeve," he agreed, wanting to stay well clear of kissing.

"That, too. But what I was thinking was that you're supposed to have a magic talent."

"Magician Murphy said so. But I'm not sure."

"We have been exposed to just enough danger to make me think that you could use more protection."

"I do have a bag of old spells the Magician gave me."

"Oh? What kind?"

"Four spells."

She nodded. "They're good ones. Not as good as one, two, or three spells, but better than five or six spells. But they can get cranky when old. Best to invoke them only at dire need."

"That's my impression."

"So maybe we should have your talent. That should be more reliable. I wish Deirdre were here."

"Who?"

"A girl I met whose talent was knowing talents. She

could touch a person and know. But I haven't seen her in years. So we'll have to find it on our own."

"But I have no idea what it is, or *if* it is."

"So maybe we should discover that, before we get into something really difficult."

"But it might be a mere spot-on-the-wall talent."

"Is that what the Magician said?"

"No. He said it was generally protective in nature. Not strong, but protective."

"That's what we need. How can we find it out?"

"I have no idea."

"Idiots," the peeve said.

Hannah glanced at it. "You have a notion, birdbrain?"

"Ask the stupid dragon."

"We have encountered only one dragon. The—" She paused. "Telepathic tunneler."

"Telepathic," Goody repeated. "Vortex can read my mind."

"And somewhere in your mind must be your talent."

"I really doubt—"

"Idiot," the peeve repeated.

Goody surrendered. "We can try it. But how can we locate the dragon? He could be anywhere on or under the ground."

"Idiot!" the bird said a third time.

"By summoning him," Hannah said. "That's what he said."

Goody remained doubtful. "How?" Then, before the bird could call him an idiot a fourth time, he got it. "Mentally."

He focused. *Vortex Dragon! This is Goody Goblin.*

Nothing happened.

"Think louder," Hannah suggested.

He concentrated harder. Then a faint response came. *I receive you. It takes a while to reach you.*

"He answered!" Goody said. "He's coming here."

"So the bird was right," Hannah said thoughtfully.

"You're just now catching on, termagant?"

"Maybe the parody wants to find a good home too," Goody said. "And knows it won't be easy."

There was a rumble and shake. Then the blue snout poked out of the ground. And a pink one. This time there were two dragons.

"Double trouble," the parody said.

The second dragon was similar in size and configuration to the first, but the colors differed: pink head, brown and green body, blue legs.

"This is my dragon lady, Vertex," Vortex said, making his thoughts sound as speech.

The parody opened its beak. Both dragons glanced at it. The bird changed its mind.

"You know what we want," Hannah said.

"Of course," Vortex said. "But this is not easy. We also want something."

"Bargaining," Hannah said. "Fair enough. What do you want?"

"This too is not easy."

"Then it's a fair exchange. What do you want?"

"A construction robot."

Both Goody and Hannah were taken aback. "That sounds like something in Mundania," Goody said.

"It is on Robot World, among the Moons of Ida," Vortex explained. "My beloved wishes to make a safe nest, but this is a new world for us, with unfamiliar dangers, especially for little ones. We lack the resources to forage effectively and simultaneously make the nest. But a robot could make a better nest than we could, faster. When it is done, we can trade the robot to other dragons, and be well off."

"But isn't a robot a machine?" Hannah asked. "Something mechanical?"

"Exactly. It has no feeling, just a program. It does what it is told, within its specialty."

"Like Anne," the parody said.

"Any what?" Hannah asked, then caught herself. "The girl."

"Not like Anne," Vortex said, reading Goody's memory. "She is a living, feeling, and beautiful human girl whose smile pacifies peeves and stuns males. A robot is dead matter, without emotions or expressions, and neuter."

"Not so, dear," Vertex said. "The robots of Robot World have gender, the males designed for brutework and the females for cutework, and their programs may have programmed feeling. They may have positive can-do and negative can't-do indications on their face-plates. We shall need a female construction robot so she won't mess it up."

"Just so," Vortex agreed, disgruntled. "That's what we require."

This was becoming complicated. "Where can we find these robots?"

"He told you, BB brain! Ida's moons."

"I don't think I am familiar with those."

"Magician Grey Murphy's wife's sister Ida has a moon, and the moon has moons," Vortex explained patiently. "Each one farther into alternate dimensionality than the last, where all creatures who exist or might exist reside. One of these is Dragon World, our origin; another is Robot World."

"Go to Castle Roogna and ask for Princess Ida," Vertex said. "She will get you there."

Goody remained borderline confused, but at least now knew where to go. "I will try," he said. "And bring back a female construction robot for you, if this is feasible."

"That seems adequate," Vortex said. "Now I shall fathom your magic talent. This may require deep reading and invocation of buried memories, which could be uncomfortable."

"So hold his hand, heathen vixen! Haw haw haw."

A wisp of steam curled above Hannah's head.

"We shall have to silence that interference," Vertex said. She glanced at the parody, and it stiffened into something like a statue.

"Wait, we can't hurt the peeve," Goody said.

"It is merely in a state of suspended awareness," Vortex said. "Vertex will release it when my business with you is done."

Oh. "Thank you." He lifted the inert bird from his shoulder and set it carefully on a low branch of a nondescript tree, where it remained without protest. "It should be safe here, out of danger," he said.

The dragon approached. "Now make yourself comfortable, for you may lose consciousness of your surroundings."

Goody found a tree trunk to lean against and settled down. "Ready, I suppose, I think. This is comfortable and convenient, and I am relaxed and at ease."

"You're repeating yourself," Hannah said.

"I am? Am I?"

The barbarian stared at the tree. "No wonder! That's a tautolotree. It makes you repeat needlessly, or say what's already obvious."

"Tautology," Goody agreed. "Repetition."

"Stop it!"

"It doesn't matter, for this purpose," Vortex said. "Just sit there and let your mind go blank."

"I am blank," Goody agreed. "My mind is either empty or not empty." He let his gaze go unfocused, twice.

Nothing changed. But he had seen that phenomenon in No Man's Land, so knew better than to assume that nothing was happening. He was merely resting here, thinking.

Then the scene faded, to be replaced by the interior of what he recognized as a goblin mound. Huge goblins were running here and there, doing mysterious things. No, they were normal goblin size; he was small. He was a goblet, a baby goblin.

His nurse was busy at the moment, changing his diaper, so he cast about for mischief. He saw a little fire ant in a niche, so he caught it on a piece of cloth and dropped it on the nurse's toe.

"Eee-yow!" she screeched, almost smacking her head on the ceiling as she leaped. The fire ant had given her a hotfoot! Gory giggled so hard he almost fell off the table.

Of course he got away with it. Even if the nurse suspected, she couldn't punish him, because he was the chief's son. He could cuss her out in language that made her faint, when he got old enough to learn how to talk.

*So he was a normal goblin male originally.*

*And the son of a chief.*

*Locate the time he changed.*

He was a chief's son? So he was; now he remembered. He had buried that memory because he was ashamed.

The scene shifted. Now he was older but still a goblet, able to walk and talk but not to do anything manly, like punching out a visitor. There was tension in the air; the adults were afraid. That made Gory afraid too.

An invisible hand took his. An adult was lending him strength, somehow. The fear receded, and he was able to study the situation as if separated from his small body.

The mound was being raided! The goblin guards were being killed, and the women were being hauled into closed chambers where they screamed piercingly. Gory found it hilarious, the way they sounded. The goblets were being rounded up separately.

"They're after loot, rapine, and hostages," Gory's nurse said. "We've got to hide you, because you're worth more than all the others combined."

Of course. He was the chief's son.

"There's no escape; the mound is surrounded. Only one ploy remains. We'll have to fix it so they won't recognize you."

Not recognize the chief's son? Impossible! He was the meanest goblet in the mound, and everyone was proud of him.

She fetched a packet from a high shelf and emptied its powder into a cup of water. "Quick, drink this, Gory," she said.

"Why, you dopey cow?" he demanded rebelliously. He didn't like anyone telling him what to do, even for his own safety.

She didn't argue with him. She pinched his nose, tilted his head back, and when he opened his mouth to breathe, poured in the fluid. He choked, but swallowed most of it.

When she released him, he opened his mouth to cuss her out properly, but the words wouldn't come. "If you please," he said politely, "what was in that water?"

"Powdered reverse wood. That makes you behave the opposite of your nature. You are now the meekest goblin in the mound. Remove your clothes."

Ordinarily he would have told her where she could go with such a directive. Not that he objected to the act; he liked to run through the girls' dorm naked, freaking them out. Once he was grown, that should be twice as much fun. But now he was unaccustomedly modest. "Please, I would rather not, lest it be unseemly."

"Then conceal yourself and change into these," she said, handing him a pile of clothing.

He obliged, for it would not have been nice to disobey the nurse, who meant only the best for him. The clothing was horrible: panties, slippers, and a dress. But he donned it meekly enough.

Then the nurse redid his hair, putting a ribbon into it. "You are no longer Gory Goblin, chief's son," she said. "You are Goody Gobliness, a common girl. Remember that; your safety depends on it."

Then foreign goblin men burst into the chamber. "Haa!" they cried. "A wench and a brat!"

They hauled the nurse into another room, where she duly screamed. Goody they hustled to a chamber with other children, then ignored them all.

After that, the raiders settled in. The older goblinesses became their servants and the younger ones their screaming partners. Goody did not know what was going on, but was glad to avoid it. He stayed with the girls, and never let on to anyone that he was not the same as them. In due course the boys were taken away as hostages, leaving only the girls.

A few days later a counterattack wiped out the raiders. The chief returned. Now at last it was safe for Goody to reveal his identity. At first the chief laughed uproariously to learn how his son had outwitted the enemy. But when it became apparent that the boy's nature had changed, he was disgusted.

*Reverse wood! No wonder he's so nice!*

*But it's not the talent.*

*It seems to be connected, though. Do a slow talent search.*

Goody moved forward through his life, growing up despised, being tacitly exiled, and finally being upset because of the nasty Finger. His original self would have loved the Finger!

Then he opened his eyes back in the present. Hannah was holding his hand. She was the one who had given him strength and courage during the flashback.

"Are you back?" she asked.

"Yes, thank you." He glanced at their linked hands. "But I thought you didn't want to—"

She let go. "I didn't want to give the bird the satisfaction. But it was clear you needed support, and that was the only way to give it. So, as a friend would—"

"A friend," he said, liking it. "It really helped. Did you see what I saw?"

"Yes, when I was in contact with you. You had a rough time as a child."

"I hate the memory."

"Of what happened to you?"

"Of what I was originally. Those women—they were being—and I laughed, though at that age I didn't know the details, just that they were suffering."

"You are not what you were," she agreed. "You are now as nice as you were mean."

"And I don't want to change back."

"But your talent—they didn't find that."

"Yes, we did," Vortex said. "We just had to analyze the subtle indications near the present. It seems to be related to your infiltration by the reverse wood. At first it reversed your personality. Now it is extending to your body."

"My gender!" Goody exclaimed, alarmed. "I don't want to turn into a girl again."

"Not that. This affects your interaction with your environment. We don't properly understand it yet, perhaps because it is as yet weak, but with time and practice it will surely strengthen. It helps protect you."

"Without Hannah's protection, the parody would have gotten me killed several times over. I'm not aware of any power of my own."

"Your talent has not yet been evoked. But perhaps we can do that now. We have reviewed its parameters, and—"

"Its whats?"

"Values, scale, compass, measure, connection, degree, limits—"

"Boundaries?" Hannah asked.

"Whatever," Vortex agreed without ire. Actually his words had been accompanied by the thought concept, so Goody had garnered a working comprehension of it. "It has variable application, depending on circumstances. It's fairly sophisticated, but as yet weak. Perhaps we can demonstrate. Strike at him with your weapon."

She shook her head. "If I do that I'll cut him in half."

"Feint, then, or use a harmless weapon."

"I won't faint!"

Goody realized that she had picked up the sound without all of the meaning, being illiterate. "Make a pretend strike."

She fetched a pillow from a nearby pillow bush. "I'll bash you with this. I'll score, but it can't hurt you."

Goody stood before the tree. Hannah swung the pillow at him. It shied off without quite touching him.

"That's odd." She wound it back and tried again. The

second time it seemed to bounce back a bit, without quite touching him.

"Something wrong with this pillow," she said. She fetched a weed stalk instead, and poked it at him. It seemed to push back in her hand.

"Weird." She fetched a light stick and rapped at his shoulder. The stick came back at her with similar light force.

"It is repelling the weapons," Vortex explained. "Bouncing them back in the direction they come from. It seems to be related to the reverse wood, reversing the thrust."

"A bounce!" Goody said. "It really is there."

"Let me make one more test," Hannah said. "I will try just to nick you lightly." She drew her sword.

Goody was distinctly nervous about this. "I'm not sure this is wise."

She brought the sword down on his shoulder. It bounced back, just missing her own shoulder. "I felt it!" she said. "A force reflected it. You *are* protected!"

"I suppose so," Goody agreed, amazed.

"It is getting stronger with practice," Vortex said. "Now that it has been evoked."

"So I really do have a protective talent," Goody said in wonder.

"You really do," Vortex agreed.

He went to fetch the parody from the branch of the tautolotree. "About time, you numskull," the bird complained. "It's been a while, bonehead."

The others laughed. "What so funny?" the peeve demanded. "Where's the humor?" But no one would explain.

# 6

# ROBOT

They set out for Castle Roogna, on the way to Robot World. They cut across to intercept an enchanted path. By the time they found it, it was getting late, so they stopped at a campsite that was convenient.

A large spotted cat was there. "Ah, I have been waiting for someone to play cards with," it said.

"A talking tabby," the parody said. "Never trust a cat."

"Cards?" Goody asked. He had not encountered a talking cat before, but perhaps it was no more remarkable than a talking bird.

"A deck of fifty-two," the cat said as a splay of cards appeared. "A good game is poker."

"If you poke me, I'll cut off your hide!" Hannah snapped.

"Very funny," the cat said, unamused. "So will you play?"

"I thought poke-her was a game fauns played, dancing around a nymph and touching her in awkward places," Goody said.

"Do you want to play?" the cat asked again, still supremely unamused. It riffed the cards.

"Let me see that deck," Hannah said, snatching it from his paw. She riffed through the cards herself. "I thought so: five aces! You're a—"

"Cheetah," the cat agreed. "What did you expect?"

Hannah returned the cards. "Let's play. What are the stakes?"

"Foraging for supper," the cat said, its eye resting on the peeve.

"Don't you touch me, you pukey puss!"

"He's a cheater, and you still want to play?" Goody asked, surprised.

"Barbarians are fools about gambling."

Goody shrugged. "But the parody is not on the menu."

The feline sighed. "You drive a hard bargain."

"I'll play too," the peeve said.

It turned out to be an interesting game. Each player started out with a stack of colored chips, and the cards were dealt in batches of five. Goody never did get quite clear about the rules, and did not do well. Neither did Hannah. The cheetah won, of course, with the parody second.

Goody and Hannah went out to forage for supper. This was not hard at all, as there were many convenient fruit trees and plants, including catnip and beefsteak tomatoes for the cheetah. The point of the card game had been diversion, and it had been fine for that.

The peeve elected to spend the night with Hannah, who was alert to things around her even when asleep, and very fast with her sword. Goody appreciated that; the big cat was not to be trusted.

Next day they walked the rest of the way to Castle Roogna. As they approached its moat, three nine-year-old girls appeared, wearing little golden crowns.

"Hello, Goblin," the first said. "I'm Princess Melody." She had greenish hair and blue eyes.

"Hello, Barbarian," the second said. "I'm Princess Harmony. She had brown hair and eyes.

"Hi, Parody," the third said. "I'm Princess Rhythm. She had red hair and green eyes.

"What a cluster of creeps!"

The three laughed. "What are you doing here, Peeve?" Melody asked.

"You're supposed to be with the Good Magician," Harmony added.

"Driving his household to 'straction," Rhythm concluded.

"I'm Goody Goblin. It's my job to find a good home for the parody. I don't suppose any of you would be interested?"

"We'd love to have the peeve," Melody said.

"It would really make things interesting," Harmony agreed.

"But Mother wouldn't allow it," Rhythm concluded.

"And I'm Hannah Barbarian," Hannah said. "So maybe you will direct us to Princess Ida?"

"Sure," Melody said.

"She's expecting you," Harmony agreed.

"Just follow the linear," Rhythm concluded.

"Ha ha ha," the parody laughed.

Goody was about to ask what a linear was, but then he saw it: a line of ears, leading across the moat and into the castle. Nine-year-old humor. "Thank you."

They followed the line. The ears faded out as they were passed. As Hannah and Goody walked on the drawbridge, a huge green head rose from the water.

"It's okay, Sesame," Melody called.

"They've been cleared," Harmony added.

"Sesame's our moat monster," Rhythm explained. "She alternates with her boyfriend."

"Moat monsters have boyfriends?" Goody asked, bemused.

"Oh, sure," Hannah said. "They're people too."

The ears led down a long hall and to a stairway, where they became a line of eyes looking up from the steps. "A stare way," Hannah said, disgusted. "I'm not walking up that in my skirt."

"Ho ho ho!"

"The princesses are mischievous," Goody said, appreciating her problem. Sneak peeks at panties were supposed to be prevented at all times, by order of the Adult Conspiracy, lest panties lose their effect and be useless. Sometimes that rule was violated, but that did not mean that violation was to be encouraged. "Do you have any way to nullify them?"

A bulb flashed over her head. "I do, now that you thought of it." She drew her sword.

"I don't think this the place for mayhem," Goody said, alarmed.

"Watch." She angled the sword. It flashed. She tilted it so that the flash reflected down onto the stairs. The eyes blinked and teared, blinded. Then, keeping the glare a few steps ahead of her, she walked up the stairs.

"That's impressive."

"I'm barbarian. That means ignorant, not stupid."

"You're just lucky it wasn't a come-hither stair," the parody said nastily. "That would have lured you up before you could get your sword out. Your panties would have panted."

"You can't distract me, buzzard brain," Hannah said, not relinquishing her focus. That of course had been the bird's intention: spoiling her concentration, so the reflection wavered, stranding her as the eyes recovered beneath her.

At the next floor the eyes gave way to mouths. Three princesses, three types of line. They were not threatening, merely painted red lips that kissed the feet that touched them. They led to a room whose doorplate said PRINCESS IDA.

Goody lifted his knuckle to knock.

"Open up, you misbegotten broad!"

Oops! Goody cast about for some fast way to explain and apologize.

The door opened. A woman Hannah's age stood there in her gown and crown. A small ball orbited her head. "You have the pet peeve!" she exclaimed.

She knew! "Yes. I'm supposed to find a good home for it. I'm Goody Goblin, and this is Hannah Barbarian. We need to visit Robot World."

"Of course. Come in."

They entered her chamber, and were soon comfortably seated, except for the bird. "What a constricted dump! Where did you get those rags you're wearing? And that crown must be made of brass."

Ida nodded. "The bird is one of a kind. You surely wish to complete your mission swiftly."

"Yes, provided there are some good fights along the way," Hannah said.

"There surely will be, considering the bird."

"Aw, what's it to you, bumbling biddy?"

Ida ignored the bird's interjections. "Are you familiar with the process of traveling to the moons?"

"No," Goody said, embarrassed. "It is complicated?"

"Not at all. But you need to understand that you can't go there physically. Only your soul can go, while your body remains here."

"Desert our bodies?" Hannah asked, alarmed. "What about my weapons?"

Ida smiled. "Your souls will form bodies like your present ones, complete with clothing and accoutrements. Your sword will be with you." She went on to explain the full process. Neither Goody nor Hannah was easy with it, but they seemed to have little choice. "I will lay a track for Robot World," the princess concluded. "You will travel rapidly there, and when you are done, you have but to release your hold on that scene and you will revert to this office."

It all seemed at once simple and frighteningly complicated. Goody and Hannah lay on adjacent couches, holding hands so that they would travel together, and the parody perched on Goody's arm. Ida brought out something for each one of them to sniff, and they were on their way.

Goody rose out of his body in the form of a diffuse cloud. One wisp of him extended to link to the larger cloud rising from Hannah's body, and another to the little cloud that was the parody. In one moment, more or less, they formed into their approximate normal shapes, and sailed upward, following a curving track of light. They did not need to make any effort; somehow the track drew them along.

Below them their bodies looked huge and clumsy, and were growing larger. Above them the track curved toward the giant Princess Ida, and to the tiny moon orbiting her head. This was Ptero, they had learned, where all people and creatures and things that might ever exist resided. It seemed impossible for such a great number to fit on such a tiny moon.

But as they zoomed toward it, it expanded, becoming a world with clouds and continents, rotating as it traveled its orbit. Then they were falling toward it, and it was huge, as big as all Xanth and Mundania combined. Now it seemed possible for many folk to be here.

They came to the surface, but the bright track continued. They zoomed across to another Castle Roogna, and into it, passing folk who seemed to be standing still, and up its stairs. Then on to Princess Ida's chamber, and in, and there she was—with a pyramidal moon orbiting her head. They went to that expanding moon, each of whose four flat triangular faces was a different color, and on to another Princess Ida. After that it became a blur, as they zoomed from moon to moon and Ida to Ida. This was even weirder than Goody would have thought of expecting.

Then abruptly they halted. They stood on a world of

solid metal, with metal things zooming every which way. This had to be Robot World, seemingly as big as any of the others, though it orbited the head of an Ida who was infinitely smaller than the original Ida. Goody found the concept daunting to assimilate, so let it slip away.

"So are you okay, goblin?" Hannah asked.

"I seem to be. If I understand the situation correctly, we are solidified bits of our souls, possessing all the attributes of our physical selves, only smaller."

"Something like that," she agreed dazedly. "Is the bird intact?"

"Who the bleep wants to know, frump face?"

"Yes," Goody answered with four-tenths of a smile.

Three figures approached them. One looked like a human woman encased fully in armor so that no flesh showed. The second resembled a metallic goblin. The third seemed to be an iron bird.

The armor addressed Hannah. "Wel-come to Ro-bot World," it said. "What is your busi-ness here?"

"What's it to you, metal mouth?"

"We are the official welcoming cohort," the robot replied, its pronunciation become more proficient. It did not seem to realize that Hannah herself hadn't answered. "Crafted to resemble the members of your party to facilitate communication. We recognize you as visitors from another planet who will require guidance around our world."

"They think I'm the leader of this group," Hannah murmured.

"Hee hee hee!"

The metal bird spoke. "It seems we are addressing the wrong entity," it said. It pointed its beak at the parody. "What is your wish aboard our world?"

"Go ram your steel foot up your copper bottom!"

There was a pause for no more than half an instant. The bird machine seemed to be heating. "That is anatomically awkward. Is it a serious request?"

The bird opened its beak, but this time Goody preempted it. "I am the leader of this mission," he said rapidly. "We have come from Xanth to fetch a female construction robot."

"We appreciate the clarification," the goblin robot said. "What do you proffer in exchange?"

"Oopsy," Hannah murmured.

But Goody had negotiated trades before. "What are your needs?"

"Information, of course."

"We have a certain amount of that. What type of information do you prefer?"

"News of other worlds, for our main database."

"Would three individual case histories do?"

"Yes."

That caught Goody by surprise. He had been stalling for time while he cast about for something better to offer. "Then you shall have them, in exchange for one construction robot."

"Agreed. But there may be a problem."

Now came the kicker. "What problem?"

"We are unable to ship a fully equipped and functioning mechanism to a downward world, because we lack substance there. We can provide only the program."

Goody realized that this made sense. A solid machine might seem large here, but would be a tiny speck on Xanth. There needed to be a mechanism to expand it. "You mean instructions to build it? We wouldn't know how to use them."

"If you provide a simple machine, and raw material, the program will construct the robot you specify."

"How simple a machine?" Hannah asked.

"A small lever. A wheel with axle. A heat source. An input/output module. A ceramic lens. Copper powder. A supply of iron."

They consulted. "Probably we could get those things," Goody said uncertainly.

"Fool!"

Goody paused. "What's foolish about making the deal?"

"How can soulless machines be fashioned from soul stuff, as everything here is? They're fooling you."

"We lack souls, true," the goblin machine said. "But not everything here is soul stuff. Only the aspects of souled creatures like yourselves. We have programs instead. They guide us as your souls do you."

"No souls," Hannah said. "That means no consciences."

Nevertheless it seemed like the best deal. "Agreed."

"Please come to the recording studio." The robots led the way to an open enclosure containing several chairs. "Please secure yourselves."

There were flexible metal straps that fit over their laps, or over the feet of the birds. They followed the examples of the robots, and fastened themselves in.

Then the enclosure took off. Suddenly they were sailing through the air, rising above the surface. The variegated surfaces of Robot World spread beneath them like an ugly tapestry. They zoomed to what might have been a huge building or a small city; it was hard to tell where one thing left off and another began, on this interconnected planet. They flew in a window or door and landed in the center of a circular amphitheater.

"Proceed with your presentations," the goblin robot said.

"Uh—"

"Kitty got your tongue, bilge for brains?"

"I think I have the idea," Hannah said. "Let's see if I can do it." She concentrated.

A picture appeared on the spherical screen surrounding them. It showed a stork flying through the air, a bundle suspended from its bill. In a moment the scene filled in from the edges, and they seemed to be floating invisibly next to the moving bird.

Goody was amazed. This was three-dimensional animation, evidently evoked from Hannah's thought. It was as real as it could be.

The stork came to a village in the jungle, and glided down. It located a particular tent and dropped the bundle before its front flap, then winged away.

The bundle bounced and fell open. A human baby was revealed, bawling lustily. A little girl, with a pink ribbon in her wisp of hair, upset about being bounced on the turf.

A barbarian woman came out. "Look!" she exclaimed. "The baby has arrived!" She picked up the little girl and took her into the tent. "We'll call her Hannah!"

This was the delivery of Hannah Barbarian! Goody was amazed all over again.

The sequence continued, fast forwarding through the early years. It seemed that every member of the village lived only to go out, seek adventure, fight monsters, and defeat civilization wherever it was encountered. Hannah was an apt pupil, soon learning to swing her little sword hard enough to brush back the barbarian boys who sought to bully her. Soon (it seemed) she made her first foray on her own, going out to slay a small dragon who had steamed the toes of one of the village steeds.

As a young adult she went on longer and fiercer adventures, developing her talent. After several years on an unusually challenging excursion she returned to the village—and was appalled. The villagers had become calm and satisfied, their wildness dissipated. In fact they were tame. Nothing she could say could rouse them. It seemed that a malign spell of civilization had been cast over the village.

There was nothing to do but depart before the awful satiety overcame her also. So she went out on her own, as a singleton barbarian wench, having adventures galore. Goody was amazed by the number and violence of them; she could have had a whole history book to herself. Until at last she got bored and made a pretext to see the Good Magician.

Goody tuned out of the reprise of their recent adventures. Now he knew more about Hannah. But one thing bothered him, and as the presentation concluded he asked it: "Why didn't you ask the Good Magician for something to banish the spell on your village?"

"Because I was too barbarian crazy to think of it."

So she had wasted her chance for a relevant Answer. "I'm sorry," he said.

"I'm not. This is a better adventure than whatever else I might have had. Maybe I'll find something for my village along the way."

Now it was the parody's turn. Goody insisted on that because he was afraid that otherwise the obnoxious bird would renege.

The peeve's scene opened out. This was a harpy's nest in a tree in the forest. An egg was just hatching, and the mother harpy was swearing a blue streak in pleasure. The streak overlapped the nest and dangled down to the ground, radiating blue. That attracted the attention of all the other harpies in the area, and they flocked in to witness the event.

But when the shell cracked asunder and the chick emerged, what was their horror to see that it was not a harpy but a full-fledged bird. Recessive genes had fouled up the egg, and there was no human element.

Not quite so, Goody realized as he watched. The parody had harpy parents, and harpies had distant human ancestry, therefore souls. So the peeve had a soul. And a voice. Two human elements that hardly registered ordinarily, because the voice was so negative.

Naturally they promptly kicked the foul chick out of the nest. It bounced on the ground, peeping pitifully. It would have perished, had not an allegory wandered by, searching for meaning in obscure parallels, and mistaken it for a parable. It was actually a pretty poor excuse for a parable, in fact almost a parody. So the allegory gave it to a family of parodies, who raised it with their chicks. Thus it became a poor parody, and quite bitter about it. But it did learn to talk, and alleviated its ire by cursing all others around it. This tended to make it unpopular with the other parodies.

Once it was grown and its wings fletched so it could fly, the parodies ejected it. The peeve was on its own, and still not very happy about it. It wandered wide and far, rejected by all it encountered. Until it found its way into the demon haunts.

As it happened, the demons were having a big event. Demon Professor Grossclout was celebrating the ten-thousandth student he had flunked out of demon school for having a skull full of mush. All the demons were there, along with lesser lights from the marching foothills of Mount Parnassus, and even a few mortal folk. And the peeve.

A rubber band was set up, elastic loops playing musical instruments. Folk were wiping their faces with napkins, and of course falling asleep along with their relatives; that was the magic of nap-kins. There was weather dancing, with some ladies with sharply pointed bosoms putting on cold fronts, and others warm fronts with rounded bosoms. Incumbents argued with succumbents, the latter always yielding in the end. In short, it was a great party.

Then the peeve started talking. "You call that music?" it demanded. "I've heard better on toilets. You call that dancing? You'd do better with hotfoots. You call yourselves demons? You're just coagulated smoke."

The demons weren't pleased, but no one wanted to spoil the occasion, so they stifled their natural reactions.

Then Grossclout stood to make his address. "Friends, Demons, and Countrymen," he began.

"What a pompous rear!" the peeve remarked.

The professor paused. "Do I hear a mush-skull?"

"It's your bloated behind that's filled with mush, freak."

There was an awed hush. No one dared speak to the fearsome Grossclout like that!

The professor peered around, spotting the bird. "One

more peep out of you, featherhead, and I'll banish you to
Hell!"

The peeve let out something slightly louder and considerably smellier than a peep. There was a gasp, not just
of shock.

That did it. Grossclout gestured, and the bird found itself in Hell.

Hell was not the nicest place to be. There were a number of brutish creatures there, and it was too hot. But
mainly it was boring, because nothing ever changed, except for the arrival and departure of individuals. No one
could be insulted, because all of them were damned anyway.

The parody had plenty of time to think. It realized that
it had made a mistake that had resulted in its getting sent
here. It resolved to correct that error, so as never to be
sent here again, assuming it ever got out. The mistake
was in the way it had insulted people. It had been crude
about it, and finally one of them had gotten the parody
back. That was no good.

So it decided to fix that problem. Instead of insulting
others using its own voice, which wasn't very good anyway, it would insult them using its companion's voice.
That way the other person would get the blame, leaving
the peeve in the clear.

Satisfied, it practiced emulating the voices of others.
When it got good enough to promote face-breaking fights
between friends, it knew it had perfected the ploy. Of
course soon enough they caught on, and started ignoring
its taunts. But that was a problem of familiarity, rather
than competence. New territory would ameliorate it.

Yet the bird remained in Hell, unable to insult innocent
folk, as none here were innocent. That was the heck of it.

Some time later the Gorgon visited Hell and took pity
on it. She had a thing for animals, especially snakes, because her hair was snaky. The bird sounded snaky when it
perched on her coils. She took the parody out and left it at

the Good Magician's castle. That was fun at first, but then the Magician, his five and a half wives, and other members of his household got savvy, and could no longer be riled.

And so it came to the present. Goody was glad to have the peeve's personal history, as it explained a lot.

Then it was Goody's turn. He rehearsed his early, middle, and late history, seeing it animate in the theater.

Was it enough? Goody was nervous as the scene faded, revealing the empty sphere.

"Here is your program," the goblin robot said, handing him a small flat package. "Assemble the tools, place it beside them, and it will proceed on its own. It is self-activating."

That seemed almost too simple, but he had to trust that it would work as represented.

"Are we ready to return?" he asked Hannah.

"More than ready," she agreed. "This mechanical world gives me the creeps."

"And you are already too creepy, Barby doll."

They took hands and released their hold on Robot World. Immediately they puffed into demonlike smoke, expanding hugely, and floated right off the planet.

They expanded past moon after moon, each one larger, until at last they came to the largest of all: so big that all they could see were several reposing giants. Two were human women; one was a goblin man. One was a desultory green bird.

Those were themselves!

Their diffuse soul substances sank into their gross bodies. Goody suffered a moment of panic as he seemed to be suffocating; then he got control of his body and looked out.

"You're back," Princess Ida said.

"No thanks to you, royal pain!"

"We're back," Goody agreed. He found the package in his hand, its substance thickening as it gathered material into itself. "Thank you."

In due course they were on their way back to meet with the dragons. "A question," Hannah said. "Do we need to trek all the way back to where we were? Why not summon the dragons here?"

"Because you're too stupid to think of the obvious, bawdy babe."

"Let's find a convenient spot and do it," Goody said.

They followed the enchanted path until they were clear of the castle area, then found a peaceful glade.

*Vortex! Vortex!* Goody thought.

Very soon the dragons appeared. "We were tuning in on the castle environs," Vortex said. "We see you have a program."

"Yes. I'm not sure it's enough, but it's what they offered.

"Let's find out," Hannah said. "First we need to assemble the required things. A lever, wheel, heat, lens, copper powder, iron, and something else."

"Input/output module, dummy," Goody's voice said.

"That's it, whatever it is."

"I know where one is," Vortex said. She slithered into the ground and disappeared.

"I can make a lever," Hannah said, drawing her sword and hacking a twig from a small poet tree, trimming its poem leaves off to make a miniature pole. Goody saw the poems fall to the ground and was sorry for the waste; a good poet tree was a creative thing that could answer questions written in verse on leaves with new poems.

"All that work to make a toothpick!"

"I can make a wheel," Goody said, and set about fashioning one from an old rim of a small branch of a defunct beerbarrel tree. He fashioned a little stand for it so that it could turn on its axle.

"And a spinner," the peeve said contemptuously.

Vortex located a hotbox for heat, and Hannah picked a lens from a spectacle tree. Goody found a cache of copper powder by the roots of a copper plant. Vortex returned with the module, which looked like a metal bird dropping with wires poking out of the sides. Hannah hacked a branch off an ironwood tree and added it to the collection.

"What a mess of junk!"

Following instructions, they set up the lever on a cleared spot of ground beside the wheel with the lens mounted on it, and hotbox, iron, and module, then sprinkled copper powder so that it dusted the dirt between objects. Finally they laid the square program in the center; it was somewhat floppy but settled down well enough.

"Now what? This will never work."

The lever moved, poking the wheel, which turned. A beam of light from the sun shone through the lens and focused on the iron, which heated and began to melt. The hotbox melted the copper powder, which formed into copper rivulets that networked the site. Some connected to the module, which seemed to animate though it did nothing they could see. Melted iron flowed into a pattern of wires, levers, and wheels that emulated the original ones. This spread to encompass the module, which disappeared into the innards of the tangle.

"Does anyone have any idea what is happening?" Hannah asked.

"The thing is mindless, so we can't fathom it," Vortex said. "But we presume it is assembling itself into a construction robot."

"Ludicrous!" But even the parody seemed impressed by this particular magic, which was unlike any other they had seen.

At last the tangle extended sticklike legs and walked around the site. It had small iron arms, and a head dome with a face-plate. It squatted and ejected the module. Then it walked to a clear patch of ground and used a limb to scratch a little picture: a blob, an arrow, and a circle.

"What does it mean?" Goody asked.

"That's akin to barbarian symbol language," Hannah said. "It means 'take me to your site.' That must be the finished construction robot."

"But it's so small!"

"Size matters less than proficiency," Vortex said. "We shall take it to our nest site and see how well it works."

"If you are satisfied," Goody said dubiously.

"We have no reason to doubt the competence of the machines of Robot World," Vortex said. "They must have seen our requirement in the experience renditions you made there, and devised a program to make what we need. Certainly you have done your part, Goody Goblin."

"Fat chance of that!" his voice said.

"We regard our deal as consummated," Vortex said. He put a foot on the little robot and nosed into the ground. In four-fifths of a moment plus a trice both dragons were gone.

"Good riddance!"

"That was interesting, taken as a whole," Hannah said. "What next, for us?"

"Now we head back into the Region of Madness to see if we can find a good home for the peeve."

"You'll never succeed, lamebrain."

"The odds do seem to be against success," Goody agreed. "But what else is there?"

"Nothing else," Hannah said. "Only a madman would adopt this abominable bird."

They set off south again. Goody glanced back, and saw activity at the construction site. At least the wheel was turning. Maybe the device was taking itself apart, now that its job was done.

Hannah saw his glance, and followed it with one of her own. "Machines give me the creeps," she said. "They're so un-barbarian. You never know what they're up to. I'll take regular garden-variety magic any day."

"You would, illiterate skirt."

"I didn't see *you* reading that robot message, fowl-mouth."

"I'm a *bird*, caveman cretin! Why should I read?"

"It would be better if you didn't talk, either, booby beak."

The parody let loose a torrent of expletives that toasted

the air around them. The barbarian had evidently scored. It was good to see the two getting along.

But Goody felt uneasy, for no reason he could fathom at the moment. It didn't help that he had the feeling that he was missing something obvious.

# 7

# Go-Go

There was no doubt they were entering the Region of Madness. While it was possible to encounter almost anything anywhere in Xanth, the oddities were thicker and odder here.

They discovered a tower that turned out to be made entirely of watches, their faces looking out, each showing a different time. They saw a tribe of hands, severed from their bodies, running around on their fingers. The largest one, evidently the leader, was labeled KER. He was the hand Ker Chief. "Handkerchief," Hannah muttered.

They navigated a kind of network of walkways through a field of tall corn. "A maze of corn stalks," Goody said.

"Maize," Hannah agreed, not seeming much amused.

They camped by a stream and settled for the night. "I don't like this region," Hannah said. "I can feel the magic intensifying. It's weird."

Goody had to agree. Even the parody seemed cowed by the environment. "Maybe it's a bad idea."

"But I really hate to be driven off by any nameless threat."

"And maybe lose a chance to place the bird."

"You fools never had a chance anyway."

"Let's consider overnight," Hannah said, "and if we don't change our minds by morning, we'll go back."

That seemed like a reasonable compromise.

As they ate supper from their supplies, they heard something odd. Hannah put her hand on her sword.

Something vaguely like a monstrous caterpillar came into sight. Each segment was a book with two little feet. It spied them, and lifted its book-head. On it was printed THERE'S NO PLACE LIKE TOME.

"Get out of here, you ridiculous bookworm!" the peeve cried.

Goody exchanged a glance with Hannah. A bookworm!

The print changed. LIBRARY ANN WOULD NOT SAY THAT.

"Librarian," Hannah muttered.

"Ann's not here, joker!"

Disappointed, the bookworm moved on.

"Are we decided yet?" Hannah asked.

"Yes. Tomorrow we get out of here."

"About time you fledgling freaks saw the light."

They slept somewhat uneasily.

The barbarian woman was up before him, out and around. Goody wasn't concerned; he was glad to leave her some privacy for female concerns. But when she didn't return soon, he became uneasy.

"Did you see Hannah?" he asked the parody.

"Why the bleep should I want to?"

So much for that. Goody did not want to go too far afield, because there was mischief all around that he was sure he could not handle on his own. True, he now knew the nature of his talent, and that might help if an ogre tried to smash his head into his feet, but he was not at all sure how much protection he really had.

"Hannah!" he called. "Where are you?"

There was no answer.

Something cold squeezed his innards. The barbarian was no joker; she would not do anything like this from humor. Neither was she a quitter; she would not desert him. That meant she was in some kind of trouble.

How was he to even think about rescuing her? He had no idea where she was, and anything that could take her out would make much shorter work of him.

He was just about to panic when he heard footsteps approaching through the forest. Someone was coming. Was it Hannah?

The figure rounded a tree and came into view. It was humanoid, but far too small. It was female, but no barbarian lass.

"A gob gal!" the parody exclaimed.

So it was. All goblin women were pretty and nice, so there was nothing to fear from her. But what was she doing out here alone? This was no safe place for anyone, particularly a lone girl.

Then she came close enough to recognize. Goody was stunned. It was Go-Go! The lovely love of his life, for whom he would have given his life if only to save hers. The one he couldn't stop loving, no matter what else happened. She would always be THE woman of his life.

But that couldn't be. His wife was most of a year dead, and there was no other like her. She had had no sister. She was unique.

She came to stand before him, silently. He knew Go-Go as well as anyone did; they had been married nearly twenty years, and he had loved her all that time. He knew her little nuances and mannerisms. No aspect of her could ever be erased from his fond memory.

This was Go-Go. Yet of course it couldn't be. So it had to be a perfect imitation.

"Who are you?" he demanded somewhat gruffly. He loved the sight of her, but hated the idea of anyone copying her appearance.

She merely shook her head.

"You can't answer—or won't?" he asked.

She spread her hands in that little way she had.

"You're mute!" he said. "You can't talk."

She nodded. It was evident that she heard and understood him, but could not speak to him.

But Go-Go was literate. "Write it," he said, clearing a patch of ground and handing her a thin stick.

Again she shook her head. She couldn't write either.

That resolved any question: She was not Go-Go. But who or what was she?

Well, sometimes the game of Nineteen Questions could help in a situation like this. "Can you answer yes or no?"

She nodded yes.

"Are you Go-Go?"

She shook her head no.

So far so good; she had his wife's appearance, but was not trying to pretend she was that woman.

For the moment his fear abated, now that he had an immediate problem to solve. "Are you some other woman?"

Yes.

"A lost gobliness?"

No.

He considered. Was she telling the truth? Suppose she were some kind of goblin-eating monster sent to lure him into a trap so he could be dispatched? How could he trust her? He couldn't ask her that, because either a friend or an enemy would answer that she was a friend—assuming she really was female.

Yet if she were a monster, she could have pounced on him already. Maybe his bounce talent would protect him—but she hadn't even tried. If she were a monster, she wouldn't know about his talent. Even if she had been lurking around watching him, waiting for him to be without his bodyguard, she would not have seen the talent in action, because he hadn't used it. So this did suggest she was harmless. It didn't prove it, but made it seem likely.

"Are you some other kind of female?"

Yes.

"Human?"

Yes.

But what human woman would be here, seeking him out?

Think outside the box.

A bulb flashed over his head. "Could you be—are you—Hannah Barbarian, transformed?"

She smiled. Yes.

He really had to believe it. Hannah was inexplicably missing, and this woman had come to him. Who else would do that? "But what happened?"

She spread her hands.

First he needed to verify her identity, as far as possible. "How did we meet? At your home village?"

No.

"At Castle Roogna?"

No.

"At the Good Magician's castle?"

Yes.

Was that enough? He doubted it. "What is our relationship? Are we business associates?"

Yes.

"Friends?"

She hesitated, then nodded.

He nerved himself for the key one. "Lovers?"

She stepped back, dismayed. No.

"So we have never seen each other unclothed?"

She hesitated again. No.

There was the error. They had stripped and bathed together. So she had guessed wrong.

"Idiot!"

The parody always insulted, but it was seldom actually wrong. Had he missed something? Then he figured it out. He had said they had never seen each other unclothed, and that was untrue. She had answered no, which was after all correct. He had tripped himself up—and been an idiot.

"We have been bare together?"

Yes.

"But did not touch?"

No.

Because they had scrubbed each other's backs. "We touched?"

Yes.

"In any romantic way?"

No.

"So we are like brother and sister?"

She paused, then slowly shook her head.

"I mean, we are friends."

Yes.

She had answered everything correctly. Had they been siblings—which was of course impossible—he would not have freaked out when she shook herself dry.

So where did that leave him? If this was not Hannah, he was surely lost, because he could hardly survive alone. If it was Hannah, he could trust her, but still had to find out how she had been transformed, and how to reverse it, because she couldn't help him much in this form. So it made sense to accept her; his only route to survival lay in recovering her as his guardian.

"I believe you," he said. "But we are still in trouble. Can you tell me how this happened to you?"

No. Further questioning determined that she had been returning to their camp when she had walked through a glowing glade, and suddenly found herself in a dusky stone chamber. Some sort of man figure was there. She had drawn her sword; he had lifted his arm; and then she was back in the glade, in this form.

Goody had heard of something once. "There is a castle kept for the three little princesses, and there's one chamber in it that is forbidden, because within it is something called the Random Factor, who does something random and horrible to anyone who enters his room. You must have entered a portal that took you there, and the Factor transformed you and sent you back the way you had come, rendered mute so you couldn't tell anyone else.

Maybe it didn't realize that there are other ways for folk to communicate."

She nodded; that made sense to her.

"But trying to return to ask the Factor to change you back won't work; he never does what anyone else wants."

"Moron!"

Both Goody and the Go-Go image smiled grimly. The bird thought they were missing something. Again.

Goody reasoned it out. "But most spells can be reversed if you know how. It's part of their balance; they are easier to do if they contain the seed of their undoing. Something like that. So maybe there's a key to reversing it, if we can only find it."

She nodded hopefully.

But something still nagged him. "How is it you assumed this form? You look exactly like my wife."

They worked it out: it could be another convenience of transformation. Rather than invent a new form, the Factor had changed her to the closest one for which there was a clear pattern. The image in his mind, of Go-Go Gobliness. Hannah had seen that when he reviewed his life history for the robots. The Factor didn't care about its relevance; the image was there, so it was used.

Could it be illusion? That could be readily checked. They embraced. She felt exactly like Go-Go. He had to stop himself from kissing her, though the urge was strong. He wasn't doing this to please himself, but to verify her situation. Had it been Hannah's form clothed in illusion, he would have found himself hugging her legs, his face in her skirt. So it was a real transformation. That also meant that Hannah had lost her weapons and muscle. She would not be able to protect him in her normal manner.

In fact, they realized, she was now more vulnerable than he. He would have to protect her. Until they found the way to change her back.

They pondered this. Then she pointed to the little bag tied to his waistband.

"The four spells!" he said, remembering. "You're

right; it's time to use them. They may be awkward and risky, but hardly more so than what we face on our own." He paused. "But should I invoke one now, to discover its nature, or wait until there is immediate need?"

They discussed it, in their fashion, and decided to compromise: invoke one spell now, and another where there was need.

"Now all we have to do is walk out of the Region of Madness," Goody said. "Protected by my talent and a four spell. We hope." He looked at her. "Probably you should stay close to me, because though ordinarily you like to range about scaring away monsters, that won't work now. You'll need to be protected by my limited magic."

She nodded meekly enough. She had always been a realist.

He opened the bag and poked in two fingers. He caught something and drew it out. It dissipated into smoke. Nothing seemed to have happened.

Then Hannah pointed. It was a dull day, but now there were two shadows in front of him, as if twin suns were at his back. He turned to look behind him, and the shadows spun around with him, but he caught a glimpse behind: there were two more there, angling out. "Fourshadows!" he exclaimed. "Magician Grey Murphy told me about them. They reflect my immediate past and future."

Hannah/Go-Go looked questioningly at him.

"I know what you mean," he said. "This bears investigation. I have no idea how they work."

She pointed to the rear shadows.

"Study them," he said, understanding again. "They should provide the key to how the front shadows work."

They discovered that the shadows to the left, fore and aft, were shorter, as if more recent, hoping that made sense. The two to the right were longer. They were not outlines of Goody, but of other things. The right rear shadow was quite dark and showed a large woman form; the left rear shadow was light and showed a small woman form.

Hannah figured it out before he did. She pointed to the short shadow, then to herself. When she stood beside it, it might have been her shadow. "It means I just encountered you!" he exclaimed. "As a goblin girl."

She nodded, smiling. Then she stood beside the longer one, and reached her hands up as high as she could. "When you were in your human form," he said. Indeed, now he recognized it as her. It even had her sword, slung by her hip.

"But why is it so dark?" he asked.

Soon they figured that out too: "The darker the shadow, the more intense the encounter," he said. "This shows when you disappeared, and I was in danger of perishing here. And the other shows that I found you, so it's lighter because there's no threat."

"So the dummy's getting smarter," the parody said sourly.

"You're getting mellow," Goody informed it. "That's really not much of an insult."

The bird shut its beak, disgruntled.

Now they considered the front shadows. The left one was dark, and flickering formlessly. The right one was also dark, and inert. "This makes me nervous," Goody said. "What am I about to encounter?"

Hannah spread her hands.

"You'll never find out if you dawdle here forever, dullard."

"Thank you for that encouragement, peeve," Goody said wryly. He looked at Hannah. "But it's right. We'd better get moving. I don't think we can avoid a threat by staying here. We just know that something odd or danger-ous is about to happen."

They set out, trying to retrace the way they had come here. But now there was no big armed barbarian glaring around, and the atmosphere of the forest was uglier. Goody remembered how he had been told that most threats would never make an appearance, with Hannah near. That had changed.

She touched his arm and pointed. The left shadow was very dark and troubled. That made him extremely nervous.

They were about to circle around a large tree. Goody paused, cautioning Hannah, then stepped forward as delicately and quietly as he could. He peered ahead.

There was a giant fireplace. Flames were flickering within it, dancing fro and to. Had he walked at speed, he would have collided with it before realizing, and gotten burned.

They stood and watched. The flames came and went, flitting through the air to reach the fireplace, and sailing away from it. Each seemed to have its own identity, maintained wherever it went. Some looked male, others female, and sometimes one of each would flicker together and brighten.

This must be where the fires of the Region of Fire went for their vacation. A place to relax well away from the burned-out home region. Indeed, they would not appreciate two goblins blundering into their sanctuary.

Now the meaning of the left shadow was clear: it was a flickering flame. And the right shadow—was dead.

They backed away, carefully. Thanks to the warning of the shadows, they had not blundered into the fireplace, and gotten themselves burned to death by outraged flames.

"How's your old flame doing with that hot tongue?" the parody demanded loudly.

The flames froze in place for a moment. Then several of them flitted directly toward Goody and Hannah.

Hannah caught his elbow and drew him toward the trunk of the tree. There was a rotted out hollow there. They squeezed into it.

"Hey!" the bird cried as the wood brushed it off Goody's shoulder. It flapped its wings, hovering in air. "You clumsy gob!"

The leading flame paused, then flickered toward the parody. It thought the peeve was insulting it.

The bird got away just before the flame could burn its tail. "Watch yourself, you clumsy candle!" Now it *was* insulting the flame.

The flame reoriented and went after the peeve again. "Oh, yeah?" the bird demanded. "Just who do you think you're singeing, you misbegotten pyre? Watch out I don't quench you with spit, hotfoot!"

Goody could do nothing, but hoped the bird was agile enough to avoid the angry flame. The peeve had brought it on itself, after all, and almost gotten them burned too. Then it had inadvertently led the flame away from them.

Now he became aware of their situation. He was jammed in the hollow, his arms around Go-Go. Hannah, really, but she looked and felt exactly like his beloved wife.

"Oh, darn," he whispered. "How I wish you were real!"

She gazed at him, her eyes every bit as big and soft as those of his beloved.

"I'm sorry," he whispered. "I know you're not Go-Go. You're Hannah, and we have no such relationship. But holding you like this—"

It was too much. The tears of his suddenly intensified grief overflowed his eyes. He knew he was acting like the unmanly wimp he was, disgusting her, but he couldn't help it.

Some time later the parody returned. "You pusillanimous jokers still necking in the tree?" it demanded. "The fires are stoked down for a break; didn't you know?"

They wedged themselves out of the crevice and unkinked their joints. "At least we figured out how to use the shadows," Goody said.

Hannah shook her head, pointing to the ground. The shadows were gone.

Oh. Well, the phenomenon had been good while it lasted.

They found a way to skirt the fireplace and moved on. No monsters attacked, so Goody didn't invoke another spell.

They came to a lake. "We got rather soiled in that tree crevice," Goody said. "This seems like a good place to wash, if there are no sharks."

Then he realized there was another problem. He and Hannah had gotten used to each other, as it were, but now she resembled the woman he loved. "Then again maybe not."

But she was already stripping, dropping her clothing at the edge of the pond so she could wash it. She might have the body of a gobliness, but her natural manner was that of the barbarian. What could he do? If he made an issue, it would just make it worse. So he stripped also.

They rinsed out their clothes and spread them on bushes to dry. Then they went deeper, for a full swim.

Suddenly Hannah screamed. Actually she made no sound, but he saw her mouth wide open as she drifted backward toward deeper water. Something was dragging her!

Goody splashed as rapidly as he could toward her. He caught her hand and tried to pull her back toward the bank, but instead she pulled him toward the center of the pond. That was no good. So he hauled her in to him and put both arms around her, shielding her with his body. He felt the dreadful force of whatever was dragging her.

Then it reversed, and they were coursing the other direction. They splashed into shallow water, gasping. Near the center of the pond a huge shape lifted out of the water, resembling nothing so much as a giant human toe. Then it splashed down and out of sight.

"The undertoe almost got you, jerk!" the parody said.

Undertoe: a big toe that dragged swimmers under. Surely related to the foothills. But why had it suddenly reversed?

Then he understood: his talent. The bounce. He had been bounced back out, and Hannah with him, because he had been clasping her. His talent had saved them.

"Hannah! My talent—" He stopped. They were lying together, naked, in shallow water.

He quickly released her. "Hannah, I'm sorry! I didn't mean to—" But what could he say? That he hated holding her like that? It would be an obvious lie.

They got up and waded back to the bank. The sun had made short work of their clothing, and it was close enough to dry to be serviceable. He noticed that her clothing had changed with her form; instead of metallic armor, it was a dainty blouse, skirt, and pan— underclothing. He faced away while she dressed.

They resumed their walk. It wasn't long before there was a stirring in the foliage, and a medium small dragon swooped down. It had sniffed them out. It paused barely half an instant before concluding that they were suitably defenseless prey, and came toward them, fire jetting from its nostrils.

"Bogey at eleven o'clock!" the parody warned, fluttering clear. Then, to the dragon: "Nyaa nyaa, hothead! You can't toast mee!"

Goody drew Hannah to the side. "Get under cover," he told her. "I'll try to stop it."

As he spoke, he bent to pick up a stone. He hurled it at the dragon. He missed, and the dragon flew directly at him, its fire intensifying.

Then the fire curled back and bathed the dragon's own snoot. It inhaled and sneezed, blowing out smoke rings. Goody's talent had worked again, bouncing the fire!

However, the dragon was still hurtling toward him. It had not been damaged by its own fire, merely annoyed. It opened its mouth to bite Goody as it closed.

And bounced back, landing on its tail, looking confused. Then, realizing that that it was up against something it didn't understand, it spun about and flew away.

Hannah and the parody joined him, and they went on. Goody was pleased that his talent was coming through; this greatly increased his confidence.

But they were not yet out of the Region of Madness. The vegetation continued weird, and he didn't trust it. He wanted to be clear of it by the end of day.

The way opened out. He recognized this section; they were near the edge. He forged ahead.

Hannah caught him about the shoulders and pulled him back. They fell to the ground together, and the bird flew up, cursing a purple streak. "What?" he asked, halfway annoyed. "Why did you—?"

She pointed. Now he saw a faint shimmer, as of a twist of air rising in the heat. A bug flew through it—and zagged crazily, crash landing, as if dizzy.

"A forget whorl!" the parody said, as they got up.

Now Goody saw a trail of dazed creatures marking the route of the whorl. If he had walked through that, he would have forgotten some or all of his nature and identity. Hannah had spied it first, and acted to save him from it.

Relief and gratitude overwhelmed him. He took hold of her, drew her close, and kissed her on the mouth. Then, realizing what he had done, he let her go. "I'm sorry. I—"

But the Go-Go form was fuzzing out and swelling. It became twice as tall, and wide and deep in proportion. Metal glinted from here and there. In fact—

"I'm back," Hannah said.

Amazed, Goody could only protest. "But you—I—"

"That was the key to restoration," she said. "I see it now. A kiss is the traditional way to banish a spell on a maiden. If only we had realized sooner."

"So you're not angry that I—"

She reached down, put her two hands on his shoulders, lifted him up to her face height, and kissed him back. Then she set him down. "Three times you saved me when I was helpless. Twice we were jammed together, once naked. You were such a bleeping gentleman you apologized! I'm no fainting girl, but I do appreciate your bravery and courtesy on my behalf. If you want to kiss me, friend, do it. It doesn't change our relationship."

"You strumpet!"

"But you looked so much like Go-Go, I was starting to fall in love with you."

"As if a goblin ever could."

"And refrained, knowing it wasn't real," Hannah said. "There are men who wouldn't make that distinction. You are a worthy person, Goody. I hope that some day you find a worthy goblin girl to make the rest of your life as happy as Go-Go made the earlier portion of it. She was obviously a very fine person too. I'm almost sorry I'm not a goblin." She considered half a moment. "Almost sorry I wasn't a goblin a little longer."

"I don't understand."

She nodded. "With luck, you'll never understand."

But as he pondered, he did understand. Hannah really did appreciate the way he had treated her when her situation had changed, and might willingly have rewarded him in the way a woman could when she chose. Knowing that for the moment she resembled the one he most desired. It was a way to thank a person that went beyond the pleasure of the moment. To give him a taste of his beloved past. Yet she wasn't sure it was right. Neither was he.

"Now let's get on out of here before dark. I don't think this is the place to find a home for the nasty bird."

"I heard that, you scheming floozy!"

She reached down and ruffled its feathers almost affectionately. "And I'll almost be sorry to be rid of you, you incorrigible squawk-box."

# 8

# ZOMBIE

They camped in a pleasant "normal" glade, foraging for pies and drinks. There were no bedding bushes, but Goody found an O-shaped plant that grew pills. Sure enough, the pill-Os made even hard rocks feel soft enough to sleep on. But as night closed, and the parody settled down on the upper pole of the lean-to, Goody was restless, though tired. "Do you mind if I—"

"I told you a kiss was okay."

He felt his skin heating in the dark. "Not that. I mean, if I ask a question."

She laughed. "Now that I have seen how manly you are under that politeness, I rather like your manners. Ask."

"It's about that. In the hollow of the tree, I—"

"You bawled, you sniveling excuse!" So the peeve wasn't quite asleep yet.

"That does seem to describe it," Goody said. "Weren't you disgusted?"

"Would Go-Go have been?"

"No. But she knew me."

"Now I know you too. As I said, it turns out that under all those layers of niceness, meekness, vulnerability, and limited vocabulary, you are a person with qualities to be respected. I hope that some year some real barbarian he-man will love me the way you loved her."

That seemed to be answer enough. "Thank you."

"You never thought about danger to yourself when you tackled those threats, did you?"

"There wasn't time. Anyway, my new talent protected me."

"But you didn't think about that either, before you acted."

"No," he admitted.

"That's what courage is. I didn't like being a helpless female, not one bit, but you were there for me. That helped a lot. Now I know that a man can be polite, and still a man. I'll bet most goblin males are cowards, too, under their bluster. It's a good lesson."

He was somewhat at a loss. "Thank you," he repeated, feeling inane. "The reverse wood powder must have reversed that aspect too."

She reached out in the darkness and found his hand. She squeezed it, gently. "Thank *you* for teaching me that."

Goody's restlessness faded, and he slept well.

In the morning they packed up and made ready to move on. "Just one thing, before we go," Hannah said.

"Of course."

"Where are we going?"

That brought him up short. "I don't know. I hadn't thought it through, beyond trying the Region of Madness. And getting out of it."

"Where else might there be anyone dumb enough to want this bird?"

"Nowhere else, you hand-holding slut!"

"I very much fear the bird is correct. It feels like an impossible mission."

"How about Castle Zombie?"

Goody considered. Zombies were stupid, because their brains were rotten. "Do zombies keep live pets?"

"Maybe if they get the chance."

It seemed promising. "Castle Zombie," he agreed.

They cut across to an enchanted path, and oriented on Castle Zombie. It would take them more than a day, but that didn't matter.

Travelers on the enchanted paths were invariably harmless, but could be interesting. Goody was glad to settle for that.

They paused for a snack on pot pies. A young human man was there. "Hello, barbarian, hello goblin," he said. "I am Phil, with an embarrassing talent."

"Not half as embarrassing as your stupid face!"

"The bird talks!" Goody and Hannah said together.

"Ignore it," Hannah concluded.

"Thank you for clarifying that."

"Goody Goblin and Hannah Barbarian," Goody said. "Talents of bouncing back threats and precise weapons control. We are trying to find a good home for the bird."

Phil burst out laughing. "I wish you every success."

"What is this embarrassing talent of yours?" Hannah asked.

"I project the most embarrassing moments of others. So my talent isn't much in demand, as you can appreciate."

"We can pass that by," Goody said, thinking of his recent crying scene. He would prefer that that never be advertised.

"Agreed," Hannah said.

"Cowards!"

They exchanged a glance. "Can you do birds?" Hannah asked.

"I think so. I'm willing to try. But really, it isn't necessary."

"Not necessary, but maybe very satisfying," Hannah said.

"It won't work. Nothing embarrasses me, you faker."

Then a scene appeared around the bird. It showed a cute little boy surrounded by slightly older girls. They were admiring the boy's just-discovered talent of turning body parts different colors. One girl had a bright green thumb, another a black eye, a third a red eye, and the forth a brown nose. They were clapping their hands with delight, knowing that the effects were temporary.

The peeve arrived, landing on a nearby branch. "OoOoo!" the girls cried in chorus. "A green bird!"

"OwWww!" the peeve said, cruelly parodying their tone. "A flock of white chicks!"

"It talks!" the girl with the brown nose said. She was always the first to cater to anyone notable.

"Can't say the same for you, crapnose."

"It insulted you!" the black-eyed girl said, clapping her hands with glee.

"And you, rot-eye."

Now they all clapped their hands, thrilled. "Isn't nature wonderful," the girl with the green thumb said.

"Too bad you don't have any."

They all laughed at this great humor.

The parody turned its attention on the boy. "You call that a talent, smudge color? What good is it?"

"I don't know," the boy said. "It's just fun."

"*It's just fun,*" the bird mimicked, the sarcasm practically dripping from the words.

But the boy was too young to get it. "Fun," he repeated happily.

Then the bird's beak turned pink.

The girls applauded. "Pretty beak, pretty beak!" they said. One held up a little mirror so the bird could see the effect.

"Pretty, my festering foot!"

Then the peeve's wings turned red.

"A red-winged greenbird!" the girls exclaimed, delighted anew.

"Ludicrous!" the bird said, outraged.

Its feet turned blue. Finally its eyes turned pink, matching its bill.

The girls cheered, thrilled. They agreed this was the best bird ever, and wanted to keep it forever.

Horribly embarrassed, the parody flew away. Its colors reverted to natural dull green the moment it left the vicinity of the boy, but that wasn't the point. The point was that no matter how hard it had tried to insult the group of children, it had done the opposite, pleasing them. What awful shame!

The scene faded. They were back in the present.

"Well, now," Hannah said. "That must have been when you were ranging the countryside, before Professor Grossclout sent you to Hell. Your one abject failure. Now we know."

The parody hung its head.

"We are all entitled to occasional failure," Goody said. "That's how we learn. I think I have failed more than I have succeeded."

"Well, you're an effeminate goblin," the bird said, hardly mollified.

"And not much of a failure," Hannah said. "Why don't we all just forget about the past, and focus on the present? We've got a meal to make and a night's resting to do."

The others were glad to agree.

Next day they marched on toward Castle Zombie. The parody recovered its spirit, and insulted everyone they encountered. These included a group of knights who were looking for adventure, and not having much luck. There was Sir Fer, who preferred to ride sea horses; Sir Prise, who liked to pop up unexpectedly; Sir Pent, who was a naga; Sir Comspect, who tended to evade casual notice; Sir Tain, who inspired confidence; and Sir Cumnavigate, who could get around anything. By the time the bird was done with them, they were more like daze than knights.

In late afternoon they spied the castle. It was decrepit,

with stones dissolving and a moat filled with sludge. Zombies were all around, shuffling aimlessly here and there.

"What a bunch of freaks!" The parody's observation was unkind, but accurate.

They paused to consider. "I don't think I would care to live here," Hannah said.

"I must admit to wondering what the purpose of a zombie is," Goody said.

"Oh, I know that. They defend Xanth from attack. There's a whole graveyard full of them at Castle Roogna. I think they also handle other jobs the regular folk don't like, such as processing organic wastes. And I think they run the dead letter office."

"Letters can die?"

"Well, I can't read them, so I don't know, but I think they do die when they can't be delivered. I hear a big snail delivers them. There was some kind of flap about that a few years ago, when some old letters got delivered after all. So maybe it's the un-dead letter office."

"Maybe a priority male delivered them."

She glanced sidelong at him as if suspecting a pun. "Maybe. I heard one was delivered to the Demon Jupiter, and it made him so mad he hurled his red spot at Xanth."

"Oh? Did it hit us?"

"I don't think so. It must have missed."

Goody gazed at the decrepit castle with distaste. "I understand that living human folk run it."

"That's what I heard. So we had better locate them, and ask whether they would like to adopt the dirty bird."

They reluctantly approached the castle. "What a stench!" the bird complained. No one debated that.

At the rickety drawbridge a zombie soldier challenged them. "Halsh! Who goesh zere?"

"Whosh the hellsh wants to knowsh?" the parody demanded insolently.

"Goody Goblin, Hannah Barbarian, and a pet peeve,"

Goody said quickly. "We would like to talk with the proprietor."

"Thish way, pleaze."

They followed the zombie across the rotten planks of the bridge and into the castle. Ichor drooled along the dingy stone walls, and rotting bits of zombie flesh were in the corners. Goody suppressed his reaction, but the parody didn't.

"This place is a rotten grease trap!" Again there was no argument.

The zombie lifted a partially fleshed hand and knocked a bit squishily on a wood door. "Mishtrish!" it called.

The door opened. A dark young woman stood there. "Yes, Benjamine?"

"Vizitshers."

The woman looked past the zombie and saw them. "Oh, living visitors! Come in. I'm Breanna of the Black Wave."

They entered her apartment, which was abruptly free of slime, rot, odor, or other zombie indications. That was a relief. "I am Goody Goblin, and this is Hannah Barbarian."

"It's so nice to see living folk for a change. The zombies are wonderful in their way, but all day every day gets wearisome. What brings you here?"

"We're on a mission for the Good Magician," Goody said. "We have to find a good home for the parody here."

Breanna looked at the peeve. "That doesn't seem difficult. Hi, birdy."

"Go soak your face, you smarmy black piece of snot!" Goody's voice said.

"Who borrows our voices to insult others," Goody said. "I apologize for its behavior. That's what makes it difficult to place."

"Now I have some faint suspicion why," Breanna agreed. "Meanwhile, there's something about you that confuses me."

"I am a polite male goblin."

"That's it! I never heard of that before. I would have expected an attitude more like the bird's. Are you a transformed human or something?"

"No, I drank powdered reverse wood as a child. It made me everything I was not. A subsequent drink did not reverse it. I am a pariah among my kind."

"And the goblin girls won't touch you," she said, appreciating it.

"In essence, yes."

She nodded. "So you can't travel with a bird like this, without a bodyguard."

"That's right," Hannah said. "But he's a good man."

"And she's a wanton wench," the peeve said.

"Not so," Goody said. "She's a good woman."

Breanna's glance hesitated halfway between them as an odd thought evidently intruded.

"No, we aren't," Hannah said. "We're not each other's types. We have just learned honest respect for each other."

"Yeah, like when you were both jammed together naked in that pool."

"Well, if it comes to misinterpreting images from the past—" Hannah said with studied lack of emphasis.

The bird's beak snapped shut.

"We were escaping a water threat," Goody explained. "The undertoe."

"Of course," Breanna said, too quickly. "I'll ask my husband, Justin Tree, about placing the bird." She turned her head and called. "Dear!"

Soon a man appeared from a back room, carrying a two-year-old child. That would be Justin, who seemed unremarkable. But the child was beautiful, with amber skin and wavy brown hair. When the man set her down, she toddled over to admire the peeve. "Our daughter Amber Dawn," Breanna said proudly.

"Get away from me, you whiskey-skinned brat!"

Justin frowned. "Who spoke?"

"I did, knothead. Are your ears stuffed with sap?"

"It's the bird, dear," Breanna said quickly. "They're looking for a home for it. Do you know of anyone who might appreciate it?"

"Baked under glass, maybe," he said.

Breanna shook her head. "So I'm afraid not. The zombies wouldn't be bothered by its words, but they don't know how to care for living things."

Little Amber Dawn had not given up on the bird. She held out a translucent stone. "Bug," she said. "In amber."

The parody was interested. It peered at the bug frozen in the translucent heart of the stone. "Looks good enough to eat, tar baby."

"Her talent is making resin that preserves insects," Breanna said. "She has quite a collection of them already."

"What a waste of bugs, blackhead!"

The child turned about and walked to her mother. So much for that acquaintance.

There was a mushy knock on the door. Justin went to open it. He talked briefly with the zombie, then faced back to his wife. "Something odd outside," he said. "I'll go check."

"We'll all go," Breanna said. "Amber hasn't been out today." She picked up her daughter. "I'm sorry we can't help you, but maybe there's someone somewhere who would like that kind of bird."

"And maybe there's a rotten zombie pie in the sky, nightshade."

They trooped outside. And stopped, amazed.

"What in Xanth is that?" Justin asked.

The zombies were standing awkwardly around a small black figure. In a moment Hannah got a look. "That's a robot!"

"A what?"

"A machine man. We saw them on Robot World. They can do things, but aren't alive."

"A type of demon?" Justin asked.

"Not exactly. They're made of metal and wires. We brought a program for one, to make a dragon's nest."

"Simpleton!"

"We must be overlooking something," Hannah said.

Suddenly Goody remembered what had bothered him two chapters ago. "That robot-making device—it remained active as we left. It must have made another robot."

Justin looked sharply at him. "Something is making these things? How do you know it stopped at one or two?"

"They work automatically," Goody said. "They just keep going. It must still be making robots."

Hannah nodded. "I think maybe we had better get back there and turn it off, before we have these things getting underfoot."

"What's this one doing here?" Breanna asked.

They looked more carefully at the robot. It was using a trowel-like extension on its arm to dig a hole in the ground. When it had dug as deep as it could go, it quit, walked a few paces farther, and dug again. There was a small hole in its backside that emitted smoke.

"Metal moron!"

The robot ignored the bird, imperturbably continuing its business.

"It's doing a survey," Justin said. "Looking for something."

"For iron!" Goody said with sudden realization. "They need it to make their bodies."

"That implies intelligence," Justin said. "Or at least some clear directive. They are reproducing their kind."

"Without limit," Hannah said. "Other than their supply of iron. We may already be too late to stop it."

"Why, beast brain?"

"Because if they're actually smart, the first thing they would do is hide their factory," she said. "So we *can't* come and shut it down."

"That makes uncomfortable sense," Breanna said.

"Bully for you, blot broad!"

A small black cloud formed over Breanna's head. "You know, I could get annoyed at you, bird brain, if I tried."

"Make the effort, zombie lover."

"Just ignore it," Goody said. "It has a high AQ. That is, Annoyance Quotient."

"Not till I put it in its place," Breanna said grimly. She moved her head near the parody. "Say something else, bantam beak." The cloud intensified.

"Go soak your coal-colored caboose! What are you going to do, blacklist me, Stygian schlep?"

A miniature bolt of lightning speared out of the cloud, just missing the bird's foot.

The peeve considered, then kept its beak shut.

"I'll send the zombies out to count robots," Justin said. "That may give us a notion how many are in the vicinity."

"There can't be many," Goody said. "It hasn't been that long since we left the dragons."

"It's been three days," Hannah said. "That first one took only about an hour."

"And their factory may be more efficient now," Justin said.

"And there may be more than one factory," Breanna said. "There could be hundreds of them already."

Worse and worse. But there was a more immediate curiosity. "Why does this one smoke?" Goody asked.

They paused to consider that. "What powers them?" Justin asked. "Magic powers zombies, but this doesn't seem to be using magic. I suspect it is burning wood inside, and using its heat for power, the way they do in Mundania."

"I never thought of that," Hannah said. "Magic things are powered by magic, but humans, goblins, and other living things are powered by the food we eat. The robots' food must be wood."

"I hate that," Justin said. "I was a tree for several decades."

"And it splintered your wits, fagot face."

"Unfortunately, there are trees everywhere in Xanth," Hannah said. "So we can't cut off their food."

Justin assembled the zombies and gave them simple instructions. They dispersed, shambling in random directions. One of them brought a wooden box and pushed the little robot into it for safekeeping. The machine was only ankle tall, so was easy to pick up and carry.

"Meanwhile, come in and have dinner," Breanna said. "It will take them a while to do their business."

They went back inside the castle. A zombie brought a bottle from the castle wine cellar, but Breanna sent it back.

"We don't mean to be choosy," Goody protested.

"That was rot gut," she explained. "Zombie whiskey." Oh.

The zombie brought another bottle. "This will do," Breanna said. "This is ale, from a local ale-ing tree. They are cousins of the beerbarrel trees." She popped it open and poured foaming glasses. "This is honey brown ale, because we have bees nearby. We avoid the ones growing near wild oats."

"Oh? Why?" Hannah asked.

"Because men who drink wild oat ale become unduly attractive to nymphs, and attracted *to* nymphs," Breanna said tightly. "And women don't like it. The ale, I mean. It tastes cheap."

Goody sipped his ale. It was heady stuff.

Breanna poured a smaller glass. "This is for you, bird brain. Gripe soda."

The bird hesitated, not trusting this.

"It's safe," Breanna said. "Here, I'll sip it first." She did so. "Awful-tasting stuff," she griped.

Reassured, the parody flapped across to the edge of the table. It dipped its beak into the drink. "Awful!" it agreed, pleased.

"I always hope she'll confuse the bottles," Justin said, smiling.

"It's bad enough when you see those show girls in the

forest," Breanna snapped, evidently feeling the effect of her sip of gripe soda.

"Show girls?" Goody asked.

"They are scantily garbed female shapes," Justin said. "That show anyone anything, though not in sufficient detail."

"More than sufficient, jerk!" Breanna said. But her mood was easing. It was clear that she and Justin liked teasing each other.

After the meal the zombie foreman reported: "Zeven roboz in areaz."

"Seven," Justin said seriously. "If there are seven here, how many are there in all of Xanth?"

Hannah frowned. "There could be a hundred."

"You had better stay here tonight," Justin said. "The zombies will verify the count in the morning. Then you can decide what to do."

"Thank you," Goody said. What a development!

He shared a room with Hannah and the parody, by mutual choice. They were accustomed to being together, and he felt safer with her nearby, though surely there was no threat from the zombies.

"Why do I think that we now have a bigger problem than placing the bird?" she asked rhetorically as they settled for the night.

"And it's my fault," Goody said, chagrined.

"It's *our* fault. I'm a warrior; I should have picked up on the threat."

"I saw the first robot factory active as we left, and didn't catch on."

"There is guilt enough to go around. What are we going to do about it?"

"I wish I knew!"

She sat on the edge of the bed. "I'll think about it overnight. They may not be dangerous. It was just a nest-constructing program we brought, after all."

"Do we know that? Could there have been more to that

program than we realized? We wanted just one female robot, but now there are males too, out searching for iron."

She grimaced. "Suddenly I fear there is. Those machines on Robot World were awfully cooperative. Maybe they just made up something to make us think we were making an even trade, when they really wanted to get that program to Xanth. Why should they care about our personal life histories, anyway?"

"To study us," Goody said. "To ascertain our vulnerabilities. So as to know whether we would fall for it."

"Now you're thinking like a warrior," she said. "Scouting the enemy. I fear we have been fools."

"Exactly," the peeve said.

"Well, I'll ponder," she said. She threw herself down on the floor and slept.

Goody had the bed to himself. It was soft, but he took time to nod off. He did feel responsible for the crisis.

In the morning there was bad news: There were now twelve little robots, including the one they had captured. It had cut a hole in the box and escaped.

"Dolts!" the parody said enthusiastically.

"Of course," Hannah said. "They're construction robots. They have tools, like drills, hammers, and wire cutters. Why should a wood box hold them? We should have realized."

"Then we'll try stone," Justin said grimly. He gave instructions, and the zombies spread out again.

"But they don't have boxes," Goody said.

"They'll carry the robots here by hand."

"But if the machines have hammers and pincers—"

"They can't hurt zombies."

Oh. Goody hardly needed the peeve's chortled reminder of his continuing idiocy. He was missing obvious things galore.

They had a nice breakfast with only one miscue: Hannah reached for a platter with pasta and cheese. "Don't eat that," Breanna said.

"Oh, I thought it was part of breakfast."

"No, that's a dish I made for a zombie wedding we'll have today. Matrimonial cheese."

"Macaroni and cheese?"

Breanna smiled. "Matrimonial cheese," she repeated carefully. "It makes those who eat it feel extremely, um, loving."

"Zombies?" Goody asked.

Breanna frowned. "They're people too, you know. When you cut them, do they not drip ichor? They have feelings. Their bodies and brains may be rotten, but they deserve their chances for satisfaction, same as anyone else. They—"

Justin made a small signal with one hand, and Breanna cut off her diatribe. "Sorry. I get carried away. Yes, zombies can love, not with living intensity, but it's real for them. So this dish is for them. It's not spoiled, but I don't think you would care for its effect unless you had a romantic relationship."

"All screwed up!" the bird said.

"Thanks for the warning," Hannah said. "When I find my brute barbarian male, I don't think we'll need it."

After breakfast they went outside. The zombies had brought in fifteen little robots; it seemed more were coming in all the time. "They are eying the castle," Justin said. "They want to check it for iron. We can't hold them long in the box. We have to deal with them."

They watched the robots working on the stone box they were confined in. They were using little drills to make holes in it, then sawing out from the holes to make larger holes, and hammering out the partitions between holes. They seemed to be as good at deconstruction as construction. The work was slow, but steady. A fair amount of smoke was drifting up from their smoke holes. They hadn't seen the robots eat any wood, but surely they did, and a meal lasted a long time as it burned.

It was obvious that no box of any kind would hold them long; even metal would merely delay them. "What are we to do with them?" Goody asked despairingly. "We can't reason with them; they're mindless machines. But we can't ignore them."

"I have a barbarian solution," Hannah said. "Chop them into smithereens." She smiled. "As it were. There's an ogre leader by that name."

A glance circulated. "Maybe that's best," Goody agreed reluctantly.

Hannah found a chopping block. She used barbarian gauntlets to fish the robots out of the box one at a time and drop them on the block. Then she used her sword to hack them into pieces. Soon there was a pile of metal kindling around the block, and all the robots were gone. Smoke still curled up from their broken fire boxes.

Goody felt queasy. He knew the robots had no feelings; they weren't alive. But still the destruction of animated, purposeful things bothered him. It had perhaps been necessary, but it was not nice.

"Blood and guts!" the parody swore.

That was exactly what those remnants seemed like.

# $\overline{9}$

# EVE

They hashed it out, and decided that they should first go to dismantle the original robot factory, and if that didn't work, inform King Dor of the problem. Meanwhile the zombies would continue collecting and disposing of robots in the vicinity of Castle Zombie.

"It won't work, jerk," the parody assured them.

"Listen, featherhead, it's your fault this happened," Hannah said. "We had to go to Robot World for you."

"You're a liar, brittle bra! You went for the dragon's nest."

"Because we had to trade for Goody's talent, tattle-tail. So we could protect ourselves while ranging dangerous regions in search of a home for you."

"I didn't ask you to find me a home, wanton wastrel! I won't like it anyway."

"Because you don't like *anything*. What's the matter with you?"

"I'm a failed harpy, scandal skirt. What's *your* excuse?"

"Maybe we should just get on our way," Goody suggested.

"Awww," bird and barbarian said together.

"We were just getting warmed up," Hannah concluded.

"Such language makes me uneasy," Goody said.

Bird and barbarian exchanged a glance, and shrugged. Obviously what bothered him, they found invigorating.

They got on the enchanted path and moved smartly along. Soon they encountered a young man going the other way. His gaze crossed Goody and the parody, then lingered on the woman somewhat overfamiliarly. "Hi. I'm Tom."

"Hey!" Hannah exclaimed, grabbing her metal halter.

"Sorry about that," Tom said, not looking sorry. "It's my talent."

"Talent?" Goody asked, confused.

"Undressing women with my eyes."

"Well, drop your gaze," Hannah snapped as she fastened her halter back together.

The man lowered his gaze—and her skirt dropped down around her knees. "Oops," he said.

"One more slip like that, and I'll undress your bones with my sword," she snapped as she grabbed her skirt.

"That might be difficult, with your clothing falling off," Tom said, unrepentant.

Hannah drew her sword—and her outer clothing dropped to the ground around her feet, hobbling her. Only her metallic panties remained. Fortunately their opaque thickness shielded Goody's eyes somewhat, so he was able to block the view with one hand while recovering his equilibrium. This was no time to freak out.

"Haw haw haw!!" the peeve laughed coarsely. "Battlebottom's getting battered!"

"I feel a barbarian berserker rage coming on," Hannah said ominously.

That would surely lead to bloodshed. "Please, not that," Goody said. "Not on the enchanted path."

"I love wild, bare women," Tom said, focusing his lecherous gaze.

Goody leaped in front of Hannah as she crouched down to recover her fallen clothing. He felt something, and knew it was Tom's eye magic, this time going for the woman's panties.

Then it was Tom's turn to grab his clothing as it fell off his body. "What?" he asked, amazed.

"Hee hee hee!" the bird laughed just as coarsely. "Eye Candy's a streaker at heart."

Goody realized that his talent had reflected the magic back at the man, undressing him. Well, it served him right.

Safely beyond the eye magic, Hannah repaired her attire. "Thanks, Goody," she said.

"I was just trying to conceal you from his lecherous gaze. I didn't know that would happen."

She grabbed his head and kissed his ear. "Thanks anyway, friend. Actually I don't care that much about clothing. It was just that I hated to let him think he was getting away with something."

"Your petulant panties!"

"Something like that, bonehead beaker," she agreed. "Goody's okay, because he never presumes. But I'd have had to slay that insolent man."

"Please don't slay anyone on the enchanted path," Goody repeated.

She considered. "True. We're not supposed to do that. I'd have had to lure him off the path first. Lack of clothing would have facilitated that."

That hadn't been exactly what he meant, but surely she knew that.

They paused at a rest stop around noon. There was a deck chair on a lawn, looking very comfortable. It was labeled ROCKET, presumably its brand name. Goody decided to sit on it while he ate his pie.

"Hold up, friend," Hannah warned. "That's off the path. I'd better check it first."

"Chicken!" the parody said, flying across to the lawn chair, perching on it.

The bird took off so suddenly that feathers scattered. "Squawk!" it cried from a high tree branch.

"I had no idea you could fly that fast, truculent tailwind," Hannah said, amazed.

"I can't!" The peeve fluttered back to ground. "That thing launched me."

Hannah inspected it closely, poking with the tip of her sword. "No wonder. This is not a lawn chair; it's a launcher."

"If I had sat on it—" Goody said, appalled.

"It might have jetted itself backwards."

"Oh—that's right. I keep not thinking of my talent."

"Fortunately you don't need to. It protects you anyway."

"An idiot-proof talent: just the thing for you, goopy gob."

They got most of the way to Castle Roogna by dusk. "We'll tackle that site in the morning," Hannah said.

Goody was satisfied with that. He was nervous about what they would find.

After they ate and washed, they retired to the convenient shelter. As usual, Hannah spurned the comfortable bunk and dropped to the floor in her clothing. Goody stripped and lay down, drawing the sheet over him.

"Well now."

He leaped out of the bed, almost landing on Hannah, who stirred, grasping her sword. There was a woman there! A sultry gobliness.

"Don't be like that," the creature said from the darkness. "I won't virulence you."

"Won't what me?"

"Gnaw, cut, lacerate, chomp, masticate—"

"Bite?"

"Whatever," she agreed crossly.

"What are you doing here, Metria?" Hannah asked.

"Trying to brighten this goblin's dull life. Go back to your floor, primitive wench."

Hannah hesitated. "She probably means you no harm, Goody. If you'd like to be alone with her—"

"No!"

"Oh, come on," the demoness urged. "I'll light your dead fire."

Almost, he was tempted. When Hannah had been in goblin form he had reacted despite knowing better. With Metria, what was the point in knowing better? She was strictly a throwaway female. He did need to get over his reserve, if he was ever going to rejoin normal interpersonal society.

"Go ahead, gallant goblin," the parody's voice came, radiating perverse humor. "Really get into it. Dip your stick."

That decided him. "No. Let me sleep in peace, demoness."

"You don't know what you're missing."

"Yes, I do. Go." That gave him a twinge, for it was the first half of Go-Go's name. That was indeed what he was missing: her loving embrace.

"Some other time," she said, fading. How she managed that in complete darkness he wasn't sure, but she was gone.

"I think you could have called it either way," Hannah said.

She was right, and it had been close. He was already half regretting his decision.

Next morning they cut south to locate where they had met the dragons and made the first robot. The site was there, but not the equipment. There was just a bare patch of ground.

"They moved," Hannah said. "They probably found a better source of iron, and set up there."

"Probably," he agreed. He was disappointed, but not wholly surprised.

"I could track a robot, using my barbarian skill, but I can see there were a number of them, and I wouldn't know which one to follow. I think we've lost them."

"Loser!"

"Bolt your beak, buzzard."

"Same time as you stop flashing men on the enchanted path, dropskirt."

"Time to go to Castle Roogna," Goody said heavily. "Maybe they'll know what to do."

They wended their way back to the path, then on toward Castle Roogna, which wasn't far.

"Bogey at twelve o'clock!"

It turned out to be a girl standing in the path, looking to the side. No, it was a gnomide, a female gnome, standing about a third Hannah's height, or somewhat shorter than Goody. Gnomes tended to be surly and brusque with strangers, but gnomides were nicer.

"Hello," Goody said. "I am Goody Goblin, traveling with Hannah Barbarian and this obnoxious bird. Is there a problem?"

"Yes, but you should go right on past, please."

"But maybe we can help."

"But you shouldn't try."

"The gnifty gnomide's telling you to gnet lost, gnoblin."

"It's the bird talking," Goody said hastily. "It insults everyone. Pay it no attention."

"Oh, it's starting already," she said, looking frustrated. "I don't understand."

"I am Kiya Gnomide. My talent is to complicate situations, though I don't want to. It started when I was delivered; I was supposed to be named Gniya, but it got complicated. I hoped you would pass me by before you got complicated too. But I fear it is already too late."

"Maybe we should heed her advice," Hannah murmured. "We have already had complications enough."

"What can be so complicated about helping a damsel in distress?" Goody asked. "Did you lose something, Kiya?"

"Yes, my mark-hers. I dropped them, and they rolled off the path. But I am concerned that it's not safe to step off it. Not for me, with my talent. So I was trying to decide whether to risk it."

Goody looked. There were three pencil-like objects. "Markers?"

"Mark-hers. They mark only women's clothing. We use them so our men don't steal our clothes."

"We appreciate that," Goody said. "We recently encountered something similar."

"No problem," Hannah said. She squatted and reached off the path toward the mark-hers. But she lost her balance, and fell against Goody, who fell against Kiya. They all wound up in an embarrassing tangle.

"Apology," Hannah said, quickly righting herself. She fetched in the mark-hers and handed them to Kiya as she and Goody got back to their feet.

"Thank you," the gnomide said. "Now you should go before another complication starts."

Then Goody saw that his bag of spells had gotten pulled open in the collision. He quickly drew it closed again, hoping that no spells had escaped.

Too late. Four bears appeared, surrounding him, growling off the others. Four tunes played simultaneously, distractingly. Two new eyes sprouted on his face, providing him four sights. "Bleep bleep bleep bloop!" he swore quadruply.

"Now you're sounding like a real man," the parody said approvingly. "Worthy of your fourbears, jangles. You look better, too."

"Get away from me!" Kiya cried. "To protect you from worse. Please."

Things had indeed become complicated. Hannah picked Goody up and carried him a distance from the gnomide. The bears ran alongside, growling, but tolerated this.

"I'm so sorry!" Kiya called. "But thank you for the mark-hers."

"You're welcome," Hannah called back. "We understand."

They went on, accompanied by the bears and tunes. "Bleep!" Goody swore. "Bleep bloop bleep! I hope some spells remain for when we need them."

Four-tunately the evoked spells did not last long. The bears, finding nothing to fight, faded out. The foursights, seeing nothing special, reverted to two eyes.

"I think the fourtunes brought you good luck to cancel out much of the rest," Hannah said. "The music must be a side effect."

"That's good," Goody agreed. "Kiya wasn't fooling about complications! That's an awful curse."

"Almost as bad as being a polite male gob," the peeve agreed.

Castle Roogna came into sight. "Whom do we want to see this time?" Hannah asked.

"I think not Princess Ida."

"Maybe the three little princesses will have a suggestion."

But when they approached the castle, no princesses appeared to greet them. Instead there was an older girl, about fourteen, dark of hair and eye, quite pretty. "Hello, Goody Goblin and Hannah Barbarian," she said softly. "I am Princess Eve. May I help you?"

"Hi, babe!"

"The bird talks," Hannah said quickly.

Now Goody saw the golden crown, almost hidden by her flowing hair. "Another princess?" he asked, somewhat dully.

"There are five of us younger ones," Eve said. "You encountered Grey and Ivy's triplets before, Melody, Harmony, and Rhythm. Dawn and I are Dolph and Electra's twins, five years older. The others are away today, so that leaves me in charge of the castle, as it were."

"Oh. Uh, we have a problem. There may be danger to Xanth."

"Then you'll need to see Grandfather Dor. He's the king."

"Um, maybe we do. If kings see goblins, that is."

"Or barbarians," Hannah said.

"He'll see you," Eve said confidently. "I'll show you in."

"Just like that?" Goody asked, bemused.

"How else did you have in mind?"

"She sure corked your spout!"

"I like your bird."

"Oh yeah, darkie? You wouldn't if you knew me better."

"I'll never know you well enough. That's my sister's talent."

That stifled the parody for the moment. Hannah picked up the dialogue. "Your sister would be a sorceress?"

"Of course. All of Bink's descendants are magician-caliber talents. Dawn knows all about any living thing she touches. I know all about any inanimate thing. So I can't touch the bird and learn its secrets."

"Praise the Demon for small favors, blackhead!"

Goody noted with private bemusement that this was the first time he had heard the bird repeat an insult. It had called Breanna or her daughter blackhead. Of course Eve's hair was jet black, so it fit.

Eve turned her head and smiled down at the parody. Its knees went rubbery (it had knees?) and it almost fell off Goody's shoulder. Goody knew exactly how that was, as he was at the periphery, not the focus of her expression, yet her dark beauty made his own knees lose cohesion. She was still a girl, but already possessed some of the womanly attributes that would make her dangerous quite apart from her magic or status as a princess.

As they crossed the drawbridge at the moat, a huge green head lifted from the water. "This is Soufflé Serpent, our resident moat monster," Eve said.

Goody nodded. That would be Sesame Serpent's boyfriend. If princesses could switch out, so could monsters.

"Whatsa matter greensnoot—you swallow a barrel of emetic?" Goody's voice called.

"It's the bird," the princess said.

The monster considered, then sank back under the water as they entered the castle.

They came to the audience chamber. Goody saw a raised platform, a dais, with two thrones, occupied by an elder man and woman. The king and queen of Xanth.

Suddenly Goody's knees felt worse than rubbery. "I—I—what do I—how do I—"

"Just bow your head briefly when I introduce you," Eve said. She was evidently used to this kind of reaction on the part of visitors. "We don't stand much on ceremony here."

"Look what's skulking in," a gravelly voice said. "A wretched goblin and a disreputable barbarian moll."

"Oh—and the furniture talks, near Grandfather," Eve said. "His talent is to talk to the inanimate, and it talks back. Close to him, it talks even when he doesn't. Grandma Irene's is to grow plants. That's the floor, just now. Just ignore it."

"Oh yeah, evening shade?" the floor said. "How would you like me to blab to the world the color of your—"

The princess stamped the floor warningly with one slippered foot, and the sentence wasn't finished. Goody found that interesting too; the floor was of course in an ideal position to see up under a girl's skirt, but could be stomped into submission.

"And get a load of that ugly bird," the wall said. "If I had a beak like that, I'd have it sawn off."

"Listen, wall-banger," the parody retorted. "If I had a paint job like that, I'd pray for a sandstorm."

"Quiet, both of you," Eve snapped, evincing sudden royal authority. Both were silent.

They came to stand before the dais, facing the king and queen, who were in their early sixties and looked quite stately. "Your Majesties King Dor and Queen Irene, this is Goody Goblin," Eve said formally.

Goody bowed his head, glad that she had told him what to do.

"And Hannah Barbarian." Hannah bowed her head.

"And their pet peeve."

"Go soak your royal snoots in boot rear!"

Goody and Hannah stiffened, appalled. But both king and queen laughed. "I see you have the unenviable task of finding a home for the Gorgon's parody," the king said.

"I can't think why that should be difficult," the queen said, tittering. She was surrounded by green plants, as if in a little arboretum.

"Uh, yes," Goody said. "But that's not—"

"Not what brings you here," the king said. "To be sure. What is your concern, Goody?"

"As if a motley goblin could have any concern other than mayhem," the dais said. "What a laugh!"

The queen tapped her toe, and the dais was silent. "Do tell us, Goody," she said.

"It—it's the robots," he said. "We didn't mean to—we were trading with the dragon, but—" He stalled out, aware that he wasn't making much sense.

"What an ignoramus!" the floor said.

"Well, he can't get lower than you, scuffle tile!"

That was a new one: the parody was defending him. Probably because that was where the best insult offered.

Hannah took over. "What my friend means to say is that we visited Robot World and brought back a program to make a construction robot for a dragon, and inadvertently loosed a robot invasion of Xanth. Now we don't know what to do about it, and thought we should tell you. We are very sorry for perpetrating this mischief."

"You are very well spoken for a barbarian," the queen said.

"I think I've been associating with this polite goblin too long," Hannah said, embarrassed. "I'm sure I'll revert to normal once this mission is done."

"A polite male goblin," the king said. "That is remarkable."

"The fool drank water spiked with reverse wood dust," the parody said. "What a milquetoast!"

"The Good Magician felt he was the only one who would not wring this bird's neck," Hannah explained.

The king and queen laughed again. "Humfrey's smart," the queen said.

"And now you feel responsible for the problem your activity may have generated," the king said.

"Yes, Your Majesty. If I'd just thought it through—"

"As if the little dope could think anything through!"

"It wasn't obvious at the time," Hannah said. "The machines tricked us. We weren't aware of what was happening until the robots showed up at Castle Zombie."

"I think this bears further examination," the king said. "Eve will go with you to investigate, and report back later to me."

"A stupid girl!"

"But we tried to—their factory was gone," Goody said.

"Thank you, Your Majesty," Hannah said. "We appreciate your decision."

"Very well spoken," the queen murmured appreciatively.

Eve led the way out. "Good riddance!" the floor called.

"What a grab-bag of characters," the wall said. "Xanth is doomed."

"Oh, yeah, you scruffy boards? Wail till the robots get their drills and saws into you."

Then they were outside the chamber, and the surroundings were quiet. "How come you were defending us?" Hannah asked.

"I wasn't," the peeve said, confirming Goody's suspicion. "I just couldn't let an insult go unreturned."

"Are you sure it is wise for you to travel with us?" Goody asked Eve. "You're a—a—"

"Pretty girl," Hannah finished. "It's a question of propriety."

"Grandma took your measure," Eve said. "She says it's all right."

Goody wondered when she could have said that. Before their audience?

"But there may be danger."

"Grandma gave me some seeds."

"Seeds?"

"You'd be surprised."

"What's to know, nightshade?"

It seemed the insults were recyclable for a new target.

Eve glanced at the parody. "Do you imitate anyone's voice?"

The bird fluttered up to land on Hannah's shoulder. "What's it to you, dark girl?" it demanded with the barbarian's voice.

"Come perch on my shoulder a while."

The peeve hesitated. The princess smiled at it. It wavered as if blown by a warm wind, then hopped across to her shoulder.

"Do you need to pack?" Hannah asked. "I mean, as a princess you must have need for special things, and of course there's the question of privacy."

"As I said, I have seeds."

Hannah shrugged. The girl seemed sure of herself.

They crossed the moat. The moat monster's head lifted from the water to inspect them.

"You still here, you oversized worm?" the princess's voice said. "Is that your tail end you're raising? It's too ugly to be your head."

Soufflé's big jaw dropped. How could the princess be saying such things to him? Then he spied the bird, and caught on. The princess was having her little joke. He nodded.

"Right, Soufflé," Eve said. "It's the bird. I couldn't resist flipping you the bird."

The monster winked, and disappeared below the surface. It was evident that he and the castle folk got along well. But if an evil intruder ever came, it might be another matter.

"We didn't see that monster the first time we came here," Hannah remarked. "We saw Sesame."

"I envy them. They have a relationship."

And she did not? Surely not from inability to attract a man.

"We don't mean to pry," Hannah said carefully. "But it seems to me that—"

"Do you have a boyfriend?"

"No. But—"

"Because you need a brute barbarian, and they're scarce in these parts."

"Yes. But—"

"Well, I need a human prince, or reasonable facsimile thereof, and any we encounter see my sister Dawn first. Her smile is like daybreak."

"And yours is like the embrace of night," Hannah said. "I see the problem. But I suspect as many men would like a night relationship as well as a day one."

"And Grandma Irene rousts out any who even begin to think of it. She thinks I'm too young."

"The dread Adult Conspiracy," Goody said. "But when you are eighteen—"

"Four years hence?" she demanded disdainfully. "I'll be dead of old age by then!"

There didn't seem to be much response to that; they were not going to pacify her.

"Good thing you two were never fourteen. You'd have messed up the whole system."

That was the peeve, still with the princess.

"Neither was Grandma Irene, really," the real Eve said. "She started the Adult Conspiracy, you know, once she was safely past the panty-showing stage. She flashed them to nail Grandpa Dor, then decreed no one else was supposed to do it. So how are the rest of us supposed to cope?"

"Oh, it can be done," Hannah said. "Stand in the way of a strong gust of wind when a man is looking, so your skirt blows up without warning. Take an accidental spill and roll heels over head. Prospects are limited only by imagination and nerve. It's almost impossible to prove intent."

"Hannah!" Goody said, horrified.

"Well, I'm a barbarian, of course. But civilized girls do it too."

"Not underaged ones."

"Of course not," Eve said thoughtfully.

They left the enchanted path, going south to the original robot factory site. Soon they were there.

"This was where we laid out the elements to make the first little robot," Goody said. "But they have moved on, and we don't know where. There are too many trails for Hannah to track."

Eve squatted to pick up a dark leaf. As she did so, her skirt hiked up slightly, showing a flash of black panty. Goody stiffened, his eyes locked in place. Black was goblin panty color! Then she shifted position, the skirt dropped down, and nothing showed. His eyes thawed. Of course it had been an unconscious accident, and he felt guilty for noticing. Especially since she was underage.

"The girl learns fast," Hannah murmured.

The princess stood, studying the leaf. "Ironwood," she said. "Once alive, but now dead, so I can fathom it. It came from an old tree in the ironwood forest south of here. They carried in the branch, used the iron, and only this non-iron leaf was left."

"All that from one leaf?" Hannah asked.

"It's my talent. I can go into more detail if you wish. My sister could have done the same with a living leaf."

"Can you tell exactly where it grew?" Goody asked. "It occurs to me that an ironwood forest would be the ideal place for their factory."

"Certainly. Let's go there now."

They marched on south. "Caution," Eve said as they approached a hillock. She was reading the leaf. "This item passed by a small dragon's lair, a smoker, and the robots had to battle it, losing several of their number, before beating it back with dented teeth. They left it in a very bad mood. We don't want to pass the same way."

"From the leaf?" Goody asked, amazed.

"And from the dragon smoke coating it," Eve agreed. "That's the thing about things, both animate and inanimate: they are composed of many elements, and each element has its own history. A lot can be learned."

Obviously so. Goody was becoming more impressed. He had never associated with a sorceress before, and had tended to dismiss their powers as more legendary than practical.

They made a detour around that section of the route, but were able to see some of the signs of the scuffle. Saplings had been beaten down and were coated with smoke, and there was a broken dragon scale on the ground. Indeed, that dragon was not in a good mood.

And the princess had called it out before they came to it. From the information in a single soiled leaf.

"We will not make it today, and it's dangerous to travel at night," Eve said. "We'd better camp."

"I'll keep an eye out for pie plants," Hannah said. "And a stream, so we can drink and wash. I'll construct a lean-to."

"No need."

Hannah paused. "Princesses don't eat or wash?"

Eve smiled. "Princesses don't rough it when they don't have to. Pick a convenient glade and I'll plant one of Grandma's seeds."

The barbarian shrugged. Soon she found a nice glade.

Eve brought out a purse and extracted a single seed. "These are pre-invoked, so Grandma doesn't need to be here to say 'Grow!'" She touched it to her mouth and set it on the ground. "Just a bit of saliva to trigger it," she said. "Then stand back."

The seed sprouted. Roots plunged into the ground, and shoots spread out in a circle. It quickly grew to considerable diameter, causing them to step back. Then the shoots made square turns and grew upward, forming eight saplings that thickened into trunks as they grew. At about head height on a human they radiated branches that reached out sideways to interlock with each other, forming a cylindrical enclosure. From there they angled up and toward the center, until they met and twined about each other, making the connection tight. Then leaves sprouted, growing large and flat, covering the slanting roof and spreading down to cover the sides as well.

In fact it was coming to look a lot like a house. "A houseplant!" Goody said, catching on.

"Duh!" the bird said with the princess's voice, as it had remained with her.

"A primed houseplant," Eve agreed. "It will serve the night. Of course we won't be able to use it again elsewhere; it is firmly anchored here. So I don't want to waste the seeds. But this shouldn't be more than a three-day excursion. If it is, we'll have to make do with your lean-to."

"Suppose a hostile creature comes?" Hannah asked.

"There are thorns." Eve carefully lifted up a leaf on the side, showing the thick spikes under it. "We'll have to use only the doorway, where the thorns retreat when requested, nicely. It's pretty tough, overall. But if a fire dragon attacks it, we'll need other magic."

"I'm impressed," Hannah said. "This is good shelter. But we'll also need food and water."

"Duh!" the parody repeated.

Eve brought out two more seeds, and touched them to her tongue before dropping them to the ground. They too sprouted immediately. One soon became recognizable as a pie plant. The other turned out to be a watermelon plant. The seeds did indeed provide everything they needed.

They ate pies and drank water tapped from the watermelons. They chatted about this and that, and Eve told them how she and Dawn had met and traveled with Forrest Faun when they were Old Enough on Ida's moons. That required some explaining. It seemed that on Ptero, the first moon, time equaled geography, or vice versa, so they could be eighteen at the same time they were only six in Xanth. They had had, Eve thought, quite a fling with the faun. But she didn't know the details, because of the Adult Conspiracy. "But I mean to be good and ready, when the time comes," she concluded.

Goody was sure she would be.

Then it was time to wash. "We girls will set up the house while you wash," Hannah said, abating a looming crisis. "Then you'll go inside while we do."

They went in, and he stripped and held a small watermelon over his head. He shook it, and it sprayed water over him. He decided not to wash his clothes; they weren't that dirty, and he needed to wear them immediately.

Then he went to the door section. "Thorns, please let me pass," he said, and the thorns turned soft so he could brush by them harmlessly.

Inside it was a delightful chamber, partitioned by a leaf wall, with two beds with leaf blankets. The house had even grown pillows. "You're over here," Hannah said. "Eve gets the other bed, and I'll take the floor."

So it was, with perfect propriety. The girls went out to wash while he rested on his assigned bed. They returned in due course, damp and cheerful. Goody got a good night's sleep, interrupted only when he heard the sound of heavy rain in the night. It beat down on the roof, but the overlapping leaves let no water through. This was a fine temporary house.

# 10

# FACTORY

In the morning, refreshed, they resumed their trip. The parody, finding the princess boring, returned to Goody. They tried to push through a patch of tall reeds, but quickly backed off: they were cutlasses, that cut only women. The adjacent patch let the girls through without obstruction, but tried to cut Goody. These were cutlad plants. Unfortunately for them, his talent protected him, and they bounced back to slice their neighbors. The plants did not seem pleased.

They came across what at first they took for a human encampment, as it was a virtual city of pitched tents. But all the tents were empty. What could this mean?

"A huge army, out foraging at the moment," Hannah suggested. "Which means we'd better move on before they return." She paused, scowling. "But I don't see any signs of human activity."

Eve touched the nearest tent. "We are in Tent City," she said. "It consists only of tents, nothing else. Many are in-

terconnected. Whoever passes through them suffers enhancement of his/her properties. It's a pun."

"A pun?" Goody asked.

"In Tent City," Hannah said. "Intensity."

"So it probably won't hurt us to pass through this," Eve
said. "The effect is temporary, anyway." She stepped into
the nearest tent.

Goody followed. The effect was immediate; he felt like
twice the goblin he had ever been, and suspected that his
bounce talent would bounce things back twice as fast. He
looked ahead, to be sure of not losing the princess in the
maze of interconnections, and froze.

"Hey, get moving, joker," the peeve said. But Goody
remained in place, blinded by dazzles.

Then something dropped over his head. "It's just a flap
of canvas from a tent," Hannah said. "To prevent you
from freaking out following the princess. I'll lead you
through." She took him by the hand.

Eve evidently paused. "What's the matter with him?"

"Your form is enhanced," Hannah said. "Just the sight
of your outline is enough to freak him out without even
any panties showing. So I'm covering his head."

"Really?" The princess sounded pleased.

"Look, doll, this isn't a game," Hannah said seriously.
"You teens who come new to it may think it's fun to see
how it works, but you can get into trouble in a hurry.
That's why the Adult Conspiracy exists: to save you from
yourselves, until you have enough experience to keep it
under control. Save it for when you need to freak out men
who mean you harm. Don't waste it on the one decent
male goblin who means no one harm. Don't be a bleeping
tease."

There was silence for a moment and a half. "Oh. I
guess so," the princess said. "I'm sorry. Let me use some
of this canvas." There were sounds of rustling and tearing. "How's that?"

"You look like a duck, canvasback!"

"Thank you, peeve. That's the object, approximately. Let's see if it helps."

Hannah lifted off the hood so that Goody could see again. There was Eve, swathed in white canvas from neck to ankle. Even so, she was dangerously alluring. He felt himself swaying on his feet.

"Maybe use the hood," Hannah said, handing it to her.

The princess dropped it over her head, opening one side so she could see out. That covered her lustrous black hair and made her black eyes fade back into the shadows like mysterious pools.

Goody steadied. "Thank you," he said. "I think I can manage now."

Eve braced herself. "I'm not good at this, but I'll try."

Not good at it? She had been dangerously proficient, as Hannah said.

The princess oriented on him. "Goody, I apologize for teasing you. Hannah's right; I was thoughtless. I am young, and this is a lesson I'll try not to forget. Please forgive me."

"Of course," Goody said, surprised. "I know you didn't mean to do it."

"Not this time," she agreed. "But I should have realized." She smiled. "And you have the honor of receiving my very first sincere apology. Was it all right?"

He was taken aback. "It was perfect," he said graciously.

"Great! Aren't you glad I didn't try a gourd-style apology!"

"A what?"

"Oh, you don't know? I'll show you."

"Don't do that!" Hannah said.

But she was too late. Eve was already dropping down to her knees and leaning into Goody. She kissed him firmly on the mouth. The world exploded into a kaleidoscopic display buttressed by rainbow-colored fireworks.

By the time he recovered, they were out of the Tent City. Hannah must have carried him.

"Goblin, you should have heard the lecture the barbarian gave the princess," the parody said zestfully from a nearby perch. "I think I learned some new words."

Goody sat up somewhat vaguely. "I never heard of a—whatever it was. How long was I out?"

"A good half hour, weak-knees. Little stars and planets and hearts were floating over your stunned puss."

"Go-Go used to do that to me. But this—"

Eve appeared. She was out of her canvas shrouding, but her hair seemed slightly singed and there were scorch marks on her dress. "A gourd-style apology," she said. "You know—the realm of dreams. They do things dreamily there. I just couldn't resist. I suppose I should apologize again."

"If you do, I'll cut your head off!" Hannah said behind her.

"Just don't tell Grandma Irene. She'd really make me hurt." The princess smiled ruefully. "I won't do it again. Anyway, it won't be half as potent, out of Tent City."

Apologizing by kissing. Goody made a mental note to be wary of things inspired by the gourd realm. He had thought it was all bad things, like horror houses and graveyards. Evidently there were other aspects.

They resumed their trek. Soon they came to a pretty little spring. "Oh, good, I'm thirsty," Eve said. She produced a dainty cup from somewhere and dipped it in the water.

"Wait!" Hannah said. "We don't know what kind of spring that is."

"Yes, we do," Eve said. She touched the water with one finger. "It's dilute healing elixir!" she exclaimed, surprised. "Good enough; I can use a drink of that." She put the cup to her mouth.

As she drank, she changed. Her hair unfrizzed and became fully lustrous again, and the scorch marks faded from her dress. The elixir had healed the damage done by the verbal hiding Hannah had given her.

Two bits of metal dropped from her ears. "My earrings!" she exclaimed. "They fell off. But they couldn't have. My ears are pierced."

"Not anymore, sweetheart," the parody said. "No more holes in your head."

Eve felt her ears. It was true. "The healing elixir—it healed my piercings."

"Serves you right, gourd head."

The princess nodded. "I suppose it does. It wouldn't have happened if I'd behaved like a lady instead of a girl." She put the earrings away. "But it's annoying as— say a word for me, peeve."

"Bleep," the bird said obligingly.

Eve blushed. "Thank you. In four years maybe I'll understand what that means."

"What a piece of work," Hannah murmured, half admiringly. Goody wasn't sure whether she was referring to the bird or the girl. Maybe both.

Goody accepted the princess's cup for a drink from the spring, and it did make him feel much better. Then Hannah took it, and finally the parody got a beakful.

They proceeded more vigorously thereafter. Suddenly they came to the ironwood forest, and were appalled. Half the stately trees had been reduced to stumps, and robots were working on others. The forest was being converted to a wasteland.

"They're cutting them all down, for the iron," Hannah said. "But clear-cutting is no good. There'll be no trees left to seed new ones."

"They don't care," Goody said. "They're machines. They're just doing the job they were made for."

"Which is why they have to be stopped," Eve said. "You're right: this is a serious threat to Xanth. We don't even need to see the factory to know that."

"Then let's get out of here before they spy us," Hannah said. "This scene gives me the crawls."

"The whats?" Goody asked.

"Creeps," Eve said.

"Barbarian version," Hannah agreed.

Goody spied something different. "This isn't an iron-wood stump."

Hannah looked. "That's weird. They're cutting some regular trees too. Why would they do that?"

Eve shrugged. "Maybe it was an accident."

"In that case, wouldn't they leave the fallen trunks here? There are none."

It was true. The mystery remained.

Then a bulb flashed over Goody's head. "They burn wood inside them! It's their food."

"That's right," Hannah agreed. "I forgot."

"Bogey at six o'clock!"

They turned. The bird was right. A robot stood there. But not a little one. This one was goblin-sized, far bigger than the others had been.

"They've got more iron now," Hannah said. "They're thinking bigger."

"We *really* need to get back to Castle Roogna," Eve said.

"But not with this one left to tell the tale," Hannah said, drawing her sword.

"That will make too much noise," Goody said. "The others will hear."

"Let me try the quiet way," Eve said. "Hey, robot, look at this." She spun around and hoisted her skirt.

The robot's eye lenses fogged, but it didn't fall. "They're machines," Hannah repeated. "They don't have feelings, so they can't freak out."

"But it did have some effect," Eve said. "So let's try this." She stepped up to the robot, dropped to her knees, and planted a kiss on its face-plate.

The robot wavered, almost losing its balance. Then it recovered. It had survived the kiss.

"It doesn't have a mouth," Hannah said. "Otherwise I think you might have had it."

The robot made the sound of a smirk. It knew it had defeated them.

"What a rusty hunk!" Goody's voice said. "I've seen better iron on an old shipwreck!"

The robot's face-plate swiveled toward Goody. Goody was silent; could the bird's insults get them out of this?

"Where is this ship?" the robot asked.

There would be a whole lot of metal there. The machine was being practical.

"Why don't you unscrew your thick metal head and throw it away so you'll look better?"

"I have no emotions," the robot intoned. "You can't annoy me. Where is the ship!"

"You have no sense either, you bleeping tin can! Now get out of our way before we grind you up for scrap."

"That would not be practical. Where is the ship?"

"Blow it out your exhaust, iron ass! You wouldn't know practical if it chomped your ugly foot."

Little sparks flitted across the robot's joints. This was not a good sign, for an emotionless machine. "I will pulver-ize you," it said, reverting to basic syllables in its distraction. "Where is the ship?"

The machine was certainly single-minded. It had taken the ship reference literally, and wanted to get to it.

"Pulverize us? You and who else, creakbolt?"

"Me and the other clones," the robot answered. And now other robots appeared, surrounding them, all of them goblin-sized. "Where is the ship?"

"I'll hack one apart," Hannah said. "The rest of you run through the gap that makes, and don't stop running." She hefted her sword.

"Don't do that," Eve said. "You'll be pulverized."

"You have a better plan?"

The princess nodded. "I have seeds. But they will need time to grow, unobserved by the robots. We need to wait until night."

"But they'll pulverize us *now*." Indeed, the robots were closing in on all sides.

"Talk them out of it."

Hannah looked helplessly at Goody. It didn't work

well; she was obviously inexperienced at such looks.

"You can't pulverize us," Goody said.

"Why not?" the robot asked.

The machine was ready to listen? He had to come up with a reason! "Because—because then you'll never find the ship."

The robots paused. They evidently had similar programs, so reacted similarly, though only the first one talked.

Then they came to a conclusion. "We need only the bird who has seen the rusty shipwreck. The others are surplus." The advance resumed.

"That's what you think, rust-for-brains," the parody said. "You can't catch me." It flew up above them.

The robots paused again. They didn't know how to deal with this complication. "We need to manufacture flying machines," the first one said.

"And that will take you, how long, hollow bottom? Two days? I'll be long gone by then."

They paused again. "How can we make you stay, bird?"

"Just treat my friends right, square nuts. I'll stay with them."

Goody was amazed. The peeve had acted to protect them!

"We will confine you until we build flying machines," the robot decided.

The robots brought metal bars and plunged them into the ground around the prisoners. They welded them together with crossbars, and constructed a barred ceiling. It was a tight cage. They were very efficient. They were after all construction robots.

Then they returned to their logging of ironwood trees, ignoring the prisoners.

"They don't hate us," Hannah said. "They just want us out of the way."

"But they seem to realize that if we escape, we'll cause

them trouble," Goody said. "So they won't let us go."

"Not intentionally," Eve said.

Hannah glanced at her. "You really do have seeds to get us out?"

"Oh, yes. But first let's eat and rest." She brought out two seeds, touched them to her mouth, and dropped them on the ground.

It seemed that the robots were not aware of living creatures' need for food and water, so had provided none. Maybe that was just as well; the less the machines understood of life, the better.

Soon they snacked on pies and drank from the princess's cup. But then another need developed.

"Oops, I forgot the potty plant," Eve said, dropping another seed. It sprouted and grew, producing several squat potties. Privacy was difficult in their cramped quarters, but dusk was coming, so they held out until shrouded by darkness.

"Somebody's pooping!" the peeve announced helpfully.

"There's a small one for you too," Eve said, tapping the side of the potty so the bird could locate it.

When the darkness was complete, Eve evoked and planted other seeds. Meanwhile the robots went right on cutting trees, needing no light or rest. They were continuous machines, never pausing. That continued to scare Goody.

"These are slow-growing plants, so we might as well rest while waiting," Eve said.

"Makes sense to me," Hannah said as a root wrestled past their feet. "Just what kind of trees are they?"

"Well, one's a steelwood that should be too tough for the iron robots to tackle. The other's a tangle tree."

"A tangler! Here in our cage?"

"But there's one thing: they are spelled not to harm me, but the rest of you lack that protection."

"Now she tells us!" the bird said irately.

"Not to worry, cutebeak. I'll protect you."

"Just for incidental information," Hannah said, "how do you mean to do that?"

"I'll put my arms around you, and they'll leave us all alone. But we must stay together, or there could be mischief."

"Such as us getting eaten by the tangle tree," Goody said uneasily.

"True," she said. "We had better get together before it gets big enough to feed."

They got together, arranging themselves for maximum coverage. Hannah sat leaning back against the trunk of the centrally growing steelwood tree, and Goody sat on her lap facing away, the bird on his shoulder. This put his head against her metal halter, which was comfortable, as the halter was flexible. Then Eve sat before them, her legs half around their thighs, and leaned in to hug them with her arms. This put her bosom almost into Goody's face. He would have freaked out, had he been able to see anything. "This should do it," she said. "The tendrils will encounter my limbs and move away."

What could he do? Shielded by both their soft bodies, he drifted off to a rather pleasant sleep. Even the irascible bird, similarly pressed, made no complaint.

He woke as Eve stirred. "Time to break out," she said. "All we have to do is climb the trunk of the steelwood tree; it has penetrated the roof of the cage."

Eve lifted herself up and caught hold of the lower branches of the steelwood. She climbed. When she was clear, Goody followed, and finally Hannah.

Sure enough, the top of the cage had burst asunder, and they were able to step out onto the twisted remnant of its framework. But next to the steelwood was the tangle tree; Goody felt its tentacles quivering as they sensed his approach. "The tangler—"

"That's to catch the pieces of the cage as they come loose, and set them down silently," Eve explained. "And to distract the robots, if necessary."

"But won't it grab us?"

"I'll have to hold you." She felt for him in the dark, picked him up, and held him close. "Okay, Tangler," she said.

Tentacles wrapped around them and heaved them both up. Then they were swinging around and down, and deposited on the ground. "Wait here while I fetch Hannah," she said as she set him down.

He waited, highly conscious of the surrounding tentacles. They could so readily wrap around him and carry him into the deadly trunk! He did not dare move anything.

"Aw, I dare you, greenie!" the parody said.

Oh, no! The bird was taunting the tree!

Then Eve and Hannah dropped down beside him. "Naughty birdy," Eve said, laughing.

They made their way quietly from the cage trees to the regular forest that surrounded the stumps of the ironwoods. They heard the continuous noises from the robot loggers not far distant. Only when they were safely within it did they pause to get some light. Hannah had some fireweed bulbs in her pack; she brought one out, and used its flame to illuminate their way.

There was a commotion back at the cage. "I think they have discovered our absence," Hannah said.

"And the tangle tree has discovered them," Eve said.

"Will they search for us?" Goody asked, worried.

"They may try," Eve said. "I just dropped a magnet tree seed."

"And that will—?" Hannah asked.

"Attract and hold any iron in the vicinity. Strongly."

"So they won't be coming this way soon."

"Not soon," Eve agreed. "We can rest until dawn in a couple of hours."

"Then hurry back to Castle Roogna," Goody said.

"Not yet," Eve said. "We haven't seen the factory."

Goody and Hannah tried to exchange a glance, but couldn't make the connection in the darkness. This teen was serious about the mission.

They settled down and slept until dawn. They had no concern about dangerous beasts; the robots had driven most wildlife away with their constant activity.

In the morning they organized and resumed their walk. They made a wide detour around the ironwood forest, which continued to resound with the sounds of its ongoing destruction.

Just south of the field of stumps they spied it: a mass of pipes, wires, and moving blocks. There was a huge fire, evidently used to heat cauldrons of iron during the night when no sunlight was available to be concentrated. "Now we know what else they're doing with the regular wood," Hannah said grimly. "Nothing is safe from them."

"Now we know," Goody echoed. "It just gets worse and worse."

"And it's all your fault, dumbbells!"

"We were fools," Hannah agreed with half a sigh.

"I don't know how you could have anticipated anything like this," Eve said. "There's been nothing in Xanth like it before. Anyone would have been deceived."

"You know, princess," Hannah said, "I could almost get to like you, if I tried."

"Too bad you're not a handsome prince who's not too fussy about age."

They laughed. Then they set about making their way back to Castle Roogna. Rather than circle the iron forest again, they cut west to intersect an enchanted path. They had to spend a third night on the road, but it was comfortable, and no more seeds needed to be planted.

Here there was nothing more dangerous than a wanna bee, which was really a fly that tried to look and buzz like a bee. They ate and washed up, reasonably well coordinated, and the princess managed not to flash anything in Goody's direction. She had indeed learned her lesson.

Then, as they were ready to retire for the night, one more traveler appeared. This was a flying centaur filly. "Oh, hello," she said as she landed. "I thought this camp was unoccupied."

"Welcome to join us," Hannah said, and introduced the others. They learned that the latest arrival was Cynthia Centaur. She was magnificently breasted, as all grown centaur fillies were. Goody struggled to avoid staring.

"A flying horse-rear!"

"The bird!" Goody, Hannah, and Eve said almost together.

"Get a load of those bare boobs!"

"It's a pet peeve who spent time in Hell," Goody said. "It is always in a foul temper, and insults everybody in range. I'm trying to find a good home for it."

"I can appreciate that your work is cut out for you," Cynthia said.

"My job is to protect him from the mischief the bird invokes," Hannah said.

The centaur turned to Eve. "And you're really a princess?"

"On a special mission," Eve said, but did not clarify. That was the hint to the others to be silent about the robot menace, at least until they had reported to the king.

They learned that Cynthia was the mate of Che Centaur, having started life as a human girl longer ago than she cared to say. But she had taken youth elixir to reduce her age to match Che's age. "There was an interesting complication," she said. "It relates to the way I fly."

"You look like a big clumsy crow!"

Cynthia smiled tolerantly. "Thank you for that insight, peeve. And I'm sure you fly like a crippled harpy."

Goody stifled a chortle. She had scored more accurately than she might have realized.

"I didn't know you had any problem flying," Eve said. "All winged centaurs have lightening magic in their tails, so they can flick bugs to make them too light to land, and themselves to become light enough to float and fly."

"That's the thing," Cynthia said. "I am not a natural flying creature; I was transformed back when Magician Trent, the transformer, was young, and he didn't get me quite right. I may even have been the first winged centaur; I don't know. At first I was ashamed of my form, and hid in the Brain Coral's pool for some time. But eventually I accommodated to my condition, and to the clotheless custom of the centaurs. So I flew by the sheer power of my wings, sending down quite a draft. Other centaurs had the lightening magic, and it was easier for them. But now I have it too. The mystery is how."

"You don't, you faker!"

Cynthia's tail flicked out and barely touched the bird. The parody sailed up into the air, squawking. "Hey, I'm too light to perch!"

"Fortunately it wears off after a while," Cynthia said. Her tone, in a less generous creature, might have sounded smug. "I didn't know I had it, until one day I flicked at a fly to scare it away, and my tail touched my own flank. Suddenly I felt light. I realized I had the power—yet I was sure I had not had it at the outset. What could explain this?"

"The three little brats—I mean, princesses—might have enchanted you," Eve said. "They can do just about any kind of magic, if they get together and sing and play it."

"No, when I thought about it, I realized there had been signs of it dating from back before they were delivered. I had the power and didn't know it. But how? Then finally a bulb flashed over my head—" She paused, smiling. "Did you know that when Queen Irene gets an idea, the bulb over her head is a plant bulb?"

"Dawn and I tease Grandma about that," Eve said, sharing the smile.

"Anyway, I remembered that at one point Magician Trent re-transformed me into a roc, so I could carry him up out of a deep cave, and later restored me." She paused, smiling reminiscently. "Gloha Goblin-Harpy and I were traveling with him, and we both had crushes on him. What a man! He made a filly of me. But of course he was married."

"To Great-Grandma Iris," Eve said. "You mean you and he—?"

"I confess Gloha and I were tempted. But he was older and more sensible than we, and nothing came of it except perhaps for some kissing."

"He kissed you?" Eve was showing the kind of shock she had not shown when she kissed Goody. Apparently it depended on perspective.

"No, we kissed him. Together, when he was frozen stiff by a snow dragon. That's a variety of steamer that lives in cold regions. We had to thaw him somehow, before it became permanent. So we hugged and kissed him, giving him the warmth of our bodies, and managed to bring him out of it. But that's beside the point. He transformed me, and when he restored me, he must have made me a regular kind of winged centaur without realizing that it wasn't quite the same. So after that I had the lightening magic."

"Fascinating," Eve said. "You smooched Great-Grandpa Trent!"

"You should have seen Eve smooching Goody," the parody said. "He barely recovered in time to see the robots."

"The whats?"

"Self-willed machines, appliances, gizmos, contraptions, motors—"

"Automatons?"

"Whatever," the bird agreed crossly.

Cynthia glanced at the others. "You saw automatons?"

The parody had given it away. "We are on an investigative mission for the king," Goody said. "There seems to be an invasion of robots. We're not sure how to stop them."

"This is something Che needs to know about."

"We were hoping to keep it quiet until the king decides what to do."

"Very well. We'll keep it quiet until we check with the king. Any kind of invasion is a serious matter."

They settled down for the night. Then Cynthia remembered something. "You kissed Goody Goblin, Eve? You are not, as I recall, yet of age."

"Oh come on!" the girl protested. "The Adult Conspiracy doesn't stop us from kissing."

"But Goody is a middle-aged adult male not of your family. He should know better."

"He does," Hannah said. "She caught him by surprise, demonstrating a gourd apology."

"Oho! That explains a lot. Still—"

"I won't do it again."

"Precisely." Then the dialogue lapsed.

In the morning the centaur flew on her way, and the others walked on theirs. Soon they saw the turrets of Castle Roogna.

What would King Dor think of their report? It would surely be much worse than he had anticipated.

# 11

# CAMPAIGN

King Dor nodded. "So now they have a better supply of iron, and are larger. They represent a greater threat than before."

"That's it, Granddad," Eve agreed. "That ironwood forest is a mess. At least they'll run out of it soon enough. Maybe that will stop them."

"I doubt it," the king said. "They will merely search for more iron, as they were doing near Castle Zombie."

"But will they find it?" Eve asked.

"The methodical way they are searching, it will not be long before they find Iron Mountain."

Goody had heard of that. An entire mountain made of iron. That would provide all the robots would ever need to conquer the rest of Xanth. "We'll have to stop them from reaching it," Goody said.

"Exactly," the king agreed. "I have summoned the human representatives of Xanth, but this is likely to be more than humans can handle alone. We shall need the assistance of the others."

"The others?" Hannah asked.

"The centaurs. The dragons. The elves. The harpies, goblins, demons, ogres, zombies, crossbreeds, and others. Those who don't necessarily answer to the authority of the pure humans. This is a threat to all of them, but it may not be easy to convince them of that until it's too late. We shall need to send persuasive emissaries."

"I hope you have good ones," Hannah said.

"We shall have to work with what we have. You, as a barbarian, can approach the barbarian humans."

Hannah was taken aback. "Oh, Your Majesty, I can't! I left them in disgust when our village was pacified."

The king turned to Goody. "And you, as a goblin—"

"I'm no good!" Goody protested. "Goblins won't listen to me. I'm exiled, because I'm too polite."

"What a washout!" the parody said.

"And we have no representatives convenient for the other species," the king said. "It seems we have a problem."

"And we don't want to alarm folk by announcing the threat before we have a way to deal with it," Eve said.

"But we may have a way to notify leaders and enlist help without making a commotion," the king said. "Because you have a pretext to travel: trying to place the bird."

Goody saw the way of it. "What do you want us to do?"

"To be my emissaries," the king said seriously. "I will give you an official letter of introduction, and arrange transportation. That is as much as I can do, in this respect."

"You could hardly have found less qualified people," Hannah said.

"Less obvious people," Eve said. "That's not the same."

Queen Irene appeared at the doorway. "The centaurs are here."

King Dor smiled. "Bring them in."

Two winged centaurs entered, a male and a female. "Good to see you again, Che, Cynthia," the king said.

"But we saw you just this morning!" Goody said, as if that made any difference.

"The king's message was awaiting my return," Cynthia said. "We came immediately, of course."

"But we hadn't even reported then," Hannah said.

Eve smiled. "Grandpa knew we had a crisis. We merely confirmed it. The humans are already organizing. If we can just get the other species to join us."

So it was that Goody and Hannah found themselves riding the two winged centaurs, after being flicked light, along with the peeve. And possessed a list of species to contact.

Goody and the parody were aboard Cynthia. "If I may comment," Goody said carefully, "I am surprised you asked to have me ride you. I should have thought you would prefer to transport a woman."

Her head turned to face him as she flew. The action caused the upper portion of her human torso to twist so that her left breast showed in splendid silhouette. "Now why should you think that, Goody?"

"Well, you're female, and—"

"So he can't gawk at your knockers," the parody suggested.

Cynthia evinced half a smile. "That too, perhaps. It is true that I feared your eyeballs would suffer damage yesterday as you attempted to restrain them. But this is a reaction we centaurs have come to expect and discount among humanoid males. You have made every effort to be restrained and polite, an unusual trait among goblin males. In fact I might have suspected you of being a female in disguise, but for those eyes."

"Thank you," Goody said weakly. "I am the only polite goblin male extant. It has become my curse."

"I sense that you are in need. This is why I wished to talk with you, and this flight seems to be a convenient time."

"In need?" Goody asked, perplexed.

"In need of a vocabulary transplant," the peeve said. "He can't even say bleep without a swearing spell."

"I can say it," Goody said. "But won't."

"Do you care to tell me your romantic background? I suspect it has been difficult."

What was the harm? He told her of his problem with goblin girls, and of his twenty-year marriage to Go-Go. "Now I am in grief for her," he concluded. "I am trying to find other things to do, to distract me."

"I had thought it would be something like that," Cynthia said. "I believe you are ready to find another woman and settle down again."

"Never!"

"Don't let your commitment to Go-Go interfere with reality. She is gone, and I'm sure she would want you to be happy again."

She had scored. "She would. Yet—"

"Yet no other goblin woman is interested in a polite male. I appreciate the problem. I will keep an eye out; perhaps there is someone for you."

"Ha ha," the bird said.

"No one can match Go-Go."

"I think it only seems that way. You are obviously aware of other females. I could tell yesterday by the way you studiously avoided looking at lovely young Princess Eve, and at Hannah Barbarian, who is a formidably mature woman."

"You should see her shaking her cheesecake!"

"I have no need of that, peeve," Cynthia said. "But the fact that you, Goody, notice female attributes means you are ready for some kind of association beyond that of convenience."

"I—" But it was true. "I suppose I see in them aspects of Go-Go. I really hate being alone."

"I understand completely. I faced a similar problem, before I got together with Che." She paused, then tackled something else. "Che tutors Sim Bird, who needs to know everything, in due course. He's a very bright bird. That keeps Che busy finding out new things. Sometimes his researches lead to obscure bypaths. There was a story a couple decades back of a goblin chief's son who was banished from his hill. We wondered what it would take to make a goblin male unacceptable. Bad language or bad nature wouldn't seem to account for something like that."

Centaur information was comprehensive! She was inquiring, indirectly. "But politeness would," he said.

"So you are that goblin?"

"That banished chief's son," he agreed heavily.

She flicked him with the tip of her tail to make him light again, lest they lose altitude. "I would think that there would be goblin girls who would be interested in any chief's son, even a polite one."

"I think they would not be the type I would care to know."

"Gold diggers!" the parody said.

"Opportunists," she agreed. "Yet if there were one who was not that type, whose interest was sincere—"

He shook his head with resignation. "She would still have to match the standards of decency and niceness Go-Go set, or I couldn't love her. That makes it just about impossible."

"Perhaps." Then she was silent for a while.

A flying dragon came toward them. "Bogey at one o'-clock!" the parody said as the dragon snorted a twin column of fire.

A bow appeared in Cynthia's hands, and she nocked an arrow. Undeterred, the dragon came on. That made Goody nervous. Dragon fire could toast them from a distance.

Cynthia drew the bowstring. The dragon inhaled, readying a deadly blast the moment it got within range. Goody's nervousness intensified. How could this filly score when flying, and wouldn't the arrow, even if on target, just bounce off the dragon's metallic scales?

Cynthia loosed the arrow. It flew into the midst of the starting flame. The dragon swerved, stung, and the flame cut off.

Then Goody saw the arrow sticking from the dragon's nose. That was one of the few soft spots. It was not a lethal strike, but it had to hurt.

"Some just have to learn the hard way," Cynthia said as she put the bow away somewhere. "Normally they feint and retreat."

"I'm sure this one will, next time," Goody said, impressed. It had not been a long or hard shot, but it had been accurate, and that was what counted.

"You should've jammed it right down its throat!"

"There was no need, peeve."

That surprised Goody again, as it implied, surely correctly, that she could have scored there. She had intended only to discourage the dragon, and teach it a lesson, not to kill it.

"How come?" the bird demanded.

"There has been a shortage of dragons recently. We don't want to take out any before their time. They perform necessary policing of untoward elements. Some merely require a bit of discipline."

And she had disciplined the dragon. This soft-breasted filly who was so concerned about Goody's romantic life—there was more to her than Goody had realized. "I'm impressed," he said frankly.

"SCP," she said. "Standard centaur policy."

So it seemed. But Goody remained impressed.

Goody snoozed as the flight continued, and so did the parody. He knew he should be marshaling effective arguments to present to the centaurs, but his mind seemed to have shut down for the day. He hoped it would reanimate when it had to.

And of course he dreamed of Go-Go Gobliness. In life she had been pretty but not outstanding, according to others, but to him she was beauty incarnate. No, there was not her like in all Xanth—and if there were, what would she want with him, a disgraced and banished male? So fleeting dreams were all he could have of fleeting happiness.

He woke as the centaur glided down to the sand of a beach. She landed running, cleverly maintaining her balance. She had allowed her weight to return so that firm contact with the ground was feasible.

"Better go to flight school, you amateur!" the parody complained as the shock of her hooves striking hard sand ran up through her body and Goody's, shaking the bird.

Che and Hannah were already down. "That was great!" she said. "I've never ridden in the sky before. And Che is the most intelligent male I've met."

Probably true, Goody thought, because chances were that Che was the smartest of centaurs, and they were generally smarter than straight human folk. It was interesting that the barbarian woman appreciated intelligence in a male. Barbarian males were not noted for that quality, which surely complicated her romantic prospects.

"Hey, you didn't take us all the way," the parody said. "Centaur Isle's across the sea, hoofheads."

Che smiled, as tolerant as Cynthia was. "True. That is because we are not welcome on Centaur Isle, or indeed, among landbound centaurs generally. They regard us as a misceginated species."

That stumped the bird. "What kind?"

"A crossbreed."

"But all centaurs are crossbreeds," Hannah said. "Between horses and humans."

"We don't like to advertise our purported human ancestry," Che said. "But the point is that ground-bound centaurs regard themselves as a pure species, and object to any dilution. They also regard magic as obscene."

"And you use magic to fly," Hannah said.

"So we are doubly obscene," Che agreed cheerfully. "We live with it."

"But how are we to get to Centaur Isle?"

"Simply walk along the beach until you come to the centaur ferry. Tell them your mission, and they will take you across."

"But we can't tell the ferryman our real mission," Goody said. "We're supposed to keep it quiet, for now."

"And your mission is to place the peeve," Cynthia reminded him.

Oh. Yes. "We'll walk," he agreed.

"We shall await your return," Che said.

"But don't you have better things to do than just wait?"

"No. This mission is preemptive."

Oh, again. Of course.

"Lazy hoofers!"

The centaurs merely smiled, unruffled, which of course nettled the bird.

They walked along the beach. Soon they came to the centaur ferry station. A male centaur stood there as if expecting them. Had word somehow been sent ahead, or did they always have an alert stallion there? Probably the latter.

Goody approached the stallion, who carried a large bow and had a quiver of arrows on his back. "Hello. I am Goody Goblin, and this is my companion Hannah Barbarian. I seek a good home for this parody."

"Not that it's any of your business, horseface."

"Who speaks with my voice, insultingly," Goody said. "So my mission is a challenge."

The centaur nodded. He gestured to the raft at the edge of the water. It was stout and broad enough for centaurs, which meant it was more than adequate for them.

They boarded, and sat in the center. The centaur stepped onto the rear of it, holding a solid pole. He angled the pole, and the raft started moving.

"But the pole's not touching anything," Goody said, surprised. "What's pushing the raft?"

"It is propelled by magic. The pole merely guides the thrust."

"But I thought—"

"A common confusion. We centaurs regard magic infestation in our bodies to be obscene, as you might regard something rotting inside your body. But we recognize magic as a viable force in Xanth, and do not hesitate to use it as required."

"Thank you for that clarification," Hannah said. "It makes sense."

"Indubitably."

The raft continued across the water, moving well.

"Bogey at nine o'clock!"

Sure enough, there was something in the water. It was large and toothy. The centaur set down the pole, and the raft slowed. He lifted his bow.

The toothy thing turned tail. It had evidently had prior experience with centaurs.

"Chicken! Buk buk buk BAWK!"

But the shamed monster did not return.

The centaur picked up the pole again, and progress resumed. "Routine," Hannah murmured.

They came to land on the large island that was the home of most of the centaurs of Xanth. They were met by a fair-haired filly, fully as full breasted as any of the breed.

"Get a load of that globe-fronted varmint," the parody said. "What a chassis!"

"Greetings, visitors," the filly said with a brilliant smile. "I am Cheery Centaur, your guide for your visit to Centaur Isle. What is your purpose here?"

"You sure got your points, creature!"

The filly paused, her smile freezing. "I beg your pardon?"

"Knockers, hooters, jugs, teats—"

"It's the bird!" Goody and Hannah said together.

"It uses my voice to insult people," Goody continued. "I am Goody Goblin, here to try to find a good home for this unusual bird. This is Hannah Barbarian, who protects me from the mischief the bird incites. As you can appreciate, it is a challenge. Please take us to your leader."

Cheery was taken aback. "I'm really not sure—"

"Because you're a simpleton, heifer!"

The centaur decided. "I will take you to our leader."

"Thank you," Goody said.

They followed the filly to an elaborate stall where an elder stallion awaited them. "This is Goody Goblin and his guardian Hannah Barbarian. They have a disreputable bird to place." She turned back to them. "This is Chevalier Centaur, our head stallion. He will give you a brief audience." She departed swiftly.

"Good riddance, founder-foot!"

Goody opened his mouth. "What is your real mission, goblin?" the stallion asked, cutting him off.

Goody had his mouth open, but was unable to get any words out. "We have a message and plea from Human King Dor," Hannah said.

"Naturally. You came here directly from Castle Roogna, as rapidly as was feasible. We knew something important was afoot. That's why I trotted here to meet you. Deliver your message and plea."

Goody finally got his mouth functioning. "Robots are invading Xanth. They are a danger to all residents, not just humans. We need to solicit the help of other organized species."

"What is this word 'robots'?"

"Machines, dumbbell!"

"They are mechanical creatures, made of iron," Goody said. "They have already ruined the ironwood forest, harvesting its trees for iron to make more robots. They are getting larger as they go. We have to stop them before they find another, richer source of iron."

"That would be Iron Mountain," Chevalier said. "That would be a virtually limitless source."

Goody nodded. "Uh, yes. King Dor mentioned it. The robots started as tiny entities. Now they are my size. If they get enough iron, they'll be full human size, or—"

"Or centaur size," the stallion agreed.

"So we feel that we must stop them before they do. Even so, it will be difficult, because they are not alive. They are machines, without feeling. They don't sleep. They just keep working, and—"

"Desist, goblin."

"But this is serious! We—"

"Hold. I appreciate the need. We will send a contingent to assist the humans in this campaign."

Goody's mouth was stifled again. Just like that, they had enlisted the centaurs!

"Thank you, Chevalier," Hannah said. "We are most grateful for your help."

"But as for the bird—"

Hannah laughed. "We'll try elsewhere!"

"Thank you."

"No thanks to you, hoof-in-mouth."

"I'm sure there is some responsible person somewhere who will appreciate the qualities of the peeve," Chevalier said with a wryness that bordered on humorous contempt.

Soon they were back on the raft, crossing to Xanth proper. "What group do we tackle next?" Hannah asked.

Goody sighed. "I dread this, but I think it has to be the goblins. There are many tribes, each more vicious than the next, and they are good at tunneling and fighting. They could really tackle the robots, especially while the robots are goblin sized."

"But your temperate language—"

"That's why I dread it."

Then a bulb flashed over her head, so bright that it startled the centaur boatman. "The peeve!"

"Present and accounted for, primitive slut."

"But the parody never says anything nice to anyone," Goody protested. "Diplomacy—"

"The irascible bird speaks the goblins' language. Carry it on your shoulder and don't let on who is speaking. They won't catch on that you're polite."

Goody stared at her. "That just might work! Except that I would have to make the case for the robot campaign, and then they'd catch on."

She nodded soberly. "There is that problem. But maybe you can delegate me to do that. I can talk their language."

"You wouldn't fit in a goblin mound. The passages are goblin sized. The chiefs would insist on talking in their official chambers."

She sighed. "Well, it seemed like a good idea."

"It *was* a good idea. I'm just not good enough to handle it. Bad enough, I mean."

"Finally the misbegotten pansy catches on!"

"Maybe we can talk them into talking outside."

"Maybe," he agreed without much hope.

They reached the shore. "Thank you, centaur," Goody said as they stepped off the raft. "We really appreciate your courtesy."

The centaur gazed down at him. "You are the oddest goblin I have encountered."

"I apologize for disappointing you."

"And that's exactly what I mean."

"But he has his points," Hannah said with a smile.

"No, you're the one with the points, peach," the parody said, peering pointedly at her halter.

"I would not be able to control my temper," the centaur said.

"That's why we are the ones with this mission," Hannah said. "It's a challenge."

They walked along the beach until they came to the two winged centaurs, who hardly seemed to have moved. "We have enlisted the landbound centaurs," Goody said. "Now I fear we must tackle the goblins."

"But—" Cynthia said.

"But it will be a disaster," Goody agreed. "Yet I see no alternative."

"He does have courage," Hannah said.

"That's not courage," the parody said. "That's folly."

Cynthia nodded. "Che and I discussed this during your absence, and we may have a viable idea."

"I had an un-viable idea," Hannah said. "I thought the peeve could insult the goblins for him. But he would still have to present the case, and that would lose it."

"True," Cynthia said. "Our thought is that he could use the assistance of another goblin."

"A regular male goblin? He'd be impossible to keep in line."

"A female goblin."

"But she wouldn't use any worse words than Goody would."

"But she would not be expected to. So the parody could insult them with Goody's voice, but the female could present the case he might seem too irate to do."

Hannah nodded. "That might work. She could fit inside their little tunnels."

"There remains one problem," Goody said. "What female goblin would care to associate with me, even in a purely business capacity?"

"Let's get flying, and we'll tell you whom we have in mind," Che said.

They mounted, and the centaurs flicked them light, spread their wings, and took off. It was weird; Goody's stomach tended to roil when it got light. But soon he adjusted. "You know a gobliness who would cooperate?"

"Some background," Cynthia said. "Che is close friends with Jenny Elf, who came to Xanth from the World of Two Moons. Jenny and Che are both friends with a single female goblin. So we thought we would ask Jenny whether she thinks that goblin would be interested. The three of them are so close that Jenny surely would know."

This was remarkable. "How did an elf, a centaur, and a goblin become friends? The three species don't associate with each other."

"It was an unusual situation. It seems the goblins kidnapped Che to be a companion for the goblin child, Gwenny. Jenny happened on the scene and was kidnapped too. There was quite a to-do about it before a compromise was reached, and the goblins released their captives. Gwenny came to live with Che's family, and their friendship endured despite the nature of their original acquaintance. Now all three are adults and living their own lives, but remain close friends."

"Why would a goblin child need a centaur companion?"

"Well, Gwenny was lame, and had an impediment of vision, so might have been cast out if those liabilities were discovered. So her mother arranged to conceal them by fetching her a steed that could see and walk for her. Actually, that was successful, and Gwenny's liabilities never became known to the goblins."

Goody felt a twinge of compassion for the goblin girl. "But you shouldn't have told me. Goblins can be quite cruel."

"As it seems you know from your own experience. But you see, by the same token she might understand your situation, and be willing to help. The mission is important enough to warrant special measures."

That was true. "If this special measure enables us to enlist the goblin hordes, then it's worth it."

"Meanwhile Che is similarly updating Hannah Barbarian, who is much concerned about your welfare."

"She takes her assignment seriously, and I think she feels the same guilt about transporting that robot program here that I do."

"Yes, for all that there is no such guilt. The robots of Robot World were simply awaiting their opportunity to colonize. You just happened to be the first to pass their way, providing them the means to put their plan into action. We were bound to face this invasion sooner or later."

"Still—"

"Yes, of course. But perhaps the guilt should be shared by the Good Magician Humfrey, who should have known that this would happen. And by the peeve, who—"

"Stifle it, airhead!"

They both laughed.

In due course they flew over an island on the west coast of Xanth that Goody hadn't known existed. "We are coming to the Isle of Wolves," Cynthia said.

"I'm not expert in geography, but I never heard of that one."

"Not surprising, as it connects only tenuously to Xanth. There's a whole line of islands that appear next to Xanth only part of the time. At other times it's impossible to reach them. But we happen to know the timing for this one. It's near Cape Flattery."

"Cape what?"

"That's a spur of land that flatters those who walk on it. That tends to distract them from the islands. But we don't need to walk on it."

"I'm sure the peeve wouldn't like it," Goody said.

"Speak for yourself, smartmouth."

"The peeve would be severely conflicted," Cynthia agreed. She hovered. "Ah, there's Wolf Isle now."

"But that's the same island you just flew over."

"It is an isle in the same place, but not the same isle. The other faded out, and Wolf Isle faded in. Now we can land." And the two centaurs glided down to the ground.

Immediately several huge wolves bounded up to surround them, snarling. "We have a pass," Che called, holding up what looked like a tuft of wolf fur. "We have come to talk to Jenny Elf about important business."

One wolf shifted into manform. "*What* business, centaur?"

"We have a cantankerous bird to find a home for."

"*What* bird?"

"What bird do you think, fur-for-brains?"

The man looked at Goody. "Listen, goblin, we don't need your kind here."

"Correct, man bottom. Our kind has some wit."

Before things could escalate, Che cut in. "Are you declining to honor our pass?"

"No, of course not," the werewolf said grudgingly. "This way." He resumed wolf form and loped along an island path.

The two centaurs galloped after the wolf. "You see," Cynthia said to Goody. "They naturally assumed you were the one talking. It was your voice and the typical goblin male attitude. With the right support you can do it."

"So it seems," he agreed, bemused.

They came to a large den. A wolf cub stood there. "Hi, Jerry," Che said.

The wolf became an elf child. "Hi, Che!"

"Tell your mother we need to talk to her."

The child became the cub and ran into the den.

"I didn't know there were were-elves," Goody said as he dismounted.

"There weren't until recently. That's Jenny Elf's son, Jerry Welf. He's five."

A large elf woman emerged, following the running child. Normal elves were half the height of goblins, but this one was taller by half than Goody. Yet there was something familiar about her. She ran up to hug Che, then Cynthia. "It's so nice to see you!" she exclaimed.

"Jenny, this is Goody Goblin, and Hannah Barbarian," Che said. Then, to the visitors: "This is Princess Jenny Elf."

Now Goody saw that she wore a small crown, similar to the one Princess Eve had worn. He opened his mouth.

"What a crappy excuse for a princess!" his voice said.

"That's the bird talking," Cynthia said. "It borrows its companion's voice and insults anyone in range. We're looking for a home for it."

Jenny gazed at the parody. "I'm afraid the wolves would eat it."

"Perhaps," Che said. "May we get private with you and Jeremy to discuss it?"

Jenny glanced at him, realizing that something was up. "Come to the royal wolfsbane patch." She led the way to a small private garden of plants with stalks bearing hood-shaped purplish-blue flowers.

"We have two things to discuss," Che said. "One with you, and one with Jeremy."

"I'll call him," Jenny said. She put two fingers to her mouth and blew a piercing wolf whistle.

Then for no good reason Goody made a connection. "We've met before," he exclaimed. "At the roster for the game of Companions of Xanth. You were chosen; I was not."

"That's right," she agreed. "I remember now. I'm sorry I didn't recognize you; to me, most goblins look alike."

"Much has happened since then."

"Indeed it has," she agreed.

"That was when Kim and Dug Mundane first visited Xanth."

"Yes. Now they are married and have a child."

In another moment a huge wolf bounded into the garden. This became a full-sized man as he landed before Jenny. "You called, dear?"

"Yes, dear. These are Goody Goblin and Hannah Barbarian, here to talk business with us."

"Bird!" Jerry said, evidently interested.

"Get lost, crossbreed brat!"

The man oriented on Goody, scowling. He too wore a small crown. Jenny put a hand on his arm. "The bird talks." Then, to the others: "This is Prince Jeremy Werewolf, my husband."

The prince cut directly to the point. "What business?"

"First, about the bird," Goody said. "That's just a pretext to mask our real mission. There is a robot invasion of

Xanth—manlike creatures made of metal—and we need the help of the werewolves and all others to stop them before they overrun it."

The prince glanced at Che. "True?"

"True. I had it from King Dor."

Jeremy returned to Goody. "I do not mean to question your veracity, but I know Che Centaur, and goblins are not known for diplomacy."

"I understand."

"There's something about you."

"I'm polite."

"That's it." Jeremy paused half a moment. "If King Dor takes this seriously, so do I. We will join the human effort to deal with this menace."

Again, it was so readily done as to be amazing. "Thank you. If you will get in direct touch with King Dor, you can coordinate your efforts. We are trying to bring all the creatures of Xanth into a coalition."

"You mentioned other business," Jenny Elf said.

Now Cynthia spoke. "Goody Goblin is at a serious disadvantage when dealing with goblins. They don't respect a clean-mouthed male. Do you think your friend Gwenny Goblin would be willing to help?"

Jenny turned a disturbingly appraising gaze on Goody. "Is he . . . qualified?" She was leaving something out; the three dots made that clear.

"Yes."

"Then I think she would be interested."

"That's what Che thought. We'll ask her."

"Qualified for what?" Hannah asked.

"Obviously to perform the mission," Jeremy said. "They would not care to waste Gwenny's time."

"I'm not qualified," Goody protested. "That's why I need help."

"Which she will surely provide," the prince said smoothly.

"Thank you," Che said. "We'll see about it immediately."

Hannah looked slightly annoyed, as if something still was not quite clear, but did not say more.

"No bird?" little Jerry asked, disappointed.

The peeve seemed to be taken aback. At least it did not muster an insult this time.

# 12

# GWENNY

Goblin Mountain was a huge heap of packed sand, much larger than the hill Goody had known as a goblet. Paths ran all over it, each leading to a guarded tunnel entrance. This was an important tribe. He surely would have known of it, if he had not tuned out of goblin matters for the past twenty years.

They landed next to it, and Goody and Hannah dismounted. They were immediately surrounded by armed warrior goblins who gawked openly at Cynthia's breasts. "Take me to your repulsive leader!" the parody snapped.

The were not fazed. "Who the bleep are you?" the troop subchief demanded.

"Why should I tell you, you bleepity bleep? Your grandmother sucks stink horns."

Goody kept his mouth shut.

"What my associate is trying to say," Che said, "is that we have an important message for your leader. See that it is delivered immediately."

"Yeah, hoofhead?"

The parody let out a torrent of invective that made the surrounding air crackle.

"Got it," the subchief said, impressed. He disappeared into the warren.

"Now let's get to the rendezvous spot," Cynthia said.

They mounted, and the centaurs flew to a nearby rest stop on an enchanted path. They relaxed and cleaned up while waiting for the response to the message.

Not long thereafter a lone gobliness arrived, garbed in work clothes. She was pretty, but of course all female goblins were. She was about twenty-eight years old, which meant she was well clear of the foolish teens without being so mature as to lose her feminine appeal.

"Gwenny!" Che said, and picked her up and hugged her.

"Now don't make me jealous," Cynthia said.

"Of course not," Gwenny said. "You get a hug too."

Che introduced Goody and Hannah to Gwenny Goblin. "What a dowdy matron!"

"And this must be your bird," Gwenny said, not fooled. Evidently the note had warned her about that too. "What a delightful creature."

"That's what you think, you black blot."

Gwenny made a restrained smile and turned to Che. "Your note mentioned something important, and I don't think it referred to the parody."

"Yes it did, fading frump!"

"Well, we are looking for a good home for it," Goody said. "I apologize for its language."

"I doubt it would fit in well in Goblin Mountain. The men would like it, but not the women."

"We have a very special mission," Che said, and explained about the robots.

Gwenny nodded. "Do you really think I could help?"

"Goody is simply too polite to make headway with goblins," Cynthia said. "But with the parody using his voice, and an assistant to clarify the details, we feel it could work. It is important to enlist the aid of as many goblin tribes as possible."

"I can see that." Gwenny paused thoughtfully. "Starting with Goblin Mountain, I'm sure."

"We thought we might enlist you to contact its leader, since you are familiar with this clan."

"I can try."

"There's something we must say," Che said gravely. "We hope that you and Goody can work together compatibly, but there is one significant aspect of each of your situations that the other does not know about. We hope that this does not interfere."

Gwenny's eyes narrowed. "What aspect?"

"Please. We fear that it could interfere with the mission if known. Let it be, for now. It is otherwise harmless."

"You are saying he is not a serial murderer."

Che smiled. "That too."

Goody coughed. "I would be incapable of that." He wondered what the centaurs were thinking of, in his case and hers. Why should there be any secrets kept?

Gwenny considered. "I agree: it is vital to stop the robots. I believe I can help persuade the other clans to cooperate. I will help you."

"We're so glad," Cynthia said. "The fate of Xanth may hang in the balance."

"Let me see if I can talk with the right person in Goblin Mountain," Gwenny said. "I will return by nightfall." She departed.

"Who is she?" Hannah demanded. "Why do you think she can help?"

"She is a clan official. She has administrative experience and knows the ways of goblin politics," Che explained. "She has assisted in the governing of Goblin Mountain, and has had indirect contacts with several other goblin clans. We think she is about as good a person for this task as any."

"And we know her well enough to trust her," Cynthia said. "That counts enormously."

"You horserears have feathers in your heads."

They laughed. "That too, peeve," Cynthia agreed.

They foraged and prepared a good evening meal. Gwenny returned just in time for it. "They will do it," she said. "King Dor will be contacted."

"We are glad you were able to persuade them," Che said.

So was Goody. Gwenny was evidently persuasive.

As night closed, Goody became nervous. "How formal are we going to be?"

"Formal?" Gwenny asked.

"He wants to see your tits, gob girl!"

Goody choked.

"Goody and I have been traveling together," Hannah explained. "I have had to stay close in order to protect him. We dispensed with formalities such as separate washings. We are after all of different species."

"And Gwenny and I are not," Goody said.

Gwenny paused, then decided. "Informal it is. But this does not imply any further relationship."

"None!" Goody agreed, not entirely relieved. He had not been alone with a gobliness since Go-Go.

"And I do want to be clean," Gwenny said. She stepped out of her clothing and waded into the nearby river bend.

Hannah stripped and joined her. Then, reluctantly, so did Goody. He really had no choice.

Once they were all three in the water, it was all right. "Oh, I haven't done this in ages!" Gwenny said, playfully splashing him. "I feel like a girl again. Except—"

"Except you haven't been a girl in twenty years, dull dowager," the parody called from the safety of the bank.

"Perhaps," the gobliness agreed. But her expression suggested that there was something else.

"Goody is good at shoulder massage," Hannah said. "Ask him."

"Oh, I couldn't—"

"My shoulders are somewhat tight," Gwenny said. "If you would be so kind."

What could he do? He moved across as she faced away from him. He massaged her shoulders and back.

"Oh, that's divine! She's right—you have the touch. How did you come by it?"

"I, well, I was married, and—"

"You were married?" she asked somewhat sharply.

In Xanth marriages were permanent. He had to explain. "My wife—Go-Go Gobliness—was cursed to die before her time. We had twenty years together, and our goblets are grown. But we couldn't abate the curse."

"So you lost her."

"Yes."

"Oh, I felt the pain coming through your hands."

He snatched his hands away. "I'm sorry."

She turned to face him, the thin covering of water making an intriguing mystery of her front. "No, no, Goody. You weren't hurting me. It was good pain, if there is such a thing. I felt your grief for your wife. I apologize for making you speak of it."

"Gourd style!" the parody called.

"No!" Goody said, alarmed.

Now Gwenny laughed. "So you have run afoul of that. I promise not to kiss you. But I am sincerely sorry to have reminded you of your pain."

"Well, you couldn't help it."

"Yes, I could. I had no business prying into your past."

"That wasn't it. I—" But he stalled out.

"It wasn't? Then tell me what *was* it, so I can avoid doing it again."

"That's not possible. Please, I'd rather not."

She gazed at him with big black eyes. "Goody, if we are to work together, we must understand how not to give each other offense. What did I do?"

There was no help for it. "It's what you are. A gobliness. You can't help reminding me of Go-Go."

She considered. "Let's swim out beyond the range of that bird so we can have some privacy."

"There's no need."

"Yes, there is. Come." She glanced at Hannah, and set out for the far side of the river.

Goody had to follow. Hannah remained behind, giving them privacy.

They reached the shallows of the other bank, and sat in the water. He tried not to notice her pretty knees as they poked through the surface, or the rest of her translucently shrouded body. All female goblins were pretty, but she seemed more than pretty, now that she was out of her dull work clothes. Probably it was just his imagination.

"Now tell me. What is there about me that reminds you of Go-Go?"

It remained supremely awkward. "I—I don't want to bore you with a long explanation that seems foolish."

"Bore me."

She was certainly assertive. "I—you may have noticed that I'm polite. You have been too polite yourself to re-mark on it, but I'm sure it turns you off. That's the way goblinesses feel about non-abusive males. Of course they don't say so, but they do stay clear. So I have had little experience with them."

He paused, but she merely gazed at him, her black hair framing her face and disappearing into the water, where it tended to float. Go-Go's hair had done that.

"So no gobliness was interested in me. But Go-Go had the curse, so no goblin was interested in her. So she com-promised and accepted me. And—" He choked off.

"And it became love," she said. "A marriage of conve-nience that worked out."

"Yes. I loved her, and believe she loved me. So I have been with no other gobliness. Except you, now. So you remind me of her simply because you are female and you are close. You can't help it, and I can't help it. We hardly know each other, and it's just a business association, but that's the way it is. I am—inevitably attracted, despite knowing better."

She nodded. "Now I understand. Thank you for clari-fying that."

"Thank you for understanding."

"Don't thank me yet. I fear I must make it worse. I did not expect to be so candid so soon, but I see I must."

"You don't have to explain anything to me. I know you don't like—"

"Be quiet, Goody. I do have to explain, and in the process perhaps hurt you, but I see now that it is better done at the outset. Three things, positive or negative depending how you see them. First, I am not turned off by your politeness. I spent years of my young life living with a centaur family and Jenny Elf, and I came to appreciate politeness and courtesy. In fact I rather lost my taste for the opposite. It repels me. This is surely why Che and Cynthia believe I could work with you. I am not like most goblin females."

He was amazed. "Then—"

She lifted a hand from the water and touched his lips, silencing him. "And I have liabilities of my own that could have meant my death as a child had they been known. Perhaps the centaurs mentioned them."

"They did. Your vision, and lameness. Though you do not look as if you suffer from either."

"I use contact lenses so I can see well, and my knee has healed with time and treatment so that nothing is visible. Only if I walk more than a short distance, or try to run or dance, does my limp manifest. But the point is, I understand about liabilities, and would not condemn yours even if I liked foul mouths. So in that way I resemble your wife."

Goody opened his mouth, but she silenced him again. "Which is why I must say at the outset that our relationship is and must remain purely business. I am under a kind of curse that limits my marital prospects. It is one reason I remain unmarried." She paused, taking several breaths, which caused the water to ripple delicately in front of her. "So do not get interested in me in any social manner, because even if I liked you in that way, there could be no future in it. We can be friends, nothing more."

Goody had to smile, ruefully. "As with any goblin girl, in effect."

"Yes. It is ironic, because you are the type I could like, and I expect our association to be pleasant. Your loyalty to your wife is a social asset, not a liability. But it will end when the mission is done. Just as will your association with Hannah Barbarian."

It was a nice parallel, for he respected and liked Hannah, and recognized her female qualities, but there was no question of romance. "I appreciate your straightforwardness. I much prefer that to avoidance of the issue."

"I learned straightforwardness from the centaurs, along with things like reading and archery. But when dealing with other goblins we shall have to practice some deception. I regard this as an aspect of a war mission."

"Yes. That's why I'll carry the parody on my shoulder, and let you present the case."

"In other matters I prefer candor and clarity. If there are things I conceal from you, it is because that seems a necessary policy."

"Of course."

"And there *are* things."

"I understand."

"Then let's rejoin the others." She oriented on the other shore, wading to deeper water. He followed. "Oh—I would like, if possible, to defuse the bird's remarks, or turn them to advantage. Therefore it may be better if it assumes that we do have a secret social relationship."

"But it would tease us unmercifully."

"Exactly. Instead of saying things that could prejudice our mission. So I apologize, but feel I must do this."

"I don't understand."

She moved into him, face to face, and kissed him on the mouth. It was shockingly sweet. He was highly conscious of her bare body momentarily against his. Then she broke, turned her head as if only then aware of the watching bird, and pushed quickly away from him.

Oh. The show was for the parody, and its blabbing beak.

Gwenny was no tease, just doing what she felt necessary. The fact that it nearly knocked him out was incidental.

They swam back across the river. "Ooo, you naughties!" the peeve exclaimed as they came within range. "And what went on *under* the water?"

Goody felt himself blushing, and saw that Gwenny was blushing too. He knew hers was forced, but his was real. Neither answered the taunt verbally, and none of the others commented. Probably Hannah thought they were fools for kissing when the bird could see them.

They waded out of the water. Hannah had two towels for them. They dried and dressed, encouraged by the continuing japes of the parody, still not responding to it.

"Something we need to clarify," Che said to the parody. "Tomorrow we go to a dangerous goblin mound. You may curse them all you want, but if you blab anything secret, you'll be broiled and eaten with the rest of us. So it is to your personal interest to cooperate with us, in your fashion. Do you get that, peeve?"

"I'm not a complete twit, donkey rear."

"And we will not be able to find you a good home if we all perish. So I recommend caution."

The bird was silent, having no rebuttal. As it said, it was not a complete twit.

Che turned to Gwenny. "And you will have to change your mode, too. We know you for an intelligent, independent woman. But there you will have to be a servile wench. Goody will be your master. He may even have to hit you on occasion."

"Oh, I could never—"

Che turned to him. "You do know what goblin males do to goblin girls of other mounds they catch?"

He knew. "Still, to actually—"

Gwenny smiled. "You can fake it. Pretend to strike me."

"But even in pretense, the implied violence—"

"Goody," she said seriously. "I will be depending on you to protect me from the very real damage those brutes would do me. Surely a little pretense is better than that."

He hesitated. She smiled at him. He melted. She had feminine power over him, since that kiss, and knew it. "I can try."

"Now make a realistic strike at me. Knock my head back."

He tried. He stepped toward her, swinging his open hand at her cheek. He stopped it just before contact. He thought.

There was a sharp smacking sound, and her head went back as she fell against the wall of the cabin with a cry of dismay. She put her hand to her stinging cheek.

Oh, no! He must have misjudged it, though he hadn't felt the contact. "Gwenny! I'm sorry!" He hurried to help her stand up straight again.

"You didn't touch me," she said.

"But—"

"It's a trick Che and I devised long ago. Let's do it again, in slow motion." She turned to the centaur. "Che?"

Che glowered. "You dare talk back to me, doxie? Take that!" He swung at her, slowly.

As his hand came near her face, Gwennie clapped her own hands together, making the smacking sound, and flung herself back, her head leading, as if struck. She put her hand up to slap her own face, reddening it.

It was an act, a playlet, obvious now. But it had fooled him. It well might fool another goblin, particularly one who was accustomed to treating women that way.

"Yes, I think I can do that," he agreed. "If I have to." This woman had devices he would never have guessed.

They settled for the night, the centaurs standing outside, the others in the handy cabin. Hannah took the floor, as usual, leaving the two bunks for the goblins.

"Why don't you get under one blanket together?" the peeve asked, chortling, and made several loud vulgar smacking sounds. They ignored it. Yet on a half-suppressed level, Goody wished that such a thing could have been possible. Gwenny was no Go-Go, but she had her own appeal.

Next morning they set off for the next major goblin clan. This was the Goblinate of the Golden Horde, reputed to be the meanest of them all. "I think you had better have one of your bagged spells ready," Cynthia said as she carried Goody. For some reason the centaurs had decided to have Che carry both women, though Hannah more than outweighed both goblins. Of course weight didn't matter, with the lightness flicking. "And hope that your bounce talent is effective. Their leader is Gaptooth Goblin, and he's a really mean one."

"Goblins aren't supposed to molest goblins. We should be all right as long as they don't catch on that I'm polite." He didn't say that he wasn't sure how many spells remained in the bag, if any.

"True. And they know better than to attack centaurs. They have enough firepower to shoot the two of us out of the sky, but then they would face the disciplined onslaught of a significant flight of centaurs, and that would be mischief even they would not care for."

"Like the way goblins learn not to attack an ogre," he agreed. "Some of them get their heads rammed through knotholes, others wind up in orbit about the moon, and the rest are less fortunate."

She laughed. "Exactly. But it is best not to tempt fate, regardless. And certainly they will be an asset in the war against the robots."

"Pity the poor robots!"

She laughed again. "You seem to be in a good mood. That surprises me."

"Well, you saw Gwenny kiss me." Now he realized why he got to fly alone, as it were. Cynthia wanted to ascertain his reactions to Gwenny. He was happy to oblige.

"I saw her stage a show for the public. Had she kissed you seriously, you would have sunk under the water and drowned without realizing."

"True. She explained that ours is to be a business relationship."

"Perhaps."

"She has some sort of curse that prevents her from marrying. I understand about curses."

"It's not exactly a curse, but that is the net effect. At any rate, she is a lovely and talented person we believe can do this job if anyone can."

So the centaurs did know more than they advertised. "I must admit it is pleasant to be with a woman of my kind, however temporarily."

"We had hoped you would feel that way."

In the afternoon they came to Goblinate territory. "We will remain close and alert," Cynthia said. "If any seem bent on mayhem, the first to attempt to strike you will be skewered by arrows. Then you must mount rapidly, because there are more goblins than we have arrows."

"But we'll have to go inside the mound to talk with the chief. You can't watch us there."

"That is what makes me nervous."

It made Goody nervous too, but he shrugged it off. One of the ways in which the reverse wood drink had changed him was to make him quietly courageous instead of a loud bluffer. He seldom had to call on that quality, and was no warrior, but he could do what he had to do.

They crossed over a small lake. "That's a hate pond," Cynthia said. "That's what makes these goblins so mean. They drink it to refresh their attitude."

"Hate elixir!"

"The complement to love elixir," she said. "Like the other, its effect is temporary, but overwhelming in that period. A normally placid person will kill his companion when dosed with it. If there is love between them, it will become similarly strong hate; there's a reversing effect, I believe. The goblins are used to it, and all hate each other anyway, so can control its effect to an extent. But don't touch it yourself."

Goody shuddered. "Never!"

They landed on a plateau near the goblin mound. Gesticulating goblins swarmed, as they always did, quickly surrounding them.

Goody dismounted and faced the throng. "What a paltry greeting this is!" the parody said with his voice. "I've seen better turnouts on an anthill!"

This met with gruff approval. "What the bleep is your business here, stranger?" the troop chief demanded menacingly.

"Think I'm going to talk to *you,* dungface?" the bird demanded. Then Goody added, as nastily as he could: "Take us to your chief."

"Not till you tell us why, sucker snoot."

"Oh, suddenly you're the chief, clubfoot?" the bird said. "Where I come from, you'd be dipped in hot dirty oil for interfering with the chief's business."

"You are not where you come from, joker."

"Get out of my way, lard-butt, before I start slicing fat off it to clean my rotten teeth."

The guard considered. It seemed the stranger's responses were all correct. "This way."

Goody turned to Gwenny. "Follow me, doxie." Hannah of course could not go there; she would have to crawl on hands and knees, and that would be no good. The goblins would overwhelm her and use her as a novelty female, once they got her armor off.

Gwenny bowed her head meekly and followed them into the tunnel.

They came to the central chamber, where an imposingly ugly goblin sat on a battered stool. This was the monarch of the mound. "Who the bleep are you, and what do you want?" the chief demanded, showing the gross gap in his teeth that gave him his name.

The parody let out a torrent of profanity that heated the chamber.

"All well and good," Gaptooth replied amiably. "Speak your piece."

Goody snapped his fingers. Gwenny stepped forward.

"My master does not deign to concern himself with details. But I will present them."

Gaptooth eyed her appraisingly. "Come sit on my lap, honey, while you do."

"Hardly," Goody said as grimly as he could muster.

Gaptooth jumped off his stool and approached Gwenny. "Yeah?"

This was mischief. Goody poked a finger into his bag of four spells and pulled one out, hoping it would help defuse what could become an ugly situation. At least the bag wasn't empty.

It was the fourwarned spell, enhancing his senses of sound, sight, touch, and smell. It was that last that amazed him. The goblin chief was wearing female panties under his armor! He was a cross-dresser.

Gaptooth reached for Gwenny. Goody jumped forward, interposing himself. "Touch my moll and you die, feces-face!" the parody said.

Gaptooth didn't reply. Instead he punched Goody in the gut. The woman might have been merely a pretext to set up what he really wanted, which was to beat the intruder into a pulp. *Then* he could safely take the woman.

But his fist bounced back, repelled by Goody's defensive talent. He stared at it, amazed. Then he readied a roundhouse punch.

"I wouldn't," Goody said evenly.

The punch came swinging at his ear—and bounced back.

Undismayed, Gaptooth kneed him in the groin. The knee bounced back so hard the foot beneath it slammed into the dirt floor. Goody had not moved.

"What the bleep?" the chief demanded.

"You're the bleeping bleep!" the parody said. "You punch like a gigglesome girl."

Gaptooth tried again, this time swiftly drawing a knife and stabbing at Goody's chest. The knife bounced back, twisting out of his hand so that it dropped to the floor.

It was time to make his mark. "Note that I have not attacked you, baby-face," Goody said temperately. "I have merely blocked your feeble thrusts in a pacifistic manner. That's because I am feeling good. Were I annoyed, it would be another matter. You wouldn't like me when I'm annoyed."

Gaptooth stared at him with a certain dawning respect. "Yeah? What would you do?"

"I would hang you up by your dainty pink panties along with the other girls."

The dawning respect converted to dawning horror. "What do you know?" Now the cowardice beneath the brutality was beginning to show.

"Nothing, of course, as long as I am not annoyed. Now suppose you listen to my doxie's presentation?"

Gaptooth shrugged. He started to turn toward Gwenny. Then he rammed his head forward in a violent butt, trying to catch Goody off guard. The chief's head was thrown back so hard he landed sprawled across his stool.

"Would you like to see that block again, in slow motion?" Goody inquired. "I am beginning to tire of these routine games."

"You're more of a Goblin than you look." Gaptooth picked himself up. Then another evil thought crossed his cranium; Goody's spell-enhanced sight picked it up. "Have a drink." The chief fetched two mugs of liquid, sipping one himself.

Goody lifted the mug to his face—and smelled poison. Specifically, hate elixir. His new senses evidently had a database of information.

He dared not drink it. That might make him go berserk, and possibly attack Gwenny, reversing his positive feeling for her. How glad he was that Cynthia and the spell had warned him!

But what was he to do with it? Gaptooth would become suspicious if he didn't partake.

Then a faint bulb flashed. Suspicious? What did it matter? The chief already meant him ill. This drink was proof of that. Indeed, the goblin was watching him cannily. Let him drink the elixir, turn on his companion, then be destroyed by massed goblins—and the secret of the panties would be protected.

He steeled himself for the violence, then acted. He threw the water in Gaptooth's face. "I am disappointed that you should try your cheap tricks on me. If you don't give over immediately, I shall definitely be annoyed."

The parody, taking the hint, let out another mind-numbing burst of expletives. Gwenny's ears reddened with the impact.

Gaptooth was defeated. He definitely did not want to see Goody annoyed. "Tell it, doxie."

"We bear a message from Human King Dor," she said evenly. "Xanth is being attacked by metal machines called robots, and will be overrun if we don't stop them before they get to Iron Mountain. We need stout fighters from every species, to join with the humans in this campaign, and yours are the stoutest."

"We don't want to join humans, we want to destroy them!"

"If the robots destroy the humans, they will come after you later, much stronger. Better to stop them, and save your battle with the humans for another time."

Gaptooth's desire to destroy Goody warred with his desire for a really good fight elsewhere. Goody's enhanced senses could practically read the chief's body signals as the thoughts forged that way and this. Finally they took the more expedient course. "Sign us up."

Thus it was done. They left the mound, rejoined the centaurs, and soon were on their way to the nearest enchanted camping site. This time Gwenny rode on Cynthia behind Goody.

"You were magnificent," she said warmly. "You never said a bad word, but you beat him down anyway."

"Thank you. I couldn't have done it without the peeve's cussing and your cooperation."

"You got that right, pantywaist."

"How did you know that drink was bad?"

Goody explained about the fourwarned spell he had activated. As he did, he realized that the spell had worn off. It had been critically useful, but now was gone.

"And the way you stopped him from molesting me was marvelous."

"Well, I couldn't let him touch you!"

"I know. But the way you did it was elegant. You were being your pacifistic self, I know, but to him it seemed as if you held him in so little regard you weren't even bothering to hit him back. That shook him up."

"I was lucky."

"You made your own luck." She kissed the back of his head. "I'm so proud of you."

By the time his head stopped floating, forcing the centaur to correct for elevation, they were at the campsite.

# 13

# RECRUITS

They flew from goblin mound to goblin mound, recruiting them all. They made a good team: Goody, Gwenny, and the parody. They didn't necessarily fool all the chiefs, but their coup in enlisting both Goblin Mountain and the Goblinate of the Golden Horde made the others more amenable.

The trickiest, for Goody, was his own mound, where he was banished. He did not want to advertise to Gwenny his shame of being a disowned chief's son. But he was lucky: his mound had suffered hard times, and was now allied with a stronger neighboring mound. It was to that other mound they went, where he was unknown. Probably no one in his home mound would have recognized him anyway, twenty years later, but he did not have to risk it.

"Soon you can return to Goblin Mountain," Goody said regretfully. "You have helped immeasurably recruiting the goblins, but of course you have your own life to lead."

"I have changed my mind," she said. "I want to continue helping. This mission is too important to neglect."

Goody was pleased, but still argued the case. "There is danger, and it is surely an inconvenience for you."

"True, and true. But I like your company."

Goody felt profoundly flattered, but controlled it. "Thank you. But since there is no social future for us, my company becomes irrelevant."

"Perhaps. Yet I confess I have not had the pleasant company of a goblin male in some time, and I am inclined to indulge myself. I think Goblin Mountain can survive a while longer without me."

He laughed, as this was obviously humor. Any goblin mound could survive indefinitely without any of its members, other than the chief. But he was very glad to have her continued company, however long she cared to extend it. Also, she was quite competent, and would be a real help with other species.

After all the significant goblin clans were recruited, they turned to the dragons. This turned out to be relatively easy.

"Vortex!" Goody called mentally from the region south of Castle Roogna where they had last been in contact. The robots had started there, but long since had left it for more metallic pastures.

Soon the two dragons appeared, tunneling through the ground. *There is a problem?* Vortex asked with thought projection.

"Yes." Goody introduced Gwenny and the centaurs.

"The robots!" Vortex said, reading his mind. "What have we started?"

"You didn't know," Goody said. "Any more than we did. But now it is a serious problem we must deal with. We would like to enlist your help in contacting the other dragons."

"You shall have it, of course. We are not leaders, but can rapidly contact the leaders."

"The dragons," Gwenny said. "They suffered a

plague, and had to be replenished last year. But there hasn't been time enough for them to expand their numbers significantly."

"True," Vortex said. "So we may be of limited assistance. Still, the big ones should be able to chomp a good many robots."

"That will surely help," Gwenny agreed.

"Dragons are just oversized worms anyway," the parody said.

Vertex spoke. "How is it that you are doing this dangerous chore yourself, Chiefess, rather than assigning lower-ranking goblins to do it?" Then she slithered back. "Oops; I see that wasn't supposed to be known."

"What?" Goody asked. Had he misheard?

Gwenny sighed. "I would be in danger if it were generally known I was outside my mountain. Especially from the males of other goblin mounds." She turned to Goody. "I apologize for deceiving you. I wanted to work with you without any problem of status between us."

"You're a chief?" he asked, stunned.

"I govern Goblin Mountain, yes. That is why our relationship had to be limited; I can marry only royalty: a goblin chief, or chief's son, or a prince of some other species, to form a strategic liaison."

"But you're a lovely woman! You should have no trouble finding a chief."

"All you have to do is lift your skirt and bend over!" the peeve said zestfully.

"I find I have lost my taste for brutishness. Could you see me marrying Chief Gaptooth? I'm sure he would be willing, and it would be an advantageous liaison."

"So that's what you call it!" the bird said. "He might even share his panties with you."

"Or an elf or naga or even human prince," Goody said. "With an accommodation spell—"

"She doesn't need it! Just tear her clothing off."

"Yes, I have seriously considered that. But Jenny and Cynthia got the good ones."

"I'm not a prince!" Che protested, embarrassed.

"She is teasing you," Vertex said.

"The vixen does that."

"So you see, my options are limited," Gwenny said. "I fear I am doomed to a bad marriage, for the sake of my mound. At least these past few days I have had a pleasant association with an unassuming goblin male. I will cherish the memory."

"It's not necessarily finished," Cynthia said. "We told you that Goody, too, has a secret."

"He's a real clam!"

"We wanted you to get to know Goody first," Che said. "Rather than as the son of a chief."

"What?" Gwenny asked.

"You heard, dottle ears!"

"So if you didn't like him, you could let him go without considering his lineage," Cynthia said. "That's more romantic."

Gwenny focused on Goody. "You never said a word!"

"He's a dummy!"

"I'm not proud of it," Goody said. "They don't want me at my mound."

"But then you qualify!"

"Qualify for what? I'll never govern there."

"You don't have to! You just have to be of chiefly lineage. You could come to Goblin Mountain, where you would be respected. Your home mound would have to accept the liaison, by goblin custom."

"We had something of the sort in mind, if it worked out," Cynthia said.

The two goblins stared at each other. The parody made vulgar kissing and smacking noises.

"I believe we should redefine our association," Gwenny said. "From business to social."

"But I never intended such a thing!"

She smiled. "You may not have a choice. As the ranking goblin, being a chief rather than a chief's offspring, I have the prerogative of proposing a liaison, if I find it expedient. You would then have to accept or decline. Do you think you could decline?"

"Ha ha ha!"

"I—" He would not be able to decline, and she knew it. Even the peeve knew it.

"But I am not yet certain that such a liaison is appropriate," she said. "So I am not putting you to that question. But I reserve the right to do so, at my convenience."

"Of course," he said weakly.

"Now can we be friends?"

He hesitated. "I don't think so. Not now."

"Haw haw haw!"

"I mean boy and girl friends. Dating."

Oh. "If you wish."

"Then we can kiss openly."

"I'm not sure that's wise."

She stepped into him, put her arms around him, and drew him in close. She was all softness and niceness. "All you have to do is tell me no," she murmured. "You do have that prerogative, during the courtship."

"Tell her to buzz off, weak knees!"

"I—"

She drew his head down. "Are you saying no?"

"No!" Then he corrected himself, embarrassed. "I mean, I'm not saying no."

"That's what I thought." She put her face to his and kissed him on the mouth, sweetly and lingeringly. Little hearts flew out so hard they ruffled the parody and smacked into the surrounding trees.

When he recovered, he was lying on a bed of grass someone had provided, gazing blankly at the sky.

"You should have put up more of a fight, mush mind," the parody reproved him.

"I couldn't fight," he said, sitting up.

Hannah came across to help him stand. "You never had a chance, once she oriented on you. The centaurs were smart to hide your chiefly lineages from each other, or we'd have gotten nothing done."

She was probably correct. "Hannah, you're a woman. Can you tell me—"

"She's not a woman, she's a slut in a tin can."

Hannah didn't bother to correct the bird about the distinction between metallic armor and a tin can. "Yes, she likes you, and means to marry you. But two things hold her back: she wants to be sure it would be good for Goblin Mountain, and she wants to give you more time to get over Go-Go."

Go-Go! She had been well away from his mind, amazingly. "How can I even consider—what would Go-Go think?"

"We already know she would want you to be happy, Goody. And Gwenny can do that. I have talked with the centaurs. She really is a nice person, quite apart from being a chief. So I think you will have to relegate Go-Go to the past, with no disrespect. Gwenny is your future, if she chooses to be."

So it seemed. "Thank you."

"As if you helped, cave girl."

"If we knew your gender, peeve, we might find a mate for you too," the barbarian said evenly. That shut the bird up for the moment.

"Now we need to see about recruiting the dragons," Goody said.

"Vortex and Vertex are already on it. They feel responsible for bringing the robots. They were tricked too."

They rejoined the others, who were holding a dialogue. Gwenny beckoned, and he went to her without question. She took his hand. "We think the naga should be the next recruited, or the harpies. We can't decide. What do you think?"

That was tough, because goblins had had many wars with both species. "Do we have any contacts who might help?"

"Princess Nada Naga," Che said. "She could also help with the demons."

"But they're an entirely different species."

"She married a demon prince, forming an interspecies alliance," Cynthia said. "They have a child."

Oh. "Then maybe we should seek her first. I know we'll have to approach the harpies too, but they give me the creeps."

"They are foul birds," Gwenny agreed, giving his hand a squeeze. "But perhaps Gloha Goblin-Harpy will help us there."

He vaguely remembered. "Gloha would be a crossbreed? Between a goblin and a harpy?"

"Yes. She looks like a winged goblin girl. She married an invisible giant."

"Ho ho ho!"

"This is no joke, peeve," Che said. "Magician Trent transformed the giant to a winged goblin male, and they are starting a new species of winged monster."

"Then she seems like another good contact," Goody agreed. "We'd better get on it, because those robots are surely multiplying."

"They are," Che said. "But they haven't found Iron Mountain yet. They could have, had they had the wit to befriend and question the right living creatures. But they don't think the way living folk do, and that limits them. But they are steadily canvassing, and it can't be long before they find it. That will be the end."

They got on it. The centaurs flew them to the naga tunnels near Goblin Mountain. Gwenny rode behind Goody again, wrapping her arms around him for security, she said. He felt her softness against his back, and wondered whether she had to cling quite that closely, but could hardly object.

"Yes, I am being seductive," she murmured. "I am trying to fathom what marriage to you would be like. I have not had a fraction of the experience with the opposite gender that you have."

"Hee hee hee!"

She nevertheless controlled their relationship, as the bird understood. He was delightfully powerless.

A cloud of smoke appeared, pacing them. "What have we hearken?"

"Look what the wind blew in: a stinking ball of smog."

"Have we what?" Goody asked.

"Sound, noise, blare, racket, listen—"

"Hear?"

"Whatever," the cloud agreed crossly.

"Fade out, Metria," Gwenny snapped. "That's a homonym, not a synonym."

"A what?"

"A word that sounds the same, but means something else," Gwenny said. "What you wanted was 'here': 'What have we here?' not 'hear.' "

"How the bleep can you hear the difference between hear and here?" the peeve demanded rhetorically.

"You know Metria?" Goody asked Gwenny, belatedly surprised.

"We all know the demoness," Cynthia said. "Wherever something interesting is happening, she pokes her nose in."

"And sometimes sets up embarrassing confusions," Gwenny said.

"But there's nothing interesting here," Goody protested. "We're just flying to see the naga folk."

"Hoo hoo hoo!"

"The bird's right," the cloud said, forming into a face. "Gwenny's seducing another innocent man. Naturally I had to investigate."

"Another?" Goody said, before thinking.

He felt Gwenny's flush against his back. "She told me a human man was a prince looking for a match, three years ago. He wasn't."

"Wasn't a prince, or wasn't looking for a match?"

"Wasn't either one," she said. "Can we drop this?"

"And Surprise Golem had already spoken for him," Metria said smugly.

Goody fathomed that this had been a considerable embarrassment. So he decided to get rid of the demoness. "As it happens, we have an important mission," he said. "We need to contact the demons, to enlist their aid. You would be ideal to—"

He broke off, because she was gone.

"Thank you," Gwenny said, giving him a squeeze.

They came toward a mountain. A winged dragon circled it and came toward them, but neither centaur lifted a bow. "That's Draco," Cynthia explained. "We know him from winged monster conventions. He knows we wouldn't try to molest his mountain den."

The dragon came close enough to recognize them, did a wings wigwag, and flew away.

They landed on a strip near the base of the mountain. There was a shelf cut into the mountain slope, piled with folded cloth and clothing. "What are those rags for?" the peeve demanded.

Cynthia smiled. "You'll see in a moment."

A large snake slithered up, and formed a human head. "Who are you?"

"Who wants to know, fang face?"

"That's an obnoxious talking bird," Cynthia said quickly. "Ignore it."

"Che and Cynthia Centaur," Che said, answering the challenge. "Bringing Goody and Gwenny Goblin to see Nada Naga."

"The princess does not see goblins."

Gwenny jumped down. "Are you sure, naga?"

The naga took a better look at her, and bowed his head. "Apology, Chief. I did not make the connection." He slithered into a hole.

Soon another snake appeared. This one formed a lovely female head with a small crown. "Welcome, Gwenny! Cover me while I change."

Gwenny looked to Hannah. "Would you bring a cloth, please? You are tall enough."

Hannah picked up a section of cloth and spread it to

mask the naga. A breathtakingly lovely human woman head appeared above the cloth, her body moving intriguingly behind the shroud as she garbed herself.

Then she stepped out in fully human form, in princessly garb, lovely in every nuance. "Hello, visitors. I am Princess Nada Naga. Of course I know Che, Cynthia, and Chief Gwenny, but don't believe I have had the pleasure with Hannah or Goody."

"You missed one, serpent shank."

"Or the bird," Nada added with a quirk of her lips. She was another female who could evidently tame demons with a smile, and the parody was silenced.

"Hannah Barbarian is along to guard Goody Goblin, because the peeve tends to get him in trouble," Gwenny said. "Goody is trying to find a good home for the bird, but it seems to be difficult to place." She kept her face straight for a moment; then they both laughed.

"The children might be interested," Nada said. She turned her head. "Ted! Monica!"

Two nine-year-old children appeared, literally: they did not run or walk, but manifested in place. One was a naughty-looking boy in shorts, the other a naughty-looking girl in a short skirt.

"This is Demon Ted, Metria's son," Nada said, cupping the back of the boy's head with one hand. "And this is DeMonica, my daughter. Ted is half human, having a human father, and Monica is a quarter human. Their demon ancestry enables them to change forms and do some tricks. We take turns babysitting them, as they like to be together."

"Can we go play now?" Ted demanded impatiently.

"We've got a spring," Monica said.

"First say hello to the parody."

Both children glanced at the bird, plainly bored.

"What's it to you, brat britches?"

Two expressions changed, becoming interested.

"Come on, poop feathers," Ted said, lifting one arm.

The peeve hopped to that arm. "Is that mess your hair,

or did you lose a gutter mop?" the boy's voice demanded of the girl.

Both children giggled. "My turn," Monica said, lifting an arm.

The parody hopped across. "Your mother's a stinky cloud!" her voice said. "And she garbles her interjections."

"Her whats?" Ted asked.

"Declarations, enunciations, verbalizations, assertions, briefings—"

"Words?"

"Whatever," the peeve agreed crossly.

There were more giggles as they moved away. "Stay in sight!" Nada called.

"Awww," three voices said together.

They squatted by a patch of turf and brought out their spring. This was a bouncy metal coil that splashed as it bounced. Soon there was a depression in the soil, filled with water. "Their new toy," Nada said. "A magic spring."

"Something I've wondered about," Hannah said.

"Yes?"

"When demons marry mortals, don't they get half souls?"

"Yes. Vore got half of mine, but of course mine regenerated in time. He is limited to his half, however."

"And your children?"

"Monica started out with a quarter soul, half of my half. But because she's part human, that regenerated, so now she has a full soul of her own. The same is true for Ted. He got half a soul from Metria, leaving her with a quarter soul. But now his soul is complete. The children tease each other about what fraction of a soul each has, but it's not so."

"That's what I wondered. Thank you."

"Welcome, barbarian." Then Nada got serious. "Surely the bird is not the only reason for your visit."

"Your turn, Goody," Gwenny said.

"There is a serious menace to Xanth," he said. "Goblin-sized metal machines called robots are mining all the iron they can find to make more of themselves, and overrunning the land. We're afraid they'll push out all the other species if we don't stop them before they reach Iron Mountain. So we need all the help we can get. The goblins have signed up, and the centaurs, and maybe the dragons, but we'd like to have the naga too, and the demons."

"How do you propose to stop them?"

"There doesn't seem to be any way other than bashing them into junk metal," Goody said. "They aren't alive; they don't have feelings. All they do is make more robots."

Nada nodded. "Dear," she said.

There was a swirl of smoke that coalesced into a handsome male demon. "You conjured me, beloved?"

"This is my husband, Prince Demon Vore," Nada said to the others. "D. Vore has a considerable appetite."

"And I can't wait to get her alone," Vore said.

"He's never sated," Nada said, flushing fashionably.

"You dumbbells can't spell," the parody said. "That should be D. Vour."

"Depart," Vore said firmly. The bird fled back to the children. "Dear, we need the demons to fight the robots."

"If there's a good fight to be had, we're for it."

Nada clarified the situation. "You tackle your father the king, and I'll tackle mine." He vanished.

"Keep an eye on the children," Nada said, and shifted to full serpent form. Her gown was now a pile of cloth on the ground as she slithered away.

"I'll watch them," Hannah said, and walked to where the children were dunking themselves in the growing spring.

"So far so good," Gwenny said. "But time is surely short. We need to enlist the harpies, elves, and ogres. They're the last of the populous species of Xanth."

"What about the walking skeletons?"

"They're largely confined to the gourd realm. The robots won't go there, having no minds to dream with."

She was right. "And the fauns and nymphs?"

She laughed. "Have you ever had direct experience with them?"

"Well, no, but—"

"All they do is chase each other around and celebrate, as they call it. They have no memories beyond the day, unless they happen to leave their retreat. Then they become mortal. But not many do that, and most are empty-headed."

"But I thought some trees had them."

"Some do—and they seldom stray far from their trees. In any event they are not good at fighting. They constantly make love, not war."

"Still, if they understood the robot menace—"

"Pretend there's a robot coming," she said. "You're a faun. You have to tackle it. Meanwhile, here's a nymph." She pulled her blouse tight and took a breath, compelling his gaze. "Now go see to that robot."

He started to turn away. She twirled, flinging her hair about. It was nice hair. "Are you going?" she asked.

He tried again. She made a cute little scream and kicked one foot high in the air. He felt a guilty shock as she almost showed a panty. "What, not gone yet?"

"How can I go when you're doing that?"

"I'm being a nymph. This is what they do." She spun around again, so that her hair and skirt both flared. She had nice legs. "All the time."

And he was compelled to watch. All the time. But he tried once more.

She turned again, then screamed, but this time in pain. "Oh! My knee!"

He caught her before she fell. "I'm so sorry," he said.

"I overdid it. I'm not a nymph, and my knee can't stand up to that much stress. My fault."

"I shouldn't have made you do it."

"You're such a gentleman." She caught his shoulders, twisted him into her, and kissed him. They sank to the ground together in half a tangle of limbs.

"Mush! Mush!"

"Oh, mice!" she swore. "The kids are back."

So they were. "Sorry," Hannah said. "Little hearts started flying by, and I couldn't stop them. They're so curious about what they shouldn't be."

"Storks," Ted said eagerly.

"How are they summoned?" Monica asked.

"Wouldn't you like to know!" the parody chortled. "Go eat some bratwurst."

Goody and Gwenny separated. "At any rate, I trust I have made my point," she said. "The fauns and nymphs won't help."

Neither would goblins, he realized, if subjected to similar temptations. "We'll let them go."

Nada Naga appeared, having changed into her body and clothes while they were distracted. "The naga are in," she said. "How are the children doing?"

"They like the parody," Hannah said. "I wonder if—"

The peeve let out a marvelous burst of profanity. Nada blanched. "I think not."

Goody sighed inwardly. Every time they had a prospect, the parody destroyed it.

D. Vore appeared. "And the demons." He frowned. "Father went farther. He ordered us to help you recruit the last of the viable species, because he says the robots will reach Iron Mountain in just two more days."

"Two days!" Goody said. "But it takes us more than a day to recruit one species, and we have three species left."

"Precisely. You can no longer afford to fly economy class. You need instant travel."

"But how—"

"Demons," Vore said. "Ted, call your mother."

"Aw, she won't come one minute before your babysitting time is up."

Vore smiled. "Repeat after me, with feeling: 'Oh, look at that faun and nymph! What a celebration!' "

Monica clapped her hands. "OoOoOo Daddy! You naughty!"

Ted took a big breath. "OH, LOOK AT THAT FAUN AND NYMPH! WHAT A—"

Demoness Metria appeared. "Stop that! You know it's a violation of the Giant Conjugation!"

"The what what?" Ted asked innocently.

"Grown Cartel, Big Alliance, Mature Coalition, Aged Association, Ripe Collusion, Senior Confusion—"

"Adult Conspiracy?" Monica asked just as innocently.

"Whatever!" Metria agreed crossly. Then she looked around. "Oh, bleep! It was a set-up."

"You take Gwenny," Vore said. "I'll take Goody."

"I will not!"

"Very well. *I'll* take Gwenny." Vore smiled. "Come here, you delightful little package. I've wanted to get you in my arms for the longest time."

Gwenny went to him, trusting him, especially since Nada Naga did not look worried, as well she might not. No female could rival her for beauty.

Metria hesitated, starting to lose cohesion in her distraction.

The parody flew back to perch on Goody's shoulder. "I dare you, fog face."

The demoness puffed into smoke. The smoke popped out of existence, only to reappear around Goody. "Where to, guileful goblin?" it asked.

"The elves," he said.

The smoke coalesced around his body, squeezing him in awkward spots. "Done."

There was a moment of disorientation. Then Goody and Gwenny stood before a towering Elf Elm tree. "The elves won't let demons into their tree," Vore said. "You'll have to go alone. But they will give you a fair hearing."

"I know," Gwenny said.

The demons faded out.

Elves appeared, swinging down on vines from the high

foliage. They wore green uniforms and were half the height of the goblins, and much less in mass. Both had glossy gray hair, not a sign of age but of elfin health. "Ho, goblins!" one said. "What is your business here with the Warrior Elves?"

"What's it to you, greenface?"

"It's the bird!" Gwenny said quickly, and explained. The elves nodded, understanding.

"I am Goody Goblin. We come to enlist your help in saving Xanth from disaster."

The elves exchanged glances. "This seems worthy. Come this way." He climbed up his vine.

"Uh, we lack—"

"Oh, that's right. You aren't strong at the tree. Very well, take hold of Amazonia's feet. I'll take the gobliness. I am Mace Elf."

"But—"

"Do it," Gwenny said. "And don't let go." She reached up and caught the elf man's ankles with her relatively huge hands. Mace immediately climbed his vine, using his two hands, hauling her up with him.

Then Goody remembered: elves were very strong near their elms. The nearer, the stronger, until they were perhaps the strongest creatures in Xanth. He looked up, saw the elf girl's feet, and took hold of her ankles. She too climbed hand over hand, taking him up without seeming effort.

"You haven't been to an Elf Elm before," Amazonia said.

He looked up to talk to her, and saw up under her green skirt. He hastily looked away. "True."

"Get a load of those green p—"

"Perfect legs," Goody said, overriding the peeve.

"We'll use accommodation spells to make it easier. Just call us by our names, nothing else."

"But your king—"

"Is Sword Elf. Call him Sword. That's all. He knows his rank."

"Thank you." They were now about halfway up the trunk toward the foliage.

"Is the gobliness your woman?"

How was he to answer that? "She may be."

"Then we will spare you amour, though it is customary for important deals."

"Hoo man!"

Just how did the elves usually make deals? He decided not to ask.

They reached the foliage. "Step onto the branch," Amazonia said.

He found a branch almost hidden amidst the leaves. He put his feet on it, got his balance, and let go of her ankles. He walked carefully to the central trunk, which was still quite large at this height. He saw Gwenny approaching along another branch.

Mace and Amazonia appeared. "We have a modified accommodation spell," Mace said. "Do you understand?"

"Yes," Gwenny said.

"No," Goody said.

"Then we shall explain," Amazonia said. "A normal accommodation spell is used for occasions such as summoning the stork, when the participants are of different sizes, such as a human and an elf. It makes them seem to be the same size, the human one-eighth his normal mass, the elf girl eight times her normal. But this modified one will affect only you goblins, making you seem an eighth of your mass, while we are unchanged."

Goody realized it made sense. An elf was half the height of a goblin, but in terms of mass that was not half, not a quarter, but an eighth; it had to do with the magic of numbers, that liked to multiply when they weren't being closely watched. "Now I understand, thank you."

The elf maiden glanced sharply at him. "You don't talk like a goblin male. Only your bird does."

"I am cursed to be polite," Goody said.

"We would prefer to have more like you," Amazonia said. "Goblin girls are in demand by elf men with accommodation spells, but goblin men are not in demand by elf girls." She glanced appraisingly at him. "Are you sure you don't wish to indulge in our—?"

"How fast can you get out of that armor, you luscious little lass?" the parody asked. Naturally the one time it didn't insult was when a compliment would do more damage.

"He's sure," Gwenny said.

"Now I shall invoke the spell," Amazonia said. She waved her hands. There was a flash, and suddenly the tree trunk expanded to double its former width. Rather, they had seemed to shrink by that amount.

"King Sword will now receive you," Mace said.

A door opened in the trunk of the tree, and they walked inside. There was a bare wood chamber. The door closed behind them, and the chamber abruptly lifted. They were rising farther in the tree.

The ascent slowed. The door opened, and they stepped out into a bower crafted of foliage. There stood an elf man wearing an impressive sword. This was obviously King Sword of the Warrior Elves.

"Greetings, Chief Gwenny and consort," the king said.

"And our greeting to you, King Sword," Gwenny replied. "I had not realized that you knew me."

"I know *of* you, Gwenny, and respect what you have done with Goblin Mountain. In time those goblins may even become civilized."

"Never!" the peeve said.

"What is your business with us?"

Goody explained about the robots.

Sword nodded. "Of course we shall do what we can. But you must understand that we can be effective only near our Elf Elms, where our strength is greatest. There are several near Iron Mountain, and I will send word to those trees. You can complement our forces with others that can operate freely between trees."

"Thank you, Sword," Goody said, gratified. "That will surely help significantly."

"Then it is done." Sword glanced at Gwenny. "You are a winsome lass; are you sure you would not like to indulge our hospitality for a night?"

"Ordinarily it would be a pleasure. But we have two more species to contact today," Gwenny said diplomatically.

When they returned to the lower trunk station, a number of the elf maidens had changed to flowing green dresses that enhanced their excellent figures. "If you care to dally, goblin man—" one said.

Goody borrowed Gwenny's phrasing. "Ordinarily I would be delighted. But we have a short deadline." Indeed, had he found himself in this situation before meeting Gwenny, he would have been seriously tempted. There might be ways in which elven maidens were inferior to goblin maidens, but there was no evidence of that here.

They rode ankles back down to the ground. "Some other time, perhaps," Amazonia said as they parted, giving her green skirt a flounce.

"Any time, bonny belle!" the bird said.

"I'm almost sorry to haul you away from that," Gwenny murmured as they walked from the tree.

"First you would have to tell me that you have no further interest in me."

"Haw haw haw!"

She smiled and squeezed his hand.

The demons reappeared. In half an instant they were on their way to the harpies.

That turned out to be easy: "We love to fight!" the harpy leader screeched. "Now that we're not fighting goblins—" She looked at Goody as if truly regretting that. "We need something else. The robots sound ideal. We'll bomb them to oblivion."

"They may have developed flying machines," Goody warned her. "That could make the air dangerous."

"Then we'll take losses. We're used to that. What counts is the fight."

Almost before they knew it, they were on their way to

the last of the contacts: the ogres. Goody was wary of this, because ogres and goblins did not necessarily get along, but Gwenny happened to have an ogre contact.

"My friend Okra Ogress," she explained. "She was an outcast because she wasn't ugly enough."

"That's the sort of thing I can understand."

"I thought you would." She kissed him. "Her husband is Smithereen, the Ogre Overlord. We call him Over Ogre, because he's too stupid to remember the whole title."

Okra lived in a huge cave near Lake OgreChobee. As they walked beside the huge shallow lake a group of burning letter O's sailed up, startled. "Watch it, Flaming O!" the parody squawked as one passed close enough to almost singe a feather.

"Jenny Elf calls them flamingos," Gwenny said. "She heard the term from the Mundane she was being a Companion for. Isn't that funny?"

"Mundanes don't know anything," Goody agreed.

They came to the cave. Goody picked up a rock and pounded it against the wall.

Two shaggy young ogres appeared, an ugly male and an uglier female. Each was twice human height, which was four times goblin height. Goody and Gwenny were barely knee-high on them. "Who you?" the male demanded truculently.

"Who do you think, meathead?" the parody said.

Pleased by the compliment, the ogre smiled. The effect was horrendous. "Me think goblin stink."

"You stink worse, horse hide!"

Both ogre youths smiled. This was going very well.

"Let's exchange introductions," Gwenny said. "Me Gwenny Goblin."

"Me Og Ogret," the boy said.

"Me Goody Goblin."

"Me Not-Og Ogret," the girl said.

"You will soon be able to curdle milk with just a smile," Gwenny said.

The girl blushed with pleasure. Fleas leaped from her skin as the heat became unbearable.

"I came to see your mother Okra Ogress," Gwenny said.

Not-Og turned her head. "Maaawww!" she bellowed.

In barely a moment an ogress appeared. She was not a whole lot larger than Hannah Barbarian, and hardly ugly enough to impress an ogre. How had she managed to marry an ogre overlord?

"She kissed him," Gwenny murmured.

Oh. Of course.

"Gwenny!" the ogress exclaimed. "I haven't seen you in ages!"

She wasn't talking like an ogre. What was going on?

"She's not stupid enough," Gwenny murmured, again answering his thought. Then, to Okra: "We came to see your husband on important business."

Okra shook her head. "He'll never understand if you talk like that. Maybe you should tell me, and I'll translate for him."

"That makes sense."

Okra turned to the ogrets. "Go fetch your father."

The two lumbered off, jostling each other. "Aren't they darling?" Okra asked. "There's not a trace of intelligence or prettiness in either. Smithereen is so pleased."

Just as Go-Go was pleased when their children had no trace of politeness. Goody understood.

"Wonderful," Gwenny said. "They are doing you proud."

"Come in," Okra said. "You can stand on the table."

They entered the cave. In the center chamber was a huge table crudely chiseled out of a giant slab of granite. "Smithereen chewed it into shape with his front teeth," Okra said as she lifted them up to its surface. "It took him a whole hour."

The cave shook as heavy footsteps approached. The ogre male appeared, almost as wide as he was tall, and muscular in proportion. "You give beefcake a bad name," the peeve said.

"The cake? Me take."

Okra hastily brought a huge cake. The ogre stuffed it into his mouth.

"You're so stupid, it's a wonder you remember to breathe!"

"It's the bird," Goody said. "It talks."

The Over Ogre focused on the parody. "Me heard. Like bird."

"Maybe we should let the children play with the bird," Okra said. "We'll never get anything done if it keeps flattering him."

Goody agreed. He carried the bird to the ogrets. Meanwhile Gwenny walked out to stand directly before Smithereen.

"Me see goblin she," he said, surprised.

"It's Gwenny Goblin, Chiefess of Goblin Mountain," Okra said. "Jenny Elf's friend. Remember?"

He struggled to remember, throwing off more fleas than his daughter had as his head heated with the effort.

"Lift me up to your ugly face," Gwenny told him.

The ogre put out a monstrous ham hand. Gwenny sat on it, and he lifted her up for a closer inspection. She leaned forward and kissed him on the horny nose.

Stunned, he crashed back into the stone chair Okra had providently placed behind him. "Now me remember, little goblin her," he said, dazed.

"I thought you might," Gwenny said, climbing off his hand as it sank back to the table.

Goody knew how that was, too.

Then Gwenny explained about the robots and the need for all the creatures of Xanth to help beat them back. It was a well-turned paragraph.

"Ogres bash, robots crash," Okra translated.

Smithereen's smile was so broad that the roaches in the corners fainted and fell to the floor. "Grate fate!"

"That's 'great fate,'" Okra told them. "He can't spell, of course. It means the ogres will join the effort."

"Thank you!" Goody said. "Tell them to be at the Iron Mountain tomorrow if they can make it. And not to fight with all the other species that will be there."

"I will," Okra agreed.

The parody fluttered to rejoin Goody. "Would you like to stay with the ogrets?" he asked it.

"Too stupid to be insulted," the peeve said peevishly.

Goody sighed. Another prospect hadn't worked out.

# 14

# COORDINATION

**B**ack at the naga landing strip they consulted. "All those troops are going to be converging on Iron Mountain," Hannah said. "Some are natural enemies. It's going to be chaos unless there's someone to organize them."

"You're right," Gwenny agreed. "But who? None of them are going to take directives from a natural enemy."

"Ha ha ha! Let the gobs fight the ogs!"

They ignored the parody, which annoyed it.

"I can think of someone," Cynthia Centaur said. "Human King Emeritus Magician Trent. He's a manly man with a lot of governing experience and a potent talent. I think he is universally respected by the major species."

"You've still got half a crush on him," Che chided her.

"Ooo, kisses and smacks! Do you do it frontwise or rearwise?"

She nodded, still managing to ignore the peeve. "I suppose I do. But I've got more than half a crush on you, and you return it."

Che nodded. "I think your idea is viable. He could command the human contingent, and direct the others through their leaders. They would not be giving up their independence to the humans, merely coordinating. But he'd need a demon to move him around rapidly, so he could be aware of the big picture."

"Dad," Vore said. "Demon Professor Grossclout. He's the one who is organizing the demons, and who assigned us to transport you two goblins. Now it's his turn."

"Oh, let me tell him!" Metria said eagerly.

Vore looked at her. "You'd flash your polka-dot panties with the empty dots at him and do your best to annoy him."

"Yes! Let me do it." She flicked her skirt, showing a dot. Goody barely managed to avert his eyes in time.

"I will do it." Vore vanished.

Metria glanced at the parody. "Come here a moment, bird." It obligingly fluttered across to perch on her shoulder. "Bleepity bleep ka-bleep!" her voice swore, browning the nearby foliage. The bird returned to Goody, its job done.

"My job is to guard Goody," Hannah said. "But I can't do that if you demons are transporting him and Gwenny to places I can't go."

"You should go too," Gwenny agreed. "He'll be no good to me if he gets skewered by a robot. Is there a demon we can trust to transport you?"

"Dara," Metria said, perking up. "Magician Humfrey's first wife. She's off duty now, so is available. She has a bit of a soul, so can be trusted. And she won't feel you up the way I do Goody."

"You what?" Gwenny asked sharply.

"Caress, fondle, cuddle, massage, goose—"

"You do not!" Goody protested.

"Pet?" the parody asked.

"Whatever," Metria agreed, not very crossly. "I'll go fetch her. If I have to be stuck with this chore, she does too." She popped out.

Gwenny faced Goody. "And Vore has not been handling me, either. They're both married, you know."

"Married? I did suspect," Nada said with half a smile.

The children and bird laughed. "Dad doesn't even get it on with Metria," Monica said. "Mom's such a spoilsport."

"Fortunately those two demons don't really like each other," Nada agreed.

It occurred to Goody that the half-demon children liked to flirt with violations of the Adult Conspiracy. They probably knew more about it than they let on. Their parents seemed remarkably tolerant. They probably had to be.

There were two pops, and Metria and another demoness appeared. The second was dusky in a sexy sort of way. "Here's Dara," Metria said. "Sometimes called Dana because Humfrey can't keep her name straight. And I didn't even have to show her my polka-dot panties."

"Those were *my* panties," Dara said severely. "You stole them two centuries ago. If I'd had them when Humfrey rescued his wives from Hell, I wouldn't have had to settle for one month in six."

"And this is Hannah Barbarian," Metria continued. "You will transport her where I take Goody."

"Hello, Hannah. If you guard Goody, who guards you?"

"I don't need a guard!"

"But you do need a man, don't you."

"Are you teasing me?"

"Maybe."

Hannah nodded. "We'll get along."

Vore returned. "Dad's on board."

"Because he knows where the action is," Nada said.

"He'll fetch King Trent, and meet us tomorrow at Iron Mountain."

"But we told the other species to be there two days from now," Goody said.

"That's why we need to be there the day before," Hannah said. "So we can direct them to their quadrants. We'll need to survey the region beforehand."

"You're pretty good at this," Vore said.

"Well, I'm a barbarian. We like to fight."

"Maybe we should go there now and make camp," Goody said. "So we won't have to do it tomorrow."

"It works for me," Vore said. "We'll drop you off now."

Metria took Goody, Vore took Gwenny, and Dara took Hannah. There was a wrench, and they stood before a mountain made of iron. It was impressive, towering above them, with iron steps cut into its side leading upward, and an iron guardrail. An almost invisible river gushed from a coiled spring and cascaded down the side.

"What a pile!" the parody exclaimed.

"South is Lake Wails," Dara Demoness said. "East is the Kiss Mee River, newly restored to friendly curves. Nearby is the Singing Tower. Immediately west is Mountain Lake. It's an interesting location."

"You're familiar with it?" Gwenny asked.

"I pop by every so often. Once I found an ogre and a number of damsels stuck atop Iron Mountain without proper water or a bed, and was able to help them. I try to do a good deed every day, if I can."

That explained something about Dara. She was definitely nice for a demoness.

Hannah got busy preparing a lean-to, with the parody staying to criticize her efforts. Goody and Gwenny set off in search of pillow and pie plants. They found a few, but that suggested a problem. "What's the army going to eat?" Goody asked.

"I think we'll have to import supplies."

"From where?"

"I think we have a problem."

They harvested what they could, and started back. "Oh, I meant to inquire, now that we're alone," Gwenny said, setting down her bundle. She stepped close to Goody. "Did Metria do this to you?" She squeezed him in a private place.

He started to protest, then realized that she was teasing

him. The absence of the peeve was a rare chance for private interaction. So he squeezed her in a naughty place. "Did Vore do this to you?"

She considered. "Maybe." She kissed him. "Did the demoness do this to you?"

"I'm not sure. Try it again."

She tried it again. "No, I don't think so. Did Vore do this to you?" He stroked her in an intriguing place.

She pondered, not withdrawing at all. "Probably not. Did Metria—"

Goody leaped into the air. "Hoo!"

"I didn't do that to you either," Metria said, coming into sight after doing it invisibly. "What are you two up to?"

"Nothing you wouldn't understand," Gwenny said with resignation.

They picked up their bundles and returned to the developing camp. "We found some pies and pillows," Goody said. "But the full army will need a hundred times what's here."

"Food!" Hannah said. "Why didn't *I* think of that?"

"Because you're an uncivilized dunce."

"Thank you so much, peeve. That explains everything." She looked around. "What *will* they eat? We don't want them to start in on each other before the robots even get here."

D. Vore appeared. "I'll check with Dad." He vanished.

"I'll check with Humfrey," Dara said, fading out.

"I'll check on the children," Metria said. "Nada may be getting tired of minding them both on her own."

They were alone. They ate the pies and washed in Mountain Lake. This was in the shape of a mountain, of course, with the water angling up to the peak. It seemed to be a big wave that got caught on land, so stayed put. The land beneath it was fairly level, but the rising surface soon made it too deep to wade in.

"This is weird, swimming uphill," Hannah said, doing so. Then she heaved herself out of the water, spread herself flat, and slid down the slope to the shore.

They settled down for the night, lying side by side on their bed of leaves, with Hannah on the hard ground as usual. "Does it seem cool to you?" Gwenny asked.

"No, it's warm."

"Dumbbell!"

"Are you sure?" She squiggled up next to him.

Oh. "Maybe it *is* cool," he agreed.

"That's good."

She rolled into him. Then he discovered that she wasn't wearing anything. "But I thought—you haven't—"

"I haven't decided whether to marry you," she said. "I'm still gathering evidence. Do you have any?"

"I—"

"I think you do."

"With Go-Go, we waited until we were married to—"

"I am nothing like Go-Go. Hadn't you noticed?"

He hadn't thought about it. She was right: she and Go-Go were both female goblins. Both were comely. There the resemblance ended. Go-Go had been content to be a homebody; Gwenny was a lady chief. Go-Go was inclined to go along with whatever was usual; Gwenny was an assertive leader. Go-Go had liked to dance in her special way; Gwenny couldn't dance. Go-Go had been cursed; Gwenny seemed blessed. They were different in practically every way he could think of.

Except one. He loved them both.

"Oh, Gwenny," he said. "Whatever you want—I want too."

"I haven't decided," she reminded him.

"Of course."

"This is merely an interaction."

"Yes."

It turned out to be some interaction. Fortunately the parody had gone to sleep, or had the wit to keep its beak shut. The same, perhaps, went for Hannah Barbarian.

The first to arrive next day were the centaurs: a hundred archers, male and female, led by Chevalier himself, flanked by Cheery.

"The dumbbell and the knockers," the parody said loudly.

The filly frowned. "You can't fool me again, parody. I know it's you, and will not tolerate it."

"Yeah, boobsy twins? You and who else?"

Her bow appeared in her hands, an arrow nocked. She loosed it without seeming to aim. It flew between Goody's shoulder and the bird's feet, the fletching scraping the peeve's tail. "Squawk!" it protested. "You almost hit me!"

"Next time I'll aim more carefully. Now fetch me back my arrow."

"What?!"

The second arrow oriented. "Dart, shaft, quarrel, bolt, barb—"

The peeve was on its way. Soon it returned with the spent arrow held in its beak. Evidently the arrow had been lightened to make this possible. Cheery's bow had disappeared. She lifted one hand. The bird dropped the arrow into it.

Chevalier's mouth barely thought about twitching. He had remained studiously indifferent, but the point had been made. The filly's first arrow had gone exactly where she intended, making its point. The centaurs would not be subject to more harassment by the bird.

"You are the first," Goody said. "I suppose you can pick the area you wish to defend. We'll need to circle the mountain so the robots can't reach it from any direction."

"We'll require a territory with good foraging for food and supplies," Chevalier said.

"This area is lean," Goody said. "We'll have to bring in supplies."

"Past the robots?"

"I hope Magician Trent will have an answer for that. He has agreed to supervise the operation."

"Excellent. We know of him from way back. But we thought he had retired as the human monarch."

"He did. That's why he is available."

There was a muffled pop, and a puff of smoke formed and dissipated. "Did I hear my name?" Trent inquired.

"Spoken with respect," Chevalier said. "I am Chevalier Centaur, head stallion of Centaur Isle."

"We know of you, too," Trent said. "We're glad to have your contingent." The two shook hands. "Now what is your question?"

"We and the other contingents will need supplies, especially food. We can ring the mountain, but the robots may in turn ring us. We will not be as effective if hungry."

"I believe we can handle that," Trent said. "I discussed it with the Professor."

There was another puff of smoke, and a grim older demon appeared. He had to have been there, invisible, because Trent could not have traveled in such manner by himself. "I heard my name," Demon Professor Grossclout said. "Food will be provided."

Chevalier nodded. "Thank you, Professor."

"Bogey at two o'clock!"

A flight of ungainly birds was arriving. These manifested as harpies as they came closer. "Very good," Trent said.

The lead harpy spied them and flapped in. "Fowlmouth Harpy here," she screeched. "Where can we land?"

"Good to see you, Fowlmouth," Trent said. "Settle adjacent to the centaurs. We have special use for you."

The harpy leader eyed the centaurs. "We don't do it with their breed. Too big."

The Magician did not smile at her crude humor. "As I remember, the harpies have control of the lunch box plantation."

"That's right," she screeched. "We could feed an army."

"That's exactly what is required. We have an army to feed. Can you ferry in enough boxes?"

Fowlmouth looked doubtful. "We have enough, but can't carry more than two at a time. How many troops do you have?"

"Thousands, we hope."

"Thousands! It would take us a month!"

"Suppose they are made light, so you could carry twenty at a time, in bags?"

"That would help. But how would that be done?"

"We have two flying centaurs you can guide to the plantation."

"We don't associate with that kind," Chevalier said grimly.

"Nor do you need to," Trent said smoothly. "They will not be on the field of battle."

"Making things light," Fowlmouth screeched. "It will do. But we hear there will be flying machines. We can't fight and carry at the same time."

"The centaurs will shoot those machines out of the air as they approach you," Trent said, "providing a safe corridor."

"That we can do," Chevalier agreed.

Goody saw that it was working out. Magician Trent was already taking charge and addressing the problems. Harpies were leading the two flying centaurs away.

Now there was a series of pops as demons materialized. "Here to me, demons," the Professor called. "Mush! Mush!"

The demons coalesced around him. "Good to work with you, Grossclout," one said. "We remember your classes."

"You had better," the professor said gruffly. "Follow me." He vanished. So did they.

Now a pack of wolves ran in. Their leader approached Trent and transformed to manform. "Prince Jeremy Werewolf," he said.

"Magician Trent. We met when you married Jenny Elf."

"I remember. What can we do for you?"

"We have not as yet decided, but I'm sure you will be effective."

"If I may make a suggestion. My wife had an idea."

"Let's have it."

"We understand you also recruited elves."

"True."

"They can be doughty warriors, but are known to lack strength away from their trees."

"They will have to operate near their trees," Trent agreed.

"Suppose we gave them rides?"

"I am not sure I understand."

"Where Jenny comes from, elves are wolf riders. She knows how it is done. We could carry them, greatly increasing their range. They could use their weapons from our backs, protecting us."

Trent nodded. "This may have merit. We'll consult with the elves when they arrive."

The parody noticed something. It flew high in the air, peering beadily about. "Bogey at twelve o'clock!"

"What species?" Trent asked.

"Goblins. A gang of them."

"That would be my contingent," Gwenny said. "Goody, I must go supervise them." She kissed him quickly, then vanished as Vore carried her away.

Magician Trent glanced at Goody. "So Chiefess Gwenny Goblin has finally found a partner?"

"She is considering," Goody said uneasily. "I am Goody Goblin. I—we—seem to have been responsible for bringing the first robot here."

"The dope was suckered," the peeve explained.

"I am Magician Trent. My talent is transformation. I am glad to meet you, Goody." He reached down, extending his right hand.

Astonished, Goody just stood there. "Shake his hand," Hannah whispered. "That's how humans greet folk."

"But I'm not a chief or anything!"

"Idiot!" the bird said.

Goody reached up to shake the Magician's hand. He was able to grasp only two fingers. Trent seemed not to notice. "You have, I believe, already met the representatives of the dragons, other goblins, naga, and ogres?"

"Yes, Magician."

"We are expecting the dragons to converge at Lake Wails, not far to the south. The ogres are marching north from OgreChobee and should arrive soon near the Singing Tower. I would appreciate it if you would meet both contingents and help them orient. They need to be sure that no robots penetrate their quadrants."

"But I have no authority!"

Trent smiled. A tiny fly buzzed by before his face. He made a slight gesture, and the fly became a large shiny bug. He caught the bug and set it on Goody's lapel, where it held on firmly. "You do now. The demons have told them to heed a coordinator, as identified by this scarab badge. They will be expecting you."

The Magician had evidently come prepared. It was becoming clear why so many species respected him. "Yes, Magician."

Trent glanced at Hannah. "And since you are assisting him, you should have a badge too." He looked for another fly, but found none, so he reached down to gesture at a little yellow flower. It became another scarab. He picked it up and set it on her halter.

She was taken aback. "Thank you, Magician."

"Humfrey spoke well of you. On your way."

Metria and Dara gathered them in and transported them to Lake Wails. This was set in an old volcano cone, with steep sides and very deep water. There was room to walk around the rim, but not a lot to spare. "It's a fun milieu," Metria said as they stood by the placid lake.

"A fun what?"

"Tract, environ, abode, spot, address, terrace, habitat, billet, space, quarter, city, hinterland, locale, street, arena, niche, scene, range, forum, pad, point—"

"Place?" He had been curious how long she could continue with the wrong words, but there seemed to be no limit.

"Whatever," she agreed crossly. "Haven't you heard of it?"

"I didn't get around much for twenty years."

"I did," Hannah said. "This is where the fabulous Wailing Monster runs, leaving little footprints on the surface of the water. The prints of wails."

Goody looked across the water. "I don't see any monster."

"It's shy. We may not see it at all. But we know it's there."

"Bogey at six o'clock."

They looked. A flight of dragons was coming in. Soon they glided to a landing near Goody and Hannah, perching neatly on the rim. Metria and Dara were normally invisible when not active.

Their evident leader was a giant fire breather, big enough to take them both in with one chomp. He folded his wings and moved toward them as if they looked good to eat. Goody and Hannah hastily pointed to their scarab badges. The dragon looked, and nodded regretfully; these morsels were not for eating.

"I am Goody Goblin," Goody said, feeling weak in the knees. Would the dragons really honor the truce between species? "This is Hannah Barbarian. We—"

The dragon shook his huge head. He couldn't understand them.

Then the rim rumpled. A snout poked out. *This must be the place.*

"Vortex!" Goody cried, vastly relieved. "We need translation."

The dragon drew himself out of the ground. "Of course. I came as fast as I could. Just let me check in." He oriented on the giant dragon leader. "This is Firestorm Dragon, leader of the flying dragon contingent. He is of the Rational persuasion, meaning he is smart rather than telepathic. He is indifferent to the fate of other species, but realizes that if the machines overrun Xanth, it will spoil the hunting. He recognizes your badge of authority, so will refrain from toasting you, with regret. I will translate your directives, and he will command the contingent."

"Very good," Goody said, his knees stiffening somewhat. "There are several things he needs to know. First, leave the local denizens alone, such as the Wailing Monster. Second, the harpies are ferrying in food: lunch boxes."

"What?" Vortex translated, fire flickering across the word. "We require quivering live meat and plenty of it."

"Uh—"

"I will check," Dara said, flickering momentarily in and out of view. Then a lunch box appeared in her hands; she had checked rapidly. "Try this. It is tightly packed."

Goody took the box. It had a broken-off stem on the bottom. It had evidently grown on a plant or tree and been harvested. "This is a sample lunch," he said, unlatching the lid and lifting it.

A monster leaped out, a globular cluster ten times the size of the box. It had eyeballs and tentacles galore, and a fat center. It landed on the rim and scrambled away.

Firestorm jetted a lance of fire from one nostril. It speared the monster and fried it in place. Then he flicked the tip of his tail around to wrap around the morsel and drop it into his mouth. He chomped. He nodded.

"It will do," Vortex said. "Surprisingly tasty."

"We try to do things right," Goody said, relieved. "More will be delivered soon by a flight of harpies." He fixed Firestorm with what he hoped was a steely glare. "*Do not toast the harpies.* You need them to deliver the lunch boxes, and they don't taste very good anyway."

"We know," Vortex translated.

Hm. "Set up a defense line circling south of the lake. The terrain should help, but it's not the lake we're defending, but Iron Mountain to the north. Your line should reach around east and north to meet the line the ogres will set up, and to the west and north to where the—" He paused, uncertain who was assigned to that quadrant.

"The naga," Dara murmured invisibly in his ear. She was more responsible than Metria, so was paying attention.

"The naga," Goody continued. "Are you familiar with them?"

"Yes. Good folk," Vortex translated. "Apart from their human contamination."

"This is Xanth proper," Goody said. "We have many crossbreed species, even one or two human/dragon ones. It's not like Dragon World."

"Unfortunately," Vortex translated.

"We expect the robots to arrive tomorrow, but they might surprise us. Remember, these are metal entities. They aren't edible and they don't think, at least not the way we do. You will have to crunch them carefully so as not to chip your teeth, and let the refuse pile up. If you allow a gap to open in your line, they may rush through it. *Don't let them reach Iron Mountain!* If they do, they'll make more and larger robots, and be much harder to stop."

"Got it," Vortex said.

"If you need help, ask for it," Goody said. "This is a community effort, with everyone helping everyone against the common enemy. After we defeat the robots, we can all go back to normal activity. But not until we all return to our natural haunts. No predation on other species here."

"Got it," Vortex repeated. "We won't need help, of course, but if by some incredible chance we do, how do we ask?"

"I will be passing by frequently. Failing that, send a telepathic dragon to Magician Trent at the mountain."

Firestorm nodded, then flew off to direct his minions, most of whom had landed at the base of the volcanic slope. "Nice job," Hannah said. "You may be cut out to be a leader."

"Never that! I just do what I have to, as competently as I can."

"Exactly."

The demons took them to the Singing Tower. It was set in pretty gardens and seemed to be warming up. "Do ra me so fa so good," it sang with ascending notes.

Hannah smiled. "I don't think it takes us seriously. If there gets to be a real audience, it will surely sing arias."

There were no ogres in sight. That was all right with Goody, as it would give them a chance to rest.

Hannah rubbed her belly in the barbarian way she had. "I'm hungry."

"One moment, please," Dara said. She flickered, and two lunch boxes appeared in her hands. One for each of them.

"What about me, you smoky stench?"

"Oops. Of course, peeve." She flickered again, and produced a third box. She opened it for the bird.

It contained an assortment of crystallized honey bees and fried meal worms.

The parody opened its beak to say something nasty, but couldn't manage it. Instead it pecked up a bee and gulped it down with avian gusto. This was obviously its favorite meal.

Goody hesitated before opening his. "I'm not sure I want to fry and eat a globular cluster, or a meal worm."

"I can handle it if I have to," Hannah said. She gripped her sword, then opened her box.

Nothing happened. She flipped up the lid. There was a milkweed pod, a beefsteak tomato, and a collection of roasted grasshoppers. "Ideal fare!" She tossed a grasshopper into her mouth, then chewed on the beefsteak. "It's been so long since I've had a real barbarian meal."

Goody hadn't realized that he was crimping her style. He opened his own box. There was a bottle of boot rear and two banana-turnip sandwiches. "My favorite!" he said, biting into one. It was delicious. He hadn't had this since Go-Go died.

Which abruptly sobered him.

"Chew on bad software?" Metria asked.

"On what?"

"Virus, blemish, fungus, maggot, insect—"

"Bug?"

"Whatever. You look as if you just swallowed a rotten tooth."

Oh. "I remembered Go-Go Gobliness."

"Who?" Dara asked.

"My long-time wife. She died."

"That's miserable," she agreed. "Marriage is better."

She was a demoness, but probably serious, since she was one of Humfrey's wives. "But the lunch is very good. I hadn't realized they were so carefully personalized."

"The harpies take good care of their garden."

Soon after they finished their boxed lunches, the tower really did sing an aria. Something was coming.

"Bogey at four o'clock!"

Indeed, the ground was shaking with the heavy tramp of many horny bare feet. The ogres were arriving.

They went to meet them. Smithereen was leading a troop of about twenty ogres, each almost as brutish and ugly as himself. "Me see Good-ee," he said, spying Goody. "Who she, pee-wee?"

"Hannah Barbarian," Hannah said.

"What a bunch of hairy ugly stupes!"

There could hardly have been a better greeting for ogres. They liked the bird.

Goody explained about forming a line to connect with the dragons on the south and the goblins on the north, but he wasn't sure they were getting it. "Bash all robots," he concluded. "No one else."

Then a flight of harpies appeared, coming in from the west. Each was carrying a huge bag. "Me see har-pee," Smithereen said, lifting a hamfist.

"No, no! Har-pee friend-lee," Goody said. "Bring food."

"Food! Shrewd!"

The harpies dropped the bags, which were becoming heavy after their long flight. They burst open and mounds of lunch boxes tumbled out. The ogres gazed at them in dismay, surely thinking they contained effete human food.

"Look," Goody said. He picked up a box and opened it. It was filled with assorted bones.

The ogres smiled. Goody did his best not to wince. They swept up the boxes and began crunching bones. When the bones were done, they crunched the boxes too. It seemed that everything was edible, ogre style.

They were done here. The demons carried them back to the main base. "The troops are bivouacked in place," Magician Trent said, pleased.

"Are what, royal jerk?" the parody asked.

Trent smiled. "Camped." He never got a word wrong. "Go settle. We have a big day tomorrow. The robots are proceeding on schedule, as machines seem to do."

Goody went to their lean-to. Gwenny was already there. She greeted Goody with a hug and kiss. "We don't know what's going to happen tomorrow, so let's make the night memorable."

More so than the prior night? He doubted it was possible. So did the peeve. "Ha haw ho!"

Both of them were mistaken.

# 15

# BATTLE

They had time for excellent lunch-box breakfasts. Then the robots arrived. They came initially from the northwest, where the elves and werewolves were defending. "Watch that quadrant, Goody," Trent said grimly. "If they can't handle it, notify me immediately."

The demons took Goody and Hannah to the northwest front. This was beyond Mountain Lake, and suddenly the line looked dangerously thin. The robots came like a massive carpet, rank on rank, marching in metallic step, every one alike. They remained goblin size, which meant they had not found any other source of iron, but it seemed the whole of the ironwood forest had gone into their legions. Much of the natural forest must have gone into their bellies, too, because their emitted smoke was forming a haze that partly shrouded them.

The werewolves carried elves, and it did seem to be working. They ran up to the robot vanguard and paused, and the elves fired tiny arrows. That seemed laughable, but the arrows went unerringly to crevices in the robots' joints, and caused them to jam, handicapping them. They stalled, and the following robots crashed into them, and the ones after them crashed too, making a considerable jam before they managed to halt their blind advance. The haze of smoke became worse, because it was no longer dissipated by their motion.

"Know something?" Hannah murmured appreciatively. "I think those robots never thought there would be any resistance. Assuming that they think at all. They just used up their iron, then organized their march to the new supply they discovered. They're confused by the obstruction."

"That gives us an initial advantage," Goody agreed. "But they won't stay confused long. They'll tackle the obstruction."

"Yes. But I think the werewolves and elves have this quadrant under control for now. Let's check the next."

They went south to the centaur quadrant. The harpies were still bringing in bags of boxes, and flying back for more. But now the robots were reaching this region, and the threatened flying machines were appearing. They trailed messy contrails of smoke as their flapping metal wings disturbed it.

Now the centaur archers went to work. Their arrows scored unerringly, striking through the hot bellies of the robots and letting more smoke out. Their heat power weakened, the metal birds flapped less vigorously, and spiraled down toward the ground. They couldn't get at the harpies.

But more were coming. Could the centaurs keep up with them? Suppose they attacked the harpies farther back, behind the robot vanguard? "I see mischief," Hannah said.

"So do I," Goody said. "I think we should report to Magician Trent."

The demons took them to Trent, who had climbed high on Iron Mountain so as to oversee the complete surrounding region. It was impressive; the top was flat enough for a camp, though completely bare. Goody could see all the way south to Lake Wails, east to the Singing Tower, and west to Mountain Lake. He could see the werewolves to the northeast, the centaurs west and south of Mountain Lake, the naga south of them, the dragons surrounding Lake Wails, the ogres surrounding the Singing Tower, and the goblin hordes covering the entire north quadrant. Iron Mountain was well guarded.

But the robots were coming on in waves, blanketing the entire western front and converging on the north and south. Soon they would completely surround the defensive circle. There were just so many of them! And if they won through to Iron Mountain, there would be several times as many more.

"It is true," Magician Trent said, as if reading his thoughts. "We have the massed might of Xanth here, yet we must manage carefully or the outcome will be in doubt."

"Oh. Yes," Goody agreed, embarrassed by his distraction. "We came to report a possible problem in the centaur sector. They are protecting the harpies now, but if the flying robots attack the harpies farther to the west, beyond the range of the centaur arrows—"

"Excellent point. This is why we have reserves." Trent snapped his fingers.

Two young human women detached themselves from an admiring throng of men and ran to join Trent, their tresses flying out behind their heads. One was as bright and fair as sunrise, the other as dark and fair as sunset. Both were uncommonly comely. Goody watched them running. The iron ground tilted crazily.

"Boom-boom, boom-boom!" the parody remarked.

"Steady," Hanna murmured as she steadied him. "Haven't you learned? Gaze at their faces, not their chests, especially when they're running."

He wrenched his eyes up, and the ground steadied.

"Thank you." He had forgotten about that particular form of female magic.

By the time Goody was back to normal, the girls had arrived. "These are my great-granddaughters, Princesses Dawn and Eve, the children of Dolph and Electra," Trent said. "Girls, these are Goody Goblin and Hannah Barbarian, coordinators."

"We've met," Eve said with a dusky smile as she gave her black hair a flounce.

"You bet, soot head!"

"No, we haven't," Dawn said, giving her flame-red hair a similar flounce. Her eyes were bright green.

"We traveled with Eve," Hannah said. "To locate the robots."

Dawn turned on her twin sister. "You didn't tell me!"

"I'm a creature of dark secrets."

Dawn turned back to Goody, and smiled. The day turned three shades brighter. "Hello, Goody Goblin."

Eve poked her in a rib with an elbow. "Stop charming him. I got dibs on that."

Goody remembered how Eve had said that her sister dazzled boys away from her. Now he understood how that could be. "Hello, Princess Dawn."

Dawn stepped forward to shake hands, surprising him. She was almost twice his height, but her hand was delicate enough to clasp his. "And you're of chiefly lineage, as well as being uncommonly polite and in grief for your late wife Go-Go." She squeezed his hand, holding her forward-leaning pose.

"Stop flirting with him!" Eve snapped.

"And watch out those nags don't slip their halter, fire-head."

This time Goody had had the wit to keep his eyes on Dawn's face, so wasn't freaked out by her loose décolletage. Even so, peripheral vision could tolerate only so much. "How did you know—if Eve never said—"

"My talent," she said with another day-brightening

smile as she released his hand and straightened up. "I can tell anything about anything living. So when I touched you, I knew. You're cute." She dodged her sister's kick.

That was right: Dawn and Eve were sorceresses. He had seen the power of Eve's talent; now he appreciated her sister's complementary talent. It was also instructive to see their sibling rivalry, even when it came to impressing a goblin neither had any real interest in. They were princesses and sorceresses, but they were also teen girls, alternating flaunting and quarreling. They would be a terror when they forged into adulthood.

"What a load of zombie tripe!"

Eve masked a knowing smirk, leaving it to her sister to figure out.

"Who spoke?" Dawn asked. "I thought at first it was the male goblin, but now I know it wasn't."

"I did, you twitchy teen tease."

"The parody insults people," Hannah explained. "We're looking for a home for it."

"Really," Dawn said. Then she oriented directly on the peeve and loosed her brightest smile yet.

"Awk!" it half squawked, as the air near it seemed to sparkle and tiny yellow birds flitted around it in twittering circles. The parody's green feathers intensified.

"Insult me," Dawn breathed. But the bird had been blissfully stifled. It seemed she could do more than merely know about living things; she could affect them, when she tried.

"Girls," Trent said with a faint great-grandfatherly hint of a smile, "there is a problem. Go with Hannah to the centaur quadrant, clarify the situation there, and assign your men to handle it. Do not get into the fray yourselves."

"Awww," they said together, bouncing a smile back and forth between their faces. Sunlight and shadow seemed to flicker around their heads. Then they turned together and lifted beckoning hands.

A column of human soldiers formed and marched to-

ward them. "This way," Hannah said, and headed down
the iron slope toward Mountain Lake and the centaurs.
The princesses followed her, and the human troops followed them.

The parody finally regained its volition. "And don't
come back, nymphets!"

"But—" Goody began.

"You will direct the demon contingent," Trent said.
"Take them to the harpies and clarify the problem. You
will rejoin Hannah once they are in action." He snapped
his fingers again.

A cloud of smoke appeared, the apex of a triangular
formation of clouds. "We hear and obey," a demon voice
said. Then: "Oh no! Not her!"

Metria appeared. "I'm just here with Goody," she said.
"You have an anxiety with that?"

"A what?" the cloud asked.

"Predicament, annoyance, infirmity, aggravation, complication, trouble, bone of contention—"

"Problem?"

"Whatever," she agreed crossly.

"Yes, we have a problem. You're nothing but mischief."

"And you're nothing but a scatology!"

"A what?" the cloud demanded, swelling menacingly.

"She means an unkind term for a dung heap," Trent
said. "Metria is merely transporting Goody Goblin. She
has no authority. You may ignore her."

"That helps," the cloud said. "Lead, goblin."

"To the harpy supply line," Goody said.

Metria dissolved into smoke, surrounded him and the
bird, and heaved them up. This time she did goose him in
the process.

"How can you goose a process?" the peeve demanded.

"Like this," Metria's voice said. Suddenly the bird
squawked and jumped.

Goody almost smiled. The bird had asked for it.

They floated down the iron slope, gathering speed. The
clouds followed, maintaining their formation. They

floated over the column of marching men and went on to Mountain Lake.

Fowlmouth Harpy spied them and flapped across to intercept them over the lake. "What's this?" she screeched. "A convention of smokers?"

"Ha ha ha, vulture face!"

"This is a squadron of demons, here to help you clear out the flying robots," Goody explained from his hovering cloud. "How can they best assist you?"

"They can brush back the machines to give us a broader corridor," Fowlmouth screeched. "And patrol the rest of our supply line where the centaurs can't."

"We hear and obey," the lead cloud said. The clouds flew across to the line of harpies and enveloped flying robots. The machines started dropping to the ground. They evidently did not appreciate being goosed in their crevices.

Meanwhile the human contingent arrived below, and soon moved out to break up the robots that fell, and any on the ground near them. They had stout clubs that bashed the machines, knocking them out of whack, and shields that prevented the robots from bashing them back very effectively. The size differential helped; it would have been more difficult with human-sized machines. Soon the supply corridor was widening.

"That does help," Fowlmouth screeched. "We were starting to take losses."

"We need those lunch boxes," Goody said.

It was time to check on the next quadrant. Goody got back together with Hannah, and the demons took them to the naga section.

The robots were encroaching, but the naga were ready for them. They had erected barriers that made the machines form into single-file columns, and naga in their human form were bashing them as they passed key stations. Others were hauling away the broken parts and tossing them onto a growing pile. Still others were slithering around behind robots, then changing to human form, grabbing whatever was handy, and bashing them from behind. Some were slithering through holes in the ground, reappearing unexpectedly.

There were both male and female naga, and all of them were naked in human form, because they couldn't keep their clothing when changing forms. Goody and Hannah both were set back for a moment, for the human-form naga were well formed, male and female.

"Maybe we should go check another quadrant," Hannah murmured. "They seem to be doing well here."

"Yes. They may not appreciate being spied on when unclothed. There's no need to embarrass them."

"Get a load of those flagrant naked bodies!" the parody said loudly. With Goody's voice, of course. "What a pile of fresh meat!"

Heads turned toward them. So much for delicacy.

"We're coordinating for Magician Trent," Hannah called. "Is there anything you need?"

"Not at the moment," a male naga called back. "Thank you. Check back again in an hour."

"We will," Hannah said.

"To see more bare buns and b—"

But the demons transported them to the next quadrant before the peeve could finish.

This was Lake Wails, and the dragons were there in force, all sizes and types. But so were the robots. Dragons were toasting them with fire, causing them to melt; smoking them, causing them to clog; steaming them, causing them to rust; sucking them in for careful crunching; and catching them with prehensile tongues, pulling them apart.

A snout appeared in the ground. "Hello, Coordinators," Vortex said. "Is all going well elsewhere?"

"We have checked the werewolf, centaur, and naga sectors," Goody said. "They are all handling it. But the battle is yet young. How are you dragons doing?"

"Well enough so far. But aerial reconnaissance reports that such a massive wave of robots is coming that we must inevitably retreat or be overwhelmed. We are too few in number; otherwise we could take on anything."

"I'll tell Magician Trent now," Goody said. "I will return soon with his response."

The demons took them back to Iron Mountain. "What sector?" Trent asked.

"Dragon. They say—"

"That they are spread too thin," Trent said. "I was concerned about that; they haven't had time to fill out their populations, following the plague and recolonization. So I arranged for support, but it is late."

"Support?"

"The zombie contingent. They can't move rapidly, shambling, so are still on the way. They should arrive in another two hours. Tell the dragons that if they can hold out that long, the zombies will relieve them. If they can't, let me know and I'll see what my regular support troops can do. I don't want to commit too many of those until I have to, lest there be trouble elsewhere."

"Thank you, Magician." Metria enveloped Goody and kissed him on the back of the neck as she took him back to the dragon sector. He had to tolerate her teasing, and refused to give her the satisfaction of reacting.

Vortex was there. "He has a plan?"

"A contingent of zombies is shuffling this way. They should arrive in two hours to relieve you. Can you hold out until then?"

"Zombies? We dragons don't especially like them."

"They are people too," Goody said, echoing Breanna. "But you don't have to touch them. Just stand back and let them tackle the robots. Every robot they take out is a robot you don't have to. They should make good allies."

"We can hold out," Vortex said. "They should be messy but effective."

They moved on to the ogre sector. The ogres were having a great time bashing robots into flying parts, but again it was evident there were too few of them. Only the vanguard of machines had arrived; when the main party came, it would be impossible for just twenty ogres to bash them all.

Goody sought out Smithereen, who was in action beside the Singing Tower, which was singing a battle song. "There will be too many robots," he said. "Some will get by."

The ogre nodded as he bashed another robot into scrap metal. "Me see, Good-ee."

"Maybe if you make barricades," Hannah said. "So they can't sneak by you."

"Show me, Good-ee."

"Heave some boulders into a wall high enough to stop them, then guard that wall."

"No fear," Smithereen agreed. "Guard here." He stomped off to tell the other ogres.

"We weren't supposed to get into the action," Hannah said as a robot came toward her.

"I don't think we have much choice at the moment."

"My sentiments exactly." She drew her sword and zestfully cleaved the robot in half.

"Metria, Dara," Goody said as he grabbed a stick and ran to intercept another robot. "Pop off and tell Magician Trent. Barricades may not be enough."

There were two pops as they went.

Goody reached the robot. He swung his stick, clouting it on the dome. "Take that, iron pants!" his voice said. It fell over, its arms and legs flailing the air. Then it righted itself. He swung again, but this time it caught his makeshift club and jerked it out of his grasp. It grabbed him. Apparently Goody's bounce talent didn't stop a grab. "Hey, watch who you're handling, oil brain!"

Then its head flew off as Hannah's sword scored. The remainder of the robot fell to the ground, unable to function. "You're not cut out to be a warrior," Hannah said.

"I'm afraid you're right," he agreed ruefully.

"Why don't you retreat to the Singing Tower while I hold the fort here? That way I can do the job without worrying about your delicate hide."

"Agreed." He ran for the tower.

But a robot was also approaching it. Goody beat it to the small door set low in its square base, braced himself, and lifted a foot to shove it back. Then he entered and slammed the door shut, and bolted it.

He turned to survey the gloomy interior. A circular stair led to the upper sections. He ran up this—and encountered a robot coming down. Oh, no—they were already inside!

They collided. The robot grabbed him. Its metal arms were stronger than his arms; he couldn't break free. But he could shove it around, preventing it from doing him any harm at the moment. They were at an impasse, here in the confinement of the stairwell. But soon enough the robot would be able to manhandle him into mischief, either banging him into the wall or throwing him down the stairs.

"We're in trouble, gob," the peeve murmured. "Another fine mess you've gotten us into."

Then Goody remembered the bag of spells. He wrestled one arm around until he could poke a finger into it. Were any left? He hooked it, hauling something out. Whatever spell it was, it would have to do.

Something changed. His chest throbbed, somehow shifting in some fashion. What was happening?

"Four arms!" the parody exclaimed.

That was it. He had sprouted two more arms below his natural ones. They seemed to be just as sturdy as the originals. He lifted them, looking at his two new forearms—fourarms—and hands.

"Surprise, iron sides!" his voice said.

Then he put those two free hands on the robot's head and twisted. The face-plate showed no surprise, but the voice said, "Ungh?"

Goody twisted harder. The robot let go of Goody's original arms to grab the new ones. Then Goody used his natural hands to grab the head again, twisting it another notch. The robot took a new grip, but whatever it did,

Goody had two arms free, and kept twisting its head. He twisted it all the way around until the face-plate faced him again, then farther yet, until it snapped with a "sproing" and came off in his hands.

The robot collapsed, letting go of him. He squeezed to the side and let it tumble down the stairs. Then he went on up. He wanted to reach a window so he could look out and see how Hannah was doing.

He reached the next level. There was more light, from a stained glassy window. He stepped toward it.

There was a pop, and a goblin-sized figure appeared before him. He grabbed it before it could grab him, and squeezed. And paused, surprised.

"Hey, gob chief," his voice said.

"Hello, peeve," a dulcet voice replied.

"Gwenny!" He was so surprised and pleased that he hugged her with all four arms. Two hands spread out against her back; two against her bottom. All four squeezed.

"What a grope, groupie!"

"Well, now," she said. "I could swear you had four hands!"

"I do," he said, guiltily removing the lower two. Meanwhile the tower was singing a romantic ballad.

"Dara said you were in trouble, so I had her bring me."

"I *was* in trouble. I invoked a four spell."

"So you could grope me?"

"I—"

"I was teasing," she said, and kissed him. "Use your four hands again."

"But the ogres need help. They—"

"The demons are helping them make barricades, per your suggestion. Now, if you're quite done with my posterior, I have troops to direct."

"I—of course."

She kissed him again. Then the demoness's smoke surrounded her, and she vanished.

"What a darling doll," the parody said.

"What, no parting insult for her?"

"I'm trying," the bird said crossly. "It's hard to find anything wrong with her."

Goody knew how that was. He went to the window and looked out. Stone walls were forming. Ogres were tromping along beside them, bashing any robots trying to get over. The situation seemed to have improved.

He went back down the stairs, passed the metal body, opened the door, and stepped out. There was another robot. He grabbed it with two hands on each of its arms, and swung it into a tree. He swung it again, bashing its head into the trunk. He swung it a third time—and his two extra arms shrank back into his body. The spell had expired.

Well, it had been fun while it lasted, in more than one sense. He grabbed the confused robot by the head before it could realize it was no longer overmatched, and twisted.

Hannah appeared. "Maybe I spoke too soon about your not being a warrior."

"No, you were right. I had four arms, for a while. Now I'm back to anemic normal."

"Fourwarned is fourarmed," she agreed. "The ogres have things under control now. Our demons are back. Time for us to check the next sector."

"Good enough."

Metria formed her cloud around him. "What's this I hear about four arms and Gwenny?" her voice murmured in his ear. "Did you do this to her?" Two arms seemed to press against his back. "And this?" Two more squeezed his rear.

"Something like that," he agreed.

"He gave her the groping of her life," the peeve reported helpfully.

"What about this?"

"OoOoOo!"

"Not yet," the bird said.

They arrived at the goblin sector. "I heard something," Hannah said. "Were you in pain?"

"Not exactly."

"The demoness gave him the goosing of his life," the parody reported.

"Oh? Did he deserve it?"

"Pretty much, tomato tush."

"Now if we can get back to business," Goody said with a slight edge.

"Of course." The demons caught them up and carried them to the final front.

They were on a hill. They gazed down on the battle below. There were several distinguishable goblin hordes engaging a massive robot incursion from the north. The goblins were chopping, bashing, and twisting, but they were taking losses too. It was impossible to tell which side had the advantage.

"I don't like this," Goody said.

"Why not?" Hannah asked. "It looks like a great battle all around."

"That's what I don't like. Our forces have been holding back the enemy everywhere, but reserves have had to be used, and still more robots are coming, and they are indefatigable."

"They are what?" Metria asked.

"Tireless," Hannah said quickly. "I see your point: our troops will tire, and their number is limited. By the end of the day they'll be giving out. Then we'll lose."

"We have a traitorous defeatist in our midst," the parody said. "I'd be ashamed, if I had any shame."

Goody sighed. "I had hoped you would refute me, Hannah."

She patted his head. "You have a sensible mind. You'll make a good chief consort."

"A what? Oh—you mean if Gwenny marries me."

"Not if, when. She's decided."

"She hasn't told me that."

"Why would she tell *you*, stupe?" the peeve demanded.

"She wouldn't," Hannah said. "But she will, when the time comes."

"I'm not at all sure of that," he said, both flattered and alarmed. "I'm still in grief for Go-Go."

"Good thing you didn't remember that when Gwenny tumbled you those nights," the bird said.

Hannah shrugged. "What do you demonesses think?"

"She'll marry him," Dara said. "She'll tell him, and he'll say yes, and it will all be over except for the big dull wedding."

"His fate is pickled," Metria agreed. No one asked her to clarify the word, but she nevertheless looked cross.

It was past time to change the subject. "Should we tell Magician Trent of our concern?"

"We'd better," Hannah said. "Though he's probably way ahead of us."

The demons took them back to the peak of Iron Mountain. Magician Trent was there, with the two princesses. "What can we do for you, Coordinators?" he inquired.

"We're afraid we're in trouble," Goody said. "Because the robots are too numerous and tireless."

"Of course. Our forces will have to make a strategic withdrawal."

"A what?" Metria asked.

"Retreat," he clarified. "Up the slope of Iron Mountain."

"But then the robots will get to the base of the mountain," Goody protested.

"So they will," Trent agreed.

"But then we'll have lost!"

"Not necessarily. The girls and I may have a surprise for them."

"I don't understand."

The Magician smiled tolerantly. "Do you need to?"

Goody stared at him, unable to answer.

"Feline got your gizzard?" the parody inquired snidely.

"What Grandad means," Dawn said brightly, "is that if a smart goblin like Goody doesn't get it, and if a battle-hardened barbarian like Hannah doesn't get it, neither will the robots."

"That's important," Eve agreed darkly. "Of course they're only machines, but they have mechanical sense. I have fathomed considerable potential in their program."

"What should we do?" Hannah asked.

"Circulate to the sectors and tell them to fall back as necessary to preserve their formations. To withdraw to the upper slopes of Iron Mountain. The robots will cease engaging them when they reach the base."

The demons closed in about Goody and Hannah and bore them away. "Has Trent lost his statues?" Metria inquired as she pinched his bottom.

"His whats?"

"Sculptures, granites, concretes, stones, rocks, glass spheres—"

"Marbles?"

"Whatever. Once those robots have access to the iron, they'll be unstoppable."

"That is my thought," Goody agreed glumly. "Yet the princesses seem to agree with him."

"They do have talents."

"Which hardly seem to apply here."

They arrived at the werewolf sector. The wolves and elves were clearly suffering. The animals' sides were lathered, and the elves were almost out of arrows, yet the robots were coming on unabated.

Prince Jeremy spied them. He loped up and changed to naked manform. "We need support," he gasped. "We are taking losses and the robots seem innumerable."

"The Magician says to withdraw up the slope of Iron Mountain when you have to," Goody said. "Keep your formation."

"But that will give the robots access to the iron at its base."

"Yes. He has a plan."

"That's good to know." He changed back and ran to rejoin his pack.

"I'm glad he had the sense to leave Jenny behind," Hannah said.

They moved on to the centaurs. This time it was Cheery who spied them. She trotted up, but the peeve did not make any comment about her bouncing front. "The demons and humans really helped, but they had to move on to support the naga, and we're low on arrows. We'll have to shut down the supply line soon."

Goody relayed the Magician's message.

Cheery looked relieved. "Chevalier's injured, but he won't quit. A strategic withdrawal, however, might appeal." She trotted away.

It was similar with the naga. The straight humans were helping them, and the demons were carrying robots high into the air and dropping them so that they broke, but it wasn't enough. "Withdraw to Iron Mountain!" Hannah shouted. "In orderly manner."

The zombies had arrived to assist the dragons, and were gumming up many robots with their rotten parts. But here too the sheer numbers of the machines were slowly overwhelming them.

Vortex's snout appeared in the ground. "Brilliant!" his image said. "What a leader you have in Magician Trent!"

"But we don't even know his plan," Goody protested.

"Oh, but we do! It's in Hannah's mind. I'll relay the news." He tunneled out of sight.

Goody turned to Hannah. "You know?"

"Well, Dara and I discussed it. It seems she overheard Magician Humfrey discussing it. We hope it works!"

"You're all addle brained," the parody remarked.

"What—" Goody started. But then Metria enclosed him, and they were on their way to the ogre sector.

They were doing all right. It resembled a goblin/ogre battle, only it was robot heads rammed through knotholes and orbiting the moon. The tower was singing of glorious deeds of valor and sacrifice. Still, there were too many machines.

"Go to Iron Mountain!" Goody called to Smithereen. "After you bash enough robots." That was about as complicated a statement as the ogres could understand.

"We gain mountain," the ogre agreed as he twisted a robot into a metal pretzel shape.

Then on to the goblins. Goody didn't see Gwenny, but found Gaptooth of the Golden Horde and relayed the message. "Got it," the chief said, and went to direct his battered troops.

"We've done what we can," Hannah said. "Time to report back."

That reminded him. "What is the plan?"

"That's right, I didn't tell you. Eve analyzed the mountain, and found—"

Then Metria enclosed him, and they were on their way back to Iron Mountain. "You should have let me hear the rest of it," he chided her.

"You'll get to in a moment."

Sure enough, one moment later they were back at the iron peak. "And if it works, every robot on the mountain will be finished," Hannah concluded. The trip had blotted out her intervening clarification.

"Isn't it brightly brilliant?" Dawn asked.

"And darkly imaginative," Eve agreed.

"Fascinating," the parody said sardonically.

Well, maybe he would find out soon enough.

They had a panoramic view of the battle scene. Unfortunately it was contracting, as the six sectors gave way before the onslaught of the robots. They were fighting brave rearguard actions, but there was no stemming the metal tide. The robots were definitely winning.

As the day waned, they reached the base of the mountain. The werewolves were panting, their elves just hanging on. The centaurs hardly had strength to climb the gentle slope, and the harpies were riding their backs, exhausted. The naga made it to an iron gully and lay strewn out in snake form. The dragons found a higher ledge and clung to it, pretty much out of fire, smoke, and steam. Even the ogres looked worn out, their knuckles dragging. Only the goblins, small but ornery, still showed fight;

their lines roiled as they sallied to beat back the machines. The robots tried to press between them and Mountain Lake, but they rallied and shoved them back. But finally even the goblins had to seek the refuge of the mountain, following paths to assorted holes and caves.

The robots reached the base and found the iron. There was a fluting cheer from them as they achieved their objective, while Goody, Hannah, and the battered troops looked down in dismay.

"Is it time?" Magician Trent inquired, as if in doubt.

"Yes, Grandpa, I think it is," Dawn said.

"If the big birds are ready," Eve said.

"I will notify them," Grossclout's voice said. Goody hadn't realized that the demon professor was present, but of course demons were normally invisible unless they chose to become apparent. There was a pop as he departed.

"There," Dawn said, pointing north.

Goody strained to see. On the horizon were several dots. These expanded rapidly, becoming birds. The birds seemed to grow larger as they approached, and larger yet. Finally they were huge: they were rocs.

The rocs carried some sort of lines strung out between them. At first they looked like spider strands, then like string, and finally like cables. They were heavy; a roc could carry a Mundane elephant, but the cable was making them struggle. It looped around in a complete circle, a number of strands, with rocs supporting it all around. It seemed to be metal wire wrapped in cloth. Goody had no idea what the point of it was.

The big birds flew right over Iron Mountain, carrying the giant ring of wrapped wires. Then all together, they let it go. The cable dropped down to circle the base of the mountain close to where the robots were. The robots looked at it, but saw no purpose in it, any more than Goody did. Why drop wrapped metal wire on a metal mountain?

Then demons materialized, detaching individual strands and connecting them to large plants growing in sheltered gullies. "Those look like electric plants," Goody said.

"Oh, yes," Eve breathed. Like her sister, she breathed very well. "The perfect mating of animate and inanimate."

And they were the sorceresses of animate and inanimate things, at least in knowledge. They surely knew what they were doing.

But meanwhile more and more robots were reaching the mountain, clustering there, delighted with the presence of all that iron. Soon they would be setting up a factory to make more of themselves.

Suddenly it happened. The robots fell to the iron ground with audible clanks and lay there unmoving.

"What a lazy bunch!" the peeve said.

"What are they doing?" Goody asked, surprised.

"They're dead, if machines can be dead." Eve said. "The battle is over."

"I don't understand."

"But I explained it to you," Hannah said. "The coils, the electric power plants, the coiling current—it's the magic of magnetism."

"The magic of what?"

"Allure, glamor, charisma," Metria said. "Appeal, potency, seduction—"

"No, this is electric attraction," Eve said. "Specifically, iron. We have made Iron Mountain magnetic. The iron bodies of the robots are helplessly attracted to it, and that's their doom, because when their heads come up against all that power it blows their programs. They are done for."

"But why didn't it do the same to us?"

"It doesn't affect living organisms," Dawn said. "Or even all metal. Just iron."

"Which I appreciate," Hannah said. "My armor is aluminum. I'd hate to have it pulled off by a magnet."

So, just like that, they had won the battle and beaten

the robots. Who had not thought of magnetism any more than Goody had.

"Tomorrow we'll start picking up the pieces," Magician Trent said, satisfied.

# 16

# LOST THINGS

I t was too crowded on the mountain to go anywhere or
do anything other than stay put and rest. The harpy
supply line resumed, bringing box suppers for all, and
facilities for washing and refuse were set up in mountain
crevices. The invisible river that sprang from the side of
the mountain provided plenty of translucent water.

They settled down for sleep where they were. Dawn
and Eve argued over which of them would get to be a pillow for Goody to sleep on, until Hannah settled it by doing that job herself. Her metal armor wasn't very soft, but
he knew better than to complain; he definitely did not
trust the teasing mischief of the princesses.

In the morning Goody, Hannah, and the princesses
were drafted to relay Magician Trent's parting message
to the troops. "You have all done well in this significant
battle. You held the robots back long enough for us to
craft the magnet that destroyed them. You can all be
proud. But take this warning back to your people: we

have won the battle, not the war. It was not possible to destroy all the robots, and those that remain will surely resume construction of more of their kind. Next time they will profit from experience, and organize with leadership instead of pushing blindly toward Iron Mountain. They will insulate themselves from damage by magnetism. They will seek not merely to pass by the opposition, but to destroy it. So do not rest easy; we must remain vigilant, and prevent the robots from ever becoming numerous enough to defeat us."

That was a sobering statement. The threat had been abated, not ended. They relayed it to the several contingents as they organized to go home.

Only then did Goody feel free to seek Gwenny, who he knew was busy organizing her goblins for the return. They went to the Goblin Mountain section and asked for her.

A goblin subchief was surprised. "We thought she was with you and Magician Trent. She's not with us, dunce."

It felt as if a cold hand gripped Goody's innards. What had happened to Gwenny?

They questioned the other subchiefs, trying to ascertain who had seen Chiefess Gwenny last. It turned out that she had been rousing the troops everywhere, doing a fine job (for a female), going constantly back and forth. She had been there as they started the retreat up the mountain. And not since. She had simply disappeared, and no one had seen her go.

"I hate to say this," Hannah said. "But many goblins were slain in the melee. She—"

"Croaked?" the peeve asked.

"No!" he cried.

"May have been abducted by the robots," she concluded. "To be a hostage for their safe escape. If some of them suspected that Iron Mountain was a trap."

He stared at her. "They did catch us and hold us prisoner before," he said. "They do know about that sort of thing."

"Yes. And as Magician Trent said, they can profit from

experience. So they might take her away, knowing her value to us, and maybe use her to bargain for a better deal."

Goody didn't like the notion, but it seemed better than the alternative, which was unthinkable. He had to believe that she was alive and well. "But then how can we find her?"

"We can look around the area. They can't have gotten far."

But a quick search revealed nothing. It seemed Gwenny Goblin was nowhere in the area, dead or alive.

By the time Goody gave up the search, the assorted contingents had departed, leaving the robots littering the scene, especially on Iron Mountain. Magician Trent and the princesses were gone, together with the demon and human contingents, including Dara and Metria. There was no one left but Goody and Hannah.

"I don't know what to do," he said. "I can't rest until I know where she is."

"Give it up, joker," the parody said. "She ditched you, one way or another."

Goody stiffened. His hands twitched.

"Maybe I should carry the bird for now," Hannah said.

"That seems best," Goody agreed with a controlled voice.

"I can tell you how to find her," the peeve said in Hannah's voice.

Goody was so on edge that he took the bait. "How?"

"Look in the gourd, idiot. If she's alive, she's dreaming of you, ha ha."

Goody and Hannah split a glance. The obnoxious bird just might have something.

They found a live gourd plant growing in one of the few untrampled sections of the shore of Mountain Lake. "Now this has to be careful," Hannah said. "Suppose I watch you and break the connection every hour? That way you won't get stuck forever, and can take rest and food breaks. It might be a long search."

"Yes." He lay down beside the gourd, propped himself comfortable, and peered into its peephole.

He found himself standing before a haunted human house. He had heard of this; it was one of the gourd's standard entry points. He could get anywhere from here, once he found the way. But where would she be?

He wasn't partial to haunts, but if there was any chance she was there—maybe having entered via the same portal—he had to check. So he braced himself and marched up to the rickety door. He lifted its cobwebbed knocker and let it fall, once. Somehow he was able to reach it though the house was obviously sized for human dreams.

There was no response. Well, he had tried the polite thing. Now he took the handle, which was at head height on him, and turned.

Zap! He got a shock. But the door opened and he saw inside the gloomy edifice.

"Oooo!" It was a ghost making its eerie noise as it fled. Of course. But since Goody knew these were all bad dreams, having no physical reality, he took them in stride.

He entered the house and explored it, setting off all manner of ugly things. The most insidious was a can of eyeballs staring out at him. He lifted it out of his way, and it sent some kind of signal through his hand and body. "I can do anything!" he exclaimed. He knew this was a trick of the eye can, but it did give him confidence. He proceeded on through the house with improved efficiency.

There was no sign of Gwenny. But he had only begun. He passed on out of the house and came to a graveyard. He walked across it, and skeletons hauled themselves out of the graves and converged spookily on him.

"I'm looking for Gwenny Goblin," he said. "Have any of you seen her?"

The skeletons were taken aback. Screams and fear they could handle, but not a straightforward practical question. They passed an eyeless glance around. Then one came forward. "I saw a note signed by a goblin," it said.

"Where?"

"I don't remember. My head is empty."

Oh. Of course. But it was useful information. "Thank you."

The skeletons retreated into their graves, and Goody went on to the next setting. This was a desolate wasteland resembling a trash heap. Odd items were strewn everywhere. But it did not seem that they had been thrown away, because each was carefully labeled. Could the goblin note be here?

He investigated the nearest. This was a large curved sword labeled CUTLASS. Well, he had heard of that; barbarians used them.

Then he saw that there was small print under the note. "For use only against women."

Goody recoiled. What a vile notion! Then he smelled the pun: cut-lass.

He checked the next. This was a small section of cloth with print all over it. CANTEEN = ADOLESCENT CAN. FEE-MAIL = ADDITIONAL LETTER COST. FAST FOOD = RUN TO CATCH IT. SOFTWEAR = VERY SOFT CLOTHING.

Goody shook his head. These were nothing but bad puns!

Then he saw the label: PUNTIES. Panties made up of puns. He had been handling panties without realizing. Why hadn't he freaked out? Maybe because they weren't the same when not filled by fee-mail, correction, female flesh.

The next was a picture of a rowdy-looking man. But as Goody approached it, something struck his knee. It was a wad of spit. He tried to brush it off, but was hit by another. They were coming from the picture! The face was spitting at him. Ugh.

Then he saw the label: SPITTING IMAGE. Double-ugh.

Now he came to a harpy sitting on a perch. She was nipping toenails off with her teeth. She was unclothed, of course, but unlike centaur fillies, harpies were not very attractive bare.

"Hello, harpie," he said politely.

She glanced at him. "What's it to you, goblin?" she screeched. "Can't you see I'm pruning?"

That set him back. "I'm afraid I don't understand."

"Birds preen, mammals groom, crossbreeds prune, dumbbell." She returned to her nipping.

He let her be and investigated the next: a small furry creature. "Hello," he said cautiously.

It paused to study him. "You're a really handsome goblin."

Goody was set back again. "Oh, I don't think so. I'm quite ordinary. But if you don't mind telling me, what are you?"

For answer, the creature held up its tag: LITTLE WHITE LIE.

This was becoming wearing. Everything here seemed to be a bad pun.

Then he saw two young men walking toward him. Maybe they would be able to help. "Hello," he called. And felt a kind of wrenching, as if he was no longer quite there.

"What have we here," the man on the right said.

"I believe it is a lost goblin," the other said.

"Well, as the pro-tagonist it surely is up to me to deal with him."

"Aw, you never let me do anything. How can I ever get beyond being the amateur-tagonist if I can't deal with things?"

"Perhaps you have a point. Very well, you may take over the viewpoint for this one." He held it out.

The amateur-tagonist smiled, accepting it. Immediately the realm was seen through his eyes and no one else's. It was a glorious feeling. He leaned down to address the goblin. "You may be feeling a little strange right now," he said. "That is because while you may have been the main character in your own story, you are now in our story, so have been relegated to secondary status. Probably you should leave now."

"I agree," the surprisingly polite goblin said. "Just where is this?"

"This is Pungatory, where bad puns are stored until there is use for them," Amateur explained patiently.

The goblin seemed not wholly surprised. "No wonder I was encountering so many! How can I best depart this site?"

Amateur pointed. "Cross the com-plain until you reach the doors. Be sure to exit through the one saying DO NOT LINGER."

"Thank you," the goblin said, and set off across the plain.

Once he was away from the tagonists, Goody's awareness settled back on him, and he felt in charge of his life again. That was weird, losing it like that! It was as though he had briefly become part of someone else's story.

"You're hurting my surface with your big feet," the ground beneath him said.

"I beg your pardon," Goody said. Was King Dor somewhere in the vicinity, causing the inanimate to talk?

"And your voice grates," the ground said.

Then Goody got it: this was the com-plain. A plain that grumbled. Part of Pungatory.

Then came an animal that really gave the plain reason to object: a galloping bull. Goody was alarmed as it headed right for him, but then it stopped. "Would you like to have your fortune told?" it inquired.

A bull telling fortunes? Where was the awful pun? But he didn't want to rile the beast. "Perhaps. Who are you?"

"I am Ptero Bull, from the planet of Ptero, of course." Then Goody got it: the name sounded like "terrible." "I read Ptero cards and tell fortunes." Which sounded like tarot cards.

That might be useful. "Can you tell me whether I will find my love?"

"Certainly." The bull produced cards with pictures and

laid them out on the sand, not seeming to have any problem handling them with his hoofs. This was after all the dream realm. "Yes, you will. But you may not keep her. There will be a key choice, and you may choose wrong. That's as close as I can define it, because telling you more might cause you to change it and invalidate the reading."

There always seemed to be a fudge factor. Still, it was good news. "Thank you."

"By the way, if you prefer to avoid all these bad puns, walk in the lee of the pun shield there." The bull waved a hoof at a wall Goody hadn't seen before. "That was erected to protect the sanity of the innocent, and you certainly seem innocent."

"Thank you." Goody quickly walked to the wall. But he had a problem: which was the lee side?

Fortunately a young human woman was standing beside it. "Please, miss—which is the lee side?"

"This is," she said.

"Thank you." Then he saw that objects were piled up along that side of the wall, and not on the other. Was he being misled?

He decided to think just a bit outside the box. "I am Goody Goblin."

"I am Lee Human."

And this was her side of the wall. "Nice meeting you, Lee." He moved to the other side.

There was a frustrated roar from the massed puns as he walked, as they tried in vain to get past the wall and blast his sanity. He was afraid it would fall and leave him to their horrible mercy, but it managed to hold.

At last he reached the edge of the site. There was a wall, inset with two doors. One said DO NOT LINGER, and the other said DO NOT ENTER. He was supposed to exit through the first. He put his hand on its knob.

He paused. Had the tagonists told him right? This was the region of stored puns; was this a devious pun? He couldn't fathom it, but neither did he trust it. Maybe the secret was that he couldn't enter, because he was already here; he would be exiting regardless which door he used.

He wasn't at all sure of his logic, but since his purpose was to find Gwenny, if she were here, he needed to check every possible place she might be, not just the one approved for visitors. He moved to the second door, turned the knob, and exited through it.

He was in an endless pasture with fine grass growing thickly. To the right was a nice stall, similar to those used by centaurs. To the left was another stall. And another, and another. It appeared to be an endless line of stalls at the edge of the endless pasture.

He considered. This did not seem to be a scary or punnish setting. So what was it? Was Gwenny likely to be here, or at least a message from her?

He stepped into the nearest stable. Suddenly he saw a huge horse standing in it. It was male, midnight black of hide and eye and tail. This was surely the dreaded Night Stallion!

But it did not seem to be quite real. For one thing, it took no notice of him, though he was standing close before it. Was it a statue?

He walked up and put his hand on the stallion's right front knee, which was what he could comfortably reach. He didn't quite touch it; his hand sank in slightly, encountering obscure resistance.

This was weird. It was as if he didn't belong here, so didn't properly register. That could be why the door said DO NOT ENTER: it meant it literally, like the NO MAN'S LAND gate. Still, he wasn't sure, so he explored further.

The next stall looked empty until he entered it. Then, suddenly, it was partly occupied. The horse was leaving it, or frozen in the act, with only the tail inside. The rest was in the pasture.

Goody considered, then walked back to the first stall. There was the horse inside, as before. This time he walked on to the next stall behind the horse. Sure enough, the horse was just entering it. This was Trojan's recent past.

Now he saw a sign with two words: PASTURE and FUTURE, with arrows pointing opposite directions. The past and the future, of course. He had taken the pasture for a mere grazing place, and not realized that the other direction represented things to come. So, bit by bit, it was coming clear. He had always to be wary of puns and alternate explanations.

How far did this go? Goody hurried on to the next stall, and found the horse farther away. Now that was interesting: the faster Goody went, the more time he seemed to cover. Could he reach the end of it, and maybe discover what it all meant?

He ran through the next stall, and the next. The horse retreated farther, faster, but somehow not out of sight. The stables became a blur.

Then he came to the end. He stood before a great ancient Mundane city. Trojan was there. From somewhere came words, or at least that was how Goody heard them.

"You lost, Trojan. Therefore your status as a Demon is revoked, and you are confined to the Realm of Dreams until you are able to purchase your freedom with the souls you collect. Only then will you be eligible to court the fair Helen of Troy again."

That was all. Apparently the scenes covered only spot samples of the Night Stallion's history. Before this it had been outside the dream realm, so was not represented here.

This was nevertheless phenomenal information.

Goody walked back to the next stable, set some time after that significant event. He had heard of the Demons, who were to regular demons like Metria as the whole of Xanth was to a grain of sand. They were said to be aloof, arrogant, and so powerful that the whole of the magic of the Land of Xanth was merely the trace radiation from the surface of the Demon Xanth. Their whole attention was taken by constant little contests with each other for

status, making bets on the most trivial things. Evidently
Trojan had been a Demon, and lost a contest, and his
penalty was to run the gourd world.

But what was this business about Helen? Trojan had a
girlfriend? She must have been quite pretty, because
there were lovely creatures galore in the dream realm he
should otherwise have taken. Of course that was long
ago; she would be an old hag by now, if she survived at
all. A long lost love. So why was he still collecting
souls?

Goody came to the next stable. It was empty, but there
on the floor was a scroll. He picked it up and read it.

> O, Trojan, I am so sorry you got banished! Know
> that I still love you, and will love you for eternity,
> though I dare not let my husband or lover find out. I
> beg of you, answer me if you can.
>
>                                              *Helen*

Well, that confirmed their secret love. But it had to
have faded long since.

He walked to the next stable. There was another scroll.

> Dearest Trojan, I was so glad to hear from you!
> Yes, I was serious about eternity. I have a potion to
> keep me young and beautiful forever. By the time you
> fetch enough souls to win your reprieve, the other
> men in my life will have aged and died and dissolved
> into dust. Now tell me again how you love me.
>
>                                              *Helen*

Well, now! That explained a lot. Maybe she was still
around somewhere.

The scrolls continued through the stables, later becoming flat envelopes. The final one, in the present stable—
Goody had missed it before, because it had been hidden
by the body of the horse—had a return address of Troy,
New York, Mundania. So she was still Helen of Troy. It

expressed joy that Trojan had finally collected enough souls, and agreed to meet him on the honey side of the moon for their honeymoon. Goody appreciated why; the near side of the moon was no longer milk and honey, because the honey had soured and the milk turned to moldy green cheese from constantly gazing on the dreariness of Mundania and the horrendous puns of Xanth.

As Goody set the letter down, there was a little flash. He cast about, searching for its origin. He spied a floating eyeball. It was a spy eye, hovering above the letter. Someone was spying on Trojan's love life. Who could it be?

Goody went and put his eye to the pupil of the eyeball. He saw inside it, and through it, to its other lens. There was an elegant chamber with thick curtains and an ornate bed. A lovely black-haired older woman reclined on it, reading a book. Who was she?

Now that he had the connection, Goody found he could look around the room well enough. He saw a letter addressed to Sorceress Morgan le Fay. That must be her. But why was she spying on Trojan?

He looked at the book Morgan was reading. It was titled *Greek Mythology*, and he realized she was reading it for research to learn more about Helen of Troy.

"Ah, Helen," Morgan murmured. Goody wasn't sure how he heard her; maybe it was a form of telepathy sponsored by the connection. In fact her lips weren't moving; he was hearing her thoughts. "Soon your body will be mine, and I will escape the confines of Ptero and roam the dream realm, on my way to Xanth proper. That foolish horse will never know. But I must catch you unguarded, when you are distracted by your lover's first kiss."

What an insidious plot! The aging Sorceress would steal the lovely body and use it as her own. What would happen to poor Helen? Goody had heard of the Sea Hag, who stole lovely young bodies and soon wore them out; this might be similar. And Trojan had no idea. Only Goody, who did not belong in this scene, could see what was going on. The love of centuries would be blighted by the evil selfishness of the Sorceress.

What could he do? Goody didn't know, but he would have to make the effort. He understood too well the grief of love lost, and didn't want it to happen to anyone, not even the fearsome lord of dreams.

He withdrew from the spy eye. Now he knew that Trojan was heading for his rendezvous with Helen on the honeymoon, and that Morgan would intercept them as they met. Maybe he could warn them before it was too late.

He followed the stables into the future, hurrying. Soon—it was hard to tell time in this timeless scheme, and he could make no sense at all of distance—he found Trojan arriving there. It was beautiful, but no more so than the radiant girl coming to meet him. Trojan transformed from horse to man, smiling.

They came together—and the spy eye appeared. It was going to happen!

Goody ran to them. He leaped, bounding as high as he could, landing on their shoulders. They seemed not even aware of him, and closed in for their kiss. He scrambled to get his body between their heads and the floating eyeball.

Something zapped his own shoulder and bounced back to its origin. That was his talent operating. There was a shrewlike scream. "Curses! Foiled again!"

The eyeball puffed into smoke and drifted away. Goody dropped to the ground. Trojan and Helen continued their kiss, oblivious to all else.

Goody returned to the "present" stable, then found the door. He exited the Night Stallion's private quarters, as it was clear he did not belong there. Yet he did not regret the incident.

He used the DO NOT LINGER door, and found himself in a library. A very old man sat at a desk writing on a pad.

"Hello. I am Goody Goblin."

The man looked up. "And I am Ichabod Mundane, of course. Are you my new research assistant?"

"I don't think so. I'm looking for a message from Gwenny Goblin."

*"Gwendolynius goblinus."*

Goody looked blank.

"Oh, sorry; I was locked in classification mode. I am devising scientific names for the magical creatures of Xanth, using the excellent dream library. I don't believe I have seen such a message."

Goody was curious. "Scientific names for magical creatures? Isn't that an—an—"

"An oxymoron? By no means. Anything can be scientifically classified, and ought to be. For example, this creature." Ichabod showed a picture of a bird with the head and breasts of a woman. "You see a—?"

"Harpy."

"But that could be subject to confusion, particularly when puns are involved. It could be the condition of being a harp. Whereas a proper cladistic description would be *Homogyps vulgaris.* Then there is no doubt."

"I suppose so," Goody agreed dubiously.

"And this one," Ichabod said, warming up to his subject. He showed another picture.

"Mermaid."

"Ah, but how do we know she is really a maid? Or whether she is freshwater or seawater? And what of the male of the species? But if we label this *Homopices nereadus,* or Sea Merperson, we have it properly covered."

He did seem to have a point. He went on to show off his designations for the centaur species, *Homoequis intellegus;* invisible giant, *Homotitan invisiblis;* water griffin, *Aquileo gryphonus;* white unicorn, *Monoceros alba;* naga, *Homoserpens hybris;* and the huge sphinx, *Homoleo giganticus.* He seemed quite proud of his work.

"I'm sure it will clarify things for all those who follow," Goody said politely, hoping he wasn't emulating the furry white creature he had seen in Pungatory, the white lie.

"Now that I think of it, I believe I did see a note in the adjacent lot," Ichabod said. "I am unseasonably old, and tend to forget what I don't write down."

"Thank you." Goody went on to the next setting. This was a very nice one, with a pleasant garden, gentle walks, and delightful patches of sunshine. But he didn't see the note.

He did see another young woman. He hoped she wouldn't try to deceive him punnishly the way Lee had. "Hello, I am Goody Goblin."

"I am Emily Human."

So far so good. "I am a visitor exploring the dream realm."

"And I am the keeper of this garden of the day mares."

"Day mares?"

"Night mares carry bad dreams to deserving sleepers. Day mares carry daydreams, which are far more pleasant. This is where those nice dreams are crafted."

"But I thought everything in the dream realm was for bad dreams."

Emily smiled. "Obviously not. Dreams can be of any type. It's just that there is more demand for the bad ones, and they require fancier settings, so most of the realm is allocated to them. All except this portion."

That was interesting. "Did you by chance see a note here?"

"Why yes, as it was a pleasant one. I believe a lady goblin left it."

Goody's heart throbbed. "Please, may I see it?"

"Right here," she said, presenting it to him. "I picked it up for safekeeping, as I did not know for whom it was intended."

He read the note. *Goody—meet me at the Lost & Found. Gwenny.*

"Oh thank you!" he exclaimed. "It's definitely for me! Can you tell me where the Lost & Found is?"

"Certainly. Just follow the yellow line." She pointed to the ground, where there was a line he hadn't noticed before. Had it just come into being? He decided not to question it. "Thank you, Emily."

"Welcome, Goody. We are glad to do little favors for worthy dreamers."

That made him pause. "But you don't know me."

"I don't, but the Night Stallion asked me to do you a favor. Evidently you have pleased him in some obscure manner."

Could Trojan have known after all? Suddenly that seemed possible. "I appreciate it."

He followed the yellow line, and it greatly simplified his travel. It passed through numerous other settings, but the folk there were all busy crafting their bad dreams and paid no attention to him. He had not realized that there was so much labor involved in making bad dreams; it seemed that every detail of the setting had to be correct, and actors had to act out every role, with several takes until they got it right. Only then was a dream fit to be delivered by a night mare. Even then, he gathered, the mare could foul it up.

He found himself on a path through a forest. The sign said LOST PATH, but he wasn't lost—not as long as he had the yellow line to follow—so it must be the path that was lost.

He saw a pile of oddly shaped ocean birds. One was like the letter A, another like the letter B, a third like the letter C, and so one. They looked unhappy, so he paused, always sensitive to those who were sad. "Can I help you?"

"We are lost gulls," the A bird said. "We were headed for our setting to help craft a dream, but forgot what our pun was. Until we remember, we can't get where we're going."

Goody considered. He was getting better at fathoming puns, having been exposed to so many recently. Sometimes it was just a matter of getting literal. "Let's see— you're the A-gull," he said. The bird nodded. "You're the B-gull." Another nod. "And you're the C-gull." Then a bulb flashed. "C-gull! Seagull! That's the pun!"

"That's it!" the C cried. "Now we remember!" They spread their wings and flew away.

Goody resumed his trek. Soon he met a man who was evidently looking for something. "Are you lost?"

"No, I'm looking for something."

"Perhaps I have seen it. What is it?"

"A vampire."

Goody kept being surprised. "You want to find a creature who will suck your blood?"

"That won't happen. I merely want to look at it. I'm a vamp-eyer."

"You want to watch a vampire sucking blood?"

"No. I want to watch a sexy vamp in operation."

Now Goody got it. Not a bloodsucker, but a seducer. He went on.

Suddenly there was a hand in front of his face. He blinked. Had he walked into something without looking?

"Snap out of it, Goody." It was Hannah's voice.

Oh. He was back in real Xanth, lying beside the gourd. He must have been there an hour, and it was time to take a break.

"Thank you. I have almost found her. She's the last lost thing. I'm on the way to meet her at Lost and Found."

"Good for you. Do you want another hour now?"

"Yes!"

"But first eat a bite, drink a gulp, and see about nature. You might be there some time."

It made sense. He did those things, then settled down again by the gourd.

# 17

# TRUST

Goody was back on the Lost Path, relieved to see that the yellow line remained. He had understood that a person always returned to the place in the dream realm that he had left, but he hadn't been quite sure. It was probably set up that way to prevent folk from escaping bad dreams before they ran their full course, but for him it was convenient.

He came to a brown dog that looked lost, as was natural on this path. It seemed sad, so he paused, though he was in a hurry to reach Lost & Found. "Hello, brown dog."

The canine gazed at him mournfully. Evidently it wasn't a talking animal.

"You are lost," Goody said. "Is there a reason?"

The dog nodded. Good; it understood him.

"You have forgotten where you live?"

The dog shook its head no.

"Where you are going?"

A mix, neither yes nor no.

"What breed you are?"

The dog nodded. That was its problem: it didn't know its assignment in dreams, because they were surely specified by species. Once it remembered that, it should know where to go, and would no longer be lost.

Goody sniffed. He smelled chocolate. "You're made of chocolate!" he said.

The dog nodded.

"You're a chocolate lab!"

The dog nodded, licked Goody's face with a chocolate tongue, and bounded happily away.

Goody continued—and found another dog. This one was long and low, with stubby legs. Steam rose from its body; it was obviously quite warm. He would burn his hand if he tried to pet it.

He didn't hesitate. "You're a hot dog!"

The dog bounded away. Goody felt good; he liked helping creatures.

Now at last he came to a shelter marked LOST & FOUND. And there was Gwenny Goblin.

He ran to her. "Gwenny!"

She turned and saw him. "Goody!"

They came together, like Trojan and Helen, embracing and kissing. "I'm so glad you're alive and safe," he said.

"I'm so glad you found me. I left notes, hoping you'd find one. If you thought to check the dream realm."

"I did," he said. "And did."

"I have so much to tell you."

"And I want to hear it all." But then he suffered an awful thought. This was the realm of dreams, where things were not necessarily what they seemed to be. Was this really Gwenny, or was it someone or something else emulating her, to lead him astray? He did not want to be fooled; he had to be sure of her. Because a fake would cause him to stop the search, and maybe really lose her when he might have saved her. "Gwenny—"

"You're not sure I'm real," she said. "For all that we're both dreaming. And I'm not sure you're real, either."

"Yes. How can we prove to each other that we are who we claim to be?"

"We could compare memories from before we got separated. Is there anything that only the two of us know about each other?"

"I can think of one thing, but—"

"And if one of us is genuine, and the other is fake, what would that mean about our constancy to each other?"

"Actually, we are both experienced adults," he said.

"I'm not."

"Yes, you are. We—"

She blushed. It was far redder in her dream state. "Apart from you, I'm not."

"But you were so—"

"Because you were. I pretended I was your wife. That made it easy. Otherwise—well, never mind."

Goody found that immensely flattering. But it was beside the point. A demoness like Metria could surely be more apt in that respect than any mortal woman. And while she was diverting him, the real Gwenny might be suffering or dying. So it was no good as a test.

Then he thought of something. "On Iron Mountain I happened to see the twin princesses running. It nearly freaked me out. I bet you could run just as nicely. Show me that you can."

She looked crestfallen. "Oh, Goody, I wish I could do that for you! But I can't."

"Can't or won't?"

She reconsidered. "Then again, this *is* the dream realm. Maybe I'm not limited the same way. So if you really want—"

"No need. I accept your identity."

"Yet if I can do it here, it's no test."

"A fake Gwenny bent on seduction wouldn't have hesitated. She wouldn't have known about your knee."

She nodded. "This is the first time I have appreciated my lameness. But I still need to verify your identity."

"And I'm not lame."

Then a little bulb flashed over her head. "Goody, whom do you love best?"

He paused. "You mean, among living women?"

"I accept you," she said, and kissed him.

Because she knew of his lingering love for Go-Go. A fake wouldn't have hesitated to reassure her that he loved Gwenny best.

"Then we have verified each other," he said. "Yet it reminds me of the time Hannah was transformed to the likeness of Go-Go, and I wanted to—" He shrugged, embarrassed.

She put her hand on his. "I understand, Goody. I really do, especially now, and I wouldn't have blamed you if you had. You hadn't met me yet; Hannah is the one who safeguarded you so that you could come to me." She led him to chairs in the Lost & Found pavilion. Even in the dream state, she was wary of staying on her feet too long. "But now we need to talk."

"Of course. I need to know where you are, where the robots have you, so we can rescue you."

She sat opposite him, her skirt showing her legs to advantage, surely by no coincidence. "It's more complicated than that, Goody. I think it best if I tell you the whole story, so that you'll understand."

"You're hurt?" he asked, alarmed.

She smiled. "No, not hurt. But something has changed, and I'm not sure you'll accept it if you don't have the background first."

"You love someone else?"

"Oh, come on, Goody. If I did, would I do this?" She leaned across, giving him a startling peek down her blouse on the way to kissing him.

He remained alarmed. "But something's wrong."

"Not wrong. Just complicated. The others may not readily understand."

"What's so difficult to understand about rescuing you from the robots?"

She kissed him again. "Now be quiet while I tell you."

"Yes, of course."

"I was going from section to section, exhorting the troops as they battled ever greater concentrations of robots. One group was being pushed right out of formation, to the very edge of the Mountain Lake. Goblins can't fight very well in water. So I—"

Her narrative broke off. Because she was gone.

Goody stared at the empty chair, appalled. What had happened? How could he lose her so abruptly after just finding her?

He stepped out of the pavilion, searching for her. Wafts of mist had formed around it. As he forged through one he became extremely negative; he had lost her and was never going to find her again. Then he passed through another waft, and felt far more positive; of course he would find her.

Then he remembered his spot return to the waking state, when Hannah had broken his connection to the gourd's peephole. Gwenny would have set up a similar interruption, so as not to get locked in forever. She had been returned to her natural state. Soon she should return, to the same place she had been when she left the dream realm. That was the way of it.

Sure enough, after several long moments and a few nervous instants, she reappeared. "Sorry about that, Goody. I'm set for an hour at a time, and I had been waiting for you for a while before you found me."

"I understand. It happened to me on the way here. I was really concerned, before I realized, especially as I walked through the mist."

She looked out of the pavilion. "The pessimist, the sad fog," she agreed. "I ran afoul of that too. But then the happy fog optimist restored my confidence."

"Exactly." They kissed.

"Where was I?"

He smiled. "You were providing me peeps up your skirt and down your blouse. To keep me quiet while you talked."

"Of course." She adjusted both to make sure they provided just the right amount of peep. Girls were good at that, especially in dreams. "I meant in my narrative."

"Your troops were being driven to the edge of Mountain Lake. You were afraid they'd be in trouble in the water."

"Thank you. I actually ran into the water to help a goblin get out. But a robot was pushing forward, and when my goblin moved clear, the robot charged into me. We became entangled and staggered together deeper into the lake." She paused. "You know, here in the dream realm we should be able to make a dream scene. Let's see if I can animate it."

Goody hadn't thought of that. What better place for a dream, than in the dream realm? Or more properly, a dream within a dream.

A bubble appeared over her head, like the flashing bulb, only without the flash. It expanded at a moderate rate, becoming as big as her head, then larger. It looked like a balloon, only open, so as to be seen inside. Now Goody saw that it contained a picture, with blue sky above, green water below, and a confusion of things in the middle.

The floating picture expanded further, as Gwenny got the details filled in. The cluttered center was brown land, and a lake bank, with a gang of goblins facing out from the water, and a roll of robots pressing in from beyond. The goblins had stout little clubs with which they banged the robots, denting their surfaces. The robots just had their arms, but those were iron, and dented the goblins just as badly when they connected.

Then a lovely lady goblin chief appeared. "Beware of the water!" she cried, catching a goblin by the arm and pulling him to the side. He moved as directed, and the robot he had been engaging lurched forward, crashing instead into the gobliness. They wrapped their arms around each other, trying to recover their mutual balance, but both were staggering farther into the lake.

Then they lost their footing and plunged over a nether ledge. It turned out that the bottom of the lake was not flat after all, but slanted toward the center. Still embraced, they slid down a steep bank, bubbles rising from her exhaled breath and its combustion chamber. They were drowning!

The slippery bank took them down well below the surface. The gobliness might have swum back to the shore, but she was snarled with the robot, which was much heavier. So both continued down, until at last they dropped off an overhang and landed before a rocky outcropping. Gwenny—for of course she was the gobliness—saw it, and struggled to get under it, dragging the inert machine along with her. It seemed its metal wasn't as heavy in the water, so she was somehow able to move it. But her hope of climbing back to the surface of the lake was remote; she was about to drown.

Then the space under the ledge became dimly visible. It was the opening of a cave that slanted up under the bank. There was air in it! Somehow Gwenny dragged herself and the robot into that air, so she could breathe again. She collapsed panting on the sand.

The walls of the cave glowed with fungus, outlining it; that was why it was visible. There was a small assortment of other things there, evidently washed or crawled in some time before. One was an old pot with a crack in it, probably thrown away. Another was what looked like a separated animal tail. Another was a sick bird that seemed to belong to the letters species; this wasn't a C-gull, but more like an E-gull. Another was what looked like a little pile of netting, that smelled fishy. And there was a hypnogourd.

Goody paused, reflecting. He was watching Gwenny's dream image of her memory of recent events. How was it he could smell it? Well, there could be smells in dreams, and sounds, as well as images. He stopped questioning it.

After a time Gwenny roused herself. She was sorely

bedraggled, but seemed intact. Even with her clothing stuck on her and her hair matted, she looked lovely.

*Where am I?* she thought. He was able to receive her thoughts too. Well, why not, in her dream?

She looked about. "A crock pot," she said, spying it.

"No, I'm cracked," it replied. "I am now a crack pot. I'm crazy."

"Not if you can still be used." She picked it up and carried it to the edge of the water at the front of the cave. She dipped it half full, then heaved it to a dent in the sand. She scrounged for dry see-weeds, piling their dessicated eyeballs around its base. Then she found a chip of firewood and used it to light a small fire.

"Oh, that feels good," the pot said. "I hope I don't leak on the fire and put it out."

"Your crack goes down only halfway," she reassured it.

"So am I half crocked or half cracked?"

She kissed its rim, which become more brightly burnished. Goody knew how that was, too. "You're wholly useful."

Then she pulled off her sopping clothing and dumped it in the pot for a washing. Goody's eyes threatened to freak out, but he reminded himself of two things: first, he had seen her bare before, so should be partway immune to freaking. Second, this was a dream within a dream, so its effect should be doubly diluted. He could look at her without freaking. He hoped. Still, it was a close call when she pulled off her black goblin panties and added them to the mix.

Gwenny, waiting for her washing to cook, explored the rest of the cave. "What are you?" she asked the sick E-bird.

"Oh, I'm illegal," it replied. "You don't want to associate with me."

"I didn't quite hear that."

"I am an ill E-gull," the bird repeated carefully. "You might catch my disease."

"Nonsense. Goblins don't get bird illnesses. Let's see

if I can help you." She went to the pot and fished out her panties, which were now steaming. She used them to wash off the bird's feathers, beak, and feet. The encrustations on the bird fell to the sand. They looked like little B's. "I think you were just B-fouled," she said. "You're clean now. How do you feel?"

"Much better," the bird said. "In fact now that those awful letters are off, I feel like an eagle."

Goody realized something about Gwenny: she was compassionate. She was helping things and creatures, just because they were there. He liked that.

She shook the remaining B's off her makeshift cloth and returned it to the pot. She picked up the severed tail. "I'll tell! I'll tell!" it cried.

"Tell what?" she asked it, surprised.

"Whatever bad things you're doing, you naughty girl."

"But I'm not a naughty child. I'm a grown goblin."

"Oh, phooey! I thought you were a small human."

She set it down. "Better luck next time." She went to the fishy netting and picked it up. This turned out to be a pair of fishnet stockings. "Too bad Goody's not here," she remarked. "I could really freak him out with these." She put them into the boiling pot to clean.

Then she spied something much larger in the back of the cave. It looked like an enormous tangle of seaweed. As she studied its outline she realized that it was a kraken, the deadly deep-sea weed that preyed on the unwary. What was that doing this far out of the water? Was it dead?

She squatted beside a tentacle and touched it with a finger. It quivered. It was still alive! But of course it had no power; it had to be suspended in water.

She held the tentacle in her hand, communing with the monster. *How did you come here?*

*I got lost, and wound up in fresh water. I'm a seawater monster; I had to get free of it. I dragged myself out. Now I'm stuck.*

"You must be hungry," Gwenny said aloud.

More tentacles quivered. *Very.*

Goody was amazed. Was she going to help a kraken? What was the limit of her compassion?

She returned to the pot and fished out the fishnet stockings. She put them on. Her legs became outstanding; Good almost did freak out. Then she went to the water and waded in. She reached out, holding the upper section of each stocking, and caught a fish in each hand. She tossed them to the sand and grabbed for more.

Fishnet stockings: they enabled her to net fish. Now he understood.

When she had a suitable pile, she left the water and picked up two of the fish. She carried them to the kraken and tossed them onto its mass. The tentacles writhed, grabbing the fish. There was a chomping sound.

She went back and forth, ferrying the pile of fish she had caught. Every time she walked, the fishnet stockings showed off her legs to such advantage that Goody found himself panting. Maybe they were actually pantyhose. Finally she completed the task. Only then did she remove the stockings.

So far Goody hadn't seen anything that would complicate her rescue. Now he knew where she was; when he emerged from the dream realm he could tell Hannah and they could organize the rescue. It could have been much worse. He had feared the robots had taken her hostage.

Gwenny looked around. This time her gentle eye fell on the defunct robot.

Oh, no! She couldn't be thinking of helping that!

She walked to the pile of metal. The robot was dead, in its fashion: its fire was out.

Gwenny struggled to heave it up to lean against the wall, sitting. She checked its limbs and torso. They were in order. She opened its belly door and peered inside. There was a sodden half-burned chunk of wood. She took it out, then used her panty-cloth to wipe clear the interior. Then she went on a quest for dry wood.

She was doing it! Did she have a death wish?

She gathered all the dry chips she could find, and some

more see-weeds. She packed them carefully in the fire-box, then used a chip of firewood to ignite them. The fire caught and blazed up. She shut the door and stood back.

The robot came to life, in its fashion. It got to its feet. It checked itself. It looked around with its lenses. It saw Gwenny. It spoke, using its speaker grille. "Why?"

"You were hurting."

"I do not understand."

"You fire was out. You were dead. That's not nice."

"My fire was out. I was inactive. What is nice?"

She shook her head. "Maybe you have to be alive to understand."

"I am not alive. I do not understand."

She considered. "Why did you fight us?"

"What is fight?"

"What you were doing. Coming at us in masses, shoving us around. Trampling us. Killing us."

"We were going to the iron. We forged through imped-iments."

"You mean you weren't trying to fight us?"

"We had to get to the iron. You were in the way. We tried to pass. You did not get out of the way."

She considered again. "But you were overrunning us. We had to stop you."

"All we want is iron."

"So you can make more and bigger robots."

"Yes. As long as the iron lasts."

"We can't allow that."

"I do not understand."

"You will squeeze all the rest of us out of Xanth."

"Yes."

"That's not right."

"What is right?"

She tried again. "There should be room for all crea-tures in Xanth, each in its place. Cooperating when that is mutually beneficial."

"Why?"

"Why do you do what you do?"

"I follow my program."

"Well, my program forbids me to hurt folk I don't need to hurt, or to let them hurt if I don't need to. That's why I helped you."

"Give me a program that enables me to understand."

She was surprised. "You would accept such a program?"

"Yes, because it seems to be a better program than mine. No other robot helped me. I would not have helped another robot. You helped me. You have a directive that would be useful for me. I want to be the best machine I can be. That's in my present program."

She considered again. "Maybe we can help each other. If you help me escape this cave, I will help you get such a program. Is it a deal?"

"What is a—"

"An agreement to help each other get what we need. To cooperate. Not to fight each other."

"I do not understand cooperation."

She considered yet again. "Can your present program accept something you don't yet understand but that may benefit you later?"

"Yes, conditionally."

"Then accept this: if we don't cooperate, we will not escape this cave. I will die and you will run out of fuel and become inactive. If we do cooperate, I will live and you will get out to get more fuel and a better program."

"I accept that. I do not know what to do."

"You'll have to trust me."

"What is trust?"

She shook her head. "You are really making me think! I think what you need is a soul program. That is, a program that emulates the conscience of a living creature. Then you would understand our case, and would understand the need to limit your pursuit of iron. Then maybe we could exist together in harmony. I mean all living creatures and all robots."

"What is trust?"

She smiled. "I suppose I didn't properly answer that. It means you accept that I mean you no harm, and that it is safe for you and your kind to do what I ask you to do. Until you get the program that will make it clear to you."

"What you offer will benefit me. I will trust you."

"Thank you."

"What is thanks?"

She laughed. "It is an expression of appreciation for a nice thing someone else has done."

"I merely made a statement of acceptance."

"This, too, is something the new program will clarify."

"What must I do?"

She went to the gourd. "I will lie down and look into this lens. You must put your hand between my eye and the peephole in one hour. Do you understand?"

"Yes."

She lay down, made herself comfortable, and put her eye to the peephole.

The dream in a dream dissipated. "And so I entered the dream realm, hoping you would think to search for me here," she said. "Now you know where I am, and can organize a rescue party. But you must also rescue the others. Including the kraken and the robot. I have a deal to honor."

"Now I understand," Goody said. "Trust me."

They laughed together.

Soon after that, Goody returned to the real world: another hour was up. "Hannah, I found her!" he said. "I know where she is."

"About time you quit goofing off, lazy loafer."

"And hello to you too, peeve." It was almost good to have the obnoxious bird back.

Hannah nodded. "So we can rescue her now."

He hesitated. "That's complicated."

"Too much for your simple mind?" the bird inquired.

Then he explained, and Hannah understood, and agreed. She had a soul too, and a conscience, so grasped the concepts of trust and honor.

"What a crock of spit!"

They laughed. The parody didn't get it.

When Dara and Metria checked on them, surely sent by Magician Trent, they explained. They went to the north shore of Mountain Lake. "Just about here," Goody said. Gwenny had been as specific as she could about the location.

"If you bring them out through the water, that robot will get fissioned again."

"Get whated again?"

"Disolved, consumed, atomized, decayed, oxidized—"

"Corroded?"

"Whatever," Metria agreed crossly. "And the kraken will hate the fresh water."

"Good point," Hannah said. "But why go through the water when we can dig them out? They can't be far below the ground surface."

"Great idea," Goody said.

"Well, I'm barbarian, not stupid," she said, flattered.

"Opinions differ, dolt."

"I'll tell them we're coming," Dara said, and puffed out.

"It won't work," the parody said sourly.

They scrounged iron limbs from the metal mountain to fashion spades and started digging. Soon they intersected the roof of the cave. It was a cast iron layer, evidently an extension of Iron Mountain. Their iron tools could not get through.

"Should have known there was a reason that cave didn't fall in long ago," Hannah muttered. "We're fairly balked."

"I told you, puddinghead!"

"You did," she agreed. "Do you have an answer?"

"Sure, booby."

"And what might that answer be?"

"Put a hole in it, looby."

"And how do we do that?"

"Fetch a hole from the holey land, clod."

"The what land?"

"Don't start that," Metria said. "I know where it is." She vanished.

Goody was amazed. Could the arrogant bird be right?

Metria reappeared, holding something invisible. She set it carefully in the middle of the exposed metal layer.

A hole appeared. The hole she had set there. "See, dullard?"

She nodded. "I could almost get to like you, peeve, if you weren't so obnoxious."

"Fortunately I am, cretin."

"Goody!" Gwenny called from below.

He was so excited that he jumped down into the cave to hug her.

"Why didn't the demons haul them out?" the parody demanded petulantly.

They gazed at each other. Why not indeed?

"Because goblins and demons aren't as smart as peeves," Goody said.

"The great light dawns at last!"

"Let's complete the deal Gwenny made," Hannah said. "First the kraken."

The two demons formed a double cloud around the kraken and carried it away. They had promised to take it directly to the salty ocean. That was another matter of trust.

Meanwhile the others labored to break down the edge of the cave wall to form a ramp up to ground level. Gwenny took the robot by a hand appendage and led it up though the hole.

"Now we need to make the soul program," she said. "Do you think Com Pewter can handle it?"

"Maybe we should take the robot there," Hannah said. "So Pewter can analyze it."

"When the demons return," Gwenny agreed. She turned to the robot. "Com Pewter is a machine himself, so he should understand. Maybe you should forage for some more wood before the demons return."

"I understand." The robot walked to the nearby woods.

Goody resumed hugging and kissing Gwenny, who co-operated with vigor. "When you disappeared, I was so afraid!"

"I knew you'd come for me. I trusted you."

Goody appreciated her confidence. He just wished he had shared it throughout.

# 18

# ROLAND

We need a third dybbuk," Metria said.

"A third what?" Goody asked before catching himself.

"Devil, fiend, hellion, specter, djinn—"

"Demon?"

"Whatever," she agreed crossly.

"The crazy spirit can't even get her own type right!"

"Why?"

"Because now there are three of you to transport."

"Are you sure?" Gwenny asked.

"Sure: You, Goody, and Hannah."

"And what of the robot?"

"Neither can she count," the peeve noted.

"Oh, dishwater!"

"Oh, what?" the robot asked.

"Refuse, bilge, carrion, garbage, trash, waste, s—"

"Slops!" Gwenny said quickly, lest an unfortunate word emerge.

"Whatever," Metria agreed, really crossly. "We can get a third demon we can trust, but I don't think a fourth exists."

"Why?" the robot asked.

"Because only three of us have souls," Dara answered. "Because we married mortals. Nada Naga's hungry husband D. Vore is the third."

"Take one, then have that demon return for another," Hannah suggested.

"Got it." Metria put three fingers to her mouth and made a piercing two-toned whistle.

Demon Vore appeared. "What, is it my turn to take the children already?"

"No such luck, Ravenous. We need you to carry Gwenny Goblin again. Plus a robot."

"Why carry it anywhere? Why not just dump it in the sea?"

"Not this one," Gwenny said. "I promised it a soul program."

Vore considered. "Would such a program have the effect on a robot a soul does on a demon?"

"We think so."

He nodded. "Makes sense to me." He oriented on Gwenny. "Where to, you luscious tidbit?"

"Com Pewter's cave. We'll rendezvous outside it."

"Shall we snuggle on the way?"

Gwenny paused as if considering. "My boyfriend wouldn't like it."

"He won't get it," he said, as he dissipated into smoke and surrounded her.

"That's what you think!" Metria called as the smoke faded.

In three-quarters of a moment Vore was back for the robot. This time Goody and Hannah went also. Metria did sneak in a snuggle, though Goody was sure Vore had not done so with Gwenny. Metria was an irrepressible temptress, while other demons could tempt or not, depending on mood.

They arrived outside the cave. "We demons prefer not to enter," Vore said. "You understand."

"We do," Gwenny said.

"I'm not sure I do," Goody said.

"Pewter changes reality in his cave," Gwenny explained. "And he doesn't like demons."

As they walked into the dark recess, Vore turned to Metria. "What was that about what I think?"

"He thinks you stink!" the peeve called back.

"Whatever," Metria agreed automatically. "Hey, wait—"

They lost the rest of the dialogue as the cave enclosed them. Then they came to the central chamber.

It was already occupied. A man and a dog stood before Com Pewter's screen.

A troll intercepted them. "I am Tristan, Com Pewter's mouse. Pewter is busy at the moment. Do you care to share your business with me?"

What was this—a polite troll? "Yes," Gwenny said. "I am Gwenny of Goblin Mountain."

"Welcome, Chiefess."

"And this is Goody Goblin, with Hannah Barbarian, and a robot. We need a new program for the robot."

Tristan nodded. "You are of course aware that Pewter does not do favors out of the goodness of his circuitry."

"Is there anything we can trade?"

"There may be. Our prior visitors have a problem I suspect Pewter will not be able to address directly, because it occurs well beyond the cave."

Then the chamber seemed to expand, and they were standing in a large pleasant garden. Pewter had changed local reality.

"Now I will introduce you to the others," Tristan said, picking up on Pewter's wish without any obvious signal. "This is Matt Heffelbower of Mundania, and Sam Dog." Tristan addressed the man and dog. "This is Chiefess Gwendolyn Gobliness, with Goody Goblin, Hannah Barbarian, and a nameless robot."

"How do you do," Matt said in the Mundane manner. He was young and handsome; Goody couldn't figure what he was doing in Xanth. The dog was a black lab; Goody wasn't sure how he knew that, but in this magic cave somehow did. Maybe it was because the dog looked but did not smell similar to the chocolate lab he had encountered in the dream realm.

"Matt and Sam came recently to Xanth and settled with an isolated village," Tristan said. "Now that village has a problem. The panties of the local girls no longer freak out men. This is a crisis for the local women, as they can't exert proper power over the men, and it seems the men are not entirely pleased either. Matt and Sam have come to ask Pewter's assistance for the village."

"Panties don't work," Gwenny said thoughtfully. "That would disenfranchise women." Hannah nodded agreement.

"Matt and Sam volunteered to walk here and try to make a deal," Tristan said. "Pewter is amenable, but is unable to change reality away from his cave. Here is his offer: Go to Pieria and solve their problem, and Pewter will make the program you need."

"But what if we can't solve it?" Gwenny asked.

"Then you won't get the program."

Gwenny seemed to stifle a sigh. "We'll try." She turned to Goody. "I will have to stay here with the robot, because its trust does not extend to others. Can you and Hannah handle it?"

"We'll try," Goody said. What else was there? He turned to Matt. "We have special transportation. If you will come outside with us and pick up Sam, we will take you to your village. Then we'll study the problem, and hope to find a solution."

"That seems fair," Matt agreed.

Outside, Goody introduced the demons, and explained how they could move people rapidly. "If you will carry Matt to Pieria, we'll join you there."

Matt looked doubtful, but picked up the dog. Vore dissolved into smoke.

Then Metria surrounded Goody, goosing him as she moved him. She seemed compelled to make naughty touches much the way the parody had to make insults. They landed outside a rather nice-looking village.

Matt set Sam down. "That was amazing!"

"Maybe to you, you ignorant lout."

"That's the bird, using my voice," Goody said hastily. "It insults everybody. We're trying to find a home for it."

Matt smiled. "Good luck."

Now what? This was Goody's challenge. "Maybe we should verify the effect. Um, Hannah—"

"I'm curious too," she said. "Watch." She hiked up her metallic skirt.

"Snap out of it," Hannah said as she jogged Goody's shoulder.

He blinked. "What?"

"Your mind was glop," the parody said. "As usual."

"You truly freaked out," Hannah said. "Even after I covered them. I've never had that kind of power before."

Obviously he had. That was weird, because he had seen her all the way bare; her panties should have had minimal effect. "What about Matt?"

"He's still out."

So he was. The man was standing still, staring at the spot where Hannah had stood. Even the dog seemed stunned.

Hannah went to jog the man back to life. "Oh, sorry," Matt said. "I must have—"

"Freaked out," Goody said. "We both did. So obviously the effect remains. Could it have been restored during your absence?"

"I suppose it could. I'll inquire."

They walked to the village. "What deal did you make with Com Pewter?" Goody asked.

"The village of Pieria lies near the famous fountain sacred to the Muses, the Pierian Springs. Its water inspires anyone who drinks it. We offered to deliver enough water so Pewter could have a pool of it in his cave."

"So as to have constant inspiration," Hannah said. "I can see why he would want that."

"If you're from Mundania, you don't have a magic talent," Goody said. "But the magic of the spring could work for you."

"Yes. It gave me the inspiration to go to Com Pewter. But they tell me it is possible I'll develop a talent later in life."

"Yes, it can happen," Goody agreed.

"But with my luck it will be the talent of watching pots boil."

"Ha. Ha. Ha," the peeve laughed sardonically.

"The bird laughs only meanly," Hannah said.

A young woman appeared before them. "Back already, Matt?" she asked. "You must have walked rapidly."

"I got a ride back, Cameo. Would you mind showing your panties?"

"They still don't work," she said, hiking up her skirt.

She was right: they were nice enough, pink and well filled. But neither Goody nor Matt freaked.

"Now that's odd," Goody said. "When Hannah—" He broke off, for Cameo was gone.

"She makes only brief appearances," Matt explained. "That's her nature, or her talent. But it shows you what we're up against. Those panties should have wiped us both out, but they had no effect. That's true for the other village girls."

"Maybe it's something near the village," Hannah said. "Do you care to check mine again?"

Goody looked—and it was Matt who shook him awake. "I didn't look this time," he said. "But you froze."

"So it's not the locale," Goody said. "It's the specific panties. That's a clue."

"But why should mine work, when others don't?" Hannah asked. "That girl Cameo should have had double the freakout power I do."

"No offense," Goody said cautiously, "but you're right. It's a real mystery. And I'm stumped."

"Let's go sip that spring water for inspiration."

"That makes great sense."

They walked to the spring. It was a picturesque fountain with clear water splashing merrily. There was a dipper, and they each sipped.

Suddenly Goody's mind was clear. "Your panties are new to this area," he said to Hannah. "So they haven't been nullified yet. Something around here is doing it."

"That makes me nervous," she said, pulling her skirt down to make sure no panty showed. "Let's wrap this up before it catches up with me."

"On the other hand," Matt said, "if it catches you, maybe we'll see it happening, and learn how to stop it."

Goody took another sip, and got another inspiration. "Someone or something here must dislike the panty effect, so is stopping it. Maybe he has the talent of nullifying panties."

Hannah took a sip. "Or *she*. It could be a jealous woman."

Matt took a sip. "Or maybe he/she/it merely diverts the panty effect so that it doesn't strike its proper targets."

"Regardless, we should check for it," Goody said. "Every member of the village has a talent, right?"

"All except Sam and me," Matt agreed.

"But those are known talents," Hannah said. "The one who nulls panties won't tell us that, of course."

"Not voluntarily," Goody said, taking another sip. "But we should be able to do it by elimination. The one who can't demonstrate a legitimate talent must be the one we want. We can take that one back to Com Pewter for nullification."

"But will that restore the magic to nulled panties?" Hannah asked.

"I don't know. The girls might have to put on new ones. Those ought to work."

"Maybe we should verify that."

"I'll get a volunteer," Matt said. He walked to the village, leaving them by the fountain.

Cameo appeared. "Any luck?"

"Do you have an unused pair of panties?" Goody asked.

"Sure. But—"

"Change into them and come back here. They might work."

She vanished, her brief scene done. But then she reappeared. "How are these?" She lifted her skirt to flash silken blue panties.

Hannah's strong hand prevented Goody from falling into the fountain.

"They work! They work!" Cameo exclaimed. And faded out, her next scene completed.

"We're making progress," Hannah said. "Now we know that whoever it is, is nulling new panties as they appear. So it won't take long for the village maidens to return to full strength, once we locate the culprit."

They organized it, with the eager cooperation of the villagers. Every person lined up before Goody, and one by one demonstrated his or her talent. The first was a man who actually understood women; he demonstrated that by making Hannah blush. The second had the ability to speak with anyone, anywhere; she demonstrated that by talking with Gwenny in Pewter's cave, and hearing her answer: "No, I won't dance." Another villager could tell who a person's significant other was: for Goody, Gwenny. Another could hold his breath longer than any could track it. Another had a negative talent: the inability to remember what happened fifteen minutes ago. Another could change the season: summer abruptly became winter, then returned to summer. Another could make people laugh, even if they didn't want to. Even the peeve.

Finally only one was left. This was a sour-looking

woman who claimed to be able to walk on walls or ceiling, but was unable to demonstrate it. "You're the one," Goody said.

"And what if I am? Those hussies shouldn't be showing their underwear anyway."

"Why don't you show yours, you dried-up frump?" the peeve demanded.

"That's not for you to decide," Goody said.

"Yes, it is."

"Come with us."

"I won't," she said sourly. "You can't make me."

Vore smiled. He fuzzed into vapor and surrounded the woman. They vanished.

"Com Pewter will nullify or reverse her talent," Goody explained to the others. "Panties will prevail again."

The villagers were applauding as the demons took Goody and Hannah back. They left Matt and Sam Dog; their mission had been accomplished, except for the delivery of the Pierian Springs water to Pewter's cave. Goody was sure they would honor the deal. And if the two Mundanes had not been completely accepted in the village before, they certainly would be now. Especially by girls with restored panty power.

Meanwhile it turned out that they were making real progress on the program. Working under Pewter's direction, Gwenny had removed the robot's master chip from its head, and Pewter had analyzed it. Now Pewter was designing a program to provide a conscience, guided by Gwenny's advice. Because Pewter hardly cared about such a thing, but Gwenny did.

"It's designed like a virus," Gwenny said breathlessly. Goody loved her breathlessness; it had its own magic. "If he—turns out he's male—looks into the lens of another robot, the soul aspect of the program will transfer, and the other robot will have a conscience too. In time, all of them will, and then they will be tolerable neighbors. But we see a problem: if the others catch on too soon, they may try to destroy the souled robots."

Goody still felt the effect of the Pierian elixir. "Then make him bigger, so they can't. That will also enable us to readily tell him apart from the others, so we know with whom we are dealing."

She gave him a fast but nice hug and kiss. "Oh, you're so smart, Goody! We'll do that."

They went out to tell the demons, who popped off to Iron Mountain and brought back loads of defunct iron robot parts. Pewter changed the reality of their shapes to make them fit the existing robot, and he grew until he was full human man sized.

"We need a name for him," Hannah said. "Beginning with RO. "What would be good?"

"Roland," Tristan said. "Another legendary Mundane hero." The troll was evidently partial to that kind.

"Roland it is," she agreed. "Roland Robot."

Pewter extruded the reprogrammed chip. Hannah took it and carried it to the robot. Then, caught by a sudden vapor in the air, she sneezed. Right on the chip. "Oh, no—I've given it a virus!"

"It is not the same," Tristan said, unconcerned. He took the chip and set it carefully into the robot's enlarged head. He fixed it in place and closed the face-plate. "Now he should be operative. We should test him."

"Your name is Roland Robot," Gwenny said. "You are now twice as tall as you were, and stronger in proportion. How do you feel?"

The robot animated. "I feel—strange. I—" He sneezed.

"The virus!" Hannah wailed. "It *is* the same! It's my fault."

Roland's head turned to bear on her. "What phenomenally fair creature is this?" he asked, amazed. Goody wasn't sure how metal features conveyed such emotion, but they did.

"Just me, Hannah Barbarian. I'm sorry I infected you."

"I love you."

"What?"

"Worship, desire, adore, deify, amour—"

"But you're a machine!"

"And you're a ravishingly lovely barbarian woman. Just my type."

"That infection," Gwenny said, awed. "It oriented the program on her. He really is in love with her."

Had their seeming success become disaster?

Roland crossed to Hannah and put his metal arms around her. "Embrace me, beloved. Kiss me with your splendid barbarian passion. I am yours."

"But I'm alive!" she protested. "You're iron."

"I must have you, you luscious creature, lest my unrequited desire melt my innards." He put his face-plate to her face, attempting to kiss her.

"But this is impossible! You don't have lips."

"And I must possess you, you unutterably exotic delight. Hold me close."

"But you don't have a—"

He paused. "So I don't. Make me one. I need it."

"That'll be the day!" the parody said, finding this hilarious. "The chip needs a poker."

"The brassy men have brass ones," Roland said. "I can have an iron one."

"How do you know about brassies?" Hannah asked, surprised.

"It's in my new improved data bank. A person can't have a conscience without knowing to what it applies. All species of Xanth are there, and all are to be respected on their own terms as long as they don't get in my way. It's the barbarian code."

"So it is," Hannah agreed. "I like that."

"Then get me the parts I need to love you completely." He drew her close again.

"Attaboy, Robbie! Give her an iron smooch!" the peeve said.

"Com Pewter," Goody said urgently. "Change reality! Abolish the virus."

"Pewter can change the reality of the locale and the

events," Tristan said. "But the robot is governed by the programmed chip. That must be removed and reprogrammed."

"Then remove it!"

Tristan approached Roland. "Oh, no," the robot said. "I don't want to be changed. It would deny me the great love of my unlife."

"If you love Hannah," Gwenny said, "You will want what she wants."

Roland nodded in the manner Hannah might have. "True. If my love asks this of me, I must obey, though it crack my iron heart."

"Ask him, Hannah," Goody said.

But Hannah hesitated. "He's a barbarian male. An iron one, it is true, but still barbarian. And he loves me."

"Yes, it's in his infected program," Tristan said. "He will never stop, unless that program is changed."

"And now is the time to change it," Gwenny said. "We need to get it right before we leave this cave. Pewter doesn't give refunds."

"Ask, beloved. I can deny you nothing, not even the loss of my overwhelming love."

"I—" She shook her head. "I think I want to explore this further before deciding. Could there be a trial period?"

"Hannah!" Gwenny said, aghast. "You're not thinking of keeping him like this? Of—of—"

Hannah blushed, which must have been a considerable effort for her. "I think I want to try it, just in case."

"But he's a robot!"

"He's a barbarian male machine. Those are rare."

"Pewter understands your preference," Tristan said. "Roland, come with me a moment."

Roland hesitated. "Go with the troll," Hannah said.

"Kiss me first, adorable."

"Kiss me first, addlebrain," the parody mimicked.

She planted a savage kiss on his face-plate.

"Now I go," he said. "If it be the first and only kiss I

have of you, it nevertheless fulfills my fondest desire."
He let her go and followed Tristan to another section of
the cave.

"You can't be serious," Gwenny said.

"A male troll can be decent, a male goblin can be polite," Hannah said. "Why can't a robot be a manly barbarian?"

"Because he's not alive!"

"Yet you saved him from extinction, and made a deal
to get him a better program. Did you do all that for a dead
thing?"

That set Gwenny back a bit. "But I didn't consider him
as a lover."

"What about as a friend? Didn't you trust him, and he
helped you contact Goody?"

Gwenny considered. "Yes. I suppose you're right. Give
him a chance."

Tristan and Roland returned. Now the robot had a
roughly human face, complete with lips, and a subtly re-
vised midsection. "Not all the changes show," Tristan said.

"You didn't change my program," Roland said.

"Too bad, rust bucket!" the peeve said.

Hannah was taken aback. "You thought that was what I
wanted?"

"Barbarian subterfuge. But if it was your desire, I had
to let it happen."

"That's not the way of trust," Gwenny said. "She
wouldn't do something like that sneakily."

"Some people would."

"Some *civilized* people," Hannah said. "They lack barbarian honor."

"True. But most of those here are civilized."

"You have a healthy distrust of civilization," Hannah
said. "I like that." She embraced him and kissed his new
metal lips.

It looked to be some kiss. Roland's limbs quivered and
his iron color shifted to a shade of gray. "Oh, you gorgeous mistress!" he said shakily.

"Gorgeous what?" Goody asked.

"Never mind!" Hannah snapped. "Let's go somewhere we can explore this."

Gwenny murmured something to the troll, who nodded. "Pewter has a pass for the honey side of the moon for three," Tristan said. "You may use it now."

"For three?" Hannah asked.

"For you and Roland, and a chaperon."

"A chaperon! What do you think we're going to do there?"

"That's why you need one," Gwenny said with three-fifths of a smile. "Goody can do it; I have business back at Goblin Mountain."

"But I don't—" Goody started.

Gwenny caught up to him at that point and kissed him. "Just do it, dear."

Dear? The word stunned him almost like a panty flash. By the time he recovered, he was outside the cave with Roland and Hannah. "You had to be the one," she said. "Because I can't guard you unless we're together."

"Why is Pewter being so nice? That isn't like him."

"Gwenny made some kind of deal for the electronic rights to the soul program. Pewter can use them. It seems there may be a huge market in Mundania."

"Machines with souls," Goody said, seeing it. "Machines that always do the right thing."

"That would really help with their Outernet."

The three demons appeared. "Take us to the honey side of the moon," Goody said.

"You're marrying the Neanderthal?" Metria asked, surprised.

"Marrying the what?"

"Barbarian!" Hannah said. "No, he's not. I'm going with Roland."

Dara eyed him. "This is the robot we brought here?"

"We upgraded him."

"I'll take him," Vore said.

The demons closed about them, and two pats and a

squeeze later they stood on the lovely honey side of the moon. The side facing Xanth and Mundania, of course, had long since had its milk curdled to moldy cheese by the sights it witnessed. This was the unspoiled side, a land of milk and honey, conducive to romance.

Hannah took Roland's hand and led him along a gently curving path between moon flowers. "Tell me more of what you think of me," she said.

"You are the most graceful of all women, wonderful in ways I wish I could imagine. I would like nothing better than to bask eternally in the joy of your favor."

"Sickening," the peeve said.

"That's an interesting revision of the program," Vore said.

"Not to mention the enhancement of physique," Dara agreed admiringly. "Buns of steel. What happened?"

"Hannah sneezed on the reprogrammed chip. That gave it a virus. It seems the virus made Roland a barbarian, and in love with her."

"That's so romantic," Dara said.

"So now she wants to screw with that nut," the parody said.

"Do what with what?" Metria asked.

"I think I'm supposed to prevent that," Goody said uncomfortably. "They're just supposed to get to know each other, while she decides whether to have his program cleared of the virus." He followed the couple.

Hannah glanced back at him. "Can't you give us a little more room? Three is a—" She paused, an odd look crossing her features and disappearing into her body. "Morgan le Fay?"

Oops. That was the Mundane sorceress Goody had balked in the dream realm, when she tried to take over Helen of Troy's body.

"I know that name," Dara said. "She's a mischief maker from way back. She takes over the bodies of attractive women."

"I thought that was the Sea Hag," Vore said.

"Morgan's less destructive. She can't force them, exactly. She simply instills a strong desire to do what she wants them to do, and they think it's their own. After a time her wishes become theirs. She's strong on the physical pleasures, not the moral ones. She's been confined to one of the tiered Moons of Ida and wants to find a host in Xanth proper."

"Odd that she should appear just when we are here," Vore said.

"Why should I want to get back at Goody Goblin?" Hannah asked, evidently speaking to someone unseen.

"Because I messed Morgan up," Goody said. "She must have learned my identity."

"She thinks Hannah's your girlfriend!" Dara said. "So she's infesting her."

"The word is *investing*," Hannah's voice said.

"Like a virus," Goody agreed.

"No coincidence at all," Vore said. "This is after all where lovers come."

"We've got to stop this," Goody said. "But I don't know how."

"Idiot!" the parody said. "Play it through."

Goody focused, and the bird's meaning clarified. "Roland!" he said. "Hannah has a visitor inside her head, like a new program. The visitor doesn't believe you are romantic. You're her boyfriend. Show her visitor what barbarians are made of. Make love to her."

"With your iron prong," the parody added encouragingly.

The robot required no further urging. "Beloved! Be mine!" He embraced Hannah, kissing her avidly. His reworked lips seemed to work just fine.

"What's this?" Hannah's voice screeched, sounding like someone else, possibly a harpy. "Unhand me, brute!"

"Ignore her maidenly protestations," Goody called. "She wants to be mastered barbarian style."

"Outrageous!" Hannah's voice exclaimed as Hannah's body struggled with the iron grip of the robot. "Get your face-plate out of my face, you ludicrous contraption!" But she wasn't having much success in persuading him.

"Morgan!" Goody said. "Hannah is Roland's girlfriend, not mine. You are doomed to perpetual mechanical love."

"The bleep I am!"

Something changed. Roland paused. "Hannah?"

"She's gone," Hannah said. "What a witch!"

"You don't want to be mastered?" He sounded disappointed.

Hannah considered. "Goody, go back to the cave and tell Pewter the present program is all right. We'll stay here for a while or two."

"But—"

"We no longer need a chaperon," she said firmly.

"Take a hint, simpleton!" the parody said.

Oh. And they were in the place of romance.

Metria enclosed him and transported him back to the cave. Naturally she squeezed him in especially awkward places. "Ain't love grand," she murmured. "May he never soften."

Almost, he asked for a clarification of the term, but caught himself in time.

## 19

# PEEVE

It was sheer delight waking up in a full goblin bed with Gwenny beside him. "This goes beyond niceness," he said. "I know you made a deal with Com Pewter, but Roland and Hannah's visit to the honeymoon took care of that. Why did he provide us this wonderful private room?"

"He needs Roland's agreement too, so has to wait until they return."

"They're still there?"

"Hannah has been without a man for a long time, and it seems he is indefatigable."

"Tristan made a working, um, device?"

"Tristan made an approximate one. Then Pewter changed its reality, following some sort of treatment described on the Mundane Outernet to make it bigger and harder. It surely works."

"Will it fool the storks?"

"Oh, I should think so." She kissed him. "Why this interest in them, when you've got me?"

They had had a remarkable night, but her words alerted him. "Is that a hint?"

"No. It's a seduction." She rolled onto him, making it literal.

"Oh Gwenny," he gasped shortly later. "I know I love you. I wish you'd ask me to marry you."

"In due course. There remains one thing to verify."

"What is that?"

"You will know it when it occurs. Meanwhile we still have to place the peeve."

He had almost forgotten. "The peeve! Where is it?"

"Entertaining Tristan Troll. Trolls understand attitudes like that."

"Do you suppose—"

"No, Pewter doesn't want bird droppings in his cave."

"Too bad."

"Now if you're quite done ravishing me—"

He had to laugh. "I doubt I'll ever be done with that. You make me feel young again."

"You're eleven years older than I am. Are you saying I'm getting old?"

"No, of course not!"

"So will you tire of me when I do get old?"

"No!" She was teasing him, but he couldn't help reacting.

"And you really don't mind that I'm lame?"

"I don't even notice. But if I did, it wouldn't make a difference. You're beautiful, and you have no trouble with your legs where it counts."

"Slow walking?"

"That too."

"I wish I could dance."

"Maybe you just haven't found the right dance."

She kissed him. "Maybe."

They got up, cleaned up, and went out to see whether the others were back. They were, and Roland had already given his consent for the electronic rights. Both looked about as satisfied as Goody felt.

"Now let's get that bird a home," Hannah said. "So I can stop guarding you."

"We had a small diversion," Goody said. "But now we should be able to focus exclusively on that."

"Lotsa luck, suckers!"

Goody sincerely hoped the parody's cynicism was unjustified. But he feared it wasn't.

Soon they were on their way: Goody, Gwenny, Hannah, and Roland. They walked slowly, so that Gwenny had no trouble. They stayed mostly on the enchanted paths. And they focused on the parody.

They came to a pleasant garden beside the path, tended by a young man. "Hello," Goody said. "That's a nice collection of plants."

"Thank you," the man said. "It's my talent. I can modify things to other varieties, and modify them again, in a chain."

"Modify your stupid head."

Goody hastily explained about the talking bird.

The man demonstrated. He started with a lily flower, and modified it to a tiger lily that growled and snapped at them. Then he modified it to a purring pussy willow. Then to a stiff cattail. And so on, finally back to a lion lily.

"That's beautiful," Gwenny said. "Can you modify a bird?"

"Don't you dare, turnip top!"

They had to go on, reminded of just how difficult it was to place the parody. "Do you actually want to find a home?" Goody asked it.

"Sure, if that gets rid of you, slacker."

But Goody had to wonder. A good home might leave the peeve nothing to be peeved about. It wouldn't like that.

They moved on. Soon they saw commotion across a field. A dragon seemed to be chasing down a running man.

"One hot meal coming up," the parody remarked.

"The fool should have known to stay on the enchanted path," Hannah said.

"We've got to help him," Gwenny said, stepping off the path.

"Wait, Gwenny!" Goody cried. "We can't stop a big dragon! We can't even—" He broke off, unwilling to remind her that she couldn't even outrun it long. And of course he knew she had a tender heart; it was one reason he loved her. So he followed her.

"Bleep!" Hannah swore. She followed, drawing her sword.

"Is this diversion necessary?" Roland inquired, following her.

"Yes," Hannah said. "It's my job to guard Goody until the bird gets placed. I can't stop him from being a fool meanwhile; he's in love."

"Ah, I comprehend. Shall I balk the dragon?"

"Sure. That will save me from nicking my sword on its tough scales."

Roland forged ahead at remarkable velocity, trailing smoke. He intercepted the dragon just as it was about to gobble down the man. "I say, beast: depart."

The dragon gazed down at him, then smirked. It inhaled, readying a withering (or more correctly, melting) blast of fire.

Roland stepped in and bashed it on the snout with his iron fist. "Begone, miscreant!"

The blow clearly had power. It rocked the dragon's head back. Little planets swirled around its snout as its stifled flame shot out its ears. It staggered away, defeated.

"You saved me!" the man exclaimed. "Thank you, iron man!"

"You are welcome. I did it at my beloved's request."

"I am Paine. I come from Camp Pain, where candidates grow and sling mud. I got so sick of muddy dates! My talent is getting into crises. I fear this would have been my last one, had you not intervened."

"Would have served you right, nitwit."

Goody hastily explained about the bird.

The normal dialogue reestablished itself. "I am Roland, iron-hearted barbarian warrior."

"Get on the enchanted path," Hannah said. "Before another crisis catches up with you."

"Oh, I shall," Paine agreed. "But I can't escape the crises. It's my curse."

"Maybe you should change your name," Goody said. "Such as to Painter. That might change your curse."

Paine looked at him, astonished. "I never thought of that. I'll try it." He turned to Roland. "Thank you again." He hurried to the path.

"That was beautiful, Roland," Hannah said, kissing him.

"Anything for you, my lovely," he replied gallantly.

"Disgusting," the peeve said. "She's turned hard metal into gunk."

"It's the way barbarian men are about women," Hannah explained. "They are utter adorable fools."

Goody exchanged a glance with Gwenny. It was clearly love. Hannah had indeed found her man, in the least likely place. And Gwenny had more than honored her commitment to the robot.

They returned to the enchanted path. The rescued man was gone, but there was a splatter of bright blue paint on the ground. "Why do I think that changing his name did not entirely change his curse?" Gwenny asked rhetorically.

They came to an odd tree. It was covered with musical instruments. "A music tree!" Gwenny exclaimed, delighted. "That must be where the curse fiends get their instruments for the music to accompany their plays. I wish I were musical."

"You govern Goblin Mountain, and you want to be a musician?" Hannah asked.

"Being chiefess is my business; I inherited that. My dreams are something else. I think Goody is one of them."

"I don't understand."

"You dope! She's got a ring in your nose."

"She means she wanted honest love," Hannah said. "As did I. As does any woman. It's harder for some of us to find than it is for uncomplicated damsels."

"She means you're a lovesick nobody," the peeve said.

"I'm not sick," Goody protested.

"Oh, I don't know," Hannah said teasingly. "Put a thermometer in your mouth and it would jump five degrees when you looked at Gwenny."

"Don't do that," Gwenny said with mock alarm. "Don't you know those things are spy eyes for the Demon Mercury?"

"Good point," Hannah agreed. "Better leave them to Mundania, where they don't know any better."

They were still gazing at the tree. "This violin looks my size," Gwenny said.

Roland inspected it. There was a faint whirring sound in his head. "That is in my data bank. It is a tic-kit. It sends critics elsewhere."

"You're so smart," Hannah said, giving him another kiss.

"Nauseous!"

"Com Pewter didn't have a barbarian data bank, so he used the standard one," Roland said. "It is filled with useless information."

"At any rate, it is obviously the instrument for me," Gwenny said. "Since I know nothing about music. The centaurs tried to teach me, but I wasn't very good. The critics would destroy me." She gazed longingly at the little violin.

"Take it," Goody urged her. "I'll like anything you play."

"Now that's an attitude I appreciate." She took the violin, which came away readily, with its bow attached. She played a note.

Goody managed not to wince. She was right: it was an awful note.

"It requires tuning," Roland said. "May I?"

Gwenny gave him the violin, and he tightened the strings and returned it. She tried the note again. This time it was melodic. "But that's as far as I go," she said. "I learned only the first note. I can't play a tune."

"Practice," Hannah advised.

Gwenny put the violin in her backpack, and they went on. So far they were having no luck in placing the bird. Were they ever going to find a good home for it? Goody was getting a heavy feeling about that.

They passed a man walking the other way. He paused, glancing at Goody. "You look glum, goblin."

"And you look stupid, bleephead," the parody said.

Goody hastily explained about the peeve. "So you see, I am beginning to doubt I can ever find a home for it. That makes it hard to smile."

"I can make you smile," the man said.

"Oh, are you looking for a pet bird?"

"By no means. It's my talent: making folk smile." He focused on Goody.

Goody smiled so broadly he was afraid his face was stretching out of bounds. But he didn't feel any better.

"You're so handsome when you smile," Gwenny said, kissing his cheek. Then he felt better.

They came to a lake. A fin projected from the water as something forged toward them. "A loan shark!" Gwenny said, alarmed.

Roland's head whirred as he sorted his database. "This is not a shark fin," he said. "It is a doll fin."

The water creature lifted its nose from the water. "Indeed, I am the smartest of water creatures," it said.

"The smartest Alec," the peeve said.

"But I don't believe I have seen a talking green parody or a barbarian robot before."

"The bird is one of a kind," Goody said.

"And Roland is the first of his kind," Hannah said. "But maybe not the last."

"A talking fish and a talking bird," Gwenny said sourly.

"That is a popular misconception," the water creature said. "I am not a fish."

"And what's this? A fiddle?" She drew it out.

Goody was taken aback. This was unlike her.

Gwenny put the violin to her chin and plied the bow. Lovely music came forth. She played an archaic melody, then paused. "Well, at least it's in tune."

"Thank you," Roland said.

"But Gwenny, you can't play a tune," Goody said.

"That ain't Gwenny, stupe," the parody said.

Gwenny focused on the bird. "Shut your beak."

But Goody already had the hint. "Morgan!" he said, horrified.

"The great light dawns," she said sarcastically. "You denied me Helen, and you inflicted the rattletrap robot on me. Now I shall make you pay."

"Now I recognize her attitude," Hannah said. "Don't let her stay. She's not nice."

"Thank you for that perceptive analysis, hussy."

"Gwenny!" Goody said. "That's Morgan le Fay, the Mundane sorceress. She can't control you directly. All she can do is make you think you want to do something. If you know it's not your own wish, you retain control. Don't let her run your body."

A flash of Gwenny showed. "That explains it! I couldn't understand why I was suddenly so cynical, or how I could play the violin."

"Neither do you have a magic talent, as I do. But you know you want to do my will," Morgan said. "It's like an itch: you can't rest until you scratch it. You may fight if you choose, but the end is certain."

"No, it isn't!" Goody said. "You can throw her off, Gwenny, if you try hard enough."

"But you don't want to try, dear," Morgan said. "*Do* you?"

There was a visible internal struggle. Then Gwenny spoke. "I do—do—oh Goody, I no longer want to. I'm so sorry."

Goody turned to Hannah and Roland in dawning despair. "What can we do? Morgan is *inside* her."

Roland's head whirred. "There is a way." He ran forward with surprising speed, picked Gwenny up, and ran up the path with her.

"Good riddance, harridan!" the parody cried.

"What's he doing?" Goody asked, newly alarmed. "I don't think he can kiss Morgan away, as he did with you; she knows that's no permanent relationship."

"I don't know, but I trust him," Hannah said. "I know he loves only me. Gwenny didn't sneeze on his program."

Then Roland came speeding back without Gwenny. "She is free for the moment, but it may not last."

"What did you do?" Hannah asked.

"I moved her rapidly. My data bank says that a spiritual force takes time to fully occupy a living body. If that body moves, the spirit gets left behind, and must reorient. My information does not specify how long reorientation takes."

"So she'll have to keep moving," Goody said. "But what about when she sleeps?"

"I can transport her as she sleeps," Roland said. "I do not require sleep myself, though I am satisfied to emulate it if my love desires it."

"There won't be much desire if you can never stop carrying another woman around," Hannah said, not entirely pleased.

"I will desist if that is your preference, inamorata."

"No, keep her moving. But we need to find a better way."

"Then I should move her again. Perhaps we can ascertain how long reorientation takes." He dashed off.

"Roland is more useful than I expected," Goody said.

"He is a barbarian of many qualities. It's amazing what a difference a program makes."

"And a rod," the parody said, chortling evilly.

Com Pewter had set up the program. Pewter had a lot of quirky information.

They proceeded along the path. Soon Roland came back, carrying Gwenny. He set her down before them.

"She's gone," Gwenny said. "Roland explained about the motion. But I'm nervous that she will find me again. I don't like her notions."

"I don't like anyone else's notions in you," Goody said.

"Thank you." She kissed him. "I must move."

"And they call birds flighty," the parody said.

Roland picked her up and ran back the way they had come. "Should we follow?" Hannah asked.

"No. We don't want to be predictable. Let's continue forward, hoping to find some better solution. Roland will surely catch up to us in due course."

"Good thinking." They moved on.

Something came bounding toward them, flipping over in air and turning handsprings. It paused before them. It was a man in athletic clothing. "Hello. I am Jim Nastic. I am very acrobatic." He bounded on.

"I don't want to be unduly critical," Hannah said. "But it seems to me that we're not making much progress on either placing the bird or saving Gwenny from the evil sorceress. I think we need another approach."

"I agree! But with Gwenny in danger, I can't think straight."

She nodded. "You have a good mind when you focus it. What about this: we settle down for a while, let Morgan catch up to Gwenny, and persuade her that she doesn't want Gwenny's body. Maybe she'll go away, as she did with me."

"I can't think well enough right now to know whether that's a good idea."

"Maybe I can handle it, while you observe and consider. If I can't make her go away, maybe you can."

Goody shrugged. "I hope you can do it, because I have no confidence that I can."

She picked him up and kissed him. "You do have ability. You just need that confidence. I'll take it from here, for a while. Meanwhile you try thinking outside the box. You're good at that."

"Thank you," Goody said faintly.

They passed another man. "Hello," Hannah said. "We are looking for a home for this disreputable bird."

"Watch your tongue, minx!"

The man shook his head. "I'm no good with birds. My talent is making sleeping dogs tell the truth."

"Isn't that somewhat pointless?"

"It's better than letting them lie." He walked on.

"I think I walked into that one," Hannah said.

"I would have done the same."

They came to a woman sitting beside the path. "Hello," Hannah said. "Are you interested in adopting a fowl-mouthed bird?"

"I'm not sure," the woman said. "Hello. I'm Lenora. My talent is making people feel guilty. I'm not sure it works on birds."

"Nothing works on me, you dowdy chippy."

"I see what you mean," Lenora said.

But it was working on Goody. He felt guilty for even asking.

"I apologize for bothering you," Hannah said. "I shouldn't have."

"No, that's my talent. You had every right to ask. But you'll feel guilty as long as you're near me."

Hannah glanced at Goody. "Do you think the Sorceress would be affected?"

"But Gwenny would be affected too, and she couldn't stay near Lenora all the time."

"True." Hannah faced the woman. "Thank you for your time. We'll be moving on now."

"Of course," the woman said sadly. Goody felt so guilty about leaving her.

The robot zoomed toward them, carrying Gwenny. Hannah flagged him down. "Pause a while," she said. "We have something to try."

"That's a relief," Gwenny said. She looked somewhat windblown. "Do you have a solution?"

"Maybe. I want to talk to the Sorceress, while Goody observes and ponders some better way. If I can't do it, maybe he can."

Gwenny went to him and kissed him. "I have confidence in you. But I don't want to kiss you when Morgan is with me. She would make it seem dirty or calculated."

"It *is* calculated, gamine," the parody said.

"Yes, but it doesn't *seem* so," Gwenny said with much of a weak smile.

"When the Sorceress comes," Hannah said, "put up some token resistance, but then let her have her way. Save your strength for when you really need to stop her."

"I'll try," Gwenny said. "But the way she instills urges—I hate it, but I do start to want it."

"If my idea doesn't work, Roland can carry you away again. This is just an exploration. With luck it will work."

They were walking slowly. They came to an intersection of paths. Nearby was a store in the shape of a giant chain link. Another link was connected to it, and another; there were several of them. "A chain store!" Gwenny said, thrilled. "Let's buy a chain."

They went to the nearest store and bought a chain, using little copper disks that Gwenny had. It seemed that such things were used in stores. The chain was more like a delicate bracelet that she wore with pride.

"Civilized girls like baubles," Hannah murmured.

So it seemed.

They returned to the path and sat on a green bench. Just when Goody started wondering how long it would take for the Sorceress to show up, she did.

"So you thought you could avoid me," she said. "That was a foolish ploy, running around like that. I'll always catch you; I just need to get another fix on your location."

"We need to talk," Hannah said.

"Forget it, barbarian beast. You passed up your chance. This is a prettier body, and it should be really fun educating this polite goblin male before I drive him crazy." She advanced on Goody.

"No!" Gwenny cried. For two and a half moments she resisted, but then the desire of the Sorceress prevailed.

"Let's discover what you are capable of, little man."

"You forget I am here," Hannah said.

"I am not interested in you or your robot. I want to put this goblin through his paces." She focused on Goody as if about to slice meat. "Of course after I wear you out, I will repair to Goblin Mountain and start in on the horny males there. Some may even like SM."

"SM?" Goody asked, transfixed by her gaze, which was so unlike Gwenny's despite emanating from the same face.

"Torture, guts, brutality, hurting, bondage—" the parody said.

"Sado-masochism," Hannah said grimly as Goody recoiled in horror. "Not for you, Goody."

"Oh, you never can tell," Morgan said. "A little priming can evoke wonders." She took hold of Goody and kissed him, her tongue prying between his lips as her hands stroked his buttocks in the manner Metria's illicit touches did. The weird thing was that he found himself responding to it despite his aversion, and he knew she knew it. Gwenny was a pleasant amateur in this respect; Morgan was a thorough professional.

Still, he made a show of resistance. "You'll never get me into that."

"You forget my talent, innocent goblin. It is to turn things on."

"I don't understand."

"Such as desire. Like this."

Suddenly Goody was burning with desire for her. He tried to draw her close, but now she fended him off with momentarily stiff arms. "Only when I choose," she murmured. "You must suffer some pangs first."

"You don't want that body," Hannah said.

"This is news to me. It is healthy, pretty, and reasonably young." Now the questing hands expertly groped his front. Goody was eager to take it further, but she was cruelly teasing, not indulging.

"It is lame," Hannah said.

Morgan paused. "How so?"

"It can't run or dance or even walk too long."

The Sorceress went still against Goody as she turned her attention inward. "Oh, bleep!" she swore. "It's true. This body is defective."

"So you might as well let it go," Hannah said victoriously.

Morgan let Goody go and stood back to orient on Hannah. "You think you've won, you primitive peon. Now learn reality. I don't need this body to live in. I need it to punish the goblin who balked me. First I will seduce him, making it clear it is not his paramour he is with, making him ashamed. I will tempt him into acts he finds appalling but can't resist. Then I will make him watch as I do it with other goblins, in increasingly degraded manner. Then I will instill in this innocent doxy the desire for self-mutilation in his presence. And finally suicide, delicately done. She will bleed to death while he watches. After that I will make a spancel of him. Then will my vengeance be complete. Then I will seek a permanent host, younger, prettier, fully human. Perhaps one of those nubile twin princesses. Much can be done with raw material like that."

"No!" Gwenny cried.

"Yes," Morgan said. "You feel the temptation already, don't you dear? There is a certain painful joy in cutting oneself and seeing the blood flow. You will come to crave it. You will come to delight in tormenting your lover, whoever he may be at the moment. You will thank me for bringing you this experience."

"This is barbaric," Hannah said.

"Thank you, aboriginal amah. From you that is a considerable compliment."

"Take her away," Hannah said to Roland.

The robot moved so swiftly he was almost invisible. He swept up Gwenny and bore her away.

"I'm sorry," Hannah said. "I thought she wouldn't want an imperfect body. How wrong I was."

"You couldn't know," Goody said, fighting past his horror. The urgent desire was slowly fading in the absence of its object. "This is much worse than I thought. The worst of it is that I know she's not bluffing; she made me start to want her even though she's not in my head."

"She knows how to play with bodies," Hannah agreed. "And how to torture them too, I'm sure. Now I remember something I heard once and didn't believe. Something called a spancel."

"She said that word. What does it mean?"

"You don't want to know. Trust me."

"We've got to save her!"

Hannah shook her head. "I wish I knew how."

"It'll be fun watching her mess up those other goblins."

For a moment blind fury governed. Goody grabbed for the parody, but it leaped into the air and hovered just out of reach.

Then a bulb flashed brightly over his head.

"You got a notion!" Hannah said.

"Yes, I think so. Bring her back."

"But the Sorceress will find her quickly if she returns here."

"This time I'll talk to Morgan."

She gazed at him. "I hope your idea works."

"So do I," Goody said with feeling.

They walked along the path. Roland ran back, carrying Gwenny. Hannah flagged him down again.

"But this is not far enough removed," he said. "The Sorceress will soon return."

"Yes. We have another ploy."

He set Gwenny down. She ran to Goody and hugged him. "If she starts that again, kill me," she said.

"I couldn't—"

"Then you do it," Gwenny told Hannah. "I mean it."

"I know you do. But Goody has a way to get rid of her." Hannah was trying to look sincere, but it was plain she lacked certainty.

"Oh, please have that way!" Gwenny said.

"Lotsa luck, sultry sweetheart."

Then Gwenny's expression changed. "Are you surrendering? It won't save you, runt."

"You need a proper audience, Morgan le Fay," Goody said. "Someone who truly appreciates your endeavors from the outset. Someone who will bruit them widely about."

Her eyes narrowed. "Not necessarily. Some things are best accomplished privately. Some things are their own best reward."

"Parody, it is time for your regular home," Goody said. "Join Gwenny, and stay with her while the Sorceress uses her body. After she dies, we'll find another person for you."

The peeve hesitated. "What's in it for me?"

"I suspect that Morgan le Fay has just about the highest AQ in Xanth. She absolutely hates to be balked, and she loves tormenting others, as we recently heard. Wherever she is, there is bound to be annoyance, rage, and grief. You will be in your element. Stick closely to her, but be alert, for her malice toward you will be great. Her anger will soon explode, laying waste to all around her. All you have to do is provoke it. It can be your finest effort."

The bird hopped across to Gwenny's shoulder.

"A stupid little chick?" the Sorceress asked, searching for the catch.

"I don't think you have had much experience with the peeve, Morgan," Goody continued. "So I will clarify. I have given you the bird. The parody talks often, almost always to insult those within range of its voice. It is highly observant, and its insults are precisely targeted. In fact it infuriates those who don't understand that it is not the person talking. It will delight every goblin you come in contact with, boasting of your nature and proclivities.

In fact it will egg on those male goblins you seduce. And it will advertise what you are doing to all who will listen—and everyone should be fascinated by your exploits. You will be very well known, very quickly."

Morgan frowned. "That won't do. I require a certain privacy, at least initially."

"Ha ha ha," the peeve laughed sneeringly.

She grabbed for it, but it flew up out of reach, only to land on her other shoulder. "Get off me, you pest!" But the bird would not leave.

A centaur came along the path. "Hi there, horserear!" Gwenny's voice called.

He paused. "I beg your pardon."

"You don't have it, manure-for-brains."

Goody and the others remained silent.

"I am Telliam Will," the centaur said somewhat stiffly. "So called because I had the misfortune to eat reverse wood when young, and now always miss my target. But I don't think this calls for gratuitous insults."

Morgan stood there with her mouth open, stricken by helpless outrage. She hadn't yet discovered how to warn others about the parody.

"Hello, Telliam," Goody said. "I had a similar experience when young, and now am a polite goblin male."

The centaur smiled. "You understand!"

"Oh, yes. As for the gobliness—she is suffering an evil possession. She may be trying to taunt folk into killing her."

Telliam nodded. "Now I understand. I hope she is able to escape the foul spirit." He trotted off.

"Good riddance, filthy tail!" Gwenny's voice called.

They returned their attention to Morgan. "The parody is just warming up," Goody said. "Wait till you try to seduce a goblin male. Your ears will burn, and he will likely flee, especially when the bird blabs about your intention to neuter him the moment he performs."

"Get away!" Morgan said, trying to scare off the bird with no better success than before.

"Stop harassing me, or I'll poop on your stupid head!"

"You wouldn't dare!"

The parody hopped onto her head and angled its tail. Morgan barely managed to brush it off before the dropping scored.

"And the gossip," Goody continued. "This bird has a fine memory for every notable exploit, the uglier the better. It will do you proud. Your nefarious reputation will precede you by the full range of its loud voice."

"Bleepity bleep!" Morgan swore, wilting the nearby vegetation.

"Good one!" the parody applauded. "Now say it again, louder, hag." It clearly knew the difference between Gwenny and Morgan le Fay.

"Oh!" It was difficult to imagine the frustrated fury jammed into that short word. "You are insufferable."

"And you're a bitchy body-snatcher."

"I can't function with this benighted bird!"

"Tough tittie, tootsie."

She stared at the parody. Then something shifted.

"Oh, bleep," the peeve said. "She's gone. She was so much fun."

"Sorry about that," Goody said. "We'll find you a better companion." He went to Gwenny. "Are you really free?"

"Yes!" she said gladly, hugging him. "Oh, Goody, you were magnificent. I could hardly keep from laughing. You made her so angry."

"I was just telling the truth," Goody said.

"With perhaps a bit of a stretch," Hannah said. "She wasn't planning to neuter her lovers."

"But the peeve would say it," Goody said.

"You bet I would!"

"So what I said was true."

"She knew, because I confirmed it," Gwenny said. "The parody is just as obnoxious as you said."

"Thank you, lame brain," the bird said.

"Of course you won't have that protection from the Sorceress once we find a home for it. But we'll clarify that we reserve the right to borrow it back if we need it."

Hannah shook her head. "Who would have thought that the parody would be your salvation."

"Well, I didn't mean to be, barb!"

They all laughed.

They walked on, querying folk about the prospect of adopting the bird, still without success. They came to a big crevice in the ground, wide and deep enough to require a bridge across it. As they crossed, a voice rumbled up. "A fine traveling party you are! Two goblins, a barbarian, and a robot! The heavens gaze down in sheer awe of the occasion."

"The cleft is talking," Hannah said.

"You call that a gap? I've seen a better crack on a poop pot!"

Roland's head whirred. "I have located it on my database map. This is an offshoot of the great Gap Chasm, known as the Sar Chasm."

They completed their crossing, and the sarcastic gap went silent. Beyond it was a camping site. "I think we have had more than enough of a day," Hannah said. "Let's stop here."

The others were glad to agree. It was early yet, but the business with Morgan had taken a toll.

There was a cloud of smoke. "How are you folk happening?"

"What?" Goody asked.

"Working, dealing, endeavoring, functioning, performing, proceeding—"

"Doing?"

"Whatever," the smoke agreed crossly.

"Well enough, considering, Metria."

"Considering what?"

"We had a run-in with the Sorceress Morgan le Fay."

"Stay clear of her."

"We intend to."

The demoness coalesced into her dusky sexy form. "Anything else?"

Gwenny nodded. "I think it is time to implement the test I spoke of before. Is Dara available?"

A second swirl of smoke appeared. "Present."

"What are you talking about?" Hannah asked.

"I need to make a decision," Gwenny said. "The business with Morgan reminds me that life is chancy, so I don't want to wait longer."

"Wait for what?" Goody asked, perplexed.

"For you to choose."

"Choose what?"

"That is the test. I need to know how you handle temptation."

"I don't understand."

"It is best that you don't." She took him by the shoulders and turned him around. "Give the parody to Roland and face this way until we tell you to turn around."

The bird flew to the robot. "Hi, nut screw," it said with the robot's voice.

"Hello, chicken gizzard." Evidently Roland had learned to cope.

"Turn," Hannah said. "Choose." She sounded sad.

Goody turned to face the other way. There stood three figures in a row. On the left was a breathtakingly lovely gobliness in scanty attire. On the right was Gwenny in her traveling clothes. In the center was Go-Go Gobliness in an ordinary house dress.

Of course the two demonesses were emulating goblins to make it three. He knew that. Gwenny was the one for him. So what was the point of this presentation?

The lovely gobliness beckoned to him, twitching her hips and smiling. Gwenny merely gazed at him. Go-Go started the formless dance-in-place she did.

Only Gwenny was real. But the sight of Go-Go dancing changed everything. It was as though nothing else existed.

He went to her and took her in his arms. "Beloved," he breathed, and kissed her.

She responded, holding him close and returning the kiss. For a timeless time they stood there, in deepest love.

Then she shifted, becoming Dara. "I'm so sorry," she said, and faded out.

The lovely one was gone too. Only Gwenny was left.

What could he say? He stood there, waiting for her to speak, dreading it. He knew he should have chosen her.

"You chose a dead woman over me," Gwenny said.

There was no denying it. "I did," he said, dejected. How could he explain it? No one else had known and loved Go-Go as he had.

"You didn't go for beauty."

"I guess I'm not much for beauty," he agreed.

"The expedient thing would have been to choose the one who could do you the most good."

"I'm not much for expedience."

"Or to have chosen the chief, for power."

"I'm not much for power."

"At least you could have used common sense. You knew the other two were mere images, not real people."

"I did. I guess I'm not much for common sense either."

"Why did you do it?" she flared.

"I love her."

"I thought you loved *me*."

"I do. But Go-Go was my wife."

"I'm a decade younger and prettier than she was."

"Yes. But that doesn't matter. No woman can ever come before her." There, it was said, cost him what it would. It was the underlying truth.

She nodded. "And when I am your wife, no other living woman will ever come before me." She reached out and took his gray rose, setting its stem in her hair.

"Yes, of course." Then he hesitated, startled. "What?"

"I believe you just accepted. So did your rose."

"But—"

"I am Chiefess of Goblin Mountain. It's all about

power. Every goblin wants it, and many are unscrupulous about gaining access to it. The chief consort is an avenue. There are women there who are a decade younger than I, some so lovely you have to look at them through smoked glass to protect your eyes. They will do anything to gain influence." She turned a dark gaze on him. "Anything. My father was corrupted. Most goblin chiefs are. How much easier to corrupt a consort."

Goody was appalled. "I would never—"

"I know. Not for beauty, not for power, not for common sense. Your commitment is absolute. You were never interested in me for my position."

"Never!" he agreed. "Yet—"

"I was lame and half blind and friendless as a child. Jenny Elf and the centaurs changed that. They gave me real life, and helped make me what I am. But I remember. I need the security of absolute loyalty. I won't find it in any male goblin I know, and maybe not in any other male of power in other species. But you I know I can trust."

"Yes, of course. But—"

"And you are of chiefly lineage. And you are decent. And not without imagination and courage."

"But—"

"What do I have to do to stop you from arguing?"

"I—"

She stepped into him and kissed him. "And I love you."

"That was it," he said as the little hearts orbiting his head slowly faded. He gazed at her, seeing the Rose of Grief nestled comfortably in her hair. She had taken it, and it had not stabbed her. She was definitely the one.

"It will be a big awful wedding, but we'll suffer through it. Then we'll see about settling in. But I think we'll arrange to be alone at times, or with special company, as we have been on this excursion."

"Yes!"

"Tomorrow we'll place the peeve. Tonight we'll be alone together."

"Yes," he agreed, his head spinning.

"One other thing," she said as she led him into the shelter. Hannah was staying outside with Roland, who was keeping the parody for now. "I believe I can dance, Go-Go's way. If you ever want me to."

"Please, no offense, but I'm not sure."

"It will be your choice. I simply want to please you."

"But why? Why cater to me? You don't have to marry anyone, and I'm really not much. We both know that."

"Because I like your company. I confess to being surprised when Che told me there might be something worth my while. I didn't expect much, but I trust his judgment. Our friendship goes way back; he's like a brother to me. Then when it turned out that you were of chiefly lineage I realized how serious Che and Cynthia were. I already liked you; we had been having fun together. It was a long time since I'd had innocent fun. That revelation gave me leave to love you. Yet I didn't want to make a mistake. My mother Godiva was a lovely and capable woman, but my father was seduced away from her. I didn't want to be similarly victimized."

"I understand."

"You surely do. I regret having to put you to the test."

"I thought I had failed it."

"There wasn't much chance of that, actually."

He looked at her, startled. "There wasn't?"

"I was already pretty sure of your qualities. If you had chosen me, I would have known you were ready. I doubted you would choose the beckoning beauty. So it was mainly a confirmation."

"But I chose Go-Go."

"Who can never be a threat to me."

"Yet if somehow she could return to life—"

"Just remember this: if that ever seems to happen, chances are that it's a gobliness imitating her, or a demoness. You love her yet, but you're not a fool."

He nodded. "I appreciate your insight."

"Now let's confine ourselves to *us*." She clasped him. It was the beginning of a long and wonderful night.

In the morning Hannah had a question for Gwenny. "You said today we would place the peeve. What do you have in mind?"

"Something I thought of a few days ago. Now's the time."

"A few days ago! Why didn't you say something?"

"She was too dull to remember," the parody said peevishly, rejoining Goody.

"I wanted to settle with Goody first, and there were complications."

"Such as Morgan le Fay," Goody agreed. "I wonder why she is called a sorceress, if she has only the talent of turning things on?"

"Now there's a lovely creature," the bird said. "How I miss her."

Roland's head whirred. "She was a sorceress in Mundania, so it carries across," he said. "That talent is only one. Possession of other bodies is another. She is learning them individually as she adapts to Xanth. She has more power on her resident moon."

"She can stay there," Hannah said.

Gwenny was thoughtful. "That database of yours has a lot of information. It occurs to me that Com Pewter knows considerably more than he tells."

"This is true," Roland said.

"You ought to know, rusty guts."

"That should be useful when we settle on Iron Mountain and start circulating the soul program to any other robots that show up," Hannah said. She returned to Gwenny. "But about the peeve?"

"Yes, let's do that now. I'll call my friend Surprise." Gwenny put her fingers to her mouth and made a whistle similar to the one Jenny had made when calling her husband.

A young human woman appeared, just barely under age to enter the Adult Conspiracy. "You called, Gwenny?"

"We may have something of interest to you," Gwenny

said. "Folk, this is Surprise Golem, daughter of Grundy Golem and Rapunzel Elf. She can do anything once." Then she introduced the others to the girl, including the bird. "We wish to give the bird to someone."

"Get lost, chaste chick."

"The parody likes to insult others, using its companion's voice," Gwenny explained. "It is extremely imaginative in its choices of words and concepts."

"Unlike certain scheming limping gobs."

"We're trying to find a good home for it, but it alienates everyone it encounters. That's why Goody needs a bodyguard."

"He wouldn't, if he weren't so piddlingly puny."

"I begin to see why," Surprise said, smiling.

"Who asked you, junior jade?"

"Can you possibly think of anyone who would want to adopt this obnoxious bird?" Gwenny's tone sounded rhetorical.

An expression of delighted mischief crossed the girl's face. "I'll fetch Dad."

"Fetch both your parents," Gwenny advised. "Rapunzel should be in on the decision. She may not wish to be given the bird."

"I suppose so." Surprise disappeared.

"How does that girl relate?" Goody asked.

"Surprise is special," Gwenny said. "She can use any talent once, and only once. So she seems like a sorceress, but is short of it. Fortunately there are so many variations of similar talents that she'll never run out. She is limited only by her imagination. But it's her father we really need to talk to."

Surprise reappeared. "I brought the whole family," she said. She gestured, and there appeared a nondescript young man with a picnic basket.

"Uh, hello," the man said awkwardly.

"My fiancé Umlaut," Surprise said.

"Oh, he's cute," Hannah said. Roland turned a lens on her, though of course a machine couldn't be jealous.

"He has that effect on women," Surprise said. "And here are my parents, Grundy Golem and Rapunzel Elf."

Umlaut opened the basket to reveal a tiny couple. The man could have sat comfortably on a human hand, or even a goblin hand, and the woman was no larger. The remarkable thing about her was her hair; it flowed about her body like a living cloak, changing colors as it went. She resembled a beautiful, elaborately coiffed doll.

These miniatures were Surprise's parents?

"I have some human ancestry," Surprise said, answering their unvoiced question. "So I revert naturally to human size. Mother can be any size she wants. Dad is the size he is."

"What a picayune pipsqueak!" the parody said.

Grundy looked at the bird. "Look who's talking, you undernourished popinjay."

"Oh, it talks! Is there a brain in with the sawdust?"

"Is there a tongue in that big mouth?"

"It's a wonder that doll beside you doesn't dump you out of your basket, you pitiful basket case."

"It's a wonder that gassy poop keeps coming out the wrong end."

"The giants and ogres must cringe in fear of your approach, you peewee midget."

"You must have hatched from a sick stinkhorn, you nauseous avian peeper."

There was a pause as a significant gaze passed between golem and bird.

"How would you like to come home with us, peeve?" Rapunzel asked. "We can give you a prominent perch overlooking a well-traveled path."

The parody flew to their basket and landed beside them. "Ditch these losers," Rapunzel's voice said.

Umlaut carefully closed the basket. He and his burden disappeared.

Only Surprise remained for a moment. "Dad loves that bird," she confided. "Now he can insult twice as many people with half the effort. Thank you." She faded out.

"I'm almost sorry to see the peeve go," Goody said.

"I promise to make it up to you," Gwenny said, kissing him. "Even though I'll never match the parody's language."

"Somehow I'll endure," Goody said, kissing her back. Little hearts orbited them.

"I believe you no longer require a bodyguard," Hannah said to Goody. "So Roland and I will head for the Iron Mountain, after we see you to Goblin Mountain."

"Thank you."

"It has been a great adventure." Hannah paused, and Goody knew why: it had become automatic, to allow for the peeve's insult. It would take a while for all of them to get used to its absence. Then she looked surprised.

"Is there a problem, wild wonder?" Roland asked.

"No problem! I just realized what the answer is to my question to the Good Magician: What is the nature of ultimate reality?"

"I am curious about that," Goody said. "What is it?"

"It doesn't matter."

"Yes, it does! You are supposed to have the answer."

"That *is* the answer. Once a person discovers love, ultimate reality doesn't matter. I have found love." She kissed Roland.

Goody thought about it. Then he kissed Gwenny. "You're right: it doesn't matter."

"Make sure to come to the wedding," Gwenny said to them.

"We will."

Goody wished that subject hadn't come up. He dreaded the threatened occasion.

# AUTHOR'S NOTE

I allow about three months to write a Xanth novel, because such light fantasy is easy for me to do. Other
types can take twice as long, or more, depending.
Even so, this one was special, because I had been looking
forward to it for two years. I loved the notion of the irascible bird! Then my fan Marisol Ramos-Lum, who runs
*P.A.T.H.*—the Piers Anthony Thread Homepage—
*http://home.comcast.net/~ramoslum/PATH/*—suggested that
Goody Goblin marry Gwenny Goblin, and that I have a
female barbarian hero. I thought of Hannah Barbarian,
who appeared briefly in *Geis of the Gargoyle,* and things
started coming together. Goody could be the one to accompany the peevish bird, with Hannah as his bodyguard. In case anyone doesn't get the pun, it's a takeoff
on the movie cartoon maker Hanna-Barbera. But I knew
that endless insults and battles with outraged ogres, dragons, tangle trees, and women would get tiresome after a
while; I needed a central theme, something for them to
accomplish along the way. One reader wanted to see a big

battle in Xanth. I'm not much for violence; I prefer humor and naughtiness, as is surely apparent, but the last big Xanth battle was in Castle Roogna, twenty-six novels ago, so it did seem about time. But against whom? I hate to do things the same way as everyone else does them. Then I thought of robots: there hasn't been a robot in Xanth, so it was about time for that too. And now you know the genesis of this novel, and I hope it doesn't spoil it for you. Some readers are heartbroken to discover that these novels are actually written by an aging, dull, mundane man according to a formula: there must always be a challenging visit to the Good Magician's castle, a romance, and more puns than the average person can stomach. But that's the way it is. I do have serious novels elsewhere, if you can't stand fun.

I did enjoy writing it. It's fun insulting every character that comes into range, and I liked Hannah and Gwenny as I got to know them better, and I think the robots will be a permanent future category, like the dragons, ogres, centaurs, and oh, yes, humans. I think it's about as funny and naughty as Xanth gets. I suspect some readers will blanch at the peeve's language, but the bird had to be obnoxious enough to make its placement a real challenge. No, I don't know its gender. Indications are equivocal, such as when it entered No Man's Land without changing, but I can't see how a female would make such sexist remarks.

I maintain a Web site, *http://www.hipiers.com*, where I have a long bimonthly column and a feisty listing of electronic publishers that inspires the thanks of aspiring writers and the ire of some publishers. (Don't look for *www.piersanthony.com;* that was hijacked by a Web squatter. Similarly don't try to call my old 800 number; that was taken by a porno outfit, leaving me to get the blame, costing me angry readers. Welcome to mundane morality!) I do it because I want to make things easier for others than they were for me. It took me eight years of submitting material to publishers before I made my first sale, and then I got cheated, and blacklisted for protesting the cheating. Even a writer's organization tacitly sided with the wrongdoing publisher and badmouthed me. So I have an ornery attitude—no more Mr. Nice Ogre—and I'm not getting mellow in my dotage, as those who tangle with me know. But most of my interactions with readers are quite positive, and the site facilitates this. This novel was affected by that.

I expected to have to do a lot of reading in the same time period I had allotted for writing this novel, because I had a huge galley proof coming, and was to judge an electronic publisher's fantasy novel contest. I'm a slow reader; that dates back to my early trouble in school when I couldn't learn to read. Today things like learning disabilities and dyslexia exist; my daughter suffered with those, and required special attention early in school. But in my day there were only stupid or lazy students, who required discipline rather than extra attention, so it took me three years and five schools to make it through first grade, finally learning to read. I was the stupidest student I know of. When I finally did catch on, I loved it, and in the end became a professional writer, as some may have noticed. It's a fine escape from the dreariness of Mundania. But I never did speed up a lot; I read every letter of every word, every sentence, every paragraph. That makes me a good proofreader but a slow regular reader.

So I was afraid I would use up too much time, and not be able to complete this novel on my schedule. That could be mischief, as there was a deadline. So I hurried, avoiding distractions, focusing on getting the job done. Fortunately it was a fun job. But in my hurry I had to shortcut anything that threatened to consume too much time. So when I came to Iron Mountain and Lake Wails I wanted to look them up in prior Xanth novels, to get their details straight; sharp-eyed and sharp-tongued readers constantly lurk to catch me in an error. But I couldn't find them. I turned the pages of *The Color of Her Panties,* because I thought they were there, but couldn't find them

without doing an actual (slow) rereading. I wasn't even
sure that was the right novel. What to do?

Here's where the Web site comes in: I asked my readers, and promised to give credits to the first five who located novel and page for me. Within a day after that
column was published, I had five responses: Lake Wails
is in *Ogre, Ogre,* and both Wails and Iron are in *Panties.*
That enabled me to do my homework efficiently, and stay
on my accelerated schedule. So here are those credits:
Krysta Barcok, Cynthia McSorley and Rob Doherty,
Michael Ratcliff, Rachael Biggs, and Kristina Keller. I
regret that I am unable to give credit to #6; Mike Sloan
just missed the cut. Thank you, all, and all the others who
followed.

Then the other books to read did not come. The result
was that I broke my record for writing, doing 81,000
words of novel text, and that HiPiers column, in Septem-
ber 2003. With that head start I had no trouble complet-
ing the 120,000-word novel the following month. It
turned out that the fantasy contest deadline wasn't until
after my novel was to be finished anyway; stupid Ogre-
fashion, I had gotten it wrong.

Here, then, are the rest of the credits, for about 140 notions. Most were suggested via e-mail, and sometimes all I
had to credit was a first name or a net name. Barbarian female main character, Goody marrying Gwenny—Marisol
Ramos-Lum. Jack and Jill rabbits—Phillip J. Houx. Song
and Ownlee Human—Justin Amy. Mournful gravestone,
modification talent—Chris Ricketts. Line of Sight, Where
daydreams are made—Emily Gertrude Alden. Mirage
Mer-naga—Lisa Rufer. Maggie Wolf-Alicorn etc.—
Maggie Foster. Bird dog, Vamp-eyer—Thalnos the En-
chanter. Cowl—Katie Todd. Meloncollie—Kathy Harvey.
Talent of making mountains from molehills, Talent of seeing most embarrassing moments, Pierced ears healed by
elixir—Catty Philpot-Hogan. Gravi-tree—John Clay. Vegetables that stalk, Margarine fly, Watch dog having ticks,
Paine—Jeanette Nelson. Bi-polar bear—Adam Bracken.

Toilet-tree—Christy Hodge. Fourwarned, Fourshadowed—
Avi Ornstein. Gumption tree—Jenna. Rusty, who makes
things rust—Mathew Matthews. Mary Annette—Raymond
Kyosei. Car tunes—Bridgett Allen. Car-pet—Karl Martin.
Lorelei—Daley and Justin Reed. No Man's Land—Zach
Robison. Ignor-ant, Ant-icipation—Rheanna Montoya-
Childers. Cookie batter—Cindi Weng. Loon-a-tick, Talent
of creating what's most needed, Tic-kit—Rusty Johnson.
Candy corn fields and farmer, A-, B-, C-gulls—Bethlyn
Erin Richard. Hazel—Suza Beth Spurlock. Metria's trip—
Christopher Walsh. Metria's work, Bookworm, No place
like tome—the Bolger Family. Olive Hue (I love you)—
Tammy Yuen. Talent of making imaginary friends—Evan
McVey. Lorlai Fiona—Diz Denner. Sharina and Suretha—
Sharina Van Dorn. Twins who turn day to night, night to
day—Thomas Jacobs. Hot crossed puns, Cheetah, Metal
coil spring, Talent of watching pots boil, Talent of making
sleeping dogs tell the truth—Matt Hill. Conundrum—
David Kaplan. Brigitte—Boni Abbruzzese. Daze-E's—
Joan O'Bryan. Billboard, Leigh and Anne—Brioney Leigh
Anne Logan. Rek King Ogre—Elizabeth Hessom. Colt—
Joy Bennet. Snow fakes, Chain stores—Vivian Baker. Talent of knowing talents—Dierdre King. Tautolotree
tree—Thomas Whapies. Poker, Fauns dancing around
nymphs, Nap-kin—Joey Morris. Come-hither stair—Judy
Herndon. Rubber band—Donna Edgar. Foot-hills of Mount
Parnassus—Nehemiah Lewrel. Incumbents and succucum-
bents, Camp Pain—Melinda Anderson. Poet tree, Fishnet
stockings—Susan Cormier. Anni Mae, Un-dead letter of-
fice, Cutlass/cutlad plants—Catie Webber. Watch tower—
Andrea Krause. Hand Ker Chief—Adam Beame. Maize of
corn stalks—Patrick Kelley. Library Ann, Eye can—Andy
Giblin. Fire place, Pill-O—Kate Wilson. Undertoe—
Tanya. Talent of changing colors of body parts—Carter. Six
Knights—Alasdair Rodgers. Priority male—Deanna and
Laurie Yamasaki. Rot-gut, Ale-ing oak trees, Gripe soda,
Show girls—Marvin J. Cox. Matrimonial cheese—Tim
Vige. Talent of undressing her with his eyes—Tom Becker.

Rocket lawnchair—Jennifer Lawrence. Talent of complicating situations—Kiya Alexander. Mark-hers—Chad Daelhousen. Cutlass, Punties and the puns on them—Robert Price. In Tent City—Joel Nielson. Sound of a smirk—Krystalle Double. Wanna Bee—Brendan Long. Queen Irene's plant bulbs for ideas, Com-plain—Gabe Pesek. Cape Flattery—Nyssa P. Hamilton. Flaming O's—Lisa Shawn Fischer. Half-demon's souls regenerating—Sabrina Smith. Lunch boxes—Annemarie de Lavelle, Terese Couture. Pungatory—Chris Efta. Spitting image—Brin Rosenthal. Crossbreeds prune—Shannon Clay. Amateur-tagonist and pro-tagonist—Sean M. Watkins. Ptero Bull, Pun shield—Henry Wykoff. Pasture/Future—Natalya Bree. History of Trojan—Kathlynn Grey. Ichabod's fantastic classifications—Oscar Kelly. Chocolate lab dog—Dawn. Hot dog—Denise Morris. Optimist, pessimist—Tim Bruening. Crock pot/crack pot—Brendan Moore, Doug Laird. Ill eagle—John Gills. Tattle tail—Scott M. Stelle. Matt Heffelbower—Shane A. Henderson. Sam Dog—Naomi Elaine Goodwin. Panties stop freaking men, Talents of all the villagers except Cameo—Adam Michael Smith. Cameo—Mark Minson. Tree growing musical instruments—Joe Haughton. Demon Mercury's spy eyes—Dana Crincic. Talent of making people smile—Ainsley Whalen. Doll fin—Sandra Heiler. Jim Nastic—John Larr. Talent of making people feel guilty—Lenora Kenwolf. Talent of turning things on—Breanna Kay Larsen. Telliam Will—Elizabeth O'Neil. Sar Chasm—Sean Wilson.

No, I didn't use all I received. I made a computerized list, and highlighted ideas as they were used, but it was like being a tortoise chasing after a running rabbit. A number are earmarked for future novels, and some came in too late to make this one. Some just didn't fit here, so have to wait. Some were too good to waste on a passing reference, so are likely to have more significant treatment in the next. All kinds of reasons. So if you sent in a suggestion, and didn't find it here, be patient; chances are it will appear in the next novel. Frankly it's a job keeping up; I do the best I can, but my readers have more good notions than I have novel to fit them into.

From Piers Anthony

# STORK

# NAKED
(0-765-30409-0)

**Available now in hardcover!**

*Turn the page for a preview*

# PARADISE LOST

H ow come that stupid bird is green?" Ted asked. "Is it sick?"

"No, it's just too small to manage a better color," Monica said.

"Children!" Surprise exclaimed. "Don't tease the pet peeve."

"Aw, why not?" Ted asked. "It's just a dumb cluck."

"It can't understand a thing we say," Monica agreed.

Surprise Golem was babysitting the half-demon children, Demon Ted and DeMonica. Her husband and parents were away, scouting for a suitable home for the new family. With her magic talents she could handle the children, but they were trying to set off the peeve. That was mischief.

The peeve eyed Ted. "Your father can't get out of bed. Want to know why?" It spoke in Ted's voice.

Ted swelled up indignantly, but the peeve was already eying Monica. "Your mother slithers on her belly," it said with her voice.

Monica opened her mouth angrily.

"Because it may tease you back," Surprise said. "And nothing teases worse than the peeve."

But the battle was fairly started. "I know why he can't get out of bed," Ted said. "It's because mom keeps him there, blissed out, so he won't be in the way."

"And how does she do that, you ignorant juvenile crossbreed?" the peeve demanded insolently.

"Don't try to answer that!" Surprise said.

"Why not?" Ted asked.

"Because of the Adult Conspiracy, dummy," Monica informed him. "You're only ten years old."

"Well so are you, double dummy!"

"Children, don't fight," Surprise said. "It's no shame to be ten. I was ten once."

"But you outgrew it," Monica said.

"And so will you, in a few more years." It was tricky keeping a lid on it, because both children knew more of the dread Conspiracy than they admitted, because of their half-demon heritage and suspiciously tolerant parents. Surprise didn't want to get blamed for a violation. She was babysitting them because their parents were busy elsewhere and few others could handle them. The two children were not related, but were like mischievous siblings with special powers. They were indeed ten years old, but often acted half that age, reveling in their childishness.

"Yeah, I guess so," Ted agreed, grudgingly satisfied.

But the peeve wasn't satisfied. "That leaves your mother, who can't stand on her own two feet," it said in Monica's voice. That was one of its annoying properties: it borrowed the voice of the one it was with, or whoever it was addressing, so that it seemed to third parties that the victimized person was talking. That could be distinctly awkward at times.

"That's because she's a naga," Monica said. "Nagas don't have feet in their natural forms."

The peeve opened its beak, ready to set the children off

again. It lived to insult people, and the angrier it made them, the more satisfied it was. It had finally found a home here because Surprise's father was Grundy Golem, the only one who could match the irascible bird insult for insult. The two got along well. But the last thing she wanted was to have the two half-demons getting into a contest with the bird. The Adult Conspiracy was bound to get tweaked if not outright abused.

"Let's tell a story," Surprise said. Children always liked stories. "About the Adult Conspiracy." Oops; she had meant to name some safe minor adventure, but her nervousness about the Conspiracy had made her mis-speak. "I mean—"

"Yes, let's!" both children exclaimed, picking up on it instantly. "With every dirty detail," Ted concluded.

"No, I meant *not* about it," Surprise said desperately.

"You said, you said!" Monica chimed. "Now we have to have it. Exactly how does it work?"

They were really trying to get her in trouble, and knew how to do it. How could she handle this?

"It's not as if it is any mystery," the peeve said with a superior tone that was also Surprise's voice. "All that is required is for the man to take the woman and—"

"Don't you dare!" Surprise said, conjuring a black hood that dropped over the bird's head and muffled it.

"___!" the peeve swore, the badness stifled by the hood. It flapped its wings, lifted into the air, did a loop, and dropped the hood to the floor, where it faded out. It opened its beak again.

"If you say one bad word, I'll lock you in a soundproof birdcage," Surprise warned it.

"You wouldn't dare, you uppity wench!"

A birdcage appeared next to the bird. It had thick sound-absorbent curtains.

The peeve reconsidered. It had brushed with Surprise before, and learned that she could do just about anything once. If she abolished the birdcage, she would not be able to conjure it again. But she could conjure a very similar one, or a bandanna knotted about its beak, or a cloud of sneeze powder that would prevent its talking for several moments and some instants left over. Her magical ability was limited only by her imagination. She was in fact uncomfortably close to being Sorceress level, and might one day be recognized as such when she perfected her ability. That was why she was able to handle the demon children, and they too knew it.

"No bad words, harridan," the bird agreed, disgruntled.

"Idea!" Ted exclaimed, a bulb flashing brightly over his head. "Have the peeve tell about the Adult Conspiracy."

Oh, no—they were back on that. No amount of magic could handle that violation if it happened. She had to change the subject in a hurry. But for the moment her mind was distressingly blank.

Monica clapped her hands. "I thought you were out of ideas, Ted, but that's a good one."

"It is *not* a good idea," Surprise said. "The peeve can't speak a sentence without insulting someone."

But the children knew they were onto something. "Is that true, bird-brain?" Ted asked.

"No, poop head. I just don't care to waste opportunity. I can cover every detail of the Adult Conspiracy without uttering a bad word."

"Wonderful!" Monica said.

"No you don't!" Surprise said. "I'll make a laryngitis spell."

"Awww," the children said together.

"I can tell about it without violating it," the peeve insisted.

"See—the bird's reformed," Ted said eagerly.

"Under a pig's tail," the peeve said. "I'll never reform."

"But you can really annoy Surprise if you make good on your pledge," Monica said with a canny glance. "No bad words, no violation, but you cover the subject and she can't stop you."

The peeve received her glance and sent it back.

"You're not half as stupid as I took you for, Harmonica."

"That's DE-Monica, greenface. As in Demon-ica."

"Ick," the bird agreed.

"So it's decided," Ted said. "The bird sings."

Surprise hesitated. The three were ganging up on her, but she was curious how the peeve could do what it said, and maybe it would help get them through until some more innocent distraction turned up. "Very well. But the rules will be strictly enforced."

"Absolutely, honey-pie," the bird agreed with her voice. But there was a shiftiness about its wings that suggested it was going to try to get away with something.

The children sat on the floor facing the peeve's perch. Surprise set about making a snack for them all, but she kept a close ear on the bird. Nothing daunted it except a direct enforceable threat.

"Long ago and far away," the peeve said, "there was no such thing as the Adult Conspiracy. People summoned storks freely and no one cared. Children knew all about it, and watched when they wanted to. That was how they learned how to do it. But then confounded civilization arrived and messed up the natural order. Adults started concealing it, and setting other ridiculous rules such as not letting children hear the most effective words. It seems the adults were jealous of the carefree life of children, so decided to keep interesting things away from them."

"Hear hear," Ted agreed.

Surprise did not see it quite the same way, but as long as the bird stayed clear of key words and concepts she couldn't protest.

"There are also stories that the adults grew fearful of a revolution by the children, so acted to prevent it. After all, suppose children started summoning babies on their own? What further need would there be for adults? They might discover themselves superfluous, and be on track for elimination. They didn't like that, so decided to stop it before the children made their move."

"That's interesting," Monica said thoughtfully. "Something should be done about it."

"Tyrants never yield their power voluntarily," the peeve said. "Power is addictive; they do everything they can to hang on to it."

Now both children were thoughtful. Surprise was disgusted. It wasn't like that at all. She had not been party to the Conspiracy long—only a year or so—but in that time had summoned the stork with her husband Umlaut, and was expecting delivery of her baby at any moment. Babies needed adults to take care of them; children were too irresponsible. So there was good, sensible reason to prevent children from summoning storks. But of course children didn't see it that way. The confounded bird was succeeding in really annoying her, without breaking any rules. In seemingly good language it was insulting the entire adult species.

"It crystallized with little Princess Ivy in the year 1071, thirty-five years ago," the peeve continued. "Adults had been preaching the gospel of secrecy, but it hadn't been very effective; most children saw through it soon, and used bad words, and could have signaled storks if they had really wanted to. They told Ivy she had been found under a cabbage leaf; only later did she learn that babies didn't just materialize under leaves, they were brought there by storks. Her talent was Enhancement, and she Enhanced the story until it became a wider reality. Later she told her twin sister Ida, whose talent is to make real what others who don't know her power believe. Thus the Conspiracy became thoroughly established, extending well into the future and half a smidgen into the past. It has been almost inviolate ever since, and most folk believe it always existed. But it didn't; it was mostly myth until Ivy and Ida made it literal."

Surprise was astonished. Could this be true? It didn't really matter, because certainly the Conspiracy existed now, but the idea of it not existing at some time in the past was subtly disturbing.

"That's really something," Ted said, impressed. "How did you learn about this, peeve?"

"I made it up, crazy boy."

Both children burst out laughing. "You're lying, bird beak," Monica said. "We can tell. You weren't lying before, but now you are."

"Just testing," the bird said, annoyed.

"Say," Ted said. "I heard about a man with a spot on the wall talent with a difference: he could summon them from elsewhere. Some spun, making folk nauseous. More fun."

"And the relevance is . . . ?" Monica inquired snidely.

"If he summoned one from where the Adult Conspiracy first got started, and took it to Princess Eve to analyze it, we could learn exactly how it happened."

The peeve looked at him. "You do have some good ideas, lunatic lad."

"No you don't," Surprise called. "That man is adult; he would never cooperate."

"Awww," both children said together.

Surprise smiled to herself. Not for nothing was it called the Adult Conspiracy. All adults participated, to the eternal frustration of children.

There was a sound outside. Surprise glanced out the window and saw a heavy bird coming to a landing. It looked like a stork.

"The stork!" she cried. "It's making the delivery!"

"Another brat on the scene," the peeve said peevishly.

"Great!" Ted said.

"We never saw a delivery before," Monica said.

Surprise wasn't sure they were supposed to, but there was no way to stop them following her to the door. She opened it, her heart pounding.

There stood the stork, a bundle before him. "Surprise Golem?" he inquired.

"That's me!" Surprise said. "I've been expecting you."

"I am Stymy Stork, with a bundle of joy. Let me handle the formalities, and the baby is yours." The stork used his beak to draw a piece of paper from his vest pocket. That was odd, as he wore no clothing, only feathers. He donned glasses so he could read the note. That was odder. "You ordered a baby, gender unspecified, nine months ago?"

"Yes!" Surprise was so excited she felt faint.

"You are duly married to one Umlaut?"

"Yes. Give me my baby."

"Not so fast," Stymy said. "I'm on probation; I have to follow every rule exactly or I'll get my flight feathers pulled. You are of appropriate age to receive a baby?"

"Yes, I'm eighteen."

The bird perused the paper. "You were delivered in the year 1093. Let's see, that would make you—I'm not good at math—thirteen years old." He did a double take. "That's too young."

"I was five years old when delivered," Surprise said. "That's why I was named as I was: Grundy and Rapunzel had almost given up waiting for me in five years, and then suddenly there I was, late but whole. I really am eighteen."

"I'm not sure of that," the stork said. "According to the rule, age is counted from the moment of delivery forward. I can't complete this delivery."

Surprise was stunned. "But that's my baby! I must have it. You can't let some idiotic confusion deny me my motherhood."

"Take your complaint to headquarters," Stymy said. He put away the paper and glasses, poked his beak into the loop of material tying the bundle together, and lifted it.

"No!" Surprise cried. "Don't take my baby!"

The stork turned, ran down the path, spread his wings, and took off, bearing the bundle away. Surprise was so amazed and chagrined that she just stood there and watched it happen.